TC

D1420882

C2 000 004 821107

HOWARD L. ANDERSON has had a varied life: he flew with a helicopter battalion in Vietnam and worked on fishing boats in Alaska, in the steel mills of Pittsburgh, as a truck driver in Houston, and a scriptwriter in Hollywood. After earning a law degree, he became legal counsel for the New Mexico Organized Crime Commission. He is currently a defense attorney in New Mexico, where he represents people from Mexico charged with crimes north of the border.

Albert of Adelaide

Howard L. Anderson

A complete catalogue record for this book can
be obtained from the British Library on request

The right of Howard L. Anderson to be identified as the author of
this work has been asserted by him in accordance with the Copyright,
Designs and Patents Act 1988

First published in the USA in 2012 by Twelve, an imprint of Grand
Central Publishing, Hachette Book Group, New York

First published in the UK in 2012 by Serpent's Tail,
an imprint of Profile Books Ltd
3A Exmouth House
Pine Street
London EC1R 0JH
website: www.serpentstail.com

ISBN 978 1 84668 840 9
eISBN 978 1 84765 788 6

Designed and typeset by sue@lambledesign.demon.co.uk
Printed by Clays, Bungay, Suffolk

10 9 8 7 6 5 4 3 2 1

It seems fitting to dedicate this book to an Australian soldier I met at a bar many years ago in Sydney. All I can remember about him was that he had a bad bayonet scar from service in Malaya and that he got me hopelessly lost on the New South Wales rail system before he passed out.

Preface

THE COUNTY THAT STRETCHES FROM Melbourne in the south to Sydney seven hundred and fifty miles up the coast is green with trees and paddocks. On the farms along the coast, sheep graze in the fields, and foxes eat the rabbits that in their turn eat the lettuce growing in the gardens. The sheep, the foxes, and the rabbits live their lives no differently than did their ancestors in England not so many generations ago.

The animals and men that used to live along the coast, in the days before the bush became suburbs, don't come to this part of Australia much any more. Kangaroos and wallabies have found ways to prosper, but the rest have been pushed back into the deserts or survive in zoos as relics of the past. Tasmanian devils snuffle along the concrete floors of their pens next to panda bears from China. Cassowaries feed in fenced enclosures next to kudus from Africa.

The original inhabitants of Australia have become curiosities to be stared at, along with other unwilling creatures from continents far away. Times have changed along the coast, and there is no room for those that used to live there. The animals living in the zoos remember that Australia once belonged to them.

They talk of a place far away in the desert where things haven't changed and the old life remains as it once was. As with most stories, hope rather than truth wins out with each telling, and in the end the only way to be sure of what's real and what's not real is to go to the source of the tale.

Albert of Adelaide

1 ≋ Desert crossing

THE TRACKS OF AN OLD railway line run from Adelaide in South Australia to Alice Springs in the Northern Territory. For many years, as each train passed by on its thousand-mile journey between the two towns, passengers threw their empty beer bottles from the windows of the cars into a landscape that seemed unimportant to them. The broken bottles accumulated along the road bed and the route from Adelaide to Alice Springs became a shining ribbon of broken glass.

At Alice Springs the railway line continues, south to north, in an almost undeviating straight line across the center of the country and passes through the towns of Tennant Creek and Katherine. The tracks parallel a road that was widened many years ago to take war materials from Alice Springs, in the center of the country, to Darwin on the northern coast. The war drifted away from Darwin to its conclusion in other parts of the Pacific, and traffic along the road slowed to almost nothing. It took almost another lifetime to complete the final nine hundred miles of track from Alice Springs to the coast. North of Alice Springs the railway line disappears into a series of mountain ranges that cross the center of the continent.

Beyond the mountains is a red desert. It is a desert of vast distances and, when closely examined, of great variety. The occasional cliffs and gorges are red in color, as is the soil and sand that covers sections of the desert floor. The color fits well with the blue and normally cloudless sky that on occasion brings water to the dry riverbeds that cut across the land.

The desert is covered in patches of short, stunted grasses that have won a marginal hold in the red, sandy soil. Scattered across the sand and grass, desert grevillea bushes seem like giants in the treeless flats. In some places the bushes grow close to one another, and small birds flutter among the branches. The birds don't sing, and the silence of the desert is broken only briefly by the flutter of their wings.

There are paths in the desert where passing animals have walked the weak grasses into extinction. These tracks, unlike the railroad, follow no set direction. They wander aimlessly through the flats and up and down the banks of the dry rivers, heading to destinations unknown. The age of the tracks is impossible to tell, for the grass grows back slowly in those parts of Australia.

In the early morning of a day long after the war, a small figure walked slowly along one of the winding tracks somewhere to the east of Tennant Creek. On close examination, the figure didn't look any different from most of his kind. He was about two feet tall and covered with short brown fur. He had a short, thick tail that dragged the ground when he walked upright and a ducklike bill where any other animal would have a nose.

The only thing that set Albert apart from any other platypus was that he was carrying an empty soft drink bottle. It was his possession of a bottle, coupled with the fact that he was hundreds of miles north of any running water, that made him different.

Albert had crept away from the railway station at Tennant Creek and into the desert three nights before. For the first day after leaving the station, he had walked along the railroad track. A train had come by late in the afternoon and Albert had hidden himself in a bush near the roadbed. No one had seen him, but he was almost hit by a half-full bottle of Melbourne Bitter thrown from a second-class coach. After that, Albert stayed away from the tracks. From a distance, he had paralleled the roadbed north for the last two days, because without that landmark Albert would have been hopelessly lost. As it was, he was just confused.

The problem was that Albert had no idea where he was going, or exactly what he was looking for. The stories had been vague at best... *somewhere in the desert... a place where old Australia still existed... keep going north... the Promised Land.* Those descriptions had sounded good in Adelaide, but they were worthless in a desert where every direction looked the same.

His escape from Adelaide and the trip to Tennant Creek had been easier than he expected. Security on the smaller animals was minimal. It had been only a matter of time before a careless attendant left his enclosure latch unfastened. Then a quick midnight run through the deserted park and a short swim across the River Torrens had gotten him into the city proper.

Some of the larger animals had been brought to Adelaide by train and then to the zoo by lorry. They told him about the trains and described how to reach the railroad yards.

Traffic on the city streets was infrequent late at night, and Albert managed to get across town to the station by hiding behind rubbish bins from the occasional passing automobile. After that, he had hopped a freight to Alice Springs and then another to Tennant Creek, the entire trip courtesy of the South Australia railway.

With the limited resources available to him, Albert had tried to prepare for the journey. He had saved part of his meal at each feeding and put the grubs into a discarded popcorn box he had pulled into his cage when no one was looking. Water he had taken from his dish and put in the stolen soft drink bottle. His planning had gotten him to Alice Springs and then to the desert outside Tennant Creek. Now, he was out of food, out of water, and out of plans.

He had filled his bottle the night he left the train at Tennant Creek, but his bottle didn't hold that much. The water had run out yesterday and Albert knew that if he didn't find more that day he would die. A platypus is an animal that lives in or near water all its life and can't survive without it. He didn't mind the dying as much as he minded not living long enough to find the place he was looking for, somewhere without people and without zoos.

Albert continued to walk north. He had decided to get as far away from Adelaide as he could before the end. His eyes were red-rimmed from the sun, and his fur was discolored from the reddish dust his feet kicked up as he walked. He had given up trying to make sense of the faint trails that occasionally crossed his path. Albert clutched the empty soft drink bottle and put one webbed foot in front of the other, moving slowly toward the distant horizon.

As the day grew longer Albert began to hallucinate. Dreams of water would mix with the heat waves rising in the air, and Albert could see the Murray River. He could feel himself slide down the mud ramp in front of his burrow and into the coolness of the river. He would float down the river and watch the green banks pass by. Just when he was sure that he was back for good in the place where he was born, the river would evaporate, and he could see faces smeared with cotton candy and jaws that dribbled popcorn. The faces laughed and handless fingers poked at him through wire mesh. The horror of the visions caused Albert to start shaking, and when he did the faces disappeared. In their place, the emptiness of the desert and the heat of the day would push their way into Albert's consciousness, and he would force himself to begin walking again.

As the day wore on, the brush became thicker and the desert began to give way to bush. Most of the brush was taller than Albert, and he lost sight of the horizon and the railroad track. As the sun changed position in the sky it became more difficult to tell exactly which direction he was walking.

After one of the series of hallucinations passed, Albert noticed something in a clump of saltbush a few yards from where he was walking, something with a rectangular outline deep in the thicket of brush. Ignoring the pain from being scratched by the branches, Albert pushed his way into the brush until he came upon a weathered sign that read:

PROPERTY OF THE SOUTH AUSTRALIA RAILWAY
TRESPASSERS WILL BE PROSECUTED
The management

Just then the wind came up, and Albert knew that it wasn't going to be his day.

He struggled out of the saltbush and once again began walking in the direction he thought was north. The wind blew harder and dust began to swirl around him. Albert shouldered his way through the dust for some distance. He ran into clumps of brush several times and instinct alone told him which direction to take. The dust in the air became thicker, and the world disappeared in a reddish-brown haze. It wasn't long before Albert lost his way completely.

When he realized he might not be going north any longer, he gave up. He was afraid that he might have turned back south, and he didn't want to die any closer to Adelaide than he had to. Albert saw a large desert grevillea through the dust and pushed his way through the wind until he reached it. He crawled under the bush and lay down. The bush blocked a little of the wind and it seemed calmer there. Albert closed his eyes and held his soft drink bottle against his chest. He began laughing because he knew the South Australia railway would never get the chance to prosecute him.

As Albert lay under the bush, red dirt and sand began to drift over him. He began to dream that the sand was the water of the Murray and that he was going home. Above him the wind rattled the branches of the bush.

As the branches rattled the bush began to sing. The song was very faint. Albert heard "glory," followed by "banks" and then "reedy lagoon." It was a song that Albert had never heard before, and he couldn't understand why a bush would want to sing it to him.

Albert didn't like the song. It took him away from the

riverbanks and brought him back to the desert. He wriggled in closer to the roots of the bush and tried to think of home, but the song wouldn't leave him alone.

"I once heard him say he'd wrestled the Famous Muldoon."

Why would a bush listen to anyone? Who was Muldoon and why was he famous? Albert lay there asking himself those questions. The bush couldn't sing very well. It was off key, and that bothered Albert. It's hard to lie down and die when you are upset. Albert slowly rolled out from under the bush and stood up in the wind. He cocked his head and listened.

And where is the lady I often caressed,
The one with the sad dreamy eyes.
She pillows her head on another man's breast.
He tells her the very same lies.

The song was scattered through the surrounding bushes by the wind. The wind would shift, and with each shift the singing could be heard coming from a different place.

Albert looked out into the dust storm that obscured the desert. He couldn't see more than a few feet, so there was hardly any chance of finding the singer. Yet it was a chance, and one that hadn't been there before. Albert put the bottle under one arm and started walking straight into the wind.

The sand in the air bit into his face and forced him to keep his eyes closed. He pushed on, walking into as many bushes as he walked around. The song flowed out of the wind and washed over Albert like the waters of the river that wasn't there.

High up in the air I can hear the refrain
Of the Butcher bird piping his tune.
For spring in her glory has come back again,
To the banks of the reedy lagoon.

With each step the song grew louder. He tried to walk faster. He was sure that around the next bush, or the one after that, he would find where the song was coming from. Just one more verse was all he needed to hear, but the last verse never came.

Albert stopped in front of a large saltbush. He stood for a long time, but all he could hear was the wind and the rustling of the branches. The feeling of hope and his last link with the Murray River collapsed, and all that remained was the certainty that this was where it would end.

All at once Albert smelled smoke and heard a gruff voice say, "If this is spring in her glory I can bloody well do without it."

Albert jumped at the sound of the voice. If he hadn't been so tired, he would have run toward it. As it was, he had only enough energy to walk around the saltbush.

There, in the middle of a clearing, with the wind scattering sparks and ashes in all directions, was a small fire. A metal tripod had been placed over the fire, and hanging from the tripod was a battered billycan. Steam was escaping from under the edge of a small plate that covered the top of the can.

On the far side of the clearing, partially obscured by the dust and the flying ashes, a blanket lay spread under a bloodwood tree. The blanket fluttered in the wind and the only thing that kept it from blowing away was the heavy pack resting on it.

Standing over the blanket, with his back toward Albert, was a bulky figure wearing a long drover's coat and a gray slouch hat, trying to tie a dirty piece of canvas between the tree and a saltbush a few feet away. Each time the creature came close to getting the rope tied, the wind blew the canvas hard enough to pull the rope from his grasp. With each failed attempt, the creature would mutter, "Spring, bah!" and redouble his efforts to tie the canvas to the bush.

After many attempts, he managed to get the canvas tied off so that it formed a barrier against the wind.

The figure in the long coat waited until he was sure the knots would hold the canvas, then nodded in satisfaction and turned back toward the fire. This gave Albert a clear view of him: a large wombat with a graying handlebar mustache.

The wombat, intent on keeping the wind from blowing the hat off his head, didn't notice Albert watching him from the far side of the clearing.

When the wombat reached the fire he turned his back to the wind, which had shifted and was now coming from Albert's direction. The wombat crouched down and fed small pieces of brush into the fire under the can. As he did, he began to sing in a whooping monotone that carried over the wind.

My bed she would hardly be willing to share
were I camped by the light of the moon...

The wombat stopped singing in midverse and began to laugh.

"Ain't that the bloody truth... not to mention if I got upwind... It's not the keeping square that has kept me single... It must be something else... I wonder what else it could be... I can lie pretty well... that can't be it... I know it's bathing... true love demands soap and water... a habit I don't intend to cultivate."

The wombat laughed again and began whistling the song as badly as he'd sung it.

If he hadn't been certain that there was water in the can hanging over the fire, Albert would have crept back into the bush and let someone more desperate than himself confront a singing wombat in a drover's coat.

Instead, he took a deep breath and started to say "Excuse me" in a loud voice. What came out was a garbled hiss. Albert hadn't spoken a word to anyone since his journey began, and he hadn't realized how dry his throat was. The wind had quieted briefly as he tried to talk, so the hissing noise carried clearly to the whistling wombat.

The wombat jumped several feet in the air and at the top of his lungs screamed, "Snake!" Upon landing, he grabbed a heavy stick that was lying by the fire and began beating the ground all around the spot where he had been crouching. After he finished pummeling every inch of ground within reach of his stick and knocking his firewood all over the clearing, the wombat stopped, looked around and saw Albert for the first time.

He stared at Albert a few moments, then began to walk toward him. Albert grabbed his soft drink bottle by the neck and prepared to sell his life dearly. Just then the wind rattled a saltbush next to the canvas windbreak. The wombat turned and ran toward the offending bush and at the same time shouted in Albert's direction:

"Thank God, reinforcements. Hurry up and bring your bottle. There's a snake around here, but I've got him on the run."

The wombat reached the bush and began beating it into pieces. Albert was too exhausted to chase a snake of his own making. He walked over to the fire and sat down.

The wombat finished destroying the bush and poked through what was left with the end of his stick. After a careful examination of the debris, the wombat looked over at Albert and said, "Hear anything?"

Albert shook his head. The wombat looked back into the remains of the saltbush and listened for a few moments, then threw down his stick.

"Damn, he got away. That's a snake's luck for you."

The wombat walked back to the fire as if nothing unusual had occurred and lifted the plate off the billycan. He peered inside the can, sniffed it, and put the lid back. "Tea's done. Want some?"

Albert nodded vigorously.

"Got a cup?"

Albert shook his head.

"I sort of figured that, you being naked and all."

Albert wasn't wearing any clothes but he was covered in fur, so as far as he was concerned he wasn't naked. He started to give the wombat a sharp retort, but he remembered what happened the last time he tried to speak. Rather than start the snake business all over again, he kept quiet.

The wombat went over to the pack lying on the blanket and rummaged through it until he found two dented tin cups. He wiped the cups with the sleeve of his coat and brought them back to the fire. He gave one cup to Albert, then filled both cups from the billy.

The wombat motioned to Albert, then went over and sat on the blanket behind the canvas windbreak. Albert got up and sat on the blanket next to him. His earlier fear of the creature had been replaced by gratitude for the tea.

They sat quietly for a while. The heat of the tea passed through the thin sides of the tin cup and burned Albert's paws. Albert ignored the pain and drank. The tea was mostly soggy tea leaves, sand, and ashes, but it was wet and that was enough.

The wombat drank his tea in gulps, ignoring the dirt that blew over him from the gap under the canvas, and stopped only to spit out tea leaves. When he finished his tea, he went over, took the billycan down from the tripod, and brought it back to the blanket. He filled Albert's cup and put the can down next to him, being careful to put the plate back on top to keep some of the dirt out. Then the wombat sat back down on the blanket and pulled out a short-stemmed briar pipe. He proceeded to fill it with tobacco taken from a pouch he pulled from another pocket.

Albert watched and wondered. He had never seen an animal smoke. Then again, he had never seen an animal with clothes on. Maybe, just maybe, he'd reached the place he was looking for, Albert kept thinking as he drank cup after cup of tea.

The wombat didn't say a word. He just smoked his pipe and stared off into the dust storm.

Albert waited until he was sure his throat was wet enough that he wouldn't hiss, then he spoke:

"Is this the place?"

The wombat looked at the pieces of desert being blown around them and took the pipe out of his mouth. "I hope not."

"What I meant was, is this the place where things haven't changed and Australia is like it used to be?"

The wombat thought for a long time before he answered. "If you mean somewhere animals run around without any clothes on while being chased by people with spears and boomerangs, the answer is no. It's not bloody likely that you'd find old Jack in a place like that."

2 ≋ Jack the Wombat

THE WIND HAD STOPPED DURING the night. The sun was high on the horizon, and the coolness of the desert morning was beginning to disappear. The bush that surrounded the camp was silent. The light woke Albert. He pulled the blanket down from his face and squinted at the sunlit tops of the bushes that circled the clearing.

The saltbush was light green against a blue sky, and some of the grevillea bushes sported small yellow flowers that were beginning to attract hoverflies.

The tripod remained standing in the middle of the clearing, a small monument to the fire that had been blown into extinction sometime during the night. The piece of canvas had long since parted company from the saltbush and hung limply from the bloodwood tree. The billycan sat partially covered by a small red sand dune next to where Albert lay.

If it hadn't been for the objects surrounding him, Albert would have been convinced that Jack was just another hallucination brought on by too many miles and too little water. His vague recollection of Jack covering him with a blanket was confused with dreams of being naked and poked with spears.

He couldn't remember very much of what happened after Jack told him the place he found wasn't the place he expected. Exhaustion had followed hard on the heels of fading hopes.

Albert lay under the blanket for a long time, trying to sort out the night, without much success. The sun rose above the bloodwood tree and dangled the possibilities of a new day over the windblown camp. Finally, Albert sat up and watched several pounds of sand slide off his blanket and onto his feet. He was preparing to stand when Jack started talking in a muffled voice:

"Sardines?"

Albert looked around. "I beg your pardon?"

"I said sardines."

Jack crawled out from beneath a sand-covered blanket. He was still wearing his drover's coat, and his hat was pulled down firmly over his ears. He poked the sand piles that were scattered around the camp until he found the pack.

"I don't know what you eat, but sardines is what we've got."

"Sardines will be fine."

Jack began pulling tins out of his pack. Along with the tinned fish, he pulled out a crushed felt hat and a coat, both articles having seen much wear. Jack tossed the coat and hat to Albert.

"Best put 'um on. It looks like the sun hasn't been treating you too well lately."

Albert reached up and felt his bill. It was blistered and hurt when he touched it. Albert hadn't realized how badly sunburned he had become during his walk north. He'd had other things on his mind.

Albert put on the hat and it fell down over his eyes. He put on the coat, and it felt like a tent had collapsed on him. Albert pushed the hat back on his head so he could see, and rolled up the sleeves, and in a little while he found his front paws.

Jack looked him up and down. "You aren't going to win any fashion shows, but those should work until we can get something better." He opened two cans of sardines, walked over, and handed one to Albert. "Jack is the name."

"I'm Albert. Pleased to meet you."

Jack sat down next to Albert and began pulling his sardines out of the tin one at a time and eating each one slowly.

"Around the district they call me Jack the Wombat... don't know why. It's not like wombats are thick on the ground. I heard there was a wombat named John east of here... never met him, though."

Albert ate his sardines quickly. He hadn't realized how hungry he was. "I guess that would make me Albert the platypus."

Jack finished his sardines. After inspecting the tin to make sure he hadn't missed one, he buried it in the sand.

"To tell you the truth, just 'Albert' will probably work. I've never seen or even heard of a platypus, and I've been here a lot of years."

Albert's heart dropped. Not only had he ended up in the wrong Australia, he was ending up as the lone platypus.

"We live in the banks of rivers and don't come out much," said Albert.

"I've never even seen a river," said Jack.

Albert put down the tin of sardines. He wasn't hungry anymore.

"Are you going to eat the rest of your fish?" Jack asked. Albert shook his head, and Jack picked up the tin.

"If you don't mind my asking, what brought you out this way?"

Albert thought quite a while before he answered the question. "Adelaide."

Jack nodded sagely. "I figured that there was a female behind it."

"Adelaide is a place."

Jack ate a sardine. "Bet you it was named after a female." He smiled as he finished the last sardine and buried the can. "Where are you headed to now, Albert?"

"I haven't thought that far ahead."

Jack started picking up the blankets. "I've got business at Ponsby Station. You can come along if you want."

Albert hesitated. "I'm not sure I belong here."

Jack cocked his head and looked over at Albert. "Maybe not, Albert, but I've walked a hundred miles in every direction, and this is all there is."

If Jack was right, and Albert had no reason to doubt him, staying alone in this desert would be the start of a short trip to the end of the line.

"I guess I'll come with you, Jack... if you don't mind."

"I don't mind. Help me break camp. Get your blanket and grab the tripod." Jack fished a canteen with a shoulder strap out of the pack and tossed it in Albert's direction. "You'd best carry your own water in case you get lost again."

Albert picked up the canteen and put the strap over a shoulder. The canteen reminded him of the soft drink bottle he'd carried into camp. He poked around the sand piles until he found the bottle. He put it in one of the pockets of his coat. The bottle was the only physical evidence of the reality of his journey from Adelaide, and Albert wasn't sure that he wasn't still in the middle of a bad dream.

He took the tripod to Jack, who tied it to the outside of the pack. After a quick look around the clearing, Jack shouldered the pack and set off. Albert followed, trying not to trip over the bottom of his coat.

They walked for several hours, heading north by northeast. Jack walked at a steady pace, not talking much but occasionally pointing out a plant and telling Albert if it was good to eat or if it had some medicinal properties. Albert was still exhausted from his trip from Adelaide, and it was all he could do just to keep up with Jack, but he kept walking and didn't say a word.

The landscape gradually began to change. The salt and grevillea bushes began to thin, and the red sand gave way to salt pans. The flats were broken only by large rock formations, and in the distance beyond the flats were low hills, and beyond the hills, mountains with gray granite cliffs.

The midday heat finally forced Jack to stop at one of the sandstone formations. There was a shallow cave at the base of the formation that had been scooped out of the soft rock by windblown sand. The cave was on the shady side of the formation. Jack walked into it and put the pack down. Albert followed Jack and sat down at the back of the cave. The sand was still cool from the chill of the previous night and felt good on Albert's feet.

Jack sat for a while, then pulled the tobacco out of his coat and began filling the bowl of his pipe. "I don't like walking in midday. It's best to stay here until the sun starts to go down."

Albert took a drink from his canteen. Jack lit his pipe

with a match he struck on the sole of his foot.

"How long were you watching me last night before you came into camp?" Jack asked.

"Not too long," Albert replied. "It was the singing that led me to you."

"I know you saw me singing and talking and making a fool of myself about that snake." Jack looked embarrassed.

"I don't remember much, Jack. I was pretty tired last night."

"I think you remember more than you're saying, and I appreciate it." Jack lit his pipe before continuing. "I've been alone a long time, Albert, and people who live by themselves do silly things because they figure no one else is watching. I try not to make a fool of myself... too proud, I guess... and I hate it when I do."

Albert didn't know quite what to say to Jack, so he didn't say anything.

Jack smoked his pipe for a while, lost in his own thoughts. When he was through, Jack knocked the dottle out of the pipe with his heel and put the pipe back in his pocket. He opened the pack and pulled out a large white rock and an old pepperbox pistol. "Excuse me a second."

He got up and carried the rock outside. He put the rock on the ground, stepped back, and fired a shot at the rock. The noise of the shot bounced off the back of the cave and nearly deafened Albert.

A cloud of smoke and the smell of sulphur drifted into the cave. Jack picked up the rock and examined it closely in the sunlight. He put the rock back on the ground and fired another shot at it. Albert had just enough time to put his paws over his ears before the second shot was fired.

Jack picked up the rock and examined it a second time.

He nodded in satisfaction and turned back to the cave. Jack put the pistol in his pocket, and when he did, Albert took his paws off his ears.

"This is a piece of white quartz I picked up two days ago, a pretty rock, but not worth much, unless..." Jack pointed outside the cave. "Take it out in the light and give it a close look."

Albert took the rock into the sunlight outside and examined it closely. "It has gold specks in it."

"It sure does, and those specks make that rock worth quite a bit."

Albert carried the rock back into the cave and gave it back to Jack. "Is it really gold?"

Jack shook his head. "A little bit of it is, but it's mostly iron pyrite, which looks a lot like gold. I take that old pistol and load up two of the barrels with thirty grains of black powder, some wadding, a little gold, and a lot of pyrite, and I shoot it at pieces of quartz. Given a minute or two I can turn any rock into the mother lode."

"What are you going to do with it?"

"I don't know yet, but I never saw a situation that was made worse by having a little gold."

Jack put the rock and the pistol back in the pack, and pushed the pack to the back wall of the cave. Jack lay down on his back with his head resting on the pack and closed his eyes. Albert had been thinking about what Jack had said about being alone.

"I was only alone once... it was after my mother died."

Jack opened one eye. Albert continued:

"When I was young, I wandered too far from our burrow. A dog attacked me and... my mother did what she could to defend me. She wasn't very big, but she had a lot of heart...

In the end a lot of heart wasn't enough."

Jack opened both eyes. "I would have liked your mum."

"I thought she was special, but I guess everyone thinks their mother is special."

After a moment, Jack turned his head and looked at Albert. "What happened to the dog?"

"I don't remember," said Albert.

3 〰 Stones that speak

THEY STARTED WALKING AGAIN a few hours before sunset. The temperature had dropped a few degrees, but it was still hot. Jack continued to walk at a steady pace, and Albert found it easier to keep up with him than he had that morning.

Albert had managed a short nap in the cave and felt better than he had in days. He still didn't know where he was going or how he got where he was, but he was moving and that was all important. Up until his escape from Adelaide, Albert's life had been one of confinement and regular habits.

His life on the Murray had taken on a dreamlike quality after so many years away from it. Albert remembered those days before his mother died as the good times, a time of warmth and freedom. But in reality the time had been very short, and most of it had been spent in a dark burrow next to the river. He had been protected by his mother and by the earth around him, and had been too young to understand how much more of the world there was.

Albert couldn't remember much of what happened during the time between his mother's death and his capture. Occasionally a memory of that time would thrust itself into his consciousness and the memory would keep him awake for days. The memories were just pictures without sound or movement: a dead dog with his lips curled back over bloody teeth, a cold and empty burrow, a net held in a gloved hand.

In some ways Albert felt his fragmentary recollections of that time, as bad as they were, might be better to have than his memories of the zoo. He remembered every endless day.

They fed him every morning at the same time with grubs and freshwater shrimp. Then he'd be harried down a tunnel from the place where he slept to a caged enclosure with a concrete water tank in the center of it. The tunnel door was shut behind him. Then, he had an hour to wait until the gates of the park opened and the visitors arrived. Albert never saw the gates—they were a long way from his cage—but he always imagined them as sickeningly ornate, replete with images of platypuses being tortured by demons.

There was someone staring at Albert every moment of the fourteen hours a day the zoo was open. He couldn't escape from sight anywhere in the enclosure. They pointed at him, talked about him, made faces at him, and sometimes would throw things at him to make him scramble into the water tank.

The water tank was the worst. There was a glass wall on one side of the tank where people could watch him swim. The glass wall was always clouded by algae growing on it, and the water magnified the faces watching him. Large mouths opened and closed and large eyes blinked ciphered messages to each other behind the blue-green scum on the glass. Albert avoided it as much as he could.

A chill in the air took Albert's thoughts from the Adelaide zoo and brought them back to the desert. As the sun disappeared below the western horizon, a cool breeze began to drift across the trail from the low hills not more than a mile ahead.

Jack pointed toward the hills. "Ponsby Station is on the other side. We'll make camp here tonight... should make the station by noon tomorrow."

Jack picked a likely clearing for their camp and put his pack in the middle of it. As Jack took the billycan and some sardines out of his pack, Albert tried to make himself useful by gathering small sticks to use as firewood.

"Keep an eye out for snakes!" Jack bellowed from where he was putting up the tripod.

"I'll do that, Jack."

Snakes didn't bother Albert. Having his own ability to poison other creatures, he had always felt a certain kinship with them. The venomous spurs on Albert's back legs set him apart from other animals and gave him an understanding of those that used poison to feed or defend themselves.

Albert dropped a pile of sticks next to Jack and went back into the bush to look for more wood. By the time he returned to the camp, Jack had a fire going and the billycan hanging over it.

Twilight was rapidly fading to darkness, and the heat and light from the fire were welcome. Jack opened a couple of cans of sardines, and as soon as the water in the billycan boiled, he poured tea into the tin cups. He and Albert ate the sardines and drank their tea in silence. The night became colder and Albert pulled his coat tightly around him. After Jack finished the last sardine, he stared at the empty tin for a moment before tossing it into the night beyond the campfire.

"Adelaide may have pushed you out into this desert, Albert, but it was claustrophobia that drove me here."

Jack paused to pour more tea into his cup. "I don't know how much you know about wombats, Albert, but we're a boring lot, let me tell you."

"I've seen one or two from a distance, but you're the first one I've ever talked to," Albert replied.

"We live in deep holes, come out in the early morning or late in the evening, eat some leaves, and then call it a day. What kind of life is that? What is there to talk about, nothing, that's what. Entire conversations consisting of 'What did you do today, Earl?' 'I ate some leaves, Frank, What did you do?' 'I ate some grass and then I slept in a dark hole for twenty-two hours.' 'What are you going to do tomorrow, Frank?' 'I hadn't thought about it, Earl, but I might eat some leaves.' My God, Albert, what kind of life is that?"

Except for all those leaves, the life didn't sound too bad to Albert. "Quiet."

"Damn right it's quiet. It was too damn quiet for me." Jack spit a tea leaf into the fire. "I never could stand the darkness. It made me crazy, and I made my mother and father crazy in return. As soon as I got out of the pouch, I started crawling toward the light. They tried to stop me for a while, embarrassed by what the neighbors would think, I guess. I got bigger and finally they stopped bothering with me. My mother cried occasionally when I'd leave, but that was all. I stayed out all day and at night I'd sleep outside the mouth of the burrow so I could see the stars... Every day I would walk farther and farther from that damn hole in the ground, and one day I walked so far I couldn't find my way back."

Jack stopped talking and stared into the fire.

"How did you get here?" Albert asked.

"I just kept walking and one day here I was. The Famous Muldoon told me once that he thought that everybody who walks far enough eventually ends up here. But Muldoon had strange ideas and I never took much stock in them."

"But where is here?" Albert persisted.

"I can't tell you that, Albert, because I don't know myself. I can tell you that where we are is real and it's a place that can get you killed if you're not careful."

"But what about the other places, the place where everything was like it used to be or the place where those men with the spears and boomerangs live?"

"You hear a lot of stories out here, Albert—some true, some not. Maybe if you'd walked in another direction you would have found those places. But you didn't."

Jack got up and took the billycan off the hook on the tripod and used the dregs of the tea to douse the fire. "They say that others were here before we were. You can see the drawings they left on the rocks, and those old ones claimed that every bush and every stone had its own spirit."

Albert got his blanket out of the pack and wrapped it around himself. "Do you believe that?"

"I don't hold much stock in those stories… Still, on windy evenings I sometimes think that the stones are singing to me. I just shrug it off, tell myself that I'm getting old and leave it at that."

"What do they say?"

"They don't say anything. It's just the imagination of someone who's been alone in the desert too long."

"What is it that you imagine they say?" Albert insisted.

"They say that there is no point to it all and that everyone that has ever sat on them, crossed by them, or picked them up was coming from nowhere and going to the same place. They giggle a bit and are quiet for a long time. Then they start singing the same song all over again."

"Are you sure it's your imagination? Maybe they are really talking to you."

Jack smiled. "Generally, rocks aren't that intelligent."

He turned away from Albert, walked to the edge of the clearing, and relieved himself on a bush before going to bed.

4 ≋ Ponsby Station

THE DIRT TRACK THAT LED to the center of Ponsby Station went through an old water course that had created a shallow gully on the edge of town. Pieces of corrugated tin had been shoved into the sides of the gully at uneven intervals, each piece shading a hole that had been dug into the dirt banks. Ragged flowers in old coffee cans or in pieces of broken crockery graced the shade under some of the protruding tin, and they were the only bits of color in a landscape made up in shades of brown and yellow.

As Jack and Albert walked down the track, Albert could hear an occasional whistle come from one of the holes. "Who lives here?"

"Bandicoots, most likely. They sleep days."

Albert was surprised. "Haven't you been here before?"

Jack shifted the pack to a more comfortable position on his back. "Can't say as I have. It doesn't matter, though. All these places are pretty much the same: bandicoots on one side of town, rock wallabies on the other, all of them working shifts in a half-played-out mine, just trying to get by."

Two hundred yards later, the track opened up into the center of Ponsby Station.

A large ramshackle building stood in the center of a flat piece of ground on the edge of a mining operation. Flat-topped hills of mine tailings dwarfed the building, and broken ore carts were scattered along a rusting track leading into the hills beyond the station.

The building had at one time been painted white, but now the walls were nothing but weathered wood with occasional patches of peeling paint. Metal signs advertising beer and tobacco had been nailed up on the ends of the building, but they, too, had weathered, and rusty streaks obscured the painted messages from better times.

The building had a tin roof extending over a long wooden verandah that ran the length of the front wall. A couple of old benches and a spittoon graced the verandah near the front door. The door was closed and the benches were empty.

On the roof was a large sign, also much faded, which read:

PONSBY STATION
GENERAL MERCANTILE
"Quality Goods at a Fair Price"
Sing Sing O'Hanlin, Prop.

Jack stopped in front of the building. He looked up at the sign and smiled. "Here goes nothin', Albert. Stay close."

He climbed up onto the verandah, opened the front door of the mercantile, and walked in. Albert followed him inside.

Inside, the store was not brightly lit. What light there was filtered in from two windows in the back and a dirty skylight over the counter that ran half the length of the store. Behind the counter were shelves of canned goods, bolts of cloth, general hardware, and odd pieces of clothing. A rifle rack holding a rusty flintlock musket and two Enfield carbines sat at one end of the counter. In front of the rifle rack was a glass case containing a few percussion pistols.

The back half of the store was a dirt floor bar and sporting arena. The bar was two wide planks set across some empty beer barrels. The arena was just an open space with a few wooden bleachers against the wall away from the bar.

A tapped beer keg rested on the planks. The back bar was a long shelf full of whiskey bottles and beer glasses. Above the shelf was a cracked mirror and a series of posters advertising prize fights that had been fought long ago. Each poster had a picture of a kangaroo wearing shorts on it. The kangaroos had their fists up and appeared to be snarling.

Behind the bar stood a large red kangaroo wearing an apron and a dirty silk shirt with garters on the sleeves. A pair of wire-rimmed spectacles rested on his nose. Across the bar from the kangaroo were two bandicoots wearing canvas overalls. The bandicoots were so drunk they were having trouble standing up.

Jack walked up next to the bandicoots, took off his pack, and set it on the bar. Albert followed him to the bar.

"I assume that's beer in the barrel," Jack said.

The kangaroo looked over his glasses at Jack. "And I assume that there's money in your pocket."

One of the bandicoots snickered. Jack pulled a couple of English shillings out of his coat pocket and put them on the bar. "My money is probably better than your whiskey, but I'm willing to take a chance."

The other bandicoot snickered.

The kangaroo looked at the money and then at Albert. "Are you the only one drinking?"

"I didn't come in here alone. I don't plan to drink alone. Two beers."

The kangaroo shook his head. "I can't serve him," he said, pointing at Albert.

At that point, Albert was much more curious than insulted. Jack's eyes narrowed and he was quiet for a moment before he spoke. "And why would that be?"

The kangaroo gestured to another sign next to the cracked mirror that read:

WE RESERVE THE RIGHT TO REFUSE SERVICE
TO ANYONE WHO ISN'T A MARSUPIAL
The Management

"He's going to have to leave. House rules."

Albert spoke for the first time. "I'm a platypus."

The kangaroo adjusted his spectacles with his front paw and took a closer look at Albert. "I never saw anything like you before, and I assume that anything I haven't seen didn't come from a pouch... until proven otherwise."

"Got to be a marsupial," said one bandicoot, nodding his head sagely.

"Marsupial," agreed the other bandicoot.

As both bandicoots and the kangaroo stared at Albert, he could feel the spurs on his hind legs start to extend themselves. The more they stared, the more they reminded Albert of the people at the zoo, and with each look the anger in Albert's soul burned brighter. At the zoo there was nothing he could do, but here he might be allowed the luxury of a violent act. The sound of Jack's voice momentarily halted Albert's downward spiral into rage and the relief of mayhem.

"I say he's a platypus, and you had best leave it at that."

Jack's voice was still calm, but the pepperbox pistol was now sitting on the bar in front of the kangaroo. Both of Jack's paws were resting on the bar next to the pistol.

The kangaroo eyed the pistol a moment before saying, "I suppose I could make an exception in this case. I just use that sign to keep the riffraff out, anyway. What's a platypus?"

The bandicoots, oblivious to what was going on, continued to stare at Albert. "We could look at his private parts," offered one of them.

Albert hit the bandicoot as hard as he could with his front paw. The bandicoot flew across the arena for a few feet before hitting the floor and rolling over to the wooden bleachers. Albert had never hit anyone before and was surprised how satisfying it felt. The spurs in his hind legs began to recede.

The other bandicoot looked over at Albert and said between hiccups, "Good shot, mate. I always thought he was a bit of a poof."

The other bandicoot got up and lurched toward the bar. "Who are you calling a poof?"

The bandicoot in front of Albert put up his fists. "Who was volunteering to look at someone's private parts, Roger?"

"I said *we* could look, Alvin."

"Don't involve me in your nasty plans, you pervert."

At that point Alvin staggered across the room and

launched himself at Roger. The bandicoots began rolling around the floor, kicking, biting, and scratching one another.

Jack took the pistol off the bar and put it in his pocket. He watched the bandicoots for a moment, then took another shilling from his pocket and put it on the bar. "A bob on the one with the other one's ear in his mouth."

The kangaroo took a shilling out of a pocket in his apron and laid it on the bar next to Jack's coin. "Done. Your bet's on Roger. He's the meaner of the two. But he gets tired quicker than Alvin."

Jack held out his paw. "Jack's the name."

The kangaroo took Jack's paw and shook it. "Sing Sing O'Hanlin, proprietor and acting captain, Ponsby Station Fusiliers."

"Fusiliers?" Jack let go of O'Hanlin's paw.

"The Fusiliers are our local militia, organized for the defense of Ponsby Station. We meet on Saturdays, march around a little bit, and then we all come over here for a drink. There's good money in those meetings, let me tell you."

Sing Sing took a couple of beer glasses from the back bar, filled them from the keg, and set one in front of Jack and one in front of Albert. "Sorry about any misunderstanding. We don't get many platypuses in here... In fact, you're the first. Have a beer... on the house."

Albert took the beer and thanked Sing Sing, but he didn't feel grateful at all. He was beginning to feel that his escape from the zoo and his flight through the desert had been for nothing. Here he was, where Old Australia was supposed to be, a place where he was to have a home, friends, and others of his kind. Now he was finding that the only way he could even get a beer in this country was at gunpoint.

The bandicoots were beginning to tire. They lay on the floor of the arena and held on to each other by the straps of their overalls, trying to catch their breath. Periodically, one would get up the energy to kick or bite the other, and the scuffle would start all over again.

"Kind of quiet around here," Jack observed, taking a sip of his beer.

O'Hanlin took a glass off the back bar and began to polish it with his apron. "Give it a couple of hours. The wallabies will be getting off shift and the bandicoots will be getting ready to go on. Payday was two days ago, and some of 'um still have money left. They'll get a two-up game going, or maybe a prize fight..."

He looked over at Albert with new appreciation. "Say, this platypus here has a good right hook and..."

"The name's Albert, Albert of Adelaide," said Albert crossly.

Sing Sing didn't miss a beat. "Albert here has a good right hook. We could probably get up a fight that could make us a little money. Nobody here has ever seen a platypus, and they'd figure he'd be easy pickings for one of the local heroes. Might get two... even three-to-one odds."

"I used to fight for money," said Jack. "There's no future in it."

"You a boxer?" asked Sing Sing.

"Wrestled, mostly."

"Boxing is what most people want to see nowadays," said Sing Sing, pointing up at the posters of the boxing kangaroos. "More blood, more action."

Sing Sing picked up another glass to polish and

continued, "If the Famous Muldoon hadn't disappeared, maybe people would still be interested in wrestling."

Jack took another drink of beer. "Muldoon could draw a crowd, that's for sure."

"Ever see him fight?" asked O'Hanlin.

"Once or twice," said Jack, "What do you say, Albert, want to make a little money punching the locals?"

Albert had never had a beer before and was beginning to get light-headed. "I've spent enough of my life having people stare at me."

Jack put his empty beer glass on the bar. "I guess that's a no, Mr. O'Hanlin." Jack picked up his pack and slung it over one shoulder. "Albert and I'll make camp outside of town and come back when things get a little more lively... Have you got a hat and coat that might fit Albert?"

O'Hanlin looked Albert up and down. "Got a vest, anyway. Let's take a look." He walked out from behind the bar and over to the store.

Just then the bandicoots, completely exhausted, quit fighting. They lay on their backs next to each other on the dirt floor.

"I'm sorry, Roger."

"So am I, Alvin."

"Even if you are a poof, Roger, you're the best mate a fellow could have."

"That's right, we're mates."

Roger began to sob uncontrollably. Alvin reached over, patted Roger, and began crying.

O'Hanlin looked at the bandicoots and shook his head. "I should have told you. They do that sometimes."

"It's not a pretty sight," Jack said, as he picked up one of the shillings from the bar, "not a pretty sight at all."

5 ≋ The evil gin does

AS THEY WALKED BACK INTO Ponsby Station that evening, Albert had much on his mind. He and Jack had set up a camp a few miles out of town. They had spoken very little during the walk to the camp, and even less as they were setting out their gear. Albert guessed that O'Hanlin's reference to the Famous Muldoon was bothering Jack. After all, Jack had told Albert that he knew Muldoon. But, when O'Hanlin mentioned Muldoon to him, Jack had avoided the subject. Albert would have liked to ask Jack more about the Famous Muldoon, but he didn't want to press him on what was obviously a sore subject.

The clothes he had gotten at the mercantile made him feel a little less conspicuous than he had felt wearing the outsized hat and coat Jack had loaned him. O'Hanlin's selection of clothing had been limited, most of the items having been taken in pawn and never claimed. However, after sorting through what was there, Albert, with Jack's help, had selected a fairly clean tweed vest and a much-repaired short canvas jacket with deep side pockets to wear over the vest. Finding a hat had been a little more difficult, but Albert finally settled on a battered kepi with a leather bill. The bill on the hat shaded the bill on Albert's face and he thought it looked rather jaunty in the cracked mirror behind the bar. Jack also found a small rucksack that fit Albert, so they took that also.

Albert had never had to pay for anything before. Life on the Murray had been a matter of digging a burrow and catching lunch in a river that abounded with shrimp and crayfish. The zoo in Adelaide fed its captives with monotonous regularity, but the animals themselves never had to collect the money or buy the food. Now, Albert found that in order to survive he was required to buy clothes and eat canned food someone had to pay for.

Jack had paid O'Hanlin for the clothes and the rucksack from a dwindling supply of coins he pulled from a pocket in his drover's coat. Albert tried to broach the subject of how he could pay Jack for the clothes on the walk to the camp, but Jack dismissed Albert's concern by telling him not to worry about the money and that they could work it all out later.

Everything Albert had he had gotten from Jack, with one exception. He still had the soft drink bottle he had brought from Adelaide. When Albert had taken it out of the pocket of his borrowed coat to put in the rucksack, O'Hanlin had noticed the bottle and expressed an interest in it.

It seemed that O'Hanlin, being in the spirits business, was fond of bottles and had a collection of them. He had never seen a bottle like the one Albert had and offered to buy it. Albert had refused to sell the bottle because of its association with his old reality.

However, while he was making camp, Albert began to think about O'Hanlin's offer. Whatever the old reality was, it was gone and a new one had taken its place. The more he thought about it, the more he realized that the less association he had with Adelaide the happier he might be. At that point, Albert decided he would sell the bottle to O'Hanlin and give the money to Jack. The money might not be enough to pay Jack what he owed him, but it was a start.

The noise coming from O'Hanlin's place broke Albert's train of thought. He could hear yelling and singing well before they even saw the lights of the building.

The Ponsby Station Mercantile was a much different place at night than it had been that afternoon. Light was streaming through the front windows and the open door. Wallabies and bandicoots congregated in separate groups on the verandah. Some were sitting on the benches talking with one another and occasionally using the spittoon. Others sat on the edge of the porch sharing half-pint bottles of gin or whiskey. The shouting and singing came from inside the building, and every so often a bandicoot or a wallaby would come flying through the open door to land face-first on the verandah. One or two just lay there, more drunk than hurt, and the rest would dust themselves off and rush back inside.

Jack stopped about fifty yards from the front of the building. "Albert, try and keep close to me. Watch my lead, and if trouble starts get out as quickly as you can. Meet me back at camp, but take a roundabout way back so no one can follow you."

Albert started to get concerned. "What do you think is going to happen?"

"Probably nothing, but you never can tell."

Jack proceeded on to the verandah, followed closely by Albert. He stepped over the fallen and walked through the front door.

The inside of the mercantile was full of smoke and noise. Miners were two deep at the bar, and O'Hanlin and two assistants were pushing beer and whiskey across the bar as fast as they could. A crowd was gathered over at the arena watching a drunken wallaby throw two coins in the air with a stick. Every time the coins landed, there was much yelling, screaming, and exchanging of money. Every other patron in the bar had a cigar or a pipe in his mouth, and the tobacco smoke hung in heavy layers in the light of the paraffin lamps that lined the walls.

Before they were three feet inside the door, they were stopped by a rough-looking gray kangaroo sitting on a stool by the bar. The kangaroo was heavyset, wearing a bowler hat with a rip in the crown and checked pants with a blackjack hanging out of the back pocket.

"You can go in," the kangaroo said to Jack, "but he's not welcome." He pointed to Albert.

"Why not?" asked Jack.

"Because I say so, and because it's the house rules." The kangaroo stood up and put a paw on the blackjack in his pocket.

"You'd better take that up with your boss," said Jack, pointing to O'Hanlin behind the bar. "Albert here is an exception to the rule."

The bouncer waved his paw toward the bar and caught O'Hanlin's eye. He pointed at Albert, and O'Hanlin motioned for Jack and Albert to come in.

The gray kangaroo sat back down on the stool. "I guess it's all right, but no trouble, you understand? I got my eye on both of you."

"We're no trouble, mate, we're no trouble at all."

Jack pushed on into the crowd. After a few minutes,

Jack was able to elbow himself and Albert a place at the bar.

O'Hanlin put a pint of beer in front of Jack and another in front of Albert. "Good evening, Jack. You too, Albert."

Jack put a couple of coins on the bar and raised his glass. "Good evening, Mr. O'Hanlin. It looks like you're doing a good trade tonight."

O'Hanlin shrugged. "It'll slow down to a trickle over the next two days. Then nothing until they get paid again in two weeks."

"Mining is a hard life, O'Hanlin, that's why I'd rather find it than dig it up."

"You a prospector?"

Jack nodded and took a sip of beer.

O'Hanlin continued: "Ever make a strike?"

Jack immediately began looking around the room in a nervous manner and put his paw on the bulge in his coat pocket. "What have you heard?"

"I haven't heard anything."

Jack leaned over the bar toward O'Hanlin. "Did you hear that Albert and I have made a big strike?"

"No."

Jack's paw shook as he took another drink of beer. "Well, it's not true. We haven't found anything, have we, Albert?"

Albert looked quizzically at Jack. "No, Jack, we haven't found anything."

"See, I told you so, O'Hanlin."

O'Hanlin looked suspiciously at Jack for a moment, then broke into a Cheshire cat smile. "Sorry to hear that. Maybe next time."

Jack nodded. "Maybe next time."

O'Hanlin took a bottle of gin off the back bar, poured three shots, and set the brimming shot glasses in front of Jack and Albert. "A drink to luck, gentlemen, compliments of the house."

Jack, Albert, and O'Hanlin lifted their glasses.

"To Luck," said O'Hanlin.

"To Luck," said Jack, and threw back the shot.

"To Luck," said Albert, and swallowed his drink. It took only a second before he thought he might have poisoned himself. His throat started burning and he felt like choking. Albert immediately grabbed his beer and took a large swallow.

"Gin goes better with a chaser, doesn't it, Albert?" O'Hanlin said, returning the bottle to the back bar.

Albert nodded and took another swallow of beer to wash the taste of juniper berries out of his mouth.

O'Hanlin finished his drink and said, "Take care of yourself, Jack, and don't leave without letting me buy you another drink." He moved down the bar to serve other customers. Jack watched him go and then turned to Albert.

"When a publican like O'Hanlin starts buying you free drinks, you can be sure your luck is going to change, and not for the better, either."

"Why is he doing it, then?" Albert asked.

"Because he's taking the bait, that's why. All you have to do is look guilty and deny everything. It works every time." Jack turned his back to the bar and started watching the game in the arena. Albert turned to watch with him.

"That's a two-up game, Albert. Ever seen one?"

"No."

"See that circle scratched in the dirt?"

"I see it."

"That wallaby with the broken ear over there is acting as the 'boxer.' He's sort of the referee; he makes sure the coins fall in the circle and calls 'heads,' 'tails,' or 'odds.'"

"What's odds?" asked Albert.

"One tail and one head—it doesn't count, and the 'spinner', the one throwing the coins, has to throw again. If they both come up heads or both tails, then whoever bet heads or tails wins. There is a little more to it, dealing with how many odds the spinner throws before he gets his called coins three times in a row, but that is basically the game."

"It doesn't sound very difficult."

"It was a game invented by alcoholics to amuse drunks; they couldn't afford to make it too complicated," Jack said, as he finished his beer. He took a few coins out of his pocket and gave them to Albert. "Stay at the bar for a while, Albert. Buy yourself another drink if you need to. I'm going to wander around the place a little and see if I can find a back door... just in case." Jack winked at Albert and pushed his way back through the crowd.

Jack's place was immediately taken by a large wallaby still covered in grime from his shift in the mine. The wallaby pounded the bar and yelled for beer, until one of O'Hanlin's assistant bartenders slammed a full glass of beer down in front of him. The wallaby threw a coin in the direction of the bartender and took a big drink. The bartender made a signal to the bouncer at the door.

The wallaby took another drink and looked Albert up and down. "What in the hell are you?"

At the zoo, Albert had been an object of curiosity and ridicule. In Old Australia he found himself an object of hate and mistrust. Albert wasn't quite sure how to deal with it, but he was becoming convinced that he had to handle the problem himself rather than passively sitting by and letting Jack stand up for him. "Why do you care?"

"Because, I don't like standing next to some sort of freak."

"Then move away. I was here first."

The wallaby slowly put down his beer. "I'll show you who's going to move!"

Albert made a fist and hoped he really did have a good right hook. Before he could take a swing, he heard a voice saying, "He's a platypus—what's it to you?"

Albert looked down, and there were Roger and Alvin.

"You stay out of this," snarled the wallaby.

"We're not stayin' out of nothin'. Albert here is our mate, isn't he, Roger?" said Alvin.

"He sure is," agreed Roger. "He hit me fair and square this afternoon, and that makes us mates."

"And any mate of Roger's is a mate of mine," said Alvin emphatically.

"You two runts better piss off before you get hurt," said the wallaby.

"Did you hear that, Roger? He told you to piss off," said Alvin.

"But he called you a runt," said Roger.

"You're right, Roger, I'll hit him first."

Just then the bouncer walked up behind the wallaby and hit him in the back of the head with his billy club. The wallaby collapsed on the floor like a puppet with its strings cut. Alvin immediately stepped over to the wallaby's body and began going through his pockets. He found some change and tossed most of it to the bouncer. "Thanks, mate. You can keep the rest."

The kangaroo caught the change in the air, pocketed his club, and started dragging the wallaby toward the front door.

"Never met a wallaby that wasn't a wanker," said Roger, watching the wallaby being thrown through the front door.

"Too right, Roger."

Alvin counted the change he had kept and then ordered three shots of gin from the bartender. "Be a mate, Albert, and hand us that beer off the bar."

Albert took the wallaby's beer and handed it down to Roger and Alvin, who managed to drink all of it before the gin arrived.

Albert was dizzy from the one beer and the shot of gin O'Hanlin had given him, but he couldn't refuse a drink from the bandicoots, not after they had come to his defense. He drank as quickly as he could, but the bad taste lingered. The bandicoots drank their gin almost immediately and started looking in each other's pockets for more money. They couldn't find any.

"Say, Albert, you wouldn't have any quid, would you?" asked Roger hopefully.

Albert took the coins Jack had given him off the bar. He held them down to Roger.

"He's only got three bob," said Roger, after counting the coins carefully.

"Not enough," agreed Alvin.

"Not enough for what?" asked Albert.

"Not enough for a proper drunk, of course," said Roger, looking very depressed. "Think of something, Alvin."

Alvin and Roger started thinking. The noise from the two-up game started bothering Albert. The gin was giving him a headache. A lot of shouting came from the arena as the latest spinner made a losing throw. It began to seem like a good idea to Albert, to go over and tell the crowd to be quiet. Albert left the bar and walked unsteadily toward the game. Alvin and Roger scampered after him.

Albert got to the center of the little arena just as the broken-eared wallaby started yelling for a new spinner.

"You are making quite a bit of noise," Albert said solemnly.

"Either take the kip or get out of the circle," said the broken-eared wallaby. He held out a wooden paddle and two pennies to Albert.

The crowd had started murmuring the minute Albert had walked into the circle. He looked into their faces. "What's the matter, haven't you ever seen a platypus before?"

The crowd started to quiet. Roger and Alvin stepped into the circle beside Albert.

"Well, now you have seen a platypus, and your life is complete. Albert's the name. I'm from Adelaide and I don't give a damn whether you like me or not."

The crowd grew silent. Albert reached over and took the paddle and put the two pennies in the holes in the paddle.

He handed the wallaby his three shillings, and said "Tails" in a loud voice. The wallaby waited, but the crowd said nothing, no one made a side bet. Finally, the wallaby yelled, "No more bets," and nodded to Albert to toss the coins. Albert flipped the coins over his head with the kip. The coins hit the floor inside the circle and rolled to a stop. The wallaby went over and looked at them.

"Tails."

The wallaby took the coins back to Albert. He put them in the kip and threw them over his head again. Again they both landed tails. The members of the crowd began to make side bets. The wallaby yelled, "No more bets," and Albert threw the coins again. The crowd was quiet until the wallaby examined the coins and yelled, "Tails." As the crowd began yelling, the wallaby took the kip from Albert and gave him two handfuls of coins in return. "You're a winner, mate."

Albert handed Roger and Alvin some of the coins and put the rest in his pocket. Someone in the crowd handed Albert a shot glass full of gin. Albert held the drink up to the crowd. "A platypus is the luckiest animal in the world—" he tossed down the drink and took the kip back from the wallaby "—so you had better bet with me because I am not finished yet."

Albert flung the pennies once again into the air and yelled, "Tails."

The copper coins rose in the smoke-filled air and hung suspended in the flickering light of the paraffin lamps for a fragment of a second before they began their fall back toward the earth.

6 〰 About the night before

ALBERT FELT THE WEIGHT ON his chest wiggle a little. He opened his eyes slowly and saw blue sky in a rectangle of rusted steel. The heat surrounding him was oppressive, and he smelled smoke. Albert tried to move his feet, but he couldn't.

He closed his eyes again. He remembered throwing the pennies in the air, the taste of juniper berries, the crowd yelling and pushing, the smell of smoke, and then nothing. Maybe it was a dream—but if it was, why could he still smell the smoke?

Then he heard a voice whispering, "Albert... Albert, wake up. We've got to get out of here."

Albert opened his eyes again. The head of Jack the Wombat had appeared in the blue rectangle. Albert looked around. He was lying on his back in what looked like a rusted metal box with no lid. Albert reached out and put a paw on the side of the box. It was warm to the touch. He looked down at his chest. Alvin, or perhaps it was Roger, was lying on his chest, snoring loudly. The other bandicoot was lying on Albert's feet. Shilling coins were scattered all over the bandicoots and the bottom of the box.

"Albert... get up!" Jack insisted. Before Albert could

reply, Jack reached down and grabbed Albert by the collar, hauling him out of the box, and shaking off the bandicoots in the process. The bandicoots didn't even wake up. They fell into a pile in the corner of the box and continued snoring.

Jack pulled Albert clear of the box, put him on the ground, and crawled back in, where the bandicoots were sleeping. Albert looked around and realized that he had been sleeping in the bottom of an abandoned ore cart on one of the tailing dumps above Ponsby Station. It was almost midday, and heat waves were starting to rise from the dumps and the ore cart. Albert couldn't see Ponsby Station, only a column of smoke rising from where the mercantile had been.

Jack climbed back out of the ore cart with two fistfuls of coins. He put the money in his coat pockets. He took a canteen off his shoulder, unscrewed the cap, and handed it to Albert. "It's just water. Take a drink and let's get moving."

Albert took the canteen and started drinking. He hadn't realized how thirsty he was, and just drinking the water began to ease his headache. After drinking most of the contents of the canteen, Albert handed it back to Jack.

"What happened?" he asked.

"I burned down the store. I'll tell you about it later." Jack screwed the cap back on the canteen. "Right now you and I have to put some distance between us and Ponsby Station."

He turned and began sliding down the tailing dump to the desert below. Albert scrambled after him, kicking up plumes of yellow dust in his wake.

At the bottom of the dump, Jack started walking at a rapid pace. "We'd better move east for a while and then circle back to the camp and pick up our gear."

"What about Roger and Alvin?" Albert asked when he caught up with Jack.

"I wouldn't worry about those bandicoots, if I were you. I'm sure they've slept off a hangover in worse places. Besides I left enough coins in the bottom of that ore cart to keep both of them drunk for a month... assuming they can find a place to drink."

The trip back to the camp was a long, painful struggle. Jack might not have liked to walk in the midday sun, but he made an exception in this case. Between the heat and the gin from the night before, each hour felt like a dozen to Albert. The only water Jack had was in the canteen that he had given Albert, and that was almost empty before the trip started. There was enough water for only a few sips each hour, and Jack rationed it carefully.

Albert was curious about why Jack had burned down Ponsby Station, but he knew that he needed to keep his mind on making it back to camp. It seemed like all he had done since he left Adelaide was to walk. None of those walks had been pleasant, but each one had seemed inevitable. Jack was beginning to teach him about the desert, but Albert knew he had a lot more to learn. It was becoming clear to him that he would soon need to strike out on his own.

Old Australia was certainly different from Adelaide. It was not the place Albert had hoped to find. There were places in this desert that the other animals at the zoo in Adelaide had never even dreamed of, and perhaps somewhere beyond the horizon was a place where he would finally find the home that had been lost to him so many years before.

They arrived at the camp north of Ponsby Station a few

hours before the sun went down. Jack had Albert wait in the desert a few hundred yards from the camp and went in alone. He returned shortly.

"No one's been there, but I don't know how long that might last." Jack motioned for Albert to follow him, and they walked back down to the camp.

At the camp Jack was all business. After a few minutes' rest and a drink of some much-needed water, he hurried Albert into breaking camp.

"Let's go, Albert. I'll tell you about the fire when we get a little farther down the road." Jack shouldered his pack and started walking west. Albert pulled on his rucksack and staggered after Jack, swearing under his breath to never touch another glass of gin as long as he lived.

Jack finally stopped when it got too dark to see the trail ahead. He led Albert off the trail for some distance before he took off his pack. Albert slipped off the straps to his rucksack and let it fall on the ground behind him. He stood for a few minutes, almost too tired to sit, but finally bent his knees and came to rest on the pack.

"I could use some tea."

Jack shook his head. "Dry camp, Albert. The light of a fire carries a long way at night. It might bring us some unwelcome guests." He took his pipe out of the pocket and looked at it briefly. "Shouldn't even smoke."

He sadly put the pipe back in his pocket and sat down. He fished a couple of tins of sardines out of his pack and tossed one to Albert. "You had a hell of a night."

"I've had a hell of a day, too," replied Albert. He played with the sardine can for a few moments. "What happened last night? I don't remember anything after I started playing two-up."

Jack nodded as he opened his can of fish. "I'm surprised you remember any of it. You and those two bandicoots had a snootful."

"I'll never do that again—you have my word on it." Albert put down the sardine can. "I could use some more water."

Jack got a canteen out of his pack and passed it to Albert. "I wouldn't be too hasty about giving up strong drink if I were you, Albert. Drunk, you're the luckiest two-up player I ever saw."

"I remember yelling something about being lucky." Albert took a drink of water. "I don't feel lucky."

"You should feel very lucky. You won a lot of money and you didn't get lynched," said Jack.

"Lynched? What are you talking about?"

"Are you going to eat those sardines?" Jack asked, pointing at the tin Albert had put down.

"No, and don't change the subject. What lynching?" Albert demanded.

Jack picked up the new tin of fish, but he paused before opening it. "You won too much money and you're different than everyone else. That combination, and the wrong crowd, will almost always guarantee a hanging."

"I didn't do anything wrong... did I?"

Jack opened the sardine can. "No, Albert, you didn't do anything wrong, and that's the sad part about it. If anybody was doing something wrong it was me, but when they saw you flipping those pennies in the air, they forgot all about me."

"I don't understand," Albert interjected.

"When we went into the bar last night, I had that piece of quartz I'd salted with pyrites in my pocket. I figured that

I'd let O'Hanlin think he'd gotten me drunk, then I'd flash the rock and let him see those specks of fool's gold, and then, depending on how the play was going, either sell him part interest in my claim for a few quid or sell him a map to the claim. At one time or another I've done both."

"I'd have to guess it didn't work out," Albert thought aloud.

"Too right it didn't work out," snorted Jack. "Nobody cares about a gold mine when a two-up player is on a streak—and let me tell you, Albert, I never saw a streak like that."

Jack separated two sardines that had become stuck together, and he smiled as he ate them individually. "The more I think of it, Albert, the whole evening was a thing of beauty. Too bad you don't remember it."

"Maybe I'm lucky I don't remember it. What about the fire?"

Jack put down his sardines and took the canteen back from Albert. "The fire was a good idea. I just got a little too enthusiastic with the paraffin, that's all."

Jack had a drink from the canteen as Albert tried hard to recall the night before. The last thing he remembered seeing was the coins flashing in the light. He could recall the smell of smoke, but nothing more.

"You were standing in the middle of the circle, winning every toss, and taunting the crowd about being losers with pouches."

Albert sat up straight. "I wouldn't do anything like that!"

Jack smiled. "Face it, Albert, you've got a mean streak."

Albert was aware of the anger that was always floating in and out of his consciousness, and he tried to keep it in check as much as possible. Obviously alcohol had loosened the reins. "What else did I do?"

"I don't recall anything else, but I got kind of busy." Jack continued to sip on the canteen as he talked. "It was clear to me that you were going to win one toss too many, or one of those damn wallabies was eventually going to take exception to being called a loser with a pouch, and when that happened all hell was going to break loose. If we were going to get clear, I figured we were going to need a distraction and we needed one pretty quickly."

"The fire!" Albert exclaimed.

"Yes, sir, the fire." Jack rubbed his forehead, and Albert noticed for the first time that his eyebrows were missing and his mustache was frizzy and quite a bit shorter than it had been yesterday.

"Is that what happened to your mustache?" Albert asked.

Jack nodded. "When no one was looking I grabbed a tin of paraffin that they had been filling the lamps with and sloshed it in a back corner of the mercantile. I threw some rags on top of the paraffin and then started looking for a match. All I wanted to do was make a small fire with a lot of smoke. After checking my pockets, I discovered I was out of matches and I had to go get one from the front of the store. I must have tipped over the paraffin tin, because when I got back the whole corner of the store smelled like paraffin. I should have known better, but the noise from the two-up game was getting louder, and I figured it was then or never, so I tossed a lit match into the corner." Jack paused for a drink of water.

"What happened next?" Albert insisted.

"Boom, is what happened." Jack replied. "I got blown

back almost to the front door. I never saw paraffin act that way, must have been mixed with some naphtha." A wry smile came across Jack's face. "It was the most excitement I've had since Muldoon killed that kangaroo in Winslow."

"Tell me about Muldoon, Jack."

Jack looked at Albert a moment and then looked away. "As I said, I was lying by the front door, and when I sat up I saw the whole back of the mercantile was on fire. The explosion had gotten everyone's attention, and there was a run at the front door. I stood up in time not to get trampled by the crowd, but they pushed me through the door so hard I popped out into the night like a champagne cork."

"And where was I when all this was happening?" Albert was disappointed that Jack wouldn't tell him about the Famous Muldoon, but he was even more disappointed that he had missed an explosion.

"That's what I wanted to know," Jack said. "I thought I might have gotten you killed. I tried to push my way back into the mercantile, but the crowd was pushing too hard the wrong way for me to get back inside. I gave up and ran around to the side of the building. Singed and smoking wallabies and a bandicoot or two were pouring out all the windows of the building, and I knew I didn't have a chance in hell of getting back inside. Then I noticed a trail of shillings heading toward the mine. I figured it had to be you or at least Roger or Alvin, so I followed the trail. I picked up the coins as I went, didn't think it was a good idea to have anyone else tag along. The coins stopped at the edge of the tailing dumps, and it took me the rest of the night and most of the morning to find out where you were. If I hadn't heard snoring coming from that ore cart, I might never have found you."

"I'm glad you found me, Jack. That's another one I owe you."

Jack shook his head. "Nothing good is going to come out of last night, Albert. All said and done, I didn't do you any favors."

"You got me out of Ponsby Station—and like you said, I didn't get lynched," Albert replied.

"Not yet, anyway, but you have to figure that O'Hanlin and some of his bully boys are out looking for us right now, and I don't think he's the forgiving sort. Even if we manage to give O'Hanlin the slip, the word is going to get around about what happened at Ponsby Station, and you're the one that is going to get the blame."

"That's because I'm a platypus, isn't it, Jack?" Albert said quietly.

"That's the short of it Albert, and there's not a damn thing either you or I can do about it." Jack stood up and started pacing up and down. "I shouldn't have taken you to Ponsby Station. One thing always leads to another, and the next thing I know something like that fire happens."

Albert let Jack pace for a few moments before he said anything. "You said last night was a thing of beauty."

Jack stopped pacing. "I did?"

"Not more than a few minutes ago."

Jack sat down next to Albert and didn't say anything for a long while. He kept looking out into the desert as if it would give him the answer to some unspoken question. Finally, he turned to Albert and spoke in a low voice.

"Albert, it would be best if I move on by myself in the morning."

Albert wasn't quite sure what to say. "You're the only friend I've ever had, Jack."

"And you're a friend to me, Albert. But I've been here before, and it wasn't a good thing. I hurt the last friend I had more than you can know. Everyone hopes that they can change, me included. It's been eight years now and I haven't changed a damned bit."

Albert had known that sometime he would have to strike out on his own again and keep looking for the place he left Adelaide to find, but he hadn't expected to have to do it so soon.

He had become accustomed to small talk and meals not eaten alone. All that would be gone in the morning, and Albert would miss Jack more than he cared to admit. No matter how he felt, there was no point in making Jack feel guilty. Jack had already done more for him than he had any right to expect.

"It's just as well, Jack. I don't belong here. If I stay, I'll never find the place I'm looking for."

Jack took the pipe out of his pocket again and put it in his mouth without lighting it. "That place probably doesn't exist, Albert."

There was a chance that Jack was right, but it didn't matter to Albert. He had come a long way on a faint hope and would continue on for the same reason.

"It might, and that's enough for me."

Albert and Jack said nothing more that evening. A cool wind came up across the desert, and each star in the night sky cast an infinitesimal amount of light on the two small and silent creatures sitting next to one another in a sea of shadows.

7 ≋ Alone again

THE NEXT MORNING JACK STARTED a fire and boiled water for tea. He kept the fire small, and the minute the water boiled he kicked some sand over the embers. Every so often Jack would look back up the trail they had taken the night before.

"We should be all right for a few hours." Jack threw a pawful of tea leaves in the billycan and after a few minutes poured some tea in Albert's waiting cup.

There wasn't much said that morning. They finished the tea and wiped out the cups with sand. Jack took down the tripod and put it and the billycan back in his pack. He pulled out a few cans of sardines and handed them to Albert. "I know these aren't your favorite, Albert, but you may need them."

He kept rummaging through his pack. "You have enough water?"

Albert shook his canteen and nodded.

Jack pulled out two boxes of matches and tossed them to Albert. "Might need a fire." He continued looking through his pack until he found what he was looking for, at the very bottom. He pulled out a small, oilcloth-covered packet and gave it to Albert.

"What's this?"

"It's a Colt pocket pistol. I keep it as a spare."

"I don't know anything about guns, Jack. You should keep it."

Jack shook his head. "This is hard country, Albert. A gun can get you into trouble and sometimes it can get you out of it. I don't know what you're going to find down the road, but it never hurts to go armed. Just pull back the hammer and pull the trigger. The caps are fresh, so it should go off."

Albert took the packet and put it in his rucksack. He didn't really want the gun, but it seemed important to Jack that he have it, and Jack was his friend.

Jack closed his pack and tossed it up onto his shoulders. "Hold out your hat, Albert."

Albert took off his kepi and held it out. Jack reached in the pocket of his drover's coat, pulled out a large handful of coins, and poured them into Albert's hat. "Don't forget your winnings."

Albert shook his head. "I can't take this, Jack. I owe you for everything I have."

Jack shrugged. "I kept enough to keep me going until I sell my rock. Don't flash that money, Albert. I knew a wallaby or two that were killed for less."

Both of them stood there awkwardly for a few seconds, not knowing what to say next. Finally, Albert put his coin-filled hat under one arm and held out his paw. "You've been a good friend, Jack."

Jack looked a little embarrassed as he took Albert's paw and gave it a shake. "I was never one for long good-byes, Albert... I figure to walk back down the trail a little way to see if we were followed, and after that I'm heading as far away as I can get from Ponsby Station. You should do the same."

"Which way should I go?"

Jack scratched his head and thought a moment. "If I knew where you were going, I might try and give you some advice. But I don't. If what you're looking for is out in that desert, you're the only one who can find it."

"I'll find it, Jack. You can bet on it."

Jack nodded. "You'll do fine."

He turned and began walking back up the trail. After about twenty feet, he looked back over his shoulder. "If you ever meet Muldoon, Albert, tell him I'm sorry."

Jack then increased his stride and moved swiftly away from the campsite.

Albert stood there in the middle of the abandoned campsite and watched Jack become smaller and smaller until he disappeared over the crest of a small rise. He had been alone for most of his life, and the few days he had spent with Jack were the only good memories he had since his mother died.

Finally, Albert forced himself into doing the little tasks that all journeys require regardless of their destination. He packed his rucksack with the money and the sardines that Jack had given him. He held back a gold sovereign that caught his attention and put it in the pocket of his coat, along with Jack's pistol.

His pack now contained money, food, Jack's spare blanket, a couple of boxes of strike-anywhere matches, and the soft drink bottle he had carried from Adelaide. Looking at the bottle made Albert realize how far he had come from his days in captivity, and he was glad he'd never gotten the chance to sell it.

A week ago he was, for all intents and purposes, a dead platypus. Now, the zoo was far behind him. He had made friends. He had more food and water than he had when he had left Adelaide, and he was still alive. Each of which was something he had not expected and, when taken together, was a small miracle. Cheered by thoughts of his survival, Albert shouldered his rucksack and began walking down the trail away from Jack and what was left of Ponsby Station.

In keeping with what he had learned, Albert walked for a few hours in the coolness of the morning and then found shelter from the midday heat. The country he passed through that morning was similar to that around Ponsby Station: low hills and barren ground. Albert could see another range of mountains far to the east of his position in the hills, and for lack of a better idea he picked the tallest mountain in the range as a point of reference and kept walking toward it.

Albert walked through the late afternoon and into the early evening. The rough trail that had led him from Ponsby Station became more and more faint until he lost sight of it completely in the fading light. He made a cold camp in a depression next to a sandstone outcrop and ate sardines washed down with water from his canteen.

He lay down on his back, using his pack for a pillow, and pulled his blanket over him as the chill of the desert night settled on the sand around him. He looked up at the stars, and for the first time he felt at one with the rocks and sand that had become his home. There was something clean about the desert that reminded him of the river where he had been born. Both the good and the bad were carried by the wind of the desert and the currents of the river, and each day brought one or the other or a mixture of both. In doing so, the river and the wind made each day different, and that difference was the salvation of the restless.

Albert remembered what Jack had told him about wombats and their desire to have the same day repeated endlessly. His days in the zoo had been the same endless repetition, and he was beginning to realize that his escape was as much about a need for change as it was to try and find an Australia where he belonged.

The stories of Old Australia had circulated every evening in the zoo, yet none of the other animals had tried to seek it out. In the end they always went back to what they knew— their pens, their cages, and their regular meals.

Perhaps those animals were wiser than Albert. He looked over at the sandstone outcrop and listened very carefully. The rocks were silent and Albert was left without an answer.

8 ≋ The Gates of Hell

ALBERT STARTED WALKING TOWARD THE distant mountain
just before dawn. The trail he had been following from
Ponsby Station and the country it passed through began
to change. Albert found himself picking his way through
undulating hills of cracked basalt and saltbush. The ancient
lava flow had cooled in folds and then pulled itself apart.
In some places the cracks had become deep crevasses, and
walking was dangerous.

Morning turned to midmorning, and the heat of the sun
began to reflect back from the black basalt. From time to
time Albert lost sight of the mountain as he moved carefully
through the ups and downs of the lava field. Albert was
drinking more water than he intended, and he knew he
was soon going to have to find a place to wait out the day.

He moved up a ridge to get another look at the distant
mountain, and when he got to the top of the ridge he found
himself looking down a gentle slope into the sandy bottom
of a large crevasse.

The crevasse formed a narrow canyon that led deeper
into the lava. It was shady in the canyon, and the black
sand of the canyon floor was easier to walk on than the
rough basalt above. The canyon seemed to be heading in

the direction of the mountain, so Albert followed it for fifty yards before sitting down. It felt good to sit in the shade with the weight of his rucksack resting against the side wall of the canyon. Albert was cool for the first time since the sun had come up.

He shook his canteen and didn't like the sound of it. His water was getting short, and he had no idea where or when he would find more. He could wait out the sun here in the canyon, but that would mean trying to walk through the lava flow at night, which given the nature of the country could be difficult if not fatal.

He took a drink from the canteen and looked up the canyon walls at the thin ribbon of sky above him. It was like looking into a river; wisps of clouds, like ripples in a current, moved slowly in the direction of the distant mountain. Albert watched the clouds for a few moments and decided that following the clouds down the canyon was as good a plan as any.

All the decisions had been made for him in the zoo, but now he had to make them for himself. The more he made, the easier it became, but it was also becoming obvious to him that some decisions were better than others and that a really bad one could have serious consequences.

Albert stood up, tightened the shoulder straps on his rucksack, and began moving deeper into the canyon. The longer Albert walked, the higher the canyon walls became. The sandy bottom of the canyon would narrow in some places and widen in others. In the wide sections the walls were too far apart to touch with both arms extended. In the narrow sections Albert's rucksack would scrape against them, but there always was enough room for him to squeeze through.

The canyon would veer to the right and then veer back to the left. Several times the canyon bifurcated, and Albert would have to choose which way to go. He would look up at the sky above the canyon walls and try to see which way the clouds were blowing. If he couldn't see clouds, he would take the gold sovereign from his pocket and flip it in the air. Heads he went to the left, tails to the right.

Albert moved through the canyon for most of the day, stopping every so often to rest and take a small drink from his canteen. He knew that he was lost in the canyon, but it didn't bother him very much. After his walk from Tennant Creek, he learned that if you don't know, or don't care, where you're going, there was no such thing as being lost. He didn't know where he was when he entered the canyon, and the fact that he didn't know where he was now didn't really change anything. It was cooler in the canyon than it had been on the lava flow, and that was reason enough to be there.

He walked on through the afternoon until the canyon began to darken and deep shadows clung to the walls. The sun was setting somewhere, and Albert knew it was time to start making a camp. He was in a narrow section of the canyon, and he wanted a wider section of the canyon floor on which to lay out his blanket. He began to walk faster, hoping to find a better place to camp before he lost the light.

Suddenly, the canyon opened up into a section that was twenty feet across with side canyons radiating out from it in all directions. It was brighter in the open section. The walls around the opening were not as high as they had been in the rest of the canyon, and they didn't block as much of the fading sunlight. The walls were still too high to climb, but the lower walls gave Albert hope that he was coming to the edge of the lava field.

Albert decided to camp in the opening and deal with which way to go in the morning. The canyon floor was covered in deep sand, which would make a comfortable place to sleep, and if he put his blanket in the middle of the open section he would be able to see the night sky.

He was in the process of taking out his blanket and a tin of sardines when he glanced up at the canyon wall across from him.

There was a very small, hand-lettered sign painted on the wall of the open space next to one of the side canyons. The uneven surface of the basalt had absorbed the paint in a haphazard fashion, making the sign difficult to read. Albert walked over and took a closer look. The sign was a few feet above his head, but even in the dim light he could read it. The sign read "HELL," with a little arrow pointing toward the side canyon.

Albert pondered the sign for a few moments. Any place called Hell was most likely to be unpleasant. Albert didn't really believe in Hell, but one could never be sure.

He could wait where he was until morning. If Hell was really down the canyon, there was no telling what visitors might show up while he was sleeping. Then again, he could immediately head back the way he had come, but there was nothing back there except dashed hopes and some angry kangaroos. Albert knew that whatever future he had lay in front of him, and the most likely path to it was down the little canyon with the sign.

Albert went back to his rucksack and put the blanket and the sardines away. He took out the matches and put them in his coat pocket along with Jack's pistol, then shouldered his rucksack and walked over to the sign pointing the way to Hell.

He moved into the side canyon and almost immediately lost the light. The walls of the little canyon were very close together and curved back and forth. Dusk was beginning to fade to darkness, and the narrow confines of the canyon added to the gloom.

Albert moved as rapidly as he could while he could still see the canyon floor, but soon it was too dark to see even a few feet ahead of him. He extended his arms, and his paws touched the canyon walls. He moved slowly ahead, using his paws to keep him in the center of the canyon. He tried going as fast as he could, until he stepped off a small ledge on the trail and fell face-first into the sand of the canyon floor. After that he moved much more carefully, extending each foot slowly to gently touch the ground in front of him. He moved forward like that for what seemed like an eternity, until he ran bill-first into solid rock.

He touched his bill to see if he was bleeding, but didn't feel any blood. He struck a match against the rock in front of him. In the flare of the match, Albert saw that he had run into a giant granite boulder that blocked the canyon exit. The boulder had a sign painted on it that said "HELL," with an arrow pointing both to the right and to the left. The match burned Albert's paw, and he dropped it into the sand. He lit another match and, holding it in front of him, squeezed through a narrow gap on the right side of the boulder.

Albert was out of the lava flow and onto a rocky plain. He could see several other large boulders in front of him, but the light of the match carried only a few feet, and it was impossible to tell how many boulders might lie ahead of him. When a gust of wind blew out the match, Albert stood quietly for a few minutes and let his eyes adjust to the darkness. There was no moon that night, but the stars were bright enough to give shape to the rocks ahead of him. Based on the shadows, Albert thought that the field of boulders went for some distance. He started making his way slowly forward, when suddenly a rocket shot into the sky from beyond the field of boulders.

The rocket arched high into the night sky and burst into a red ball of fire that lit up the field of boulders for a few seconds before it consumed itself, leaving a few sparks to fall earthward. In the brief flash of red light, Albert could see that all the boulders had the word "HELL" written on them, with arrows that all pointed toward where the rocket had come from.

Albert made his way forward. He went from boulder to boulder in the direction all the arrows were pointing. Another rocket shot into the sky and lit up the boulder field for a second time. After the rocket burned out and Albert's eyes readjusted to the darkness, he could see a faint glow of light coming from where the rocket had begun its ascent.

Albert headed toward the light, which grew brighter and brighter until he rounded a boulder and came to its source. A large one-story wooden building stood at the edge of the boulder field, and a number of lamps hung from its side. Torches had been planted around the front of the building and large canvas signs were hung from poles on the top and at the sides.

The largest sign, lit by paraffin lamps with reflectors, was on the roof of the building. It read "WELCOME TO THE GATES OF HELL." One sign on the side of the building read, "WHISKEY AND AMMUNITION"; another read "DRY GOODS." A smaller sign by the front door read "RELIGIOUS MEDALS, MAPS, FEMALES," although someone had taken a paintbrush and had crossed out the word *FEMALES* with a couple of rough strokes.

Just as Albert finished reading the signs, a large wallaby smoking a cigar walked out of the front door of the building carrying a skyrocket. He wore a white tuxedo jacket and was missing half an ear. The wallaby walked over to a section of pipe that had been pounded into the ground near the front door. He put the rocket in the pipe and lit the fuse with his cigar. Then he stepped back and watched the rocket shoot upward. After the rocket exploded in the sky over the building, the wallaby turned to go back inside. As he turned, he noticed Albert standing by the boulder.

"If you've come for the party, it's inside," he said.

Albert hesitated.

"We have cake," said the wallaby.

Albert wasn't quite sure what cake was, but the wallaby seemed friendly enough. Albert started walking toward the building. The wallaby walked ahead of him and opened the door. When Albert reached the door, the wallaby said, "Welcome to the Gates of Hell—it's our third anniversary," and escorted Albert into the building.

9 ≋ Bertram and Theodore

THE INSIDE OF THE GATES OF HELL was a large, low-ceilinged room crammed with barrels, boxes, pieces of scratched furniture, dusty bolts of cloth, and piles of things that Albert didn't recognize. The room was as dark as the outside of the building was light, and Albert couldn't see the far wall of the room.

A small table, covered by a dirty checkered tablecloth, and two ladder-back chairs had been placed in the middle of the room. The table and the room were lit by a candle stuck in the neck of a whiskey bottle sitting on the table. Melting wax from the candle had run down the bottles and pooled on the dirty tablecloth.

Sitting in one of the chairs was a ring-tailed possum wearing a cravat and a once-white tuxedo jacket, much like the one worn by the wallaby. The possum was drinking out of a shot glass when Albert and the wallaby walked into the building. The possum looked over at Albert and blinked several times.

The wallaby hurried over to a pile of furniture and started looking through the pile.

"You'll have to excuse the lack of light. Theodore is allergic to light, aren't you, Theodore?"

The possum gave a small nod and took a sip from his glass.

The wallaby pulled another chair from the pile and took it over to the table. He wiped dust off the seat of the chair with a corner of the tablecloth.

"Do sit down. Our other guests aren't here yet, so we have time for a little chat."

Albert took off his rucksack, put it by the chair, and sat down. The wallaby sat down next to him in the empty chair.

"I'm Bertram," the wallaby said, extending a paw.

Albert shook Bertram's paw. "Albert."

"Our pleasure, isn't it, Theodore?"

Theodore didn't say anything. He pushed his now-empty glass in Bertram's direction.

"Could I get you a drink, Albert?"

Jack's warning about publicans offering free drinks flashed through Albert's mind. He took the canteen off his shoulder.

"No, thank you. I have water."

"Well, then, at least let me get you a glass."

Bertram went over to one of the piles lying around the room and extracted a bottle of whiskey and two dirty glasses. He brought them back to the table, where he wiped the glasses with another corner of the tablecloth. He gave one glass to Albert, then filled his and Theodore's glasses from the bottle.

"What brings you to the Gates of Hell, Albert?" Bertram asked.

"I saw some signs pointing this way, and then I saw the rockets," Albert answered, as he poured the last of his water into the dirty glass and looped the canteen strap over his shoulder.

Bertram smiled widely. "The power of advertising... As I have said more than once, Theodore and I owe our success to advertising. Don't we, Theodore?"

Theodore nodded.

"We have even considered starting our own newspaper," Bertram continued.

"Why do you call this place the Gates of Hell?" asked Albert.

"Hell is a metaphysical concept that incites curiosity, and curiosity is a key factor in advertising. It brought you here, didn't it?"

After a brief hesitation, Albert responded, "I guess so."

Bertram continued. "We could have called the place the Gates of Heaven, but it would have attracted the wrong sort, and besides, 'Hell' has a much better ring to it, don't you think? Are you sure I can't get you a drink?"

Albert shook his head. He was beginning to get a very bad feeling about Bertram and Theodore. Albert slowly put his paw into the pocket of his jacket.

"I was wondering if I could purchase some water and supplies from you?"

Bertram looked over at Theodore. The possum gave Albert a hard look, then nodded to the wallaby. Bertram turned back to Albert and smiled.

"Actually, we don't sell supplies."

"But the signs outside—"

Before Albert could finish, Bertram interrupted him. "As I said, Theodore and I owe our success to advertising, not to being truthful."

"Then what do you do?" Albert asked, knowing he wasn't going to like the answer.

"We rob people," said Bertram.

Albert looked over and saw that a small pistol had appeared in Theodore's paw.

"It's not that we started out thieves. Originally, we had a vision of creating a vast mercantile empire, didn't we, Theodore?" Bertram said earnestly.

Theodore nodded. The barrel of the pistol pointing at Albert's stomach remained steady.

"Unfortunately, buying low and selling high is not as easy as it seems," Bertram continued. "It takes time to build a business, and Theodore became impatient."

The possum picked up his glass with his free paw, finished the whiskey in it, and, without ever taking his eyes off Albert, put the glass on the table and pushed it in Bertram's direction.

"Are you sure I can't get you a drink, Albert? I'm afraid I lied about there being cake." Bertram picked up the whiskey bottle and filled Theodore's glass.

Albert shook his head.

"We started a small store in a town quite far from here, and as I said, Theodore became impatient. One thing led to another and we had to leave. But, as someone once said, 'All's well that ends well,' and here we are celebrating the third year in our new business." Bertram lifted his glass in a toast. "To the Gates of Hell."

Albert sat quietly and made no move to pick up his glass. Bertram looked over at Albert, and for the first time his voice had an edge to it.

"It wouldn't be polite not to toast our success, Albert. You should know that Theodore gets very mean when he's been drinking."

Theodore cocked his pistol.

Albert had become convinced that the chances of him

leaving the Gates of Hell alive were rapidly approaching zero. He wasn't quite sure what to do next. Albert had his paw on the pistol Jack had given him, but he had never fired a gun, and from the looks of it Theodore was not operating under the same handicap. He decided to try and keep Bertram talking, if for no other reason than to delay the inevitable. Albert picked up his glass with his left paw.

"I'm sorry," he said, lifting his glass. "To the Gates of Hell."

Bertram nodded approvingly and took a drink from his glass. Theodore drained his glass and put it back on the table. He gestured towards Albert's pack with his pistol.

"Theodore is impatient to find out whether robbing you was worth our while. Personally, I prefer to linger over the moment." Bertram took another sip from his glass. "You're not the kind of creature we normally rob. In fact, I don't recall ever seeing anything like you before."

"I'm a platypus," Albert said quietly.

"Theodore and I have never heard of a platypus, have we, Theodore?" Bertram looked over at the possum.

Theodore continued to stare at Albert as he pushed his empty glass in Bertram's direction.

"Two strange creatures in as many days, wonders never cease. Perhaps we should put them on display, another attraction for the Gates of Hell." Bertram filled Theodore's glass.

Albert began to feel a black cloud rising from the pit of his stomach. The spurs on his hind legs began to extend themselves. "I don't think that would be a good idea," he said very softly.

Bertram smiled. "And why not?"

"Because a platypus is a magical creature, and shouldn't be made fun of." Albert began to stare back at Theodore.

"Theodore and I don't believe in magic, do we, Theodore?" Bertram continued to smile.

Albert wasn't sure he believed in magic, either, but he was beginning to believe in anger. "You will before the night is through," he said in the same flat tone he had been using since Bertram had suggested putting him on display.

Bertram hesitated for a moment, then bent over and picked up Albert's rucksack and put it on the table. The noise of the pack hitting the table covered the sound of Albert cocking the pistol in his pocket.

Bertram undid the straps on the rucksack and began to look through the contents. The smile on his face broadened as he reached in the pack and pulled out a pawful of coins. He let the coins trickle down onto the table. "I am beginning to believe in magic, Albert. Tell me more."

Albert watched the coins hit the table for a moment and then looked at Bertram. "I can summon demons."

Bertram cocked his head. "A very interesting but doubtful proposition."

Albert shrugged. "All you have to do is say *zoo* three times, very slowly and I can guarantee that a demon will appear."

Bertram filled Theodore's glass for the last time. "I don't believe in tempting fate, Albert. We have your money, and that is magic enough for me."

Theodore leered at Albert, and then hissed at him. "Zoo."

The possum's voice was high-pitched, and under other circumstances it might have caused Albert some amusement. Theodore drained the glass of whiskey in front of him and started cackling.

"Zoo!" he almost screamed.

Bertram reached out and touched Theodore on the shoulder. "Theodore, I really don't think this is a good idea."

Theodore shook Bertram's paw off his shoulder. Flecks of foam began to form around the corners of Theodore's mouth. Albert knew he was as good as dead. As Theodore started to drool, Albert attempted to pull the pistol out of his pocket. Theodore began to scream *zoo* for the third time, but before he could complete the word a terrible howl came from the darkness in the back of the store.

Theodore swiveled his gun toward the noise. When he did, Albert jerked the pistol free of his pocket and pulled the trigger. The shot missed Theodore, but the muzzle blast blew out the candle. A second before the room went dark, Albert saw a strange creature wearing red underwear and swinging a long chain come running out of the blackness toward Theodore. There was a moment of darkness, then the muzzle flash of Theodore's pistol lit up the room. Albert saw a flash of chain in the light and heard the chain strike flesh. Not knowing what else to do, Albert cocked his pistol and fired another shot where he had last seen Bertram. Before he could fire again, the front door of the Gates of Hell flew open, and Bertram was silhouetted in the doorway for the second it took him to run outside and slam the door behind him.

With the closing of the door, the room reverted to darkness, and Albert was alone with an insane possum and a demon of uncertain origin.

The mere mention of being put on display had started

Albert down a road to mindless anger. He had hoped that hearing the word *zoo* would enrage him enough not to feel the pain of being shot and would also release one of the many personal demons that he knew were just below the surface of his being. If anyone tried to torment him, that creature was going to have to pay Albert a blood price.

However, he hadn't expected one of his demons to manifest itself in the form of a creature wearing a set of long johns. Albert sat motionless in his chair and tried to see toward the back of the room. The flash of the pistol shots had temporarily destroyed what little night vision he had. He could smell the stink of black powder in the air but nothing else. Albert knew he had to move from the chair, because whoever was still standing in the Gates of Hell knew exactly where he had been when the shooting started.

Albert slipped off the chair as quietly as he could, but before he could step away from the table, someone called his name.

"Albert!"

The voice was low and had a strange accent. It had to be the demon. Albert pointed his pistol in the direction of the voice.

"Albert, we got enough problems without you pointing a pistol at the only friend you've got within fifty miles."

Albert hesitated.

"We've got to get out of here. Any minute this place is going to be crawling with dingoes. If they didn't hear the shots, you can bet that Bertram will fetch them as fast as he can."

Albert hadn't heard the word *dingo* since he had left the zoo in Adelaide. He had never seen a dingo, but the other animals in the zoo would mention the name only in whispers. It was claimed that they had invaded Old Australia in times long past and that they ate the flesh of other animals. There were some who claimed to have seen them, but the descriptions had been vague, and most of the other animals were convinced that if anyone saw a dingo he wouldn't live to tell the tale.

Albert didn't know for sure what a dingo was, but he had met Bertram, and given the choice between Bertram and a demon it was the demon every time. Albert put the pistol back in his pocket. "Where are we going?" he asked.

"As far as we can get before the sun rises."

Albert heard the rattle of the demon's chain and a furry paw took his wrist.

"I can see pretty well in the dark, but not as good as that damned possum." The demon started leading Albert toward the back of the Gates of Hell. The demon stopped for a moment, and Albert heard a rustling sound. The demon thrust a heavy cotton sack in Albert's free paw.

"Carry this," the demon said, and started moving again.

"What happened to Theodore?" Albert asked the demon.

"With any luck I killed him. I didn't hear him breathing when I took his pistol."

The demon pushed open a door at the back of the room and led Albert down a few wooden steps and onto the flats that led away from the Gates of Hell.

10 ≋ TJ

THE DEMON RELEASED ALBERT'S WRIST a few feet beyond the stairs and took back the cotton sack. The torches and the lamps from the front of the building cast a dim and shadowed light for fifty yards beyond where he was standing and, for the first time, Albert got a good look at the demon.

He stood just a little taller than Albert, had a pointed nose, pointed ears, and a band of black fur across his eyes. A bushy, striped tail stuck out the back of the ragged red underwear he had on. He had a leather collar around his neck and attached to the collar by a padlock was a section of heavy chain. The demon had looped the chain over one shoulder. He held Theodore's pistol in one paw and the cotton sack in the other.

The demon handed Theodore's pistol to Albert. "Hold this," he said, and began rummaging through the contents of the cotton sack. He pulled out a crumpled slouch hat with a wide brim, which he immediately put on. A few seconds later he pulled out a pair of dirty moleskin pants, complete with suspenders. The demon put on the pants as quickly as he could, shifting the chain from one shoulder to the other as he pulled up his suspenders.

He took back the pistol from Albert and put it in his pants pocket. Then he grabbed Albert's paw in his own and gave it a firm shake.

"I'm Terrance James Walcott, fresh off the boat from Frisco, my friends call me TJ, glad to meet you. You take the sack; I'll carry the chain. If you see anything that looks like a dog, shoot it."

Before Albert could reply, TJ let go of Albert's paw and gave him the sack, then started trotting across the desert flats.

Albert ran after him. "I left my pack inside."

TJ kept trotting. "Then kiss it good-bye. No more talking—sound carries a long way in this country."

Whatever light came from the torches of the Gates of Hell was soon behind them, and Albert found himself struggling to keep up with TJ. Albert had slung the sack over one shoulder, allowing his back to take most of the weight, but it was uncomfortable, and with each step he wished he still had his rucksack.

Albert couldn't see TJ clearly, but every so often he could see him outlined against the night sky, or hear a slight *clink* from the chain he was carrying. TJ kept up the pace and could see well enough in the dark to avoid the cracks and ridges that made traveling across the salt pans dangerous. Albert stayed close behind him.

Running was not something Albert was built for. He was good at swimming, but so far there had been little call for that. He had run from the zoo, he and Jack had run from Ponsby Station, and now he was running from the Gates of Hell.

Even though Albert didn't like running very much, he understood it was necessary. He had now walked into trouble on two occasions and managed to run his way out of both of them. It was true that walking was easier on his webbed feet. But running had proved better for his health. Maybe if he had run that day on the Murray, he wouldn't have ended up in a cage. Albert had just finished the thought when he ran into TJ's back.

Before he could say anything, TJ grabbed his bill and pushed him down into a shallow depression on the desert floor. TJ quickly got down beside him and let go of his bill. Albert stuck his head over the edge of the depression and looked out across the flats. He couldn't see anything, but the light wind blowing across the depression carried the smell of something that he hadn't wanted to ever smell again—the stench of dog.

Pictures of his mother's death started flashing through his mind, and Albert felt himself beginning to shake. The combination of fear and rage that the smell had triggered was difficult to control. One part of Albert wanted to run as far and as fast as he could, just to get away from the smell and the memories it brought with it. Another part wanted to attack something, anything. The spurs on his back legs began to leak their poison onto the alkali where he was lying.

TJ put his paw on Albert's shoulder and pushed him deeper into the depression.

The smell got stronger, and Albert could hear the soft shuffle of many paws on the desert floor. The nearness of the danger had a calming effect on Albert. The shaking stopped. He quietly reached into his pocket, pulled out Jack's pistol, and rested it on the lip of the depression. Without raising his head, Albert pushed himself forward a few inches up the slope of the depression where he could see across the desert.

Sixty yards from where he and TJ were lying, five figures moved across the desert silhouetted against the stars. They had pointed ears and pointed muzzles, and two of the figures had rifles slung over their shoulders. It was too dark to tell if the rest were armed. They were moving in the direction of the Gates of Hell. The group kept in single file and trotted past Albert and TJ's position without looking to the left or the right.

The sound of their footsteps receded into the darkness, but it was a good ten minutes before TJ took his paw off Albert's shoulder.

"If the wind had shifted, we'd have been dead meat," TJ said very quietly, as he sat up.

"Were those dingoes?" Albert asked. "They smelled like dogs."

"Not a dime's worth of difference between the two, as far as I can tell. Let's get moving. I don't want to be caught in the open when it gets light."

TJ got to his feet, adjusted the chain hanging from his shoulder, and started moving away from the depression at a slow trot. Albert put his pistol back in his pocket and slung the cotton sack over his shoulder. The contents of the sack were lumpy and dug into his back, but after his glimpse of the dingoes, Albert knew that the loss of his rucksack was a small price to pay for his escape.

They traveled across the flats for most of the night. Several times Albert started to ask TJ for a moment's rest and to see if there might be water in the sack he was carrying, but TJ didn't seem inclined to stop, and Albert kept quiet.

Since his capture those many years ago, Albert had been a solitary creature, and except for the keepers who brought his food, and occasional conversations with other animals, he had depended only on himself. His journey from Adelaide had toughened him physically and mentally more than he realized, but it had also made him realize how dependent he had become on others. If he hadn't found Jack, he would have died on the edge of Old Australia. Now he was depending on TJ, someone he had just met, to lead him to safety. Albert had become obligated to others, and with that obligation had come a connection that he had never felt before.

He knew he had been given the help freely, but he still felt he owed something in return. The debt linked him to Jack and to TJ, and maybe even to some creature he had yet to meet. Albert hoped he would be able to pay his debt when the time came. In the meantime, thirsty or not, he would just keep walking.

Dawn found them at the base of reddish sandstone cliffs that formed the eastern edge of the salt flats. To the north, Albert could see the mountain that had been his destination for the last three days. It was closer now, but still many days' journey from the cliffs.

"Another half an hour and we can call it a night." TJ spoke for the first time since they had seen the dingoes on the flats.

He led Albert up a faint trail that started on the desert floor and continued gradually up the cliff wall. Faded images of animals, snakes, and the handprints of men marked the cliff wall along the trail.

In the light of early morning Albert could get a good look at TJ as he walked ahead of him. TJ was tired, and he stumbled occasionally on the loose stones that covered the trail. The chain that TJ was carrying had rubbed a hole through the shoulder of his underwear, and the skin under the hole was seeping blood. Albert could see powder burns and a gash along TJ's neck just above the collar, and assumed that the wound came from the shot Theodore fired just before TJ hit him with the chain. Watching TJ struggle up the trail made Albert feel a little ashamed for even thinking about asking to stop for rest or water on their trek across the flats.

The trail turned up an opening in the cliff and disappeared over a rise between sandstone walls. The path was steeper, and both Albert and TJ found themselves slipping on the loose rocks and having to use their free front paws to catch themselves from falling face-first on the trail. Albert began to think he wouldn't make it to the top of the rise without stopping to catch his breath. Then he smelled it. He smelled water—and not just a little water, a lot of water.

Albert lunged forward and caught up with TJ just as he reached the top of the rise. Below him the trail led down into a small valley surrounded by the cliff walls. In the middle of the valley was a large water hole with clumps of reeds growing along its far bank. Ghost gums and bottle-brush grew in abundance in the valley, and the morning sun shining through the fronds of two red cabbage palms cast shadows across the water hole. In the brush, a few yards from the water's edge, someone had built a lean-to out of a piece of canvas and tree branches. The blackened remains of a fire lay in a circle of rocks in front of the makeshift camp.

If it hadn't been for the signs of habitation, Albert would have run down the trail as fast as he could and thrown himself into the water hole. But the time he had spent in

Old Australia had taught him caution. He waited to see how TJ would approach the campsite.

TJ took a couple of deep breaths and walked down the trail, not stopping until he reached the lean-to. He sat down next to the fire pit and dropped the chain in the dirt next to him. He took off his hat and wiped his forehead with his sleeve. He put his hat on the ground next to him, then pulled Theodore's pistol out of his pocket and put it on the hat. TJ motioned to Albert, who had followed him to the camp. "Albert, I need the sack."

Albert took the cotton sack over to where TJ was sitting and put it down next to the chain. TJ rooted through the sack and after a few minutes pulled out a large pocketknife. He opened the knife and put the blade inside the leather collar around his neck, and started sawing at the leather. "I would have done this last night, except there wasn't any time."

"Can I help?" Albert asked.

TJ stopped sawing on the collar. "Are you any better with a knife than you are with a pistol?"

Albert shook his head.

TJ started sawing on the collar again. "Then I'd better do this myself. I didn't come all the way from California to get my throat cut by a platypus."

The leather on the collar was thick, and it took TJ a few minutes to saw through it. When he finished, he took off the collar and put it down along with the chain. Without another word TJ crawled under the lean-to and lay down. He closed his eyes and immediately fell asleep. Albert had a thousand questions for TJ, but it didn't look like they were going to be answered anytime soon.

He walked over to the edge of the water hole and looked

into the water. It had been over twenty-four hours since he had slept and eight hours since he had a drink. He was tired and very thirsty, but he couldn't will himself to lean over and touch the water.

When he had seen the water hole from the rise coming into the valley, all he wanted to do was embrace it, to let the water envelop him and carry him back to those days when he was young and his whole world was fifty yards of riverbank. Those days had ended in tragedy, but the instinct of a thousand generations of his kind pushed through his thoughts and fears, demanding that he return to a home only vaguely remembered.

He slowly and deliberately took off his clothing, folding each article and placing them neatly on the bank of the water hole. He stood there naked, savoring the anticipation of both the pain of memory and the tactile pleasure of the water. He lay down on his stomach and pushed himself down the bank and into the water. His entry was soft and silent, and only a few ripples disturbed the shadows of the cabbage palms that played across the surface of the water hole.

The moment Albert hit the water, the worries and concerns of past and present disappeared. He was just a creature in the element he was born to inhabit. He didn't need to think; he just needed to do. His webbed feet drove him deeper into the pond with each stroke of his legs. The coolness of the water rippled his fur and washed away the dirt from days of desert travel.

Albert opened his eyes and watched freshwater crayfish dart among the rocks on the bottom of the pond. He grabbed one in his bill, and as he crushed and swallowed it he was overcome by hunger. Without thinking, he used his bill to push over rocks on the bottom of the water hole and ate the earthworms he found. He swam the length of the pool and dived in and out of the reeds on the far bank. Albert chased tadpoles and water beetles through the shallows. He ate what he caught and was excited by those he missed. For the hour he hunted, he wasn't Albert, late of the zoo in Adelaide. He was just an ordinary platypus in a water hole. It was a good feeling.

11 ≋ Every paw turned against him

A FAINT SPLASHING SOUND WOKE Albert from an unsound sleep. He rolled over in the sand and saw TJ kneeling on the bank of the water hole, wringing water out of his long johns. TJ had on his hat, and a blue bandana had been tied around his neck where it partially covered the gunshot wound. His moleskin pants had been washed and were draped across another patch of bottlebrush a few yards from where Albert had been sleeping.

TJ looked over at Albert. "Good morning, sunshine."

He stood up, shook out his underwear, and walked over and put it on the bush next to his pants. TJ looked up at the sun, which had passed midpoint.

"Make that good afternoon. Bring your stuff over to the camp and we'll make a plan." TJ felt his pants to see if they were getting dry, then walked back toward the lean-to.

Albert got up, brushed himself off, and got dressed. By the time he reached the lean-to, TJ was already sitting next to the fire pit pulling things out of the cotton sack.

TJ looked up at Albert. "Sorry to fade on you like that, but I hadn't slept in three days."

Albert sat down across the fire pit from TJ. "What sort of plan are we going to make?"

"I was thinking about revenge and then maybe a holdup or two. I tried claim jumping once, and let me tell you, there ain't no money in it." TJ pulled a can of black powder from the sack.

Albert didn't know who TJ was planning to get even with. On top of that, he didn't know who or what TJ was, or why TJ had gone to the trouble of saving his life. He started to ask TJ but thought better of it. Asking direct questions in Old Australia had usually not provided the answers that Albert hoped for, and he was beginning to believe that the best course was just to let things unfold of their own accord.

"I don't know anything about holdups or claim jumping."

TJ pulled a couple of small lead ingots out of the sack. "Then we'll start with revenge. Nobody chains Terrance James Walcott to a post and gets away with it. I put paid to that damned possum, now it's Bertram's turn. What do you think about burning down the Gates of Hell?"

"I hadn't really thought about it," Albert said honestly.

TJ continued looking through the contents of the sack. "It probably wouldn't be as easy as setting fire to the store at Ponsby Station, not with all the dingoes around, but with a little luck we ought to be able to pull it off."

Albert hadn't been too surprised that TJ knew his name. There was no telling how long TJ had been listening to his conversation with Bertram before the fight in the Gates of Hell. Albert had told Bertram his name, but he was sure he hadn't said anything about Ponsby Station.

"Ponsby Station? I don't think I know the place," Albert said carefully.

"They sure seem to know you." TJ pulled a folded piece

of paper out of the sack and passed it over the fire pit to Albert.

Albert unfolded the paper. It was a poster with his name on it.

REWARD

ALBERT THE PLATYPUS WANTED FOR ARSON AND CHEATING AT TWO-UP

With paraffin and malice aforethought, the above named platypus burned down the General Mercantile at Ponsby Station and cheated at two-up

DESCRIPTION

Medium height, webbed feet, has a beak, and is not a marsupial. Last seen in the company of a wombat accomplice

FIVE SHILLINGS will be paid for the capture of said platypus, dead or alive, and delivery of the corpus to the proper authorities

Sing Sing O'Hanlin, Cap't, Ponsby Station Fusiliers

"It's a bill," said Albert, after reading the poster.

"What?"

"I said it's a bill, not a beak." Albert handed the reward poster back to TJ. "That's all I've got to say."

TJ nodded, took the poster, and put it back in the sack. "I like a partner that knows how to keep his mouth shut."

Albert wasn't about to tell TJ that Jack was the one that set the fire. No platypus from Adelaide would betray a friend. Besides, he realized that TJ thought he was a tougher creature than he really was, and there was no reason to let him think differently.

"I'm not used to having a partner," Albert said after a little thought.

TJ looked Albert straight in the eye. "Hell, Albert, we need each other. I don't know straight up about this place, and from the looks of that poster, you could use someone to watch your back. Furthermore, I've seen you shoot, and you need a lot of help in that direction. Besides, robbery is always more fun if you can talk to someone about it."

After Ponsby Station and the Gates of Hell, Albert knew that getting killed in Old Australia was a lot easier than he had thought. Jack had tried to tell him, but watching Theodore frothing at the mouth had brought it home. Without help, he didn't stand much of a chance of getting to the place he belonged. TJ probably knew more about Old Australia than he did, but Jack had taught him a few things, and that might be enough to hold up his end of any deal with TJ.

"I guess learning to shoot couldn't hurt any," he said.

TJ pulled a tin of percussion caps out of the sack. "I pulled that poster off a gum tree the day before that possum caught me. I was hoping I might run into you. What did you get away with last night, besides your pistol?"

Albert searched through his coat pockets and brought out the Colt, the box of strike-anywhere matches, the gold sovereign, and the piece of oilcloth that Jack had wrapped the pistol in. Albert laid everything on his coat.

"That's the lot, except for an empty canteen."

TJ reached over and picked up the sovereign. He flipped it in the air, caught it, and bit down on the coin. Then he smiled.

"That's the stuff, Albert. It's been awhile since I put a tooth to real gold. Where did you get it?"

"The two-up game in Ponsby Station."

"Did you cheat?"

"I don't think so, but I was drunk at the time."

TJ started laughing. "You're the partner for me, sure enough. Hand me the Colt. I'll clean it up and reload it."

Albert handed TJ the pistol.

"You'd like San Francisco, Albert. Hell of a town. If it hadn't been for letting my guard down, I'd be there yet. Where are you from?"

"Adelaide, and I can do without it," Albert said firmly.

TJ put the gold coin back on Albert's coat, got up, and walked over to where his underwear was drying in the sun. He took it off the bush and brought it back to where he'd been sitting.

"I wasn't always from San Francisco. It's a place you've got to look for."

TJ searched in the sack and pulled out a needle and thread. After a little difficulty he got the needle threaded and began to sew up the hole in the shoulder of his long johns.

"I was born in the forest. I didn't like it much. It always seemed that everywhere I went was twenty miles from nowhere. Learned a few things in the forest, though: how to steal, how to run, and how to fight if I got cornered. All that came in handy when I got to California."

TJ reached over and held up the cotton sack. "I stole all this at the Gates of Hell. I'm glad to see I haven't lost my touch." He put the sack back down and continued: "After I got loose, I snuck back into the building to get my clothes and finish the job I started the night before. Then you showed up and needed a demon. I was glad to oblige."

"Bertram said they didn't sell supplies at the Gates of Hell," Albert remembered.

"Among other things, Bertram's a damn liar." TJ spit into the fire pit and went back to sewing. "They sell what they steal or what they get from the dingoes. Bertram takes it around to other towns and sells it to storekeepers."

"Who told you that?" Albert asked.

"Bertram, of course. That possum was too crazy to hold a conversation." TJ finished sewing up the hole and bit the thread loose from the needle.

"The night before, I had jimmied the lock on the back door of the Gates of Hell and was just getting ready to slip inside when that damned possum snuck up behind me and hit me with a rock. When I woke up, I was chained to a post out in back of the store. Bertram would get bored every so often and come out the store and brag on himself. He talked so much he didn't even notice I had managed get one end of the chain loose."

TJ put the needle and thread back in his sack, stood up, and started putting on his long johns. "They're still a little wet, but they should dry before evening. I can't abide being dirty."

After he finished putting on his underwear, TJ walked over and took his pants off the bush and put them on. "You might want to start collecting some firewood. I'll head over to the far side of the pond and see if I can catch some crawdads for dinner. I didn't have enough time to steal any food."

Spending the rest of his life stealing and shooting was not what Albert had in mind when he left Adelaide. He still wanted desperately to find the land that he had dreamed of for so many years, but he wasn't sure anymore what that place might look like. He had assumed that it would be something like where he was born, but he had just spent the morning in a place similar to that, and the experience had left him feeling incomplete. But to doubt in heaven was not something he could do and still go on.

He was wanted dead or alive in and around Ponsby Station, and that was going to make his journey more difficult, no matter what the destination. With every paw turned against him, shooting and stealing seemed more like educational necessities and a lot less like a couple of bad habits. The time would come for him to move on again; but for now, the valley he was in was world enough. The thought of a fire that night was comforting to him and would be enough to carry him into the uncertainties of another morning.

Fallen tree limbs littered the valley floor, and it took no time to pile up enough firewood for the evening. His days with Jack had given him a sense of how much wood was needed, and he finished the chore with enough time left to explore the valley before it got dark.

He found the spring that fed water into the valley and found more ancient paintings on the cliff walls above the spring. The drawing of a segmented serpent caught his attention at the base of another faint trail a hundred yards ahead.

He made his way up the trail and discovered a rock shelter halfway up the cliff wall, a shallow cave carved into sandstone by eons of wind and rain. Carvings of animals and stick figures of men covered the cliff wall at the entrance.

Albert ducked his head and crawled into the shelter. The ceiling of the shelter had been blackened by fires in the far distant past. Now, the only inhabitant of the cave was a brown snake coiled in the corner digesting something that had formed a lump halfway down its body.

Albert sat at the mouth of the shelter for a long time, watching the light fade in the valley and wondering whether animals or men had made the drawings that surrounded him.

12 ≋ A paradise lost

THE SMELL OF SMOKE BROKE into Albert's thoughts, and he looked down to see TJ feeding branches into a small fire he had started. The snake had stretched itself out along the back wall of the cave and appeared to have gone to sleep.

Albert quietly crawled out of the shelter and made his way down the cliff and across the valley to the fire. TJ had put the crayfish on a large, flat rock that he had slanted toward the fire, and was using the point of his clasp knife to move the ones closest to the flames when it looked like they were starting to burn.

"I used to cook in a mining camp, but the job only lasted two days, so don't expect much." TJ picked up a smaller rock, put some crayfish on it and passed it to Albert. "Remind me to steal some plates."

Albert ate slowly. He wasn't very hungry after his morning hunt, but crayfish cooked or fresh were a welcome change from sardines.

"Where was the mining camp?" he asked.

TJ scraped the rest of the crayfish into one paw and put down the knife. He juggled the crayfish between paws for a moment to let them cool. "It was a placer claim near

Coloma. First job I had after I found California." He began eating the crayfish.

"Did you have a hard time finding California?" Albert put down the rock and held his paws out toward the warmth of the campfire.

"Not really. I just walked away into the forest, got lost for a while, walked through some trees, and there I was."

TJ finished his meal, walked over to the edge of the water hole, and washed the smell of crayfish from his paws. He came back to the fire and continued:

"In the forest you always heard things about a place where things were a lot different, a place where animals got to shoot back. First time I heard the story, I said to myself, that's the place for Terrance James Walcott. Stealing bird's eggs and running from dogs might be good enough for other raccoons, but I wanted the big time, and by God, California was the place."

TJ reached in his sack and pulled out a pint bottle of whiskey. "Drink?"

Albert shook his head.

"You should have seen San Francisco, Albert. Gold coming in from the mines around the city, ships in the harbor, gambling and drinking started at noon. Every badger, weasel, and bunco artist from miles down the coast hung out there. Every night was Saturday, and shootings were a dime a dozen. It was a paradise, let me tell you."

TJ looked wistful and took a long pull on the bottle.

Albert wasn't sure what badgers, weasels, and bunco artists were, but he assumed they were animals that lived in California. San Francisco didn't seem very paradise-like to him, but good or bad it was at least a world that was different from the one he had found when he left the zoo.

If there were two places that were different from Adelaide, there were bound to be others—and if so, it was just a matter of walking far enough in the right direction until he found the one he wanted.

"When I find paradise, I'm not leaving," Albert said, thinking out loud.

TJ put the cork back in the bottle. "You might, if one dark night a mob with flour sacks on their heads started chasing you down a wharf."

He put the bottle back in his sack and took out a small pot and one of the lead ingots. "Every once in a while virtue gets out of hand, even in San Francisco. One day you're a customer, the next day you're on a list of bad apples." TJ put the ingot into the pot and placed the pot on the coals at the edge of the fire. "The local feather merchants stop watering their whiskey long enough to form a Vigilance Committee. They lynch a few creatures, just to show their wives that they believe in law and order, and then go back making money off sin and greed."

TJ took a small ladle out of the sack and put it in the pot with the lead. "I got caught up in the annual frenzy of piety, and if it hadn't of been for a strange ship at the end of that wharf, I would have ended up decorating a lamppost."

He was quiet for a while as he sat watching the lead melt into a bright silver puddle. When the lead was completely melted, TJ took a bullet mould out of the sack and began ladling the molten lead into it. Albert had watched Jack make bullets for his pepperbox pistol one evening, but TJ seemed more at home with the process.

"I ran up the gangplank of that ship with the mob a hundred yards behind me. The second I got on board I pulled a pistol, hoping they would have to come at me one at a time. I turned to shoot the first one up the gangplank, when a bank of fog closed over the ship and the wharf disappeared. That scared the hell out of me, let me tell you."

When the mould was full, TJ set it by the fire, then took off the bandana from around his neck and spread it out in front of him. "I could hear paws running along the deck and hear the captain yell up to sailors in the rigging, but I couldn't see a damned soul. Pretty soon I heard water running under the keel and knew we were under sail. Every so often I could see a faint image of some animal, but the image would fade as soon as I took a second look. I wandered around. I looked in the hold. I looked in the captain's cabin. The whole ship was empty, and except for the voices and the shadows there was no sign of life, no water, no supplies, no nothing. The fog covered everything. I couldn't see the sails, and I couldn't see beyond the railings. I sat down with my back against the quarterdeck and put my pistol in my lap. I didn't think the gun would have done much good, but it's hard to shake the habit of a lifetime.

"After a few hours, the ship became very quiet, and I couldn't hear the voices anymore. I stayed awake as long as I could, but running from a mob and hunting ghosts had taken the starch out of me. I went to sleep, and when I woke up, here I was."

TJ picked up the bullet mould and used the ladle handle to knock off the sprue. He opened the mould and let a pistol ball fall out on the bandana. He closed the mould and used the ladle to fill the mould again.

"Actually, I was off the coast of somewhere I'd never seen before. But I didn't care. I knew I didn't belong on the damned ship. I jumped overboard and swam in—lost my pistol in the surf, but at least I didn't drown."

TJ continued to cast pistol balls and drop them on the bandana. "I walked inland looking for fresh water. It was harder to find than I thought, and if it hadn't of been for Muldoon, I would have died for sure." TJ picked up one of the bullets and examined it in the firelight. He grunted in satisfaction. "I was always better at making bullets than I was at cooking."

"Muldoon?" Albert blurted out.

TJ dropped the bullet back on the bandana. "Strange creature, Muldoon. I felt a little sorry for him."

"I heard about Muldoon from a friend of mine. He wanted me to give him a message," Albert said excitedly.

"Muldoon is long gone, Albert. He doesn't like company much." TJ used the edge of the sack to protect his paw from the heat and lifted the lead pot off the coals. "I walked into the desert through a cut in the mountains along the coast. I was three days without water when I saw his tent."

"A tent?"

"Muldoon lives in an old circus tent with yellow-and-red stripes. It kind of stands out."

"What's he like? My friend Jack didn't talk about him very much."

"Well, he was an animal I'd never seen before, but that's true about everyone I've met since I got here. He looked like he had seen better days, that's for sure. He kept to himself and didn't seem much interested in conversation."

TJ put the bullet mould and the cast bullets in the cotton sack. "I doubt he was handsome when he was young, and now he's blind in one eye and covered with scars. Ugly as he is, he was there when I needed him, and I owe him. He gave me water and led me to this valley. He told me about the dingoes and the Gates of Hell."

"Where did he go?" Albert asked.

"I don't know. He just brought me to the trail that leads up here and then walked away. I never really got a chance to thank him. He only asked me one thing the two days we were together." TJ stood up. "I'm going to call it a night."

Albert looked up from the fire. "What did he ask?"

"He asked me if I had any sardines."

13 ≋ Bushrangers

"STAND AND DELIVER," said TJ, and cocked his pistol for emphasis.

The wallaby looked confused.

"Put your paws in the air," Albert added.

"Oh, it's robbery," the wallaby said, and raised his arms.

"It's not an ice cream social, bunny." TJ pushed his pistol into the wallaby's nose.

"Actually, the name's Ralph," said the wallaby.

"Don't get smart with me, Ralph. Where I come from, anyone with a snout like yours is a rabbit." TJ squinted at Ralph's nose.

"What's a rabbit?" asked the wallaby.

"Damn it! If I'd wanted to be paid by the hour I would have gone to work for the railroad. Now let's get down to it. You got five seconds. Fork over the cash or your next hop will be on the far side of the pearly gates."

Albert could tell that TJ was becoming impatient. The wallaby was their third victim in as many days, and so far they had managed to steal a worn blanket and a bag of rock candy.

Ralph put his paws down and pulled a small coin purse out the pocket of his waistcoat. As he snapped open the purse, he cocked his head and looked at Albert.

"You're Albert the Platypus, aren't you?"

Albert wasn't quite sure what to say. "It depends on who's asking."

"I knew it. I can't wait to tell the wife."

TJ shook his head disgustedly and took his pistol out of Ralph's nose. He uncocked it and put it back in the pocket of his pants. "I'm glad my mother didn't live to see this," he muttered. Then he walked over to a large rock by the trail and sat down.

"I've never been robbed by anybody famous before," Ralph continued, as he pulled a small coin out of the coin purse and extended it to Albert. "I recognized you immediately."

Albert took the coin. Not knowing what else to do, he reached into his pocket and took out the paper sack of rock candy he and TJ had taken from a sugar glider the day before. He held out the sack. "Have some candy, Ralph."

The wallaby closed his coin purse and put it back in his waistcoat. He reached into the paper sack. "The minute I saw the reward poster, I said to myself, any creature, marsupial or not, that burned down Ponsby Station can't be all bad. The place had a less than stellar reputation." Ralph took a piece of candy and put it in his pocket next to his coin purse. "If you're finished with the robbery, I really must be off. The wife hates it when I'm late for supper."

The wallaby tipped his bowler to Albert and started down the trail, being careful to give TJ a wide berth.

After much discussion, TJ had decided to stage a few robberies before trying to even his score with Bertram. It would give Albert time to learn the trade and provide them with needed supplies and maybe a little cash. Muldoon had told TJ that there were a series of small towns and mining camps that circled the desert between the distant mountain and the Gates of Hell. Trails and small roads linked the towns around the desert, and TJ thought ambushing travelers on one of the roads might prove profitable.

Albert wasn't keen on being a thief, but during his time in the desert, almost everyone he had met had made their living by stealing, cheating, gambling, or burning things down. Now that he had been labeled a cheat and an arsonist, it was only a small step to theft and a life of crime, an occupation that seemed to be much favored in the region. Jack and TJ made their living by dishonest means, but they were his friends, and thieves and killers like Bertram and Theodore weren't. Albert had come to the conclusion that another key to survival in Old Australia was in picking a criminal element you liked and sticking with it.

Also, Albert wasn't sure if he had the makings of a good thief. So far his life of crime had consisted of standing around while TJ did most of the work. He hadn't gotten a chance to draw his pistol, and wearing a mask seemed a little silly given the bill that stuck out in front of his face.

After Ralph disappeared down the road, Albert walked over to TJ, who had calmed down and now looked more disgusted than angry.

"How much did we get?"

Albert looked at the coin in his paw. "A tuppence."

TJ took off his hat and wiped his brow with the sleeve of his long johns. "If there is a sorrier place than this for honest robbery, I don't know of one. We're going to have to think of something else." He looked up at the sun. "We've got a few hours before dark. Let's try and get a little sleep before we head back."

Albert and TJ had crossed the desert from the water hole two nights before and had been making a cold camp in the hills above the road. It was too dangerous to cross the desert during the day, and even a night crossing had brought them too close for comfort to one of the packs of dingoes that roamed that part of the outback. The only advantage they had was TJ's night vision, and it had seen them safely across the desert one more time.

TJ stood up and walked out of sight of the road and around some large rocks to where they had left what few possessions they had. Albert followed him off the road.

"You can have the blanket." TJ sat down with his back to one of the rocks that had been warmed by the sun and tipped his hat over his eyes.

Albert took a drink from his canteen and then carried the stolen blanket to a sandy spot that was shaded from the afternoon sun. He lay down in the sand. The quiet of the afternoon was disturbed by the buzz of an occasional fly, but the insects were a normal part of life in the desert and Albert had learned to ignore them. He knew that he and TJ would have a long and dangerous trek back to the water hole that night and that getting a few hours' rest was a good idea. Still, it was hard for him to fall asleep.

Albert had gotten as far as he had with only bits and pieces of information. It had started with the rumors and fantasies about Old Australia he had heard at the zoo, and continued with Jack's stories about how animals got to this part of Old Australia. Jack had told him that Muldoon thought that everyone that walked far enough ended up here, but TJ had gotten here by boat and Albert had gotten here with the help of the South Australia railway. There didn't seem to be any rhyme nor reason as to why some animals got to Old Australia and some didn't. Muldoon might have some answers, but it was unlikely that Albert would find him anytime soon.

TJ hadn't been able to tell Albert much about Muldoon, except that he had been badly hurt sometime in the past and didn't like the company of other animals. Muldoon had referred to the desert between the Gates of Hell and the distant mountain as Hell itself and had told TJ that most animals from that part of Old Australia never came there. Those that did didn't survive very long.

Albert wanted to know how Muldoon had survived in Hell for so long, but TJ didn't have an answer. Albert also wanted to know what had happened between Jack and Muldoon and why Jack wouldn't talk about it. He fell asleep still wondering.

He began to dream, and those dreams became a kaleidoscope of his time in Old Australia: bottles of beer flying from train windows, Theodore screaming "Zoo!", Jack singing off-key, sand blowing so hard he couldn't see; the taste of gin, the flash of pistol shots, coins flying in the lamplight of Ponsby Station, and the yelling of the crowd.

The yelling woke Albert up. Albert opened his eyes and saw that TJ had disappeared. The sounds of a struggle were coming from the road beyond the rocks. Albert jumped to his feet, pulled his pistol, and ran around the rocks onto the road.

TJ was standing in the middle of the road holding a bandicoot by the throat with his left paw and trying to pistol-whip it with the gun in his right paw. Another bandicoot had TJ around the neck and was hanging off his back, biting TJ's ear hard enough to draw blood. TJ's hat lay on the side of the road next to an old Enfield carbine and a couple of jute bags.

Albert fired his pistol into the middle of the road, and the yelling stopped. The fighters froze and looked over at where Albert was standing and then they all started yelling again.

"Hit this one in the head!" TJ yelled, as he flung the bandicoot with his left paw in Albert's direction.

The bandicoot on TJ's back spit the ear out of his mouth and yelled, "Albert! It's us!"

At the mention of Albert's name the fighting stopped again. Albert looked down at the bandicoot that had just landed in front of him.

"Roger?"

"Too right," said the bandicoot, as he stood up and started brushing himself off.

Alvin dropped off TJ's back and ran over to where Albert and Roger were standing.

"It's good to see you, mate," said Alvin, as he grabbed Albert's paw and started shaking it.

"We've come to sign up," Roger joined in. "We want to be bushrangers."

Before Albert could say anything, both bandicoots began talking at once.

"We heard you were around here. A sugar glider showed up at Ponsby Station and said he'd been robbed by a platypus on the road to Barton Springs," Alvin said excitedly.

"I said that's our old mate, Albert," Roger interrupted.

Alvin nodded, "That's what he said for a fact."

"And Alvin said, 'Let's go have a drink with Albert,'" Roger continued.

"We grabbed our swag and came straightaway," Alvin joined in.

"The wallaby up the road said you were close by. When we got here, we were set on by that bloody foreigner." Roger pointed over to where TJ was picking up his hat.

TJ put on his hat and, from the look on his face, was considering shooting both bandicoots in the back. "Those rodents better be good friends of yours, Albert. If not, I'm going to have their guts for garters."

Both Alvin and Roger bristled.

"Fat bloody chance," said Alvin.

"Before you showed up, Albert, we had him cold," added Roger.

"Fair dinkum, and we can do it again." Alvin spit in both his paws and started toward TJ.

Albert grabbed Alvin by the back of his collar. "Who else was at Ponsby Station when the sugar glider showed up?"

"O'Hanlin and his bully boys. They're trying to rebuild the mercantile with the help of some of the miners."

Albert looked over at TJ. "Do you think that might be a problem?"

14 ≋ Last stand of the fusiliers

ALBERT HEARD ANOTHER SHOT from the Enfield, followed by the rattle of musketry. The shooting was getting closer, and darkness was still half an hour away. Albert led Alvin and Roger out of the hills onto the flats of Hell.

There hadn't been much time. O'Hanlin and the Ponsby Station Fusiliers had been only minutes behind the bandicoots. Albert and TJ had just retrieved their gear when the first kangaroo appeared on the road. TJ had grabbed the carbine from Roger and fired a shot in the general direction of the scout.

TJ's shot delayed the pursuit long enough for them to herd the bandicoots off the road and into the hills. TJ thought that the Fusiliers wouldn't follow them any farther than the edge of Hell because of the dingoes. They just needed time to get there. They agreed that Albert and the bandicoots would head directly through the desert toward the water hole, while TJ would try and slow down the pursuers. TJ took a handful of paper cartridges from Roger's bag and disappeared into the brush above the trail.

That had been an hour ago, and Albert and the bandicoots had been on the run the whole time. Roger and Alvin were not in the best of shape, and Albert was now carrying both bags of their gear. The bandicoots were panting continuously and occasionally missed their footing.

"Be a mate, Albert. Let's give it a rest." Roger was sweating, and his sweat smelled of cheap gin.

"It's not much further—you can make it." Albert slowed his pace, but the bandicoots still had difficulty keeping up. Alvin and Roger couldn't keep going much longer, but he also knew that the deeper they went into the desert the better chance they would have to see the next morning.

Albert felt sorry for Roger and Alvin, but sympathy wasn't of much use in desperate circumstances. TJ was doing his job, and it was up to Albert to do his. Albert needed to get the bandicoots to cover somewhere in the flats of Hell and beyond rifle shot of the hills behind him. Albert wasn't sure how far a rifle could shoot, so the farther the better.

For the first time in his life, Albert was responsible for the lives of others, and the effect of that responsibility surprised him. He had ceased thinking of the bandicoots as friends. They had become objects that he was duty bound to deliver safely. Friendship and sympathy had no place in the equation. All he could do was to keep pushing them to their destination regardless of the pain and discomfort it might cause them. Alvin and Roger had stood by him when friends had been in short supply, and he would stand by them now. If they didn't make it to safety, it wouldn't be because Albert hadn't given everything he had.

He eventually paused to allow each of the bandicoots a small drink of water. The shooting had stopped, and all he could hear was the sound of the wind blowing across the flats of Hell.

Low hills lay behind and to the left of them. The top of the distant mountain rose from beyond the far horizon. Termite mounds and scattered scrub covered the desert floor all the way to a stand of stunted red river gum trees growing along a dry creek bed at the base of the hills to their left. Except for the distant mountain, Albert didn't recognize any other landmarks. He knew that if he kept the hills on his left and the mountain ahead of him he would eventually come to the trail that led up the cliff walls.

Albert had just started moving toward the creek when he heard a whistle, and he turned to see TJ running toward them across the flats. His hat was hanging from his neck by the chinstrap, and he had a bandana tied around his head. TJ was carrying the Enfield in his right paw, and his face was streaked with powder residue from the rifle.

"They're not stopping," TJ said, as he slowed to a walk next to Albert.

"I was heading over there." Albert pointed to the gum trees.

TJ shook his head. "You haven't got enough time. Go another hundred yards and fort up behind a termite mound. When it gets dark, move down the creek and into the trees. Be quiet and wait for me there." Without another word TJ started running toward the trees.

Alvin started jogging toward a clump of termite mounds that lay at an oblique angle from the grove of trees. As he trotted on, he could hear the rattled breath of the bandicoots behind him. Albert had just reached the mounds when he heard Alvin squeak. He looked back to see Roger lying on the ground. Albert dropped the sacks behind one of the mounds and ran back to where Alvin was trying to drag Roger to his feet.

Roger's breathing was ragged and shallow. It was obvious that Roger had reached the end of his run. Albert grabbed the back of Roger's overalls and dragged him across the ground to where he had left the sacks. Alvin hovered behind them.

With a final rush of adrenaline, Albert got Roger behind the termite mound and let go of his overalls.

Alvin sat down next to Roger. "Is he all right?"

"He's fine, just tired," Albert whispered. He poured some water on Roger's head and neck, and Roger began to breathe a little easier.

"Lie down. Don't talk and don't move. If Roger starts to moan, put your paw over his mouth."

Albert handed the canteen to Alvin and lay down behind the termite mound. It wasn't five minutes before the wind carried the sound of voices to where they were. The voices got louder, and Albert pulled himself up on the base of the mound and looked back across the desert.

The Ponsby Station Fusiliers were milling around where TJ had parted company with Albert. They were searching the ground and babbling to one another. Albert was sure they were looking for tracks, and if the light hadn't been failing they would have already found what they were looking for.

Up close the Fusiliers were not particularly impressive. O'Hanlin had on a hussar's jacket two sizes too big for him and a shako on his head that kept slipping onto his glasses. He was using an artillery sword to direct the search. The body of the troop consisted of a dozen kangaroos and rock wallabies, all wearing bits and pieces of old uniforms. They were armed with a varied collection of muskets and pistols with which they seemed to have only a passing familiarity.

One of the rock wallabies found what he thought was a track, which immediately started an argument as to what kind of track it was and who might have made it. The Fusiliers all gathered around the track to offer an opinion. Before a definitive answer was arrived at, the meeting was interrupted by the boom of the Enfield. A rifle ball hummed over the heads of the Fusiliers, and Albert could see powder smoke drifting out of the stand of gum trees.

After a moment of confusion, the Fusiliers fired a ragged volley at the trees and charged toward TJ's position, with O'Hanlin in the lead waving his sword. Albert watched for the ten minutes it took them to reach the tree line and then slid back down the termite mound to where Roger and Alvin were lying.

Roger had opened his eyes, and Alvin was giving him some water from the canteen. Albert looked over at Roger. "How do you feel?"

Roger raised his head. "I need a drink really bad, Albert."

"Not now, Roger."

Albert crawled back up on the base of the termite mound. He watched the stand of trees, but he couldn't see any movement. After a few minutes he looked behind him. Except for some patches of brush, it was a clear run to the creek bed, and Albert felt he wouldn't have any trouble getting there, even in the dark.

Albert waited on the mound until the twilight turned to darkness. Roger and Alvin were sitting quietly behind him, and it looked like they could travel when the time came. Albert was starting to crawl down from the mound when he noticed lights coming from the gum trees. The lights flickered from behind the trees, and the smell of campfires drifted across the termite mound.

Someone had set up camp in the grove of trees, and it was a safe bet that that someone wasn't TJ. He and Albert hadn't started a fire since they'd left the water hole. Assuming that TJ was still alive, any rendezvous with him in the grove that night was now impossible. Albert had a choice: he could head back out into the flats, circle around the trees, and pick up the trail along the base of the hills; or he could take Roger and Alvin to the dry creek. Once in the creek bed he could leave the bandicoots long enough to search for TJ.

Albert looked out across the flats and thought he saw movement near one of the termite mounds. It was dark, but there was enough starlight to outline the mounds against the sky. Albert kept watching and soon saw another shadow move among the mounds in the direction of the grove of trees. The wind was still coming from the direction of the campfires, and it wouldn't carry any smell of Albert or the bandicoots to where he could see movement. Albert lay absolutely still and waited.

The moving outlines finally got between Albert and the gum trees, and the wind carried a new smell in Albert's direction. It was the smell of dog, mixed with the smell of the wood smoke from the campfires. It was the second time that Albert had smelled dingoes from close up, and this time he had better control of his emotions. The spurs on his hind legs still extended themselves, but the feelings of fear and anger were replaced by a steady calculation.

Now he had no choice. He would have to take the bandicoots to the creek bed, then try and find TJ. Albert took another long look into the night, then slid back down the mound to Alvin and Roger.

"Not a word, not a sound," Albert whispered.

Alvin and Roger nodded. They were either too tired to complain or they had gotten a smell of the dingoes. In either case they were as subdued as Albert had ever seen them.

Albert carefully picked up the jute bags and began walking toward the creek as quietly as he could. Roger and Alvin fell in behind him.

Albert couldn't see well in the dark and had to depend on his memory and sense of smell to get them there. The smell of wood smoke had become stronger and had blotted out any other smells on the night wind. Albert worried that he might walk right up on a dingo without knowing it, so he took his time. He stopped every few yards to peer into the darkness ahead of him. The hills beyond the creek bed were silhouetted by the sky and kept him going in the right direction.

Albert reached the creek and stopped by a patch of brush. He handed Alvin and Roger the jute bags.

"Lie down under the brush," he whispered. "I'll be back as soon as I can."

"What if you don't come back?" Alvin whispered back.

"Do the best you can to get back to the road." Albert handed his pistol to Alvin and started down the creek bed toward the campfires. He knew the pistol wouldn't do Alvin any good, but he hoped it would make him feel better.

Albert moved slowly. The smell of smoke became stronger, and he could begin to hear voices coming from the camp. It was the Fusiliers laughing and talking. Every so often the sound of O'Hanlin's voice could be heard above the rest. Albert was too far away to make out what they were saying, but he was as close to the Fusiliers as he wanted to get. He turned to start back up the way he'd come when TJ whispered to him:

"What took you so long?"

TJ had walked up behind Albert, close enough to touch him.

"Dingoes."

There was a moment of silence, then TJ murmured, "Where?"

"They were moving across the desert toward the trees." Albert pointed out into the blackness of the flats of Hell.

"I didn't think they'd get here that fast. Where are the rodents?" TJ took the bandana off his head and put it in his pocket.

"I left them a little way up the creek."

"Go get them and take them up to the base of the hills as quickly as you can. Wait there and I'll find you. Whatever you do, don't come back this way." TJ put his hat on and walked through the brush onto the flats.

Albert got back to where Alvin and Roger were hiding under the brush. He took his pistol back from Alvin and made sure it wasn't cocked. He had made a mistake by firing his pistol to break up the fight between TJ and the bandicoots. It had pinpointed their location to the Fusiliers, and he didn't want to make the same mistake a second time.

He got the bandicoots out of the creek and led them up to the base of the hills, high enough to be able to see the fires of the camp. They were too far away to make out individuals, but they could see movement around the fires. Occasionally, a snatch of laughter or conversation would reach them, carried on the wind.

Albert looked back down into the creek bed and saw that it had become full of shadows moving toward the fires. Two of the shadows stopped at the clump of brush where he had hidden the bandicoots. The shadows put their noses in the air. After a moment one of the shadows moved on, but the second one began to circle the brush and then started zigzagging across the creek bed toward the hills. It stopped for a moment at the edge of the creek and put its nose in the air again. It hesitated and then turned to head back up the creek to the camp. That was when Roger coughed.

The shadow spun around and bounded up the hill. Albert jumped to his feet, keeping himself between the shadow and the bandicoots. The dingo was on him in a matter of seconds. Instinctively, Albert threw his hat into the dingo's face. The dingo reared up on his hind legs and swung at Albert with a stone club. Albert ducked, and before the dingo could swing again, a rock sailed out of the darkness and hit him in the back. The dingo growled and turned toward the new assailant. Albert threw himself on the dingo's back and drove his spurs into his flanks.

Albert had been there once before, those many years ago on the banks of the Murray. He remembered his mother's torn body lying along the bank and the smell of frightened dog. The rage consumed him once again. He drove his spurs into the flanks of the dingo, one after the other like he was climbing a tree. The dingo dropped his club and tried to dislodge the enraged platypus. The dingo was still trying to reach Albert when TJ emerged from the darkness and cut his throat.

TJ took the bandana out of his pocket and wiped the blade of his pocketknife. He folded the knife, then bent over and picked up Albert's hat. He walked back into the darkness and reappeared a few moments later carrying the carbine. TJ stood on the hillside looking toward the fires of the Fusiliers.

Albert lay on the dingo's body, shaking with rage. Blood was seeping onto the ground all around him. Albert hated the smell of both the blood and the dingo, but he couldn't force himself to move. For the first time he could remember everything about his mother's death and how he had thrown himself on the dog that killed her. They weren't good memories, but they were real, and no longer the unconnected flashes of horror that had haunted him for all those years in the zoo. The sound of gunshots in the distance brought him back to Old Australia.

Albert staggered to his feet. TJ didn't say anything. He just handed Albert his hat and pointed over to the grove of trees where the Fusiliers were camped. Shadows danced in and out of the campsite; there were flashes of pistol shots, and the yelling of the maimed and the dying. The fight didn't last very long, and soon the sound of guns and struggle were replaced by screams of pain.

The screaming went on for what seemed like hours, and the wind carried the smell of burned hair, blood, and fear to where TJ and Albert were standing. After the screaming stopped it was another hour before they saw the shadows begin to slip away down the creek bed and across the desert.

TJ waited for a while after the last shadow passed, then motioned for Albert and the bandicoots to follow him back down to the creek bed. Alvin and Roger carried their jute bags close to their bodies as they started down the hill. The bandicoots glanced nervously at the body of the dingo as they walked by it, as if they were afraid that it might come to life again. As soon as they passed the body, they hurried ahead and tried to stay as close to TJ and Albert as they could.

They walked slowly toward the camp. The base of the hills came down to the edge of the creek bed and limited their passage to the sandy creek bottom. They could still see the glow and smell the smoke of the smoldering campfires.

The body of a dingo lay next to the trunk of a gum tree at the edge of the camp. Someone had scattered red ochre around the body.

"At least they got one," TJ observed quietly, as he walked past the body into the middle of the campsite.

Bits and pieces of the Fusiliers were scattered about the camp. The dingoes had carried off their guns and equipment, and left only the heads and paws of the Fusiliers they had butchered. The smell of charred flesh still hung above the camp.

O'Hanlin's head had been placed on a log. The dingoes had taken his shako, but his spectacles remained on his nose, and the glowing embers of the fires were reflected in the lenses.

15 〰 On brown snakes and bandicoots

ALBERT STOOD AT THE TOP of the trail that led up from the flats to the entrance of the opening in the cliff. He had taken to coming here each evening to look at the sun setting on the desert below. He would stand there while the shadows lengthened across the flats, then watch them slowly disappear as the sun reached the horizon.

The play of light fascinated Albert. Every day the sun shifted position in the sky ever so slightly, and the movement of the light on the desert changed with it. The change from one day to the next was too subtle to see, but Albert could feel it. He would stand there until the top of the distant mountain faded into an outline in the dusk surrounded by the first few stars of the coming night.

Albert had made the mistake of staying too long one evening. The stars had kept him on top of the trail until nightfall. When he looked down from the sky he saw the campfires of the dingoes on the desert floor.

He didn't like being reminded of what he had seen that night in the stand of gum trees. There was always the chance that the same thing could happen to him or to his friends. Albert knew that the end of the Fusiliers had resulted from their own folly, but that wasn't to say that bad luck wouldn't have worked just as well, and bad luck could happen to anyone.

It had taken them another day and night to get back to the water hole from the Fusilier encampment. There had only been a few hours of darkness left the night of the massacre, and they had gone to ground before dawn the following morning. They waited on a brush-covered rise in the heat of a long day. Albert or TJ would keep watch while the other rested in what little shade was provided by the brush. The bandicoots were quiet and spent most of their time under a stunted desert oak on the back side of the rise.

Roger had started taking nips from a pint bottle he had in his bag the minute the sun came up, and if TJ hadn't taken the bottle away from him would have been drunk by noon. Roger gave up the gin without a murmur. After watching what had happened to the dingo that had attacked them the night before, neither Alvin nor Roger were inclined to argue with TJ.

Albert really didn't know what to do with the bandicoots. There hadn't been time to sort things out on the road to Barton Springs. One minute Albert and Roger had been fighting with TJ and the next minute they had been running for their lives. If he'd had time to think about it, he probably wouldn't have taken them along. The bandicoots were just looking for someone to drink with. The idea of being bushrangers had probably been appealing in a barroom somewhere, but Albert could have told them that the reality of life on the flats of Hell was not what they had in mind. In any case, it had been too late to send them back.

Albert and TJ managed to get the bandicoots to the

water hole the next night. After they arrived, TJ immediately set off to wash and clean his gear while Albert started a fire. Alvin made a half-hearted attempt to help gather firewood, but Roger just sat by the fire circle and tried to keep his paws from shaking.

Nothing much was said that night. Everyone was hungry, but it was too dark and they were too tired to try and catch anything for dinner. Alvin and Roger had only brought a little flour and baking powder with them, and nothing to cook it in. Albert passed around the last of the rock candy. After it was eaten, everyone—everyone but Roger—sat quietly around the fire.

After awhile, TJ got tired of watching Roger shake and gave him back the bottle of gin. Roger took a few stiff drinks, then lay on his side by the fire and went to sleep. Albert and TJ drifted away soon afterward and left Alvin sitting next to his snoring companion.

The first few days after their return were spent in trying to refit as best they could. TJ washed all his clothes and, while they were drying, helped Albert catch crayfish in the water hole. Enough firewood was gathered for a week, and a few failed attempts at biscuits were made. Roger and Alvin recovered quickly and were soon bragging about what they would do to the next dingo that came their way.

Albert spent his mornings swimming in the water hole, and in the afternoons he walked up the trail near the spring and sat in the rock shelter above the camp. He thought there might be a chance that if he sat there long enough, the stones around him would begin to speak. So far the stones had remained mute, but Albert was happy enough to sit in the silence.

Within a few minutes of his arrival, the brown snake

would crawl into the shelter from a crevice in the shelter floor. The snake seemed to be attracted by the heat of Albert's body or perhaps by the noise he made on his hike up the trail. Albert was always glad for quiet company and had begun to think of the snake as some kind of totem sent by their common ancestors. The snake would coil up in the corner of the cave and remain there until Albert left.

After leaving the shelter, Albert would nap in the shade of a saltbush until the sun began to set, and then walk up to the opening in the cliff that looked out across the desert.

Just before dark, Albert would come back to the camp and eat the crayfish that TJ had cooked on the rocks by the fire. Roger and Alvin were always on time for every meal, and after eating as many crayfish as TJ would allow them, they would pass around the bottle.

It had now been four days since their return to the water hole, and both crayfish and gin were running low. Regardless of the danger involved, they decided to leave the next evening, cross the flats, and walk the road to Barton Springs. They needed food and supplies, and Barton Springs was the closest place to get both. TJ had briefly considered a raid on the Gates of Hell, but having the bandicoots along made it a dubious proposition and TJ abandoned the idea.

Robbing travelers on the road had not proven a very successful way of getting resupplied. They needed a better source, and according to the bandicoots there was a large general store in Barton Springs. Any robbery of the store would most likely result in another pursuit, and TJ and Albert wanted to avoid that if they could. Albert suggested that they send the bandicoots into Barton Springs with his gold sovereign to purchase what they needed. Once they had new packs, blankets, and food, they would be in a better position to run or fight, should it come to that.

Aside from Jack's company, the thing that Albert had missed most since he left Ponsby Station was hot tea from the billycan every morning. He hoped there would be enough money left, after they got necessities, for the purchase of a proper teakettle, some loose tea, and cups.

Albert didn't look forward to another night march across the flats of Hell, but in many ways he was glad to be leaving the little valley. He was bothered that he had created a routine that repeated itself on a daily basis, first to the water hole, then to the cave and from there to the opening in the cliff. He had spent too many days walking the limits of his cage in Adelaide not to recognize a similar pattern. It was getting time for him to move on again, but he needed supplies, and he needed to see the bandicoots safely out of Hell.

Albert watched the sun reach the far horizon and the shadows and the light end their dance across the flats. The distant mountain slowly vanished, and Albert turned to hurry back to camp before any fires could be lit in the darkness below the cliff.

16 ≋ The platypus gang

THE BANDICOOTS WERE THREE HOURS late and someone was going to have to find out why. TJ thought that if he pulled his hat down low over the black mask of fur across his eyes he might not stand out that much. Other animals in Old Australia were ring-tailed and had pointed noses and ears.

There was no question about Albert going into Barton Springs. His bill and webbed feet would make him an object of curiosity the minute he hit town. There was also the matter of the reward poster, which was still probably floating around with his description on it. If anyone was to go into Barton Springs, it would have to be TJ.

The trip to Barton Springs from the water hole had been surprisingly easy. TJ had crossed the flats enough times to be able to lead the party through the night with little hesitation. The pace was slower than it had been when they were being chased by the Ponsby Station Fusiliers, and the bandicoots had been able to keep up without too much difficulty. There had been no sign of dingoes near the trail along the foothills, and TJ had cut back into the flats before they reached the massacre site.

They had reached the Barton Springs road before dawn,

rested in a gully off the road for a few hours, then sent Alvin and Roger into town to get the supplies. Albert had made sure that the bandicoots knew exactly what they needed to buy from the store and could repeat the list of supplies back to him without error. TJ remained quiet, but he was obviously troubled about sending them into town by themselves, and he'd kept Roger's carbine to ensure his return.

But there really hadn't been any choice. It would take both bandicoots to carry the packs and supplies they needed, and to send them into town one at a time would just double the risk. After the bandicoots left, TJ said there was no point in taking chances, and he took Albert to a different location in the hills, on the other side of the road, where they could watch the road near the gully from a distance.

The road to Barton Springs was well traveled, and Albert and TJ watched several parties of marsupials move up and down the road that afternoon. With a professional eye, TJ marked out where it would be best to conduct a holdup and where best to place a lookout to prevent being surprised by other travelers.

Albert spent the afternoon thinking about what he should do next. Once he had a pack and a teakettle there would be nothing stopping him from continuing his search for a different Old Australia. Maybe TJ would want to come with him, and together they might find a way for TJ to get back to California. With enough food and a friend, there were few things that couldn't be accomplished.

As the afternoon progressed, TJ became more and more restless. Just before dusk, TJ couldn't stand the inaction any longer and decided it was time to search the town for Alvin and Roger. If he couldn't find the bandicoots, TJ planned to break into the general store. He and Albert needed food and supplies. If Alvin and Roger weren't going to deliver them, stealing them was their only option.

TJ left Albert with the worn blanket and one canteen. If he didn't return by the next morning, Albert was to make his way back across the flats of Hell and wait for TJ at the water hole. If Albert was careful, waited until nightfall, and kept to the trail along the hills, he should make the camp by the end of another night. Whoever got to the camp first would wait three days. After that the survivor would be on his own.

TJ checked the percussion caps on his pistol and the one on the carbine, then pulled his hat down low over his eyes. He took Albert's paw in his own and shook it. "Take care of yourself, partner."

"The same to you, TJ. See you soon," Albert said quietly.

"I'll be back with those damn rodents before midnight."

TJ put the carbine under one arm and started toward Barton Springs. From a distance he was difficult to distinguish from many marsupials, and Albert felt better about his chances of getting into the town undetected.

Midnight came and went and neither the bandicoots nor TJ appeared on the road near the gully. Albert moved closer to the road so he wouldn't miss TJ's or the bandicoots' return. He kept looking into the darkness and hoping that each imagined noise was the first sign of his friends. It was a long night.

At dawn, he moved back into the hills where he had been with TJ the day before, and continued to wait. Albert knew that something had gone wrong in Barton Springs. But for now, there was nothing he could do about it.

He decided that it was best to wait until late afternoon and then head back to the water hole, as he and TJ had agreed on. TJ had proven resourceful enough in the past, and there was a good chance he would get back to the valley in the cliffs before Albert could. If TJ failed to appear in three days, Albert would return to Barton Springs and look for him, regardless of the danger involved.

The road was clear when Albert came out of the hills and walked toward the gully. From the gully to the flats of Hell was about a three-hour trek. It would be dark by then and would allow Albert to start immediately across the flats to the water hole.

Albert was halfway down the gully when he heard a voice.

"A platypus returning to the scene of the crime. How trite."

Albert looked over and saw Bertram looking down at him from the lip of the gully. Standing next to Bertram was Theodore. They were both wearing black vests and slouch hats. Theodore was wearing goggles with smoked lenses and pointing a double-barreled shotgun at Albert. Peeking from behind Bertram and Theodore was a group of wallabies, kangaroos, and bandicoots carrying a variety of weapons.

Bertram turned to the group behind him.

"Congratulations, posse, you have helped in the capture of Albert the Platypus, infamous bushranger and murderer of the brave Captain O'Hanlin."

The group gave themselves a short round of applause. It was at that point that Albert noticed that both Bertram and Theodore were wearing badges on their vests. Theodore pointed at Albert.

"Some of you go down there and chain him up. Be careful—he is known to carry a pistol in his coat pocket."

There was quite a bit of milling about, but no one seemed eager to get down in the gully with Albert. Finally, Theodore jumped into the gully and hit Albert with the butt of his shotgun. After that, the rest of the posse was more than happy to run down into the gully and help subdue the already subdued platypus. In a few minutes, they had taken his pistol, his blanket, and his canteen. When they were finished, Albert had shackles on his paws and feet, a swollen eye, and a ripped jacket.

Theodore led the crowd out of the gully and onto the road. Albert shuffled along in the middle of the crowd as best he could. The chain on his leg shackles was very short and only allowed him to take small steps. Soon the entire group was spread out up and down the road.

The posse mocked him from a distance, still afraid to get too close. Theodore, though, remained close and hissed at Albert or poked him with his shotgun to move him along. Albert noticed a puckered wound on the side of Theodore's head. It was still healing.

Bertram caught up with Albert on the road and saw him looking at Theodore's wound.

"It can be very difficult sometimes to tell if Theodore is dead or not—after all, he is a possum. That said, your foreign friend came closer than most."

Bertram slowed his pace and walked alongside Albert down the middle of the road. He spoke softly so his voice wouldn't carry to the posse. "I must say that at the time I was very upset. What with poor Theodore all bloody, and tables knocked over. Even the dingoes were upset. With you and your friend gone, they had to make do with canned goods. All in all, it was not an anniversary party I would care to repeat."

Albert continued to shuffle down the road. The shackles kept tripping him, and he was more interested in keeping his feet than he was in listening to Bertram.

"However, in the end everything worked out for the best. I got to be the constable of Barton Springs and, last night, Theodore got to shoot your friend in the back."

Albert jerked his head toward Bertram.

Bertram smiled. "I thought that might get your attention."

"Is he dead?" Albert had been keeping quiet, afraid to give Bertram any information about his friends. There was no point in silence anymore.

"Probably. He left quite a blood trail behind. Theodore would have followed him, but the capture of the leader of the Platypus Gang was our first priority. Once we get you safely locked up, Theodore will go find the body."

Bertram drifted away to shake hands with the members of the posse. There was much back slapping, and congratulations were exchanged all around. Runners went back and forth between the town and the posse. Small groups of marsupials began to line the road and occasionally one of the children would throw a rock at Albert.

The pace of the procession was dictated by how fast Albert could move in shackles, and even with Theodore's prodding the trip was a long one. As it got dark, torches were brought out from town and delivered to the posse. A small band, with "Barton Springs Drum and Bugle Corp" printed on the bass drum, was waiting on the edge of town. It joined the procession playing marches and bugle solos.

The main street of Barton Springs was lined with

spectators who cheered as the first posse members in the torchlight parade passed them. The cheers changed to boos and catcalls as the chained platypus got closer. Small children waved effigies of Albert with a noose around his neck as their parents looked proudly on. A banner had been strung across Main Street that read:

HURRAH FOR CONSTABLE BERTRAM
AND HIS BRAVE DEPUTY
You Saved Our Town

17 ≋ The wages of sin

AT ONE TIME THE JAIL had been an open shed, so there was no wall on the north side. The other three sides were made of uneven planks with enough gaps in them to allow blowing dust to cover the floor. The shingles on the roof had shrunk over the years and would have leaked if it ever happened to rain in Barton Springs. Two strap iron cages had been constructed inside the shed to hold the prisoners.

Roger and Alvin shared one of the cages with a scruffy tiger cat who was doing thirty days for vagrancy. Albert had the second cage to himself.

The tiger cat had tried to strike up a conversation with Albert the night he was brought in by the posse, but Roger and Alvin had sat in the corner of their cage and kept silent. By the next morning, the bandicoots still hadn't spoken a word to Albert.

Albert asked the bandicoots what had happened, but they refused to talk to him. Roger continued to sit in the corner of his cage, but by now he was holding his knees to keep his paws from shaking. Every so often he would mutter to himself that TJ had it coming. Alvin kept telling Roger that it was going to be all right and refused to look Albert in the eye.

Neither Bertram nor Theodore had reappeared after the night they had caught Albert in the gully outside of town. Albert assumed they were looking for TJ and each day they didn't come back gave him hope that TJ was still alive.

The first day in the cage was a never-ending parade of local inhabitants coming by the shed to stare at Albert the Platypus, a nonmarsupial and soon-to-be-hanged bushranger. Most were content to look at Albert from a distance and whisper among themselves. Some of the less timid would approach close to the cage and make rude noises at Albert. If he made any movement they would back away quickly and return only after he remained still. That day in Barton Springs was the first time in his life that Albert admitted to himself there might be worse places in the world than the zoo in Adelaide.

In the evening two armed kangaroos would escort a small wallaby to the jail. While the wallaby was putting food in the cages and emptying the slop buckets, the kangaroos would describe in detail the fate that awaited Albert at the end of a noose. He was going to be the first platypus hanged in Barton Springs. The novelty of the event didn't excite Albert as much as it did the kangaroos.

The next day was quieter than the first. Scattered groups of the curious visited the jail, but after one or two looks they would pass on down the street. Albert spent the morning sitting on the floor, ignoring the visitors and watching dust particles suspended in the beams of light that came from the holes in the roof. The particles stirred with each movement of the air in the cell, and if the breeze was gentle enough the dust would create strange images in the columns of light. Albert couldn't see anything he recognized in the images, but concentrating on them took him away from the cell for a time and made the pain of knowing that TJ was dead or badly hurt a little easier to bear.

The noise of a soft cough broke Albert's concentration, and he looked up to see a wallaby standing in front of his cage. The wallaby was holding the paws of two very small wallabies. Albert looked again.

"Is that you, Ralph?"

The wallaby gave Albert a brief nod of the head. "I'm so glad you recognized me. It will mean so much to the children. Bernice. Jason. I'd like you to meet Albert the Platypus, famous bushranger and vicious killer."

The two little wallabies opened their eyes a little wider and one of them ducked behind its father.

"The wife really didn't like the idea of me bringing the twins. But I told her it would be a good object lesson, you know, the wages of sin and all that."

Albert didn't quite know how to respond. In all those years in Adelaide no one had ever introduced him to their children. He stood up in the cage. The second little wallaby ducked behind its father.

"Pleased to meet you," Albert said quietly, not wanting to alarm the little wallabies any further.

Bernice and Jason poked their heads from around their father's back but refused to get any closer to the cage.

"I'm sorry, Albert, but they seem to be a little shy. You don't mind me calling you Albert, do you?" Ralph said hopefully.

"That's fine, Ralph. I don't mind a bit," Albert said, and immediately regretted it. Emboldened by familiarity, the wallaby began speaking to Albert sternly.

"On some levels you seem like a decent sort, Albert. I

guess there is a little good in the worst of us. But one can't have platypuses rampaging around stealing and killing. If it weren't for the bravery of Constable Bertram and Deputy Constable Theodore, there is no telling how much damage you and your gang might have done."

Bertram had mentioned to the posse that Albert had killed O'Hanlin. Now here were more claims of involvement in the death of others being laid at his feet.

"What makes you think that I've been rampaging around stealing and killing?" Albert asked.

"As you are well aware, I know about your stealing firsthand," Ralph said, becoming a little petulant. "As to your murderous conduct, it has been the subject of numerous editorials and headlines in the *Gates of Hell Gazette*."

Ralph pulled a folded newspaper from inside his vest.

"The whole story is really quite chilling. Right here in last week's edition, it details how you and your gang came upon the Ponsby Station Fusiliers and murdered all of them in their sleep. You should be ashamed of yourself."

"We didn't do it, Ralph." Albert said in a pointless attempt to defend himself.

"Of course you did, Albert. It says so right here in the paper, and there was even worse to come."

Ralph turned a page in the newspaper and pointed to another article. "In this column it clearly says that a confidential source informed the editors of the paper of your plans to attack Barton Springs and subject the inhabitants to unspeakable cruelties."

He refolded the newspaper and put it back in his vest. "The town was able to hire Constable Bertram and his deputy to protect us, and as you know, they have done an admirable job."

Ralph took the paws of his children. "I must really get home. The hanging is sure to draw a crowd, and the wife and I are thinking about renting out the back room. Children, say good-bye to Albert."

The little wallabies shook their heads.

"Are you sure? There won't be a next time."

Bernice and Jason were sure. Ralph looked up.

"I guess not. Good-bye, Albert."

Albert lifted a paw and gave Ralph a wave. "Take care, Ralph."

The wallaby led his children away from the jail and down the street. Albert watched them for a few moments, then started to sit down again. He heard a voice.

"That's just an expression, right?"

Albert looked over and saw the tiger cat standing in the cage next to him. The bandicoots were still huddled in the far corner of the same cage. Roger's condition was getting worse, and he had started scratching himself.

"I beg your pardon?"

Roger started making whistling noises in the back of his throat. The tiger cat walked to the corner of the cage and absentmindedly kicked Roger a few times until he stopped, then walked back to where he had been talking to Albert.

"The wages of sin... it's just an expression, isn't it?"

"As far as I know it is," Albert answered after a moment's thought.

"Too bad. I could have used the money." The tiger cat turned and headed back toward the corner of the cell, where Roger had started whistling again.

18 ≋ "We didn't have any choice"

THE NEXT MORNING THE KANGAROOS that kept watch on the jail opened the other cage and let the tiger cat go. It wasn't clear to Albert if his sentence was up or if they were just tired of feeding him. In any case, the tiger cat seemed indifferent to his release and hung around for a while making small talk with the jailers. The tiger cat ignored the bandicoots, who continued to sleep in a pile in the corner of their cage. However, before he left, the tiger cat stopped by Albert's cage, shook his paw, and wished him well.

With the tiger cat released, the kangaroos wandered off to find breakfast and a shady spot, leaving Albert to sit in the silence of the early morning.

The kangaroos had been gone only a few minutes when Bertram and Theodore came down the street and stepped up into the shed near Albert's cage. Theodore was still wearing his goggles to protect his eyes from the light, and still carrying his shotgun.

Bertram looked at Albert and put a finger to his lips. "Shhhhh," he whispered.

Then he pulled a pint gin bottle out of his coat pocket and tiptoed over to the bandicoots' cage. Bertram then gently rapped the gin bottle against the bars of the cage.

The bandicoots were up like a shot. Roger had his paws through the bars before Alvin cleared the center of the cage.

Bertram pulled the bottle away from the cage. Roger became more and more frantic, pushing his arms through the bars as far as he could and grabbing at the bottle that Bertram kept just out of reach. In a few moments, Bertram tired of the game and let Roger have the bottle. He turned back to Albert.

"Good morning, Albert. I hope you slept well."

Albert looked up at Bertram.

"No point in being impolite, Albert. After all, I caught you fair and square, with a little help from your friends." Bertram gestured over to the bandicoots, who were rapidly passing the bottle back and forth between them.

"How's the newspaper business?" Albert asked.

Bertram smiled. "So you've come across a copy of the *Gates of Hell Gazette*. Theodore and I are quite proud of it, aren't we, Theodore?"

The possum nodded and fingered the stock of his shotgun.

Alvin handed the bottle back to Roger and then whined at Bertram. "You promised to let us go, Bertram. You promised us."

"Don't worry, Alvin, I haven't forgotten. In fact, that's why Theodore and I are here. Aren't we, Theodore?"

Theodore nodded and looked over at Alvin. Saliva began to glisten in the corners of Theodore's mouth.

"We just need you to do one more thing before you get the reward money. We would like you to take a few friends of ours to the hideout of the Platypus Gang. You'll be back in plenty of time for the hanging."

Bertram pulled a key out of his coat pocket and started to unlock the door of the bandicoots' cage. When Bertram mentioned the hideout, Albert jumped up. Bertram looked over as he continued to unlock the door.

"It seems that your friend from California had more blood in him than we thought. Theodore lost his trail at the edge of Hell. If he made it across the flats, I'm sure he went back to your little valley. Roger and Alvin are going to show us where that is, aren't you?" Bertram opened the door of the cage.

Roger staggered out first, still scratching himself. "Too right we're going to show you. That bloody foreigner stole my gun."

Alvin called over to Albert as he followed Roger out of the cage. "We didn't have any choice, Albert. He took away Roger's gin and called us rodents."

"I'm sure that was very unpleasant," Bertram said, and dismissed the bandicoots with a wave. "Theodore, please take these material witnesses over to the bar and get them ready for their trip."

Theodore got behind the bandicoots and herded them into the street with the butt of his shotgun. Bertram took a cigar out of his vest pocket, bit the end off, and spit it into the street.

"Every cloud has a silver lining—did you know that, Albert?"

Albert wasn't in the mood to listen to Bertram talk about clouds. He had to think of some way to escape before Roger and Alvin could lead Theodore or the dingoes or both to the water hole. Albert had spent so much of his life in a cage that being in the jail in Barton Springs hadn't made him frantic. He had escaped from Adelaide, and with enough time he would probably find a way to escape from Barton Springs. There was the matter of the hanging, but he had been too worried about TJ to dwell on the fact that his time to escape was limited.

"Our first meeting, except for the money in your pack, was unfortunate. Our second meeting, however, has been extremely profitable and, if I may I say so, personally rewarding. By the time I had written two editorials, I had been hired to protect Barton Springs and the price on your head had been raised to ten pounds. That kind of money tempts anyone. Ask your little friends." Bertram gestured toward the departing bandicoots with his cigar.

"Of course everyone knows that money is secondary to my sense of civic duty," he continued. "Just yesterday there was an editorial in the *Gazette* which extolled my selfless heroism in capturing the notorious Platypus Gang. According to the paper, there is even talk of me running for mayor of Barton Springs. I'm humbled by the thought."

Bertram took a match out of his pocket, struck it on the bars of Albert's cage, and lit his cigar.

"I don't care if that friend of yours dies in the desert, gets eaten by the dingoes, or runs back to where he came from. Theodore, however, holds a grudge."

He took a puff on his cigar and blew a small smoke ring through the bars of the cage. "By the way, Albert, the whole time I have been here you haven't summoned one demon." The match burned Bertram's fingers and he dropped it on the floor of the jail. "You must be losing your touch."

Bertram ground the smoking match out with his heel and walked away, leaving Albert alone in the shed.

All Albert could think about, as he watched Bertram catch up with Theodore and the bandicoots, was that TJ was badly hurt and needed him. He felt like throwing himself against the bars, but he had seen too many animals hurt themselves doing that in Adelaide. He had done it himself right after he was caught and had soon learned that fear and desperation didn't get you out of a cage.

Bertram had been right about one thing: the chance of a demon showing up was pretty slim. If anyone was going to get Albert out of the Barton Springs jail it was going to have to be Albert. All he needed was a plan.

In Adelaide he had waited until someone forgot to latch his enclosure. There wasn't much chance of him being that lucky a second time. The only other time the door to his cage was open was when they brought him food. He could probably overpower the wallaby, but the two kangaroos were another story.

The only advantage of being the lone platypus in this part of Old Australia was that no one knew about his poison spurs. TJ and the bandicoots had seen him attack the dingo but TJ had killed it before the poison had a chance to work. It was almost certain that one kangaroo would shoot him while he was poisoning the other, but with luck, he might be able to take the gun from the one he jumped and use it first.

If that was going to be his plan, someone was going to have to die. You can't poison someone halfway, and it's hard to shoot someone just a little bit. Albert had never wanted to kill anyone and didn't want to kill anyone now. He had suppressed the memories of poisoning the dog that killed his mother and had remembered it clearly only after the fight with the dingo.

TJ had saved Albert's life more than once, but that wasn't important. What was important was that TJ was

Albert's friend, and Albert was more than willing to die trying to save his life. The question was whether Albert was willing to kill someone else in the process. Albert didn't really know. He had no good reason to hate the kangaroos and probably couldn't develop one before the time came to act.

He sat on the floor of his cage waiting for the evening meal and trying to think of other ways to escape. By midday nothing had come to him. If he wanted any chance of helping TJ, he had to try to escape that evening, regardless of the consequences to himself or his jailers.

Albert got up and moved the slop bucket to the far end of the cage. Retrieving the bucket would force the wallaby to clear the door to the cage and give Albert a clear shot at the closest kangaroo. It was going to be a near thing, and he was going to need a lot of luck. Albert had told the crowd in Ponsby Station that a platypus was the luckiest animal in the world, but after spending time in Old Australia, he was beginning to have his doubts.

He was pacing off the interior of the cage, trying to estimate the time it would take the wallaby to reach the slop bucket, when he heard a familiar voice from the street.

"So you're the leader of the Platypus Gang."

Albert looked up to see Jack standing in front of the shed.

"To tell the truth, I was expecting someone a little tougher looking," Jack continued.

Albert rushed over to the side of his cage closest to the street. Jack looked over his shoulder. The kangaroo on the other side of the street was slouched in a chair with his hat pulled down over his eyes to keep out the midday sun.

"Sorry I didn't get here sooner. I don't walk as fast as I used to."

In the years Albert had spent in the zoo, he had never seen a friendly face through the bars of his cage. For a second, memories of the overwhelming loneliness of his time in Adelaide washed over him, and he was afraid to say anything just in case the figure in the slouch hat and the dirty drover's coat might disappear at the sound of his voice.

"Are you doing all right, Albert?" Jack asked.

Albert hesitated for a few seconds before he answered. "I'm doing fine, Jack, but I've got a friend that's in trouble."

Jack took off his hat with his right paw and knocked some of the dust off it by slapping it against his leg. "I guess that makes two of us." He put his hat back on. "I'll be back in a couple of hours. Don't go anyplace."

Jack walked away from the jail, and Albert noticed that he was dragging his left foot.

19 ≋ Good-bye to Barton Springs

BY THE TIME JACK MANAGED TO pry open the lock on the cage, dense clouds of smoke and ash were whirling down the street in front of the shed. The shed was one of the first buildings to catch fire, and if Jack hadn't shown up with the crowbar when he did, Albert would have burned to death. The kangaroos had long since abandoned their post, and the other creatures were too busy fleeing the fire to pay attention to what Jack and Albert were doing.

Jack wasn't able use to his left paw and had kept it in his coat pocket. As a result, he had some difficulty prying open the lock, but with Albert's help he had managed to open the cage with a minute to spare.

Albert had jumped into the street and had just helped Jack down from the shed floor when part of the roof collapsed, causing more sparks and debris to shoot skyward. Albert's hat and canvas jacket protected him from most of the sparks, but he did have to brush off one or two small pieces of smoldering wood before they burned through his clothes. Jack had brought a couple of bandanas with him, and Albert tied one over his face and helped Jack tie the other over his.

They pushed their way through the smoke and the

constantly changing wind until they came to the main street, where they joined small groups of refugees heading north out of the burning town. If any of the wallabies or bandicoots dragging children or pushing wheelbarrows full of salvaged housewares recognized Albert, they gave no sign.

Buildings on both sides of the street were on fire, and the banner that had once spanned the street had become ash that floated above the heads of the dispossessed. A few members of one of the bucket brigades along the street continued throwing water, not wanting to admit it was a pointless task. But others had abandoned their buckets and were trying to get possessions out of still-standing houses before the flames reached them.

Barton Springs wasn't a very large place, and Albert and Jack reached the edge of town ten minutes after leaving the jail. Those inhabitants that had already gotten out had stopped on the road, not knowing where to go next. They milled around the outskirts of Barton Springs, watching the fires and looking for friends to compare tragedies with.

Albert and Jack continued to walk north as rapidly as they could, and even with Jack's limp they soon left the inhabitants of Barton Springs behind them.

"I didn't expect the wind to come up like that," Jack said, as he pulled the bandana down around his neck.

Albert pulled down his bandana. "Where are we going?"

"I stowed some gear in the hills close to the road."

Jack limped up the road, stopping every so often to look back at the smoke rising from Barton Springs. Albert wasn't sure what had happened to Jack or how badly hurt he was, so he kept Jack in front of him, just in case he needed help.

As they walked, Albert told Jack about TJ, the bandicoots, and how Bertram and Theodore were in league with the dingoes. Jack said he'd heard of Bertram and Theodore before and told Albert that they had a bad reputation in Old Australia. The word was that the possum had killed a couple of miners in a not-so-fair fight.

The trip between the town and the hills took less time than Albert's walk to Barton Springs in shackles, but it was dusk when Jack turned off the road. He pulled a small pack out of the brush and passed it to Albert.

"When I read about the hanging, I wasn't sure what I was going to find in Barton Springs. There is food, water, and a blanket for you in the pack."

Then he reached in the pocket of his coat and pulled out his old pepperbox pistol and held it out to Albert. "I didn't have time to get another gun, so take this one."

Albert hesitated. "I don't know, Jack. You might need it."

"Look Albert, if I were going with you I'd keep it. But you don't have time to drag a cripple across the flats, not if you want to help that friend of yours."

Albert reluctantly took the gun. "What happened to you, Jack?"

"I'm not really sure. One minute I was walking up a hill, the next minute I was lying at the bottom of the hill with a bum leg and an arm that didn't work right. Scared the hell out of me." Jack pulled the other pack out of the bush. "Took me a week before I could get around much."

Albert didn't know what to do. Both TJ and Jack were hurt, but he couldn't be in two places at once. He knew that Jack was able to get around without him and that TJ was probably badly hurt somewhere between here and the water hole. The choice was simple, but it didn't make Albert feel any better.

"Wait here for me, Jack. I'll be back in a day or two."

Jack shook his head. "You don't know that for sure."

"Not for sure, Jack."

"I'll tell you what, Albert. If you get clear, meet me at Ponsby Station. I'll be set up near where the store used to be."

"I'm not sure that's a good idea—not after our last trip," Albert said.

"The place is pretty much deserted. They closed down the mine after O'Hanlin got himself and half the town killed."

Jack started to put on his pack, but he struggled with it as he tried to get the straps over his bad arm. Albert put the pistol in his coat pocket and helped Jack with his pack.

"It wasn't you, was it?" Jack asked.

Albert picked up his own pack. "It wasn't me what?"

"It wasn't you that killed O'Hanlin, was it?"

Albert shook his head. "Dingoes got him."

"I'm glad to hear it. I kind of liked O'Hanlin."

Jack looked over in the direction of Barton Springs. A soft glow from the burning town haloed the hills. "I think I'll wander back a little ways and watch the fire." He hesitated a few seconds, then went on. "That friend of yours is probably already dead. Don't get yourself killed over something you can't do anything about."

"I'll try not to, Jack."

Jack hobbled away toward the road. Albert shouldered his pack and walked into the hills toward the flats of Hell. It was some time before he realized that he had forgotten to tell Jack what he had learned about the Famous Muldoon.

20 ≋ "They ate Alvin"

THERE WAS NO MOON THAT NIGHT and Albert had fallen twice, once into an unseen gully and once into the bed of a dry creek. Each fall had disoriented him a little bit more, and soon one star began to look much like the next and he lost all sense of direction. Desperate to find TJ, Albert had kept walking longer than he should.

Finally, he stopped at the base of a small hill. There was a good chance that he was getting farther away from the water hole, not closer to it. He was going to have to wait until first light to start again.

Albert took a canteen and a blanket out of the pack Jack had given him and prepared to sit out the night. Continuing to travel blindly through the night would be the same as throwing himself against the bars of a cage. He took a drink from the canteen and pulled the blanket over his shoulders. Then he leaned against the rock and sat there for the rest of the night, alert for any noise or for the smell of dingoes.

The distant mountain appeared on the horizon in the faint light of morning, and Albert knew generally where he was. He would need to walk west.

Getting lost the night before had taken Albert far

enough out of his way that he didn't reach the foothills until midmorning. He had tried to veer north toward where the cliffs began, but he miscalculated the angle and missed them by a few miles. He hurried past the hills and got to the trail that led up the cliff about an hour later. He stopped at the bottom of the trail and listened.

Albert couldn't hear anything, but the air smelled faintly of dingo. He took the pistol out of his pocket and started cautiously up the trail. He reached the top and continued into the gap in the cliff walls, stopping to listen every few yards.

He had stepped out of the gap and onto the trail leading down to the valley when he found the body of a dingo. There was a flint-tipped spear by the body, which had been spattered with red ochre.

He walked carefully down the trail to the campsite. The lean-to was still standing, and TJ's coat was lying on the ground under the canvas. Albert picked up the coat. It was stiff with dried blood and had a bullet hole in the back. He held TJ's coat for a few moments before folding it neatly and putting it back where he found it. Albert held his paw over the fire pit. The ashes were still warm.

Albert took out his pistol again and began to search the valley. He came on another dead dingo lying half-submerged in the water hole. The body had been there for a while and the crayfish were beginning to feed on it. He walked the entire perimeter of the water hole but found nothing else.

Near the base of one of the cabbage palms, Albert found a set of bloodstained overalls that had been thrown on a bush next to the tree. The coveralls belonged to one of the bandicoots, he couldn't say which.

He walked up to the spring above the water hole and found a third dingo lying at the base of the path that led up to the rock shelter. Except for a blind eye and a small puncture wound on his nose, the dingo showed no signs of injury. The trail up to the shelter was spattered with blood.

Finally, he climbed the trail and crawled into the shallow cave.

The brown snake lay dead near the entrance to the shelter. Its head had been crushed, and someone had scattered red ochre over its body. Spent percussion caps were scattered around a pool of dried blood that had been smeared across the floor of the cave. Albert searched the back and sides of the shelter, but found nothing else.

He spent the rest of the afternoon searching the valley for signs of TJ but found none. Once or twice he thought he saw movement at the end of the valley, but dismissed it as just reeds swaying in the slight breeze that rippled the pond.

After convincing himself that it was futile to search further, Albert walked back to the water hole and sat on the bank, staring into his own reflection. He knew that TJ had returned to the valley. His bloody coat was proof of that. There had been a fight and someone, probably TJ, had killed the dingoes. Other than that he knew nothing for sure. Albert stayed there trying to put the pieces together until darkness covered the pond and only then walked back to the camp.

A few sticks of firewood remained near the fire pit, and Albert started a small fire with the matches he knew would be in the pack Jack had given him. There were tins of sardines there also, but Albert couldn't eat.

There was a chance the fire might attract attention. But Albert hadn't seen any sign of the living in his search of the valley, and he knew the cliffs around him prevented the light from reaching the flats below the water hole.

Albert sat and stared into the fire in much the same way as he had stared into the water hole. He wasn't sure that TJ was still alive—and if TJ was alive, he wasn't sure where to start looking for him.

The fire had been reduced to embers when Albert heard a noise in the darkness beyond the camp. He put his paw on the pistol in his pocket. The wind was behind him, so he couldn't smell anything. He sat quietly waiting for another sound. When the wind shifted direction, he smelled stale gin.

A pair of eyes, reflecting the embers of the fire, appeared in the night across from where Albert was sitting.

"They ate Alvin." Roger's voice was a hoarse whisper.

Albert took his paw off the pistol. "Where's TJ?"

"He screamed something awful."

Albert could hear Roger scratching himself.

"You wouldn't have a drink, would you, Albert?"

"No."

"You're not going to kill me, are you, Albert?" The eyes across the fire pit blinked several times.

"I thought about it."

"I saved his head." Roger's voice was becoming a whisper.

"Whose head, Roger?"

"Alvin's, of course, but don't worry, Albert. I have it in a safe place."

Albert moved slightly, and the eyes backed away from the campfire.

"I won't hurt you, Roger. I just need to know what happened to TJ."

After a moment the eyes came a little closer.

"I don't remember, Albert. It was a long time ago."

"It was yesterday, Roger."

"Was it?" The sound of Roger scratching himself intensified. "The dingoes were yelling and howling, and Theodore was hissing and shooting up at the cave. I remember that."

Roger went quiet. Albert started to reach toward his pack, and again Roger backed away.

"I have some food in my pack, Roger. Do you want some?"

Roger giggled. "Alvin and I have plenty of crawfish. I put a dingo in the pond to feed them."

Albert kept talking to Roger in an even tone, afraid that any change of pitch in his voice might send Roger back into the darkness. "I really need to know what happened to TJ. Try to remember."

"The dingoes took him. I told you that already." Roger sounded annoyed.

"Sorry, Roger, I must have forgotten. Where did they take him?"

"Bertram and Theodore were very angry."

Roger came closer to the fire pit. Albert could almost see his outline.

"Bertram is not very nice. Did you know that, Albert?" Roger started whispering again.

"I know that, Roger."

"When the dingoes took TJ out of the valley, Bertram started hitting Alvin. It wasn't Alvin's fault the dingoes wouldn't let Theodore kill TJ, was it?"

It took an effort for Albert to keep his voice from showing what he felt. "I'm sure it wasn't."

"He was afraid to hit the dingoes, so he hit Alvin. That wasn't nice, was it?"

"No, Roger. It wasn't nice."

"He took away my gin before he left. That wasn't nice, either." Roger scratched himself a few times.

Albert didn't say anything, and Roger continued scratching.

"Alvin keeps asking me why they killed him instead of me and I don't know what to tell him," Roger said, beginning to worry. "What should I tell him, Albert?"

"I don't know, Roger. I really don't know," Albert said honestly.

"They didn't like the way I smelled," Roger said after a moment.

"Who didn't like the way you smelled?"

"The dingoes. That's why they ate Alvin. I told you that." Roger started getting annoyed again.

"I'm sorry."

"They smelled both of us and then they started killing Alvin. After a while they ate most of him and then they went away." Roger continued to fluctuate between confusion and reality. "Did you hear that, Albert?"

Albert listened carefully but heard nothing except a light wind moving the branches of an acacia. "I don't hear anything."

Roger shuffled his feet in the darkness. "It's Alvin screaming—can't you hear it?"

"It's just the wind, Roger."

The pupils of the eyes darted back and forth. "Alvin needs me. I have to go."

"I can take you back to Ponsby Station." Albert didn't know what else to say.

"We like it here, me and Alvin." Roger blinked twice before he closed his eyes and disappeared.

Albert didn't sleep much that night, glad that TJ hadn't died in the cave yesterday and worried that Roger might reappear with Alvin's head.

At first light, Albert went and found Alvin's bloody overalls and burned them in the fire pit with some leaves from a eucalyptus he had discovered near the spring. He hoped there might be some magic in the gesture that would ease Roger's pain. Albert knew that one could never be sure about magic, but a lack of certainty is never a good reason to do nothing. Albert shouldered his pack and left the water hole while the smoke was still rising from the campsite.

21 ≋ A circus tent

THREE OF THEM WERE STANDING near a grevillea bush seventy yards up the shallow ravine from where he was standing. Albert had never been this close to a live dingo in the daylight, and it wasn't an experience he had been looking forward to.

One of them was carrying a short flintlock musket; the other two were armed with spears and clubs. Other than woven bags suspended from their shoulders, the dingoes were naked. Their foxlike faces were covered with a reddish fur and showed the scars of past fights. The one with the musket was older than the other two, and the fur on his muzzle was turning white.

Not so long ago Albert had assumed that fur was all anybody needed for modesty and had been insulted when Jack had mentioned he was naked. Now, the lack of clothing on the dingoes struck him as primitive. Old Australia had changed Albert in many ways, some for the better and some for the worse. Albert hoped that someday he would have the time to sort out which was which.

Albert had been glad to leave the valley. It had served its purpose in sheltering him and TJ when they were running from the Gates of Hell. Now it was just a place haunted by the dead.

He had gotten onto the flats and started walking toward the center of Hell itself. He had only a vague plan. He needed to find TJ and avoid a direct confrontation with the dingoes.

If he could locate TJ without being discovered, there was a chance he could find a way to help TJ escape and return with him to Ponsby Station. There were problems with the plan, and Albert knew it. If TJ was still alive, there was a good chance he was too badly hurt to travel. If that proved to be the case, Albert would deal with it when he had to.

His sense of smell had helped him more than once, and it stood by him that morning. He smelled dingoes from the moment he hit the flats. Albert tried to keep the wind in his face, and when he smelled dingoes, he would alter his course to the left or the right and continue walking.

But every attempt Albert made to continue in a straight line was met by the smell of dingoes on the wind or the reflection of light from what might be a gun barrel. After an hour of zigzagging deeper into the desert, the wind stopped completely. Albert stopped with it, afraid to move without some sense of what might lie ahead of him. The wind remained still, and finally he decided to try and find cover and a place to rest. Unfortunately for him, he picked the wrong ravine.

Albert's train of thought was broken when one of the dingoes made a series of yipping sounds, ran down the ravine and threw a spear at him.

He spun sideways, and the spear glanced off the back of his pack. He turned back toward the dingo, who was racing after the spear and transferring a club into his right paw.

Albert managed to jerk Jack's pistol clear of his pocket and pull the trigger before the dingo reached him.

Thirty grains of black powder blew gold dust and pieces of iron pyrites into the face of the oncoming dingo.

The dingo staggered back but didn't fall. He had been blinded by the shot, and his face was a mask of blood and gold. The dingo began moving forward again, yipping and howling and trying to use his club on an enemy he couldn't see.

Albert backed away from the wounded dingo, who kept swinging his club in wide arcs around his body and hitting nothing but air. The two dingoes at the end of the ravine watched quietly as their companion swung his club until he was exhausted. Finally, the blind dingo let the club hang at his side, then stuck his bloody muzzle in the air and let out a plaintive howl. The older dingo walked a few yards toward the wounded one and shot him with his flintlock.

The living dingoes made no attempt to move closer to Albert, and the one firearm they had was now empty. Albert wasn't sure what to do next. Running was out of the question and trying to kill the other two dingoes with gold dust was not realistic. Albert put the pistol back in his pocket. The spear that the dingo had thrown was on the ground near his feet.

At first Albert thought about grabbing the spear to defend himself, then he remembered the body of the dingo he had found at the top of the trail to the valley. Acting more on instinct than reason, Albert picked up the spear and walked slowly over to the body lying in the middle of the ravine. The two other dingoes stood quietly as Albert lay the spear down next to the dingo sprawled in the dirt in front of him and then backed up a few yards.

Albert and the dingoes watched each other for a few moments. The older dingo handed his companion his musket and walked over to the body. He reached in his shoulder bag and took out a small leather pouch. The dingo opened the pouch and scattered the red ochre it contained over the body of the slain. A moment later, the old dingo heard something and looked up the ravine. Albert followed his gaze and saw a bulky figure wearing purple tights standing where the ravine sloped back up to the desert floor.

The old dingo raised his paw toward the figure, then disappeared into the brush along the ravine, followed by the younger one. The figure in the tights looked at Albert for a second, then turned and walked away, disappearing over the lip of the ravine.

Albert wasn't quite sure what had happened, but for now, he was still alive. He walked up the ravine to where the purple-clad figure had disappeared. The desert at the top of the ravine was covered in bottlebrush and saltbush. Albert carefully wove his way through the brush until he saw the tops of gum trees growing above. He could smell water from the direction of the trees and headed that way.

The bush gave way to a series of rocky hills. At the base of the hills was a large water hole surrounded by wattle and gum trees. A circus tent stood under the sparse shade of one of the trees.

It was a small tent and had red-and-yellow stripes, just as TJ had described. A ragged pennant with the word "Champion" flew from the peak of the little tent. Over the years, the colors had faded and the canvas had been patched so many times it was difficult to determine if the stripes had originally been vertical or horizontal.

Muldoon sat on a three-legged stool in the shade of an awning that protected the front entrance of the tent from the sun. He had his paws on his knees, and his eyes were closed.

Albert approached the tent quietly. Muldoon made no movement but to cock his head, as if trying to hear a sound far away.

Albert didn't say anything. It was obvious that Muldoon did not want to be disturbed, and good manners dictated that Albert wait for a better moment to try and strike up a conversation.

There had been a Tasmanian devil in the zoo in Adelaide, and once you had seen one, they stuck in your mind. The zoo had kept animals they considered dangerous in separate enclosures, but over the years Albert had seen the Tasmanian devil twice as they moved him in a portable cage to different places in the park. The devil hadn't been much bigger than Albert, but there was a fierceness about him that Albert had never seen in any of the other creatures in the zoo. He kept striking out at the keeper through the bars of his cage, and he didn't care how much it hurt, not if there was the slightest chance of inflicting injury on the object of his dislike.

Sometime in the past, Muldoon had been terribly burned. The fur on one side of his face had been replaced by wrinkled scar tissue that covered his eye socket and left him with a stub of an ear. One of the paws resting on a knee was badly scarred and had twisted as it healed. The fur on the other side of his face was now more gray than black.

Muldoon's purple tights had been patched more times than the tent, and bits of fur showed through the places where older repairs had given way. It seemed to Albert that everything about Muldoon was being held in the present by a few pieces of thread.

Muldoon finally opened his eyes and looked over at Albert. "When I first came here, I could close my eyes and hear the crowds cheering my name." He stood up and looked out on the desert. "It's harder for me to hear them now."

22 ≋ The Famous Muldoon

ALBERT HAD SET UP CAMP near the water hole some distance from Muldoon's tent. As TJ had said, the Tasmanian devil was a creature of few words. He told Albert he was welcome to water and then had gone back inside his tent. That had been several hours ago, and Muldoon had not reappeared.

Albert had emptied his pack, and for the first time he had a chance to make a complete inventory of what Jack had put together. Along with TJ's coat, which Albert had brought with him from the valley, the pack contained two blankets, water, and some matches. Jack had also included some hard biscuits, several tins of sardines, and a half-pint of whiskey.

After his experience at Ponsby Station, Albert had given up hard liquor. But he knew TJ had a taste for it, and he was glad that Jack had included some.

Albert ate two of the biscuits but didn't open any of the sardines. He would hunt the lagoon in the morning. He knew that Muldoon liked sardines, and he was hoping to trade the ones he had for information about TJ. It was obvious that Muldoon knew much more about the dingoes than Albert did and might be in a position to help.

Darkness came without a sign of the Tasmanian devil. Albert lay out his blankets and started a small fire. He was sure that both Jack and TJ would disapprove of the fire as being a dangerous act in enemy territory, but Albert felt he could take the risk. Muldoon was close by and seemed to be on friendly terms with the dingoes. Besides, the dingoes knew where Albert was, and if they came looking they could find him, fire or no fire.

The hills blocked any view he might have had of the distant mountain, but he could see the stars beginning to appear. They were the same stars that appeared early when he watched the sky from the valley entrance not so long ago. He was glad to see them again.

Albert was just getting ready to put a few more sticks on his fire when Muldoon walked into the light carrying his wooden stool. He put the stool down across the fire from Albert and sat.

Muldoon had changed his clothes and was now wearing a dark peacoat and a watch cap. The coat was worn and missing a few buttons. The cap had been pulled over on the side of his head to cover the stub of his ear and mask some of the scars on the side of his forehead. Muldoon looked at Albert with his good eye.

"I'm Muldoon."

"I'm Albert." Albert sat down on his blankets.

The Tasmanian devil seemed hesitant, as if not knowing what to say next. After a moment he spoke again. "Do you need more blankets? I have a couple of spare ones in the tent."

Albert shook his head. "I'm fine, thanks. It looks like a warm night."

Muldoon sat and fidgeted for a minute. "You probably

need to get some sleep. I guess I'll head back."

Muldoon stood up and made a show of picking up his stool. It was clear that Muldoon was either shy or unused to conversation and would need a little help to get comfortable.

"Would you like a drink?" Albert reached in his pack and took out the half-pint of whiskey. Albert had observed that almost any friendship in Old Australia required the offer of alcohol.

Muldoon gratefully replaced his stool by the fire and sat down again. He took the offered bottle with his good paw and, with some effort, extracted the cork with the burned one. He took a small drink and passed the bottle back to Albert.

"I guess you don't get much company," Albert said, as he took the bottle and held it in his lap.

Muldoon thought a moment. "Dingoes, I get dingoes. But they don't talk much."

"I don't know anything about dingoes," Albert volunteered.

"Dingoes are pretty strange." Muldoon thought for a moment. "They like living out here."

He lapsed into silence. Albert passed the bottle back to him, and Muldoon took another drink.

"How long have you been out here?" Albert asked.

Muldoon held the bottle in his good paw for a few moments, then took another drink. "About eight years. I came out here to die, but it didn't work out."

He passed the bottle back to Albert, who once again held it in his lap.

"You don't drink?" Muldoon asked.

"No." Albert passed the whiskey back to Muldoon.

"Neither do the dingoes—they can't stand the smell of the stuff." Muldoon took a sip and stared into the small fire in front of him. The light was absorbed by his jacket and hat but was reflected by the scars on his face. There was a sadness about him that Albert had seen that morning at the circus tent, a sadness he could feel as he watched Muldoon across the fire.

The Tasmanian devil spoke again. "Nobody comes out here except the desperate."

Albert waited for a few moments for Muldoon to continue, but he remained silent. Finally, Albert spoke. "Do you remember TJ? You helped him get through here a while back."

Muldoon nodded.

"The dingoes took him two days ago and I'm trying to find him. He's a friend of mine." Albert was relieved to finally be able to get directly to the point.

"What happened?" Muldoon started putting the cork back in the bottle with his bad paw.

"I don't know for sure—I wasn't there. But it looks like there was a fight up at the water hole you took him to. TJ shot some dingoes. He was hurt and got captured, but the dingoes wouldn't let Theodore and Bertram kill him." The words tumbled out of Albert in rapid succession.

"The possum and the one-eared wallaby; I know of them." Muldoon had become focused. "What happened after that?"

"The dingoes took TJ out here someplace, and I guess Bertram and Theodore headed back to the Gates of Hell. That's all I know." Albert stopped talking and waited for some response from Muldoon.

Muldoon stood up and absentmindedly put the whiskey

bottle in the pocket of his peacoat. He started pacing up and down by the fire.

"You can never tell about dingoes. They do one thing one day and then something completely opposite the next. But one thing they like is a good fight and another is bravery. If a dingo dies well they leave him with his weapons and scatter red earth over the body."

"TJ was one to hold his own," Albert said with absolute certainty.

Muldoon nodded.

"What will they do with him?" Albert was starting to hope that TJ might still be alive.

"You said he was badly hurt?" Muldoon sat back down on his stool.

"Theodore shot him in the back."

Muldoon waited a few moments before continuing. "If he fought well at the water hole and he survives that bullet in his back, the dingoes might adopt him."

"They adopt other creatures?" The more Albert learned about the dingoes, the more strange they seemed.

"As far as I know, the last time they did it was eight years ago. But there's always a chance." Muldoon picked up a couple of sticks and fed them into the dying fire.

"What happened this morning?" Albert asked.

"You mean with the dingoes?"

"Yes."

"They'd never seen a platypus before. If the young one hadn't gotten so full of himself, they might have left you alone."

Albert sat up straight when he heard Muldoon say *platypus*. "I'm not the first platypus you've seen, am I?" It took every bit of self control Albert had to keep himself from shouting.

"There was one in the zoo where I came from," Muldoon said matter-of-factly.

"But not here. You've never seen another platypus here." Albert was afraid he already knew the answer, but he had to ask.

Muldoon shook his head. "I've fought in every mining town in the territory and walked this desert for eight years, and you're the only one I've seen." He paused a second before continuing, "I'm the only devil in Hell and you're the only platypus."

Muldoon fished the whiskey bottle out of his coat pocket and sat down on the wooden stool. He started to pull the cork and thought better of it, then tossed the bottle back to Albert. "You heard the stories, didn't you?" he asked.

"What stories?" Albert put the bottle in his pack.

"The stories about a place where nothing has changed and Australia was the place it once was."

Albert nodded. "That was what everyone talked about at the zoo in Adelaide."

Muldoon bent toward the dying fire. "Is this the place you expected to find?"

"No," Albert answered.

"When I first got here I thought there would be some of my kind in Old Australia." Muldoon stood up and used the side of his foot to push dirt over the embers of the fire. "Now I'm not sure anymore *what* my kind is."

23 ≈ Dingoes

BEFORE SUNRISE THE NEXT MORNING, Muldoon appeared back at Albert's camp, carrying a walking staff and with several canteens looped over one shoulder. He was still wearing his watch cap, but the peacoat had been replaced by a stained cotton jacket that also had seen better days.

Muldoon told Albert he was going to try and find TJ, and he cautioned Albert to wait at the water hole until he returned. Then, without another word, Muldoon walked into the brush and was soon lost from sight.

Albert had wanted to give Muldoon the sardines before he left but had hesitated. He knew that once the sardines were brought out of the pack he would have to talk about Jack, and he wasn't quite ready to do that yet. He was pretty sure that one of Jack's fires had caused Muldoon's burns, and he was afraid that Jack might be such a sore point with Muldoon as to interfere with TJ's rescue.

The weather had been hot and the air so still that the pennant on top of Muldoon's tent stayed limp in the daylight hours. The water hole was cool in the early mornings, and Albert spent the time hunting grubs and freshwater shrimp. By midday, the sun heated the shallow water to an uncomfortable level, and the little creatures that lived in the water hole went into hiding in the mud and rocks that lined the bottom.

Albert spent his afternoons lying in the shade of a blanket that he had suspended between two gum trees a few yards from the water. He would lie on his back with his head supported by his pack, close his eyes, and try to imagine what the world he was looking for would be like. It would have other platypuses in it. That was for sure. But he wasn't certain what else that world might contain. His past visions of cool water and shady river banks hadn't survived his time in Old Australia.

Dozing in the heat of those afternoons, Albert would sometimes dream that the place he was looking for would be just another zoo without bars, and the banks of any river he found would be lined with unfriendly platypuses eating cotton candy and throwing rocks.

The noise of small black flies buzzing around his face would get louder, and he would pull himself back from the dream and into the shade of his blanket. He would lie there trying to brush away the flies and worrying that TJ might be a long time dead.

The water hole became a magical place in the brief dusk between the heat of the day and the cold of the desert night. Albert would walk in the fading light around the water hole to Muldoon's tent and look at the red-and-yellow patches that covered the tent. If he were in luck, a small breeze might straighten the pennant for a moment, and the word *Champion* would flutter above the tent.

Albert wondered what the tent might contain, and what it might have looked like when Muldoon was still a champion and its stripes were new. The tent and Muldoon had become one in Albert's mind, their current shabbiness making their past glories seem grander than they might really have been.

As much as Albert wanted to know what was inside the tent, he made no attempt to go inside or to peek through the drawn curtains that covered the entrance. It would be Muldoon's life he was walking into, and one didn't do that sort of thing without an invitation—and an understanding that you never walked into someone's life without being changed by the experience.

Albert would stare at the tent for a while and try to imagine the crowds yelling Muldoon's name, but he had never seen Muldoon fight, and his imagination wasn't up to creating an entire world of mining camps and blood sports. All that came to mind was the Muldoon he knew: the one covered in scars, waiting for the cheers that he knew would never come again.

Then Albert would walk away from the tent, collect his blanket and his pack from the bushes, go back to his camp, and start a small fire. He would wrap himself in the blanket and lean against his pack. If he were still hungry he would eat a biscuit or two and then watch the fire until he fell asleep.

Five days after Muldoon left to look for TJ, Albert woke up to find an old dingo watching him from the edge of the brush near his camp. Albert wasn't certain, but he was pretty sure the dingo was the same animal he had encountered in the ravine nearby.

The dingo was squatting in the open across the coals from where Albert had fallen asleep. He had his flintlock musket in one paw and what looked like TJ's hat in the other. Albert sat up slowly and shrugged the blanket off his shoulders. He and the dingo watched one another for several minutes, neither making any sudden movements.

The old dingo got slowly to his feet and walked toward Albert. When he had covered half the distance, he put the hat on the ground and then backed his way to his original position. The dingo squatted again and waited.

Albert, following the dingo's lead, got up slowly, walked over, and retrieved the hat, then returned to his blanket and sat down. He looked down at the hat in his lap. It was TJ's hat, chinstrap and all. Albert raised his paw to the old dingo. The dingo raised his paw in return and stood up. He turned back toward the brush and beckoned for Albert to follow him.

Muldoon had told Albert to wait for him, but that had been several days ago. If the dingo was the same one from before, Muldoon had been on good terms with it—and so far, the dingo had been acting more like a friend than an enemy.

Albert had not forgotten that he had caused the death of a young dingo and that there was always the possibility that the old dingo's manner masked an elaborate plan for revenge. However, it was certain that the old dingo had some connection with TJ, and that was enough for Albert to take the risk.

He stood up slowly, took the canteen out of his pack, and went to the water hole and filled it. When he returned, the old dingo was still waiting for him.

Albert picked up his blanket and put it in the pack along with the canteen and his jacket. He left Jack's pistol in the coat pocket. It was going to be too hot to wear the coat, and the gun was almost useless. If the dingo meant him any harm he would have to depend on the weapons nature had given him. He tied TJ's hat on the back of the pack, pulled the pack straps over his shoulders, and started toward the dingo.

When he was sure that Albert was behind him, the dingo trotted into the desert. Albert followed and found himself keeping up a pace he wasn't used to. The dingo moved effortlessly through the desert, and he seemed to know just when and where to go to keep from being slowed by clumps of brush or rough terrain.

The early morning air was cool, and Albert found that if he stayed close enough to the dingo in front of him he could move along the desert floor with the same lack of effort.

But the dingo's smell was very strong, and at first Albert was repelled by it. It still reminded him of the killing of his mother, and that conjured up the zoo in Adelaide, and the horrors that had resulted from her death.

The longer the smell surrounded him the less it bothered him. As an adolescent he had smelled the dog that killed his mother and that he had killed in turn. There was no subtlety in the memory of that smell from so long ago.

The scent of the dingo in front of him was different. The odor of dog was still there, but it was only a part of something more complex. The dingo smelled like wattle, like the red earth that covered the desert floor, like wood smoke, and like the distant smell of water and gum trees. The dog had smelled of domestication and slavery.

None of the things that Albert had thought were simple in Adelaide had remained that way in Old Australia. What he had thought was evil for so long was now helping him to save a friend.

The dingo slowed his pace with the coming of the midday heat. They kept walking for a while, but before the sun reached its zenith, the dingo led Albert to a rock outcropping that provided enough shade to offer them some relief.

The dingo leaned his musket up against one of the rocks and took a paw full of dried beetles from his woven bag, ate some, and gave some to Albert. In turn, Albert took his canteen out of his pack and passed it to the dingo. The dingo wouldn't drink directly out of the canteen, but would pour a little water in a paw and lap it into his mouth.

After they finished eating the beetles, the old dingo curled up in the shade and closed his eyes. Albert prepared to wait out the heat with his new companion.

The stillness of the desert was broken by the whisper of a dry wind that came up almost as soon as they had reached the shelter of the rocks. The wind was strong enough to keep the flies away, and Albert was grateful for it. The dingo lay still, his short fur occasionally ruffled by the moving air that found its way between the stones around them. Occasionally, he would flick an ear to the left or right, as if trying to identify a distant sound, or he would raise his head, smell the wind, then settle back and close his eyes again.

Albert had known nothing of the desert when he first came to Old Australia. He had learned what he knew from Jack and his own trips across the flats of Hell. The morning he had spent trotting after the dingo had taught him a little bit more, but Albert knew it wasn't enough and never would be. The dingo sleeping near him was at home here. It was where he belonged.

Albert knew that he belonged someplace else. Where that place was, he didn't know, but it was somewhere, and as soon as his friends were safe, he would look for it again.

A light tap on the shoulder roused him from a light sleep. He opened his eyes to see the old dingo standing in front of him. The sun was getting low on the horizon, and the dry wind was cooler than it had been before. The dingo trotted back into the desert. Albert struggled to put on his pack and hurried after him.

The nature of the desert had changed that afternoon. Albert and the dingo trotted out of the flats onto a finger of red sandstone that extended into the desert from a low-lying rock ridge a mile or so ahead of them. Albert could see small columns of smoke rising from somewhere beyond the ridge.

They walked slowly up the finger of rock for an hour, and it was nearly sunset when they reached the top of the ridge. Below them a small dingo encampment was scattered across a small sandstone plateau. Near where they stood, a spring trickled clear water through the rocks and down onto the plateau. The water ran into small pools worn in the sandstone, overflowed them, then escaped over a lip of rock beyond the camp.

Small campfires were burning in front of simple brush shelters that had been built haphazardly across the plateau. Dingoes sat near the fires working on stone tools or cooking pieces of meat that Albert didn't recognize. A few dingo pups played an endless game of tag through the camp, and their yips of excitement were the only sounds Albert could hear.

Muldoon was standing in the middle of the camp, his burned paw in the jacket of his peacoat. He looked up on the ridge and waved to Albert with the paw that still worked.

24 ≋ Moonlight and laundry

TJ LAY ON HIS STOMACH on a pile of cut grasses that had been placed on the floor of one of the brush shelters in the dingo encampment. He turned his head slightly when Albert crawled through the entrance.

"I should have known better than to trust a drunk."

It was dark in the shelter, and what light there was came from a campfire not far from the entrance. It took a few moments for Albert's eyes to adjust to the dim light.

Woven bandages had been wrapped around TJ's chest, and they held a poultice of leaves pressed up against the wound in his back. His bloody long johns and canvas pants lay folded at his feet, and next to them was the cotton sack holding the rest of his possessions. The Enfield carbine had been propped against the brush wall of the shelter, close enough for TJ to reach it. A bowl of water was sitting on the ground.

Albert sat up and his hat brushed the roof of the shelter. "How are you doing?"

"Better than I was a week ago." TJ propped his head on his paws and spoke in a low voice. "How about yourself?"

"A little tired." Albert crossed his legs and leaned forward so he could hear TJ better.

"What happened to the rodents?" TJ asked.

"Alvin's dead and Roger went crazy."

TJ closed his eyes. "Not much of a loss, if you ask me."

Albert shifted position and his shadow moved on the far wall of the shelter. "Maybe not, but they were good to me once."

TJ rolled onto his side. "I'm glad to see you, Albert."

"You too, TJ. I wasn't sure you were alive."

TJ smiled. "If I'm not dead, it wasn't for a lack of trying to kill me."

"What happened in Barton Springs?" Albert asked.

"Not much to talk about. I found the general store. It was dark by then, and I thought it was safe enough. I'd started for the back door when I heard Roger call out to me. Before I could get three more steps, someone behind me fired a shot. I didn't even look back. I ran... I've run before, Albert, and I'm good at it."

"It was Theodore. He was the one who shot you." Albert took off his hat and shoved it into his jacket pocket.

TJ was quiet for a few moments. "I figured it might have been that damned possum when I saw him at the water hole. I'll make sure of him the next time." He reached out for the bowl of water and took a long drink. "Sorry I couldn't get back to you. I didn't realize how badly I was hit until I got to the edge of town."

"Don't worry, TJ. I got by." Albert reached out and gently took the bowl out of TJ's paw.

"It took me awhile, but I got back up to the water hole. I was going to wait for you in the valley, just like we said." TJ was getting tired and the pauses were becoming longer. "Two days after I got there, company showed up... It was a hell of a fight, Albert. You should have seen it."

Albert held out the water. TJ shook his head and continued.

"I shot the first dingo that came through the gap and it delayed the rest of them until I could get up to that cave of yours in the cliff. After that it got real exciting."

TJ stopped talking and rested for a few moments before he continued.

"Bertram never came within rifle shot or I would have tried for him. The possum would run in for a few shots and then run back out of range again. The dingoes were the ones that carried the fight. If I hadn't started bleeding again and I'd had a little more ammunition, me and that snake would have held that cave until hell froze over."

TJ closed his eyes again. "Funny thing about that snake. It crawled out from somewhere right after I got into the cave. It coiled up between me and the entrance and stayed there for the whole fight. I broke my wound open running up to the cave, and I had started losing a lot of blood. Late in the day I began blacking out. The last thing I remember was that snake striking at a dingo that was trying to get at me."

Albert had been saddened by the death of the snake when he had found its body at the mouth of the cave. He was glad the snake had died bravely, but that didn't make it any less dead. Albert would miss it.

"It was a good snake," was all he could think to say.

TJ opened his eyes briefly. "Would you do me a favor?"

"Of course I would."

"Would you wash the blood out of my clothes?" TJ closed his eyes. "I can't abide being dirty." TJ took a deep breath and fell asleep.

Albert gathered up TJ's pants and long red underwear

and crawled out of the shelter with the clothes under one arm.

Muldoon was sitting by the fire outside the shelter. Albert's pack was sitting next to him. The moon was full and low enough in the night sky to light up the whole plateau. The other fires in the encampment were beginning to burn out, the dingoes mere shadows that moved from time to time among the other shelters.

Muldoon looked over at Albert, the moonlight softening the scars on his face. "How is he?"

Albert walked over to his pack and opened it. "He's sleeping."

Albert took TJ's coat out of his pack and put it with the rest of the bloody clothes he had taken from the shelter. TJ's hat hadn't suffered much, so Albert put it aside. As he started to close the pack, he remembered the sardines. He was going to have to talk to Muldoon about Jack sometime, and this might be as good a time as any.

Albert reached into the bottom of the pack and pulled out the tins of sardines. "I understand you like these."

Muldoon looked at the sardines in Albert's paw and then at his face. "Who told you that?"

"TJ, for one." Albert extended the sardines to Muldoon.

The Tasmanian devil hesitated, reached out slowly and touched the tins for a brief moment, then withdrew his paw without taking the sardines. Muldoon looked back into the fire and said nothing.

Albert held the sardines for a moment more, then lay them down on the ground next to Muldoon. He picked up TJ's clothes and walked to the stream coming down from the ridge. He followed the water past the pools to where it spilled over the sandstone escarpment and flowed into a grove of gum trees a hundred yards beyond the dingo camp. The dingoes got their water from the pools close to their shelters, and Albert didn't want TJ's blood mixing with their drinking water.

The moonlight was reflected by the water and the stones around him, and there was more than enough light for washing. Albert wet the clothes, gently rubbed them on the sandstone, then rinsed them in the stream. When he finished, he stretched the wet clothes flat on the stones to await the next day's sun.

Albert sat at the edge of the plateau and looked over the treetops in the grove below him. The moon was beginning to move higher in the sky, and its light dimmed the stars around it.

For the first time since he had arrived in Old Australia, Albert felt at peace. There had been that brief two days between meeting Jack and the fire at Ponsby Station when no one was chasing him or creatures he knew weren't being shot at or eaten.

TJ was alive. Jack was waiting for him at Ponsby Station. The zoo in Adelaide was now ancient history, and Hell was proving to be a pretty good place.

Albert decided to spend the night by the stream where he could see the trees. He was just getting up to retrieve his blanket when he saw Muldoon walking toward him across the sandstone.

"They're afraid of you. Did you know that?"

"Who's afraid of me?"

"The dingoes."

Albert was always surprised by the idea that anyone could be afraid of him. It was true that the citizens of Barton Springs had kept their distance, but Albert had thought that was just the result of some bad press and hadn't taken it personally. "That doesn't make any sense."

"It does to them." Muldoon sat down next to Albert, using his good paw to ease himself onto the sandstone. "Your footprints started it, and then there was that business with the snake."

"My footprints?"

Muldoon shrugged. "How many other creatures run around out here with webbed feet? None, that's how many. The dingoes don't miss much. They've seen your tracks. They smell poison on you and they smelled poison on one of their dead. That cave where they got TJ had your footprints all over it, and when that snake killed another dingo, they began to put two and two together. Shooting one of them with gold dust just added to the legend. If I didn't know better, I might be afraid of you myself."

"I didn't think Tasmanian devils could be afraid of anything," Albert said after a moment of reflection.

Muldoon laughed. "Neither did I. Then I got famous and everything changed."

"What changed?"

Muldoon stopped laughing. "I became afraid of not being famous." He stood up slowly. "How's Jack?"

Albert hesitated. "Getting old," he finally said.

"I recognized his pistol when you fired that shot the other day." Muldoon looked down at Albert. "Are you going to see him again?"

Albert nodded. "I promised to meet him at Ponsby Station."

"Tell him I'll save the sardines until he gets here."

Muldoon made his way back toward the dingo camp leaving Albert surrounded by moonlight and wet clothes.

25 〰 A platypus unleashed

CALL TO ARMS!

VOLUNTEERS WANTED—NEW REGIMENT FORMING

All able-bodied marsupials wanted for
punitive expedition

Remember Ponsby Station!
Remember Brave Captain O'Hanlin!
Remember Barton Springs!
Civilization in jeopardy!
Dingoes and Platypuses—crimes against nature!

Report to Gates of Hell on or before June 1st next
Many medals available

Signed: General Bertram, Commanding
Col. Theodore, in charge of ordnance

ALBERT TORE THE POSTER OFF the tree and put it in his pocket
along with the reward posters he'd been saving. Every gum
tree Albert had seen since he reached the hills near Ponsby
Station had been plastered with handbills. Most were calls
for volunteers; the rest were reward posters with his name
on them. The price on his head was now up to twenty

pounds. He was being blamed for killing O'Hanlin, burning down Barton Springs, and selling guns to non-marsupials. Albert wasn't quite sure what a punitive expedition was, but whatever it was, it was being directed at him and the dingoes.

It had taken only two days to get to Ponsby Station from the dingo camp. Muldoon had told Albert that most of the trails that led into Hell went through the lava flow, but there were shortcuts through the hills if one knew where to look for them.

A young dingo had led Albert to the edge of Hell and no farther. It had been a strange trip. The dingo would walk or trot ahead of Albert but wouldn't look at him. He would disappear at night only to reappear in the morning. When they reached the hills, the young dingo disappeared for the last time.

Albert was glad to be back on his own. His silent companion had made the trip across the flats much quicker, but it had also been a reminder of how deep the gulf was between the dingoes and himself.

Muldoon had told Albert that while TJ's fight at the water hole had been good enough for his possible adoption, the major reason the dingoes took TJ away from Bertram and Theodore was because of Albert.

His looks and actions had become the subject of much conjecture around the campfires. TJ and Muldoon had pointed noses and pointed ears, and the dingoes could understand bravery in creatures that looked much like themselves.

In Albert's case, it was unimportant to the dingoes whether he was brave or not. It was clear to them there had to be some magic associated with him and the events that he played a part in. The dingoes had learned that trying to hurt a friend of Albert's could get you bitten by a snake and that trying to hurt Albert personally could get you a face full of gold dust.

Dingoes weren't stupid. If they couldn't find a stranger to fight with, they were more than willing to fight among themselves, but they weren't suicidal. Albert was obviously too foreign or too dangerous to take lightly. Helping him or his friends was a cheap price to pay to stay on his good side. After reading the recruiting posters, Albert was afraid that the price might turn out to be more expensive than the dingoes had expected.

He reached the trail he had taken from Ponsby Station to the lava fields shortly before noon and turned south toward the settlement. The trail was familiar, and Albert was able to reach their old campsite by nightfall.

Albert made a cold camp that night, partially in memory of his and Jack's flight from the wreckage of the mercantile, but mostly because he was a wanted animal in Old Australia. He wrapped himself in a blanket and lay back against his pack, glad to be alive.

He tried to remember what he had been like when he first came to Old Australia, but that had been some time ago and the animal that had arrived in that dust storm was long gone. He had been replaced by an animal that carried a pack, slept under blankets, and had an unflattering description of himself posted on every tree in the territory. He could remember all the things that happened to him and all the things that he had learned, but in living those events he had become what he was, and the animal he had once been was now a stranger. He fell asleep dreaming of dust storms and singing wombats.

Before the sun showed itself over the hills, Albert had already begun walking down the trail to Ponsby Station. The holes that lined the gully leading into town were quiet. No whistles came from the empty burrows, and the flowers in the coffee cans at the entrances had died from lack of water.

The silence of the morning was broken by drunken laughter drifting up the gully from the center of town. Albert hurried down the trail and onto the flat piece of ground next to the mine.

The rock foundations of the mercantile were still standing, but the building itself had been completely destroyed by the fire. Someone had cleared the site. Piles of burned timber, broken glass, and rusted tin had been shoveled to one side of the rock footings. A construction scaffold was still standing at one corner of the foundation, and a few uprights and wooden beams had been put into place. Work on the building had stopped long enough ago for the uprights to become covered with posters and broadsides.

Jack was standing on the foundation under one of the beams with a rope around his neck. The rope had been thrown over one of the beams and then secured to one leg of the scaffold. Jack was trying to keep his balance, but his crippled leg was on the verge of collapsing.

Two kangaroos and a large wallaby were standing in front of Jack, laughing and drinking from half-pint bottles. One of the kangaroos had on a bowler hat and was wearing checked pants. The other kangaroo and the wallaby were roughly dressed and carried rifles in their free paws. Two grubby adolescent bandicoots were sitting on the footings on the other side of the foundation. They wore overalls and had on tweed caps.

In between drinks, the kangaroo in the bowler would demand that Jack tell them where Albert was. When Jack wouldn't answer, the kangaroo would slap him across the face and take another drink. With each slap, Jack would wobble on the footing and the noose on his neck would tighten. The noise from the blow would carry across what remained of O'Hanlin's store, and the eyes of the young bandicoots would widen at the sound. The last rational thought Albert had, before he went berserk, was that the kangaroo in the checked pants looked familiar.

The rage didn't spiral up from inside of him as it had done in the past. It was just there and it was complete.

He felt his pack fall away and heard it hit the ground behind him. Ahead of him everything moved in slow motion. He could see the bandicoots point toward him and the kangaroos and the wallaby turn their heads. Albert looked down and saw small puffs of dust rise in the air with each footfall as he ran across the flat ground toward the mercantile. He looked up again and saw a cloud of smoke as the wallaby fired his rifle, and he heard the ball pass by his head.

Before another shot could be fired, Albert was in the air with his feet in front of him. He hit the kangaroo with the rifle and felt his spurs sink into its chest. As Albert fell backward, the other kangaroo struck him with a billy club.

The blow caught Albert on the shoulder, but he couldn't feel it. He could hear the kangaroo that he had just poisoned start to scream. The uninjured kangaroo bent over to try to hit him again. He kicked up as high as he could, and his spurs caught his attacker in the throat. The kangaroo looked surprised and dropped the club he was holding. He slowly sat down in the dirt, and the bowler hat slipped from his head and rolled a few feet away.

Albert jumped to his feet and ran at the wallaby, who was trying to put another paper cartridge in his rifle. The wallaby turned to run, and Albert jumped on his back and spurred him in the flanks. The wallaby carried him for a few feet, then fell on his face. Albert jumped up again and spun around. He and Jack were the only creatures still standing.

The young bandicoots had taken cover behind the foundation and were peeking at Albert over the stone footings. The kangaroo he had hit in the chest was still screaming. The wallaby was moaning and twitching in the dirt. The kangaroo in the checked pants was bent over and making a gurgling noise. One of Albert's spurs had caught him in the jugular, and blood was pouring down his front and over his pants.

Albert stood there, shaking his head, and tried to make some sense of what just happened. The screaming bothered him a little bit. He remembered that the dog on the banks of the Murray had screamed after he had spurred it, and he wondered abstractly how badly it must hurt to be poisoned by a platypus. He looked over at the bowler in the dirt and recognized it. The bleeding kangaroo had been the bouncer at O'Hanlin's.

The screaming stopped, and the wallaby stopped twitching. The kangaroo in the checked pants finished bleeding to death, and everything came back into normal time. Albert's shoulder began to hurt. He walked over to Jack, took the noose from around his neck, and helped him sit down on the foundation. Jack didn't say anything but kept glancing at the bodies scattered around him.

The bandicoots made their way carefully around the foundation and stopped by the scaffolding. They stared at Albert for a moment and then whispered to each other. One of them reached up and tore down a reward poster from the upright on the corner. They looked at it and whispered some more. The one holding the poster started walking toward Albert but hesitated. His friend gave him a push.

The bandicoot came over and stood in front of Albert. He reached in the pocket of his overalls and took out a pencil stub. The bandicoot wiped his nose with his forearm and held the poster and the pencil up to Albert.

"My mate wants your autograph."

26 ≋ Good intentions

JACK HAD SET UP THE TRIPOD and billycan with the use of one arm, and he'd gotten upset when Albert tried to help him. It was obvious to both of them that Jack's condition hadn't improved since Barton Springs, and it wasn't likely to in the future. Jack could still carry his pack and do the chores necessary to survive. But he was slow at it, and each time he struggled with something that had once been easy, he became irritated.

The cup was warm in Albert's paws, and the smell of the tea helped mask the odor of death that he had carried with him from Ponsby Station. It had been two days since they had left that place, and he and Jack had encountered nothing but open desert during that time.

Muldoon had told Albert that as soon as TJ was able, they would go back to Muldoon's camp by the water hole, and Albert and Jack were to meet them there. The word would be out among the dingoes to watch for them and guide them back across the flats of Hell.

No dingoes had appeared, and Jack and Albert had been on their own since they had come out of the hills. Each morning Albert would start walking toward the mountain on the far horizon. He knew that the camp he was looking for was between himself and there, but not much more.

When Albert had told Jack that Muldoon wanted to see him, Jack just said that he expected it to happen someday, and now was as good a time as any. They had moved slowly, not covering much distance each day. Albert was glad for the pace. It gave him time to think, and it gave the dingoes more time to find them. Jack moved ahead in a stoic fashion, favoring his bad leg and keeping quiet about what he expected out of his meeting with Muldoon.

They hadn't spoken about the killings at Ponsby Station. Jack had given Albert a gruff thanks and left it at that. Albert had returned the borrowed pistol and considered taking a gun from one of the dead, but thought better of it. What had happened there was done, and he wanted no souvenirs of the event.

Jack hobbled over from the tripod with the billycan and refilled Albert's cup. It was late afternoon, and they had stopped for the day in a grove of acacia. A breeze was coming out of the west. It was sufficient to cool the afternoon but not so strong as to kick up any dust. Albert sat leaning against his pack, sipping his tea and hoping the clear skies would hold through the night.

Jack returned the kettle to the tripod and moved away from the small fire to the sparse shade of a nearby acacia. He sat down in the shade, took a last drink from his cup, and threw the dregs into the bush behind him.

"So this is Hell."

"That's what the signs said." Albert looked up at the sky, but no clouds had appeared.

"Looks pretty much like everywhere else… Sardines?" Jack started digging in his pack.

"No thanks."

Jack found a can of sardines, opened it, and ate half the contents before speaking again.

"I looked for Muldoon, Albert. Did I tell you that?"

"No, Jack, you didn't."

Jack thought for a moment and then shook his head. "I could of sworn I said something about it." He went back to eating the sardines.

"Muldoon told me that he was afraid of not being famous," Albert said, trying to keep Jack talking.

Jack looked over at Albert and shrugged. "That's because fame was the only thing he ever had, except maybe me and a few cans of fish." He looked at the can he was holding in his good paw. "Muldoon came out of the desert looking for a place he heard about that didn't exist. He had to settle for being famous."

He got up and wandered into the bush, looking for a place to bury the sardine can. Then he spent a few minutes looking for snakes that might be hiding in the brush, but his heart didn't seem to be in the hunt, and he soon retreated to the shade of the acacia. Albert spent the rest of the afternoon lying against his pack, getting up only to collect firewood for the evening. Whatever thoughts they may have had they kept to themselves.

With the coming of darkness they built up the fire and waited for the dingoes to find them. The dingoes should have seen the fire the night before. If they didn't see it tonight, something had to be wrong. Albert was beginning to think he should have picked up a gun when he had the chance.

Jack hadn't said much about coming into Hell when Albert told him where they were heading. He had shrugged and said if it was a good enough place for Albert and

Muldoon, it was a good enough place for him. He was a little more curious about the dingoes, whom he had only heard of in whispers. After Albert told Jack what he knew about the dingoes, Jack said that he was glad to hear they were friendly, but that he was going to reload his pistol with lead balls, just in case.

Albert was surprised at how quickly he had come to accept dingoes as a natural part of his world. Other than their eating habits, which took some getting used to, the dingoes were straight-up creatures. They had proven to be brave and loyal, which was more than he could say for most of the other inhabitants of Old Australia.

Muldoon had told Albert that the dingoes never left the flats of Hell. If someone was imprudent enough to come to where they lived, the dingoes ate them and that was the end of it. They made exceptions to the rule as it pleased them. Muldoon, Albert, and TJ were the beneficiaries of a dingo logic that required no rule ever to be written in stone.

The dingoes had also made an exception for Theodore and Bertram when they built the Gates of Hell. The building straddled the line between Hell and the rest of Old Australia, which created a certain territorial ambivalence in the dingoes. In addition, Theodore and Bertram would trade them guns for the coins and equipment they took from trespassers on the flats, and would give them the marsupials that had fallen victim to advertising and the killer possum. As TJ had pointed out, no intelligent animal ever passes up a gun or a free meal.

When Bertram had proven himself a coward at the fight at the water hole and Theodore had shown that he was willing to kill someone protected by a platypus, the dingoes knew that no good would come to them if they continued to associate with creatures that spineless or that reckless. They warned Bertram and Theodore never to return, and the pair had shunned the Gates of Hell ever since.

Albert shifted his position against the pack. His shoulder was still sore from the blow he had taken at Ponsby Station, and sitting in one position too long caused it to stiffen up. Jack had been quiet since they'd finished gathering firewood, and he had stayed in the shade of the acacia smoking his pipe and swatting flies.

When it began to get dark, Jack put some twigs on the coals under the tripod and brought the fire back to life.

"I tried to stop," he said suddenly.

"Tried to stop what?" Albert asked.

"Setting things on fire." Jack sat down under the bush and relit his pipe. "I thought that after what happened to Muldoon at Winslow I'd never set another one."

He took a draw on his pipe. "But I was never sure. So I stayed away from towns as much as I could. I'd go in somewhere, sell a map or a rock I'd salted, get supplies, and get out. It worked for eight years."

"Ponsby Station." Albert was pretty sure what was coming next.

"And then we got to Ponsby Station and I burned the damned place down." Jack nodded sadly.

"Not all of it," Albert said thoughtfully.

"There is that, I suppose." Jack stopped talking and took in an occasional mouthful of smoke from his pipe.

"You set the fire to help me, Jack. You can't blame yourself for that." Albert was beginning to feel a little guilty that he had been responsible for Jack's relapse.

Jack shook his head. "Every fire I ever set, I set with good intentions. At least that's what I told myself. The problem is, Albert, if you like a thing too much you can always find a reason for doing it. I might have been able to get Muldoon out of Winslow without setting fire to the hotel, and I might have been able to get you out of Ponsby Station without burning down O'Hanlin's place. But a fire was always the first thing that came into my mind, and once that happened I never considered trying anything else. If I had, there's a good chance Muldoon wouldn't have been killed and you wouldn't have a price on your head."

"Muldoon's not dead," Albert said quietly.

Jack didn't hear what Albert said, or if he did he ignored it.

"Muldoon wanted to fight in Winslow, but I was against it. Winslow was a tough town and a hard place to get out of if things went bad. But Muldoon was famous by then and felt his reputation was at stake. There was a pretty tough kangaroo in Winslow who had challenged Muldoon to a fight, no holds barred. The kangaroo had killed two opponents and was known as quite the wrestler in some parts of the territory. The locals thought highly of him... a little *too* highly, as it turned out.

"If Muldoon had let the fight go on for a while, we probably would have been all right. He knew how to string out a match. We had made a lot of money on side bets when we first started. He and I would do an exhibition match every so often and make it look like I came close to beating him. I couldn't beat him—nobody could—but we were pretty good at selling the illusion.

"Anyway, when Muldoon walked into the ring in Winslow and the crowd stared booing him, I had a bad feeling. Muldoon hated being booed, and he hated having things thrown at him.

"The kangaroo was late in coming, and the longer Muldoon was in the ring by himself the worse the crowd got. Pretty soon empty bottles and rotting vegetables started flying out of the crowd. Muldoon just stood there and didn't flinch even when he got hit.

"When the kangaroo finally showed, the crowd started to settle down. The kangaroo climbed into the ring and called Muldoon a couple of names. Muldoon didn't say anything, he just walked over to the kangaroo and broke his neck. I'd never seen anything like that, and I know the crowd hadn't, either. It took them awhile to come after us."

Jack took another draw on his pipe, but it had gone out.

"We got back to the hotel ahead of the mob, but not by much. I set the place on fire to cover our run for the edge of town. The fire was going pretty good when Muldoon ran back inside."

Jack tapped his pipe on his knee for a few moments and then looked over at Albert. "It never crossed my mind that Muldoon would run back into the hotel, but it should have. I knew the medals were important to him, and I'd forgotten he'd left them in his room."

"Medals?"

Jack looked away from Albert and back toward the fire. "I didn't think they were much. But Muldoon set quite a store by them. He was never interested in the money we made. He'd buy sardines, and maybe a drink every so often, and not much else. But he liked medals, and he liked being carried on the shoulders of the crowd. He was the only one of his kind that ever got here, and I think the medals and the cheers made him feel a little less alone."

"What kind of medals were they?" Albert asked.

"What you'd expect. A piece of pot metal with a ribbon

that said 'Champion' or 'Winner' or some such thing. Some local dignitary would hang one around his neck when he won a fight and tell him how great he was.

"I don't know if he believed what they told him—he didn't put much trust in others. But the medals were different, they were solid. He could carry them with him and hold them long after the crowds had disappeared."

Jack picked up a small stone at his feet and tossed it toward the fire. "At least, that's what I think now. We never really spoke again. But he had a partially melted medal in his paw when I pulled him out of the hotel."

"What happened after you got him out?"

Jack shrugged. "Not much else to tell. He was hurt a lot worse than I was, but I got him clear of the town and eventually got both of us back to our camp. I put him in his tent and nursed him as best I could. A few weeks later I went into a town to get supplies—and when I got back, both Muldoon and the tent were gone."

Jack got up slowly and looked out into the night beyond the camp.

"The Famous Muldoon died in that fire, and that was the only Muldoon I ever knew. A shadow is waiting for me out here, Albert. The shadow of a time long past, and I'm afraid of what I might find."

Before Albert could say anything, he heard what sounded like thunder coming from the distance. He stood up and walked over to where Jack was standing. The sky above them was clear, and the stars were bright as far as they could see.

There was a flash of light on the horizon, and a few seconds later another clap of thunder rolled over the camp.

27 ≋ Marsupials forever

ALBERT LEFT JACK AT DAWN, carrying nothing but a canteen, and walked the desert in the direction of the explosions he had seen light the sky the night before.

It was clear that things were happening on the flats of Hell that did not bode well for Albert and his friends. After what had happened at Ponsby Station, Albert was worried about leaving Jack alone. But it was clear that they needed information as quickly as they could get it, and he was the only one fit enough to act as a scout. He gave Jack the pistol and careful instructions: if a dingo showed up, Jack was to ask questions first and, if need be, shoot afterward.

Albert kept a brisk pace through the morning and came across a dingo encampment at noon. He searched through what remained of the camp, but he didn't find anyone still alive. The smell of black powder hung in the air, and brush shelters scattered around the small clearing were still smoldering. The midday sun had already dried the pools of blood around the bodies, and bush flies were everywhere in great numbers.

It hadn't been a big camp. Albert counted only twelve bodies, mostly females and pups. It was hard to tell what had killed the dingoes—the bodies were badly torn, and all of them were missing their ears.

The camp had been built near a small spring, and the minute Albert approached it he could tell something was wrong. He might not know much about the desert, but he knew something about water.

There were footprints all around the spring, and none of them belonged to the bodies in the camp. Albert bent down and took a little of the water in one paw. It smelled of cities and had the color of tarnished copper. A few crawfish floated on the surface of the pool along with some dead insects. Whoever had killed the dingoes had also poisoned the spring.

Albert stood up and wiped his paw on the front of his jacket. Poisoning water was a crime of such enormity that he couldn't understand it. Water was where a platypus lived. It was the center of his being.

In some ways, he could understand the killing of other creatures. He had done it himself and could point to reasons, both good and bad, for having done so. He could find no reason in destroying that which was freely given to everyone. The spring was neutral. It had provided life for anyone that came to drink there, even to the ones who had poisoned it. There had been no passion in its death, only a sad desire to kill the future.

He began to worry that some other passerby that didn't know water as well as he did might stop to drink there. He was looking for something to mark the spring when he heard another explosion in the distance.

The noise wasn't as far away as it had been the night before, and Albert thought he could get to the source in a fairly short time. What he would do when he got there depended on what he found.

He quickly made an arrow of rocks on the ground pointing to the spring and piled the dead crawfish at the point of the arrow. It wasn't much, but it was better than nothing. Albert took a last look at the spring and shook his head before jogging into the bush in the direction of the noise, which was continuing to repeat itself.

A mile from the dead dingoes Albert located the source of the explosions. A group of marsupials were entrenched around the base of a low hill that rose no more than twenty feet above the desert floor. On top of the hill a group of kangaroos were loading and firing a small cannon. A small figure was directing the gun crew and every so often Albert could see flashes of light reflected from the goggles it was wearing.

Albert had never seen a cannon before, but this was obviously a big gun. It was firing large bullets into the bush somewhere beyond the hill.

Every time a shell exploded, the militia in the trenches would wave flags and cheer. Albert could hear faint cries of "Death to Dingoes" drifting in the wind from the hill, as well as the singing of a song that had "Marsupials Forever" as a chorus.

The hill gave those on top a good view of the surrounding desert, and Albert was afraid to get any closer than a thick stand of grevillea about half a mile from where the kangaroos were firing the gun.

He had been crouched in the bush for about twenty minutes when the firing stopped. He watched as the militia left the trenches and headed out into the bush toward where the shells had landed. Theodore and the gun crew stayed with the cannon.

A figure in a plumed hat climbed up the hill from the

trenches and stood next to the gun. The figure took off its hat and waved it over its head. The cheering from the gun crew got louder. Albert thought the figure was probably Bertram, but it was difficult to be sure at that distance.

He turned to head back to where he had left Jack and almost ran into a dingo that had come up behind him. Startled, both Albert and the dingo jumped backward, but after the first moments of confusion things began to settle down.

The dingo was young, with just a few scars. Albert couldn't remember having seen him before, but he seemed to know Albert. The dingo pushed Albert back down behind the grevillea and watched the hill for a few minutes. When he was sure that their movements hadn't been seen, the dingo beckoned Albert to follow him and set off into the bush, keeping clumps of brush between them and the hill.

The young dingo led Albert away from the hill for some distance before angling back toward the militia trenches. They came to a shallow ravine and followed it to a small grove of acacia not very far from where Albert had watched the cannonade.

The early afternoon sun was filtering through the leaves of the trees, and the contrast between the light and small shadows made the center of the grove a study in two dimensions.

TJ was sitting on a log in the middle of the grove, surrounded by half a dozen silent dingoes. The dingoes raised their paws to the young one as it led Albert into the grove, and their salute was returned with the same quiet dignity.

TJ motioned to Albert to join him. He had on the clothes

Albert had washed, and Albert could see a lump in his long johns where it covered the bandages. TJ looked very tired, but he smiled as Albert walked over to the log.

"Good to see you, partner."

"You too, TJ."

The young dingo found a place among his kind and became one with the shadows of the grove.

"Sorry we couldn't get to you sooner. The dingoes didn't spot your tracks until a few hours ago. It's been kind of busy around here."

Albert sat down on the log next to TJ.

"That possum may be crazy, but he's not stupid, and that's for sure." TJ tipped his hat back and wiped his forehead with the back of his paw. "They've been bombarding a camp about a quarter mile from here. I think most of the dingoes got out before it started, but I'm not sure."

Albert took the canteen off his shoulder and offered it to TJ. "How are you doing?" he asked.

TJ shrugged and took the canteen. "I'm a little peaked yet. My lodge brothers over there had to half-carry me out here." TJ gestured to the dingoes with the canteen. "I needed to know what we were up against, and I don't speak dingo real well." He took a drink from the canteen. "They keep those toy soldiers of theirs in groups and cover them with the cannon. Dingoes wouldn't have a chance going up against anything like that... It could be worse, I guess."

"What do you mean?" Albert asked, as TJ handed back his canteen.

"They move real slow and have to set up the gun each time they come to a camp. The dingoes travel light and can keep away from them. I figure after a while they'll run out of food or get tired of chasing dingoes around Hell and head back to where they came from."

Albert shook his head. "It will be too late by then."

"Why?"

"They're poisoning the water."

TJ didn't say anything for a moment. Finally, he pulled his hat down. "Well, that puts the icing on the cake, doesn't it." He stood up. "Come on, boys, it's time to head back."

The dingoes moved out of the shadows, and one of them came over and stood next to TJ.

Albert jumped off the log. "TJ, we can't let them kill the springs."

TJ put his arm over the dingo's shoulder and leaned on him for support. "And we're not going to. It will be a cold day in hell before a damned possum and a one-eared rabbit outsmart Terrance James Walcott, and you can bet real money on it."

28 ≋ An illusion of the present

JACK HAD BEEN EXHAUSTED when they reached Muldoon's camp. They had come a long way that day, and even with a guide it had been a hard trip. The young dingo, like most of his kind, wasn't used to dealing with cripples and didn't have much patience with Jack. Bad leg or not, he had to keep up.

Albert had carried Jack's pack for most of the day, but Jack was still a long way back when he walked into the center of the camp. TJ and a number of dingoes had already arrived, and there was a lot of activity going on around the water hole. Albert quickly took the packs he was carrying over to the edge of the water hole where he had slept before. He was heading back to collect Jack when Muldoon walked out of his tent.

At that moment, Jack stumbled out of the bush at the edge of the water hole, dragging his left foot and doing his best to keep upright. He and Muldoon saw each other at about the same time. After a moment's hesitation, Jack squared his shoulders and walked toward Muldoon, trying to disguise his limp.

Muldoon ducked back into his tent and came out with a canteen and two stools. He put the stools down by the tent entrance and waited for Jack with the canteen in his good paw. Muldoon made no move to help Jack, but let him make his way to the tent as best he could.

Jack reached the stools and sat down heavily. He looked up at Muldoon. "It's been awhile."

Muldoon gave the canteen to Jack. The cork was still in the canteen, and Jack and Muldoon had only two good paws between them. Jack held the canteen as Muldoon pulled out the cork with his good paw.

Jack took a drink. "Did I miss anything?"

Muldoon shook his head.

"That's good to know," Jack said, as he gave the canteen back.

Albert walked away from Muldoon's tent and set up a place for him and Jack to sleep. He never again went near enough to hear what Muldoon and Jack said, but he watched them from time to time as he moved through the camp.

Jack's guilt had always been of his own making. If Muldoon had been hurt, he could blame only himself and the past events in his life that had driven him into the ring in Winslow. Albert was pretty sure they both understood this, but he couldn't be certain.

When Jack came back to Albert's camp later, he was too tired to say very much. Before he went to sleep, he told Albert that he was glad he'd come and that it had been important to both him and Muldoon.

Jack had been right when he said the Muldoon he knew had died in the hotel, but what he didn't say was that the Jack from those days was just as dead. The Jack that saved Albert was not the same creature who had limped into Muldoon's camp, and he would be a slightly different creature yet when he limped out.

Albert was beginning to believe that he might have died in the desert near the railroad, and that TJ might have died on the gangplank in San Francisco, and all they had before them was a chance to die another time in a different place. The coming morning might be the time, and the clearing he was sitting in could very well be the place.

The only lights in the desert that night came from Muldoon's camp and the fires of the militia on the rise a half mile away. Two days after Albert and Jack arrived at Muldoon's camp, TJ had sent word across the flats that no fires were to be lit in the dingo encampments beyond the water hole, and since that time there had been no other fires lit in Hell.

TJ had suspected it was the firelight that had brought the militia, and he had been proven correct. The fires that had been left burning every night around Muldoon's tent had drawn the milita to the water hole and, if the patterns of the past repeated themselves, the bombardment would begin just before dawn.

The glow of the fires and the light reflecting from the water, from the tent, and from the ragged canopy of the gum trees created a sense of theater in the camp that fore-shadowed what was to come in the morning.

In a few hours, the dingoes were to let the fires die, and everyone in the camp except Albert would slip back into the bush beyond the range of the gun. TJ had said that if he had any choice he would have picked someone with longer legs, but Albert was the only chance they had.

In the last two attacks, after the initial bombardment, the militia had left the trenches they had dug and had gone into the deserted camps to poison the water and take trophies from the dead. There was no reason to believe they wouldn't do the same in the morning.

The militia needed to be given a reason to go far enough beyond their camp that the shells of the cannon couldn't protect them. TJ hoped that a short-legged platypus worth twenty pounds sterling dead or alive would be reason enough.

If he survived the bombardment, Albert was to wait in the camp until the militia spotted him, then run into the bush, making sure that Bertram's troops gave chase. The farther they chased him, the better. The militia had met no opposition so far, and they had likely become convinced of their invincibility.

TJ had originally considered using a few dingoes as bait—they were brave enough to do the job, and they could run a lot faster than Albert. But they looked pretty tough, and TJ was afraid the militia might have second thoughts about chasing them into the bush. He would hold them in reserve in case Albert was killed at the water hole.

Albert had dug a shallow burrow at the water's edge to use during the bombardment. He had taken the reward posters he had been saving and placed them on stunted trees between the water hole and the militia camp, just to make sure the coming marsupials knew that chasing a platypus could be a worthwhile endeavor. Albert had done all he could, and if it wasn't enough, he'd worry about it in another life.

He sat by himself in the middle of the camp. He would send his pack out with TJ and the dingoes when they left, keeping only his canteen. TJ wanted nothing left in the camp that the militia could use. He had asked Muldoon if he wanted to strike his tent and move it beyond the water hole and out of range of the cannon, but Muldoon just shook his head, and TJ let the matter rest.

TJ and some of the older dingoes were now gathered at one edge of the camp conversing in signs and monosyllables. Every so often young dingoes would come in from the darkness bringing information, then be sent back out again with a response from TJ or one of the elders.

Jack and Muldoon waited for word to leave the camp sitting under the canopy of Muldoon's tent. When they spoke, they spoke in low voices and Albert couldn't hear what they were saying.

He knew that eight years had passed since they had seen each other, and that those years had been hard on both of them. He thought there would be an awkwardness between them born of the pain they both carried from Winslow, but time had erased none of the familiarity they had shared so long ago. Albert watched as one or the other would cock his head or use a paw for emphasis, casting moving shadows on the wall of the tent.

The dingoes stopped feeding the fires, and one by one the lights around the water hole went out for the last time. Jack put on his pack and Muldoon came out of his tent wearing his peacoat. He had made a bundle of his wrestling tights and was holding them under his good arm.

All that needed to be said had been said that afternoon, and with a brief wave Jack and Muldoon walked away. Two dingoes, one carrying Albert's pack and the other carrying TJ's carbine, helped TJ into the night. Albert was now alone in the deserted camp.

29 ≋ The winners

THE FIRST SHELL SENT UP a geyser of water in the middle of the water hole, and the second hit Muldoon's tent. After that, Albert stopped paying attention. The morning air was dead still, and smoke from the explosions hung low on the ground. It wasn't long before Albert couldn't see more than a few feet from the edge of his burrow.

The shots came at measured intervals, and Albert had enough time between each explosion to consider his mortality. He began to wish that the intervals were shorter and gave him less time to think. All he could do was lie in the burrow, covered in pieces of yellow-and-red canvas, listening to each shell whistle as it dropped into the camp and hoping his luck would hold one more time.

As the morning passed, he became used to the noise of the cannon in the distance, the whistle and the detonation of the shells. Once or twice dirt had been thrown on him by shells that exploded close to his burrow, but he hadn't been hurt. Fatalism replaced fear as Albert realized it would take a direct hit to kill him.

He became more concerned with what was going to happen when the bombardment ended. The wind hadn't come up and the smoke had gotten thicker. If it weren't for the water hole at his back, Albert would have no idea which way he was facing and where he expected the militia to enter the camp. Between explosions he tried to listen for movement, but all he could hear was the ringing in his ears.

It was quiet for a long time before Albert realized that the cannon fire had stopped. He stuck his head over the edge of his burrow and looked out into a gray haze. He could hear the faint sound of music in the distance beyond the smoke.

He crawled out of the hole he had dug and stood up. The music wasn't very good—it was just drums and bugles, one ragged, the other off-key, but it gave him some sense of the direction of oncoming militia. It wasn't long before he began to hear voices mixed with the beat of the drums.

He was going to have to start running pretty soon, but the militia would have to be able to see him first. The smoke wasn't something he or TJ had considered; it made everything more difficult and had lessened his chances of survival considerably.

Albert could smell the water behind him, and the instinct of untold generations of his kind told him that he would be safe there. He had learned the hard way that nothing was ever safe in Old Australia, but the urge to dive into the water hole was becoming stronger and stronger. Rather than risk a victory of instinct, Albert threw himself into the smoke and began running in the direction of the music.

He was only about ten yards from his burrow when he ran bill-first into a large kangaroo carrying a musket. They both jumped back in surprise.

"Platypus!" the kangaroo screamed.

Albert turned and was two steps back into the smoke when the kangaroo fired his musket. The shot missed, but it started a chain reaction. Guns began going off all around him. The air was full of the sounds of shots, screams of pain, and then more shots.

Albert had gone only a few more yards when he ran into a wallaby, armed to the teeth with rifle, pistol, and sword. The encounter scared the wallaby enough that he didn't have time to swing his sword before Albert disappeared again. He heard the wallaby yell, "There's another one over here!"

There were more shots, more yelling. Albert kept bouncing off marsupials as he ran through the smoke. He tried to keep running in a straight line, but each collision shifted his direction and produced more high-pitched yells of warning.

Gunfire rattled through the smoke and bullets were flying everywhere. Every so often, Albert would see a dim muzzle flash through the thick smoke and shift his direction to avoid the shooter.

Screams of "Platypus!" were coming from directions he'd never been, and with each scream, shooting throughout the camp intensified.

The cannon had started firing again, and Albert could hear the shells whistle overhead and explode somewhere beyond the camp. The sound of the gun gave Albert a vague sense of its location and he started running away from the noise.

He tripped over a dead bandicoot with a spear in it, and he lay in the dirt next to the body for a few moments. He could hear the yips of dingoes in the smoke around him and the thud of clubs mixed with pistol and rifle shots. The air was clearer close to the ground and Albert could see feet running past him, dingo feet and marsupial feet mixed together. Occasionally a body would drop out of the smoke near him to lie on the dirt whimpering or choking.

It was obvious that TJ's plan had unraveled and the fight was not happening beyond the range of the cannon. Albert's day as decoy was going badly, and he had no idea what he should do next. As he lay there, hoping for inspiration, the instinct that he had suppressed all morning began to reassert itself. The smell of water was very faint and was mixed with the stench of blood and black powder that surrounded him, but it was enough.

If he closed his eyes, Albert could sense where the water was. He began crawling forward. He opened his eyes every so often to make sure he wasn't crawling into someone being killed. If the way ahead of him was clear, he would close his eyes again and let his sense of smell guide him. The noise of the guns and the screams of the dying faded into idyllic scenes of the river of his childhood, and Albert began to crawl faster.

He could see his mother on the far bank, and he knew if he could reach her everything would be all right and he would be safe forever. He jumped up and started running. As he reached the bank of the river, he tripped over something and fell headfirst into the water.

Albert opened his eyes and found himself in the water hole with his hat floating next to him. A cannon shell exploded over his head and blew shrapnel across the water in front of him. Albert grabbed his hat, shoved it in his vest, and dove under the surface.

He swam across the water hole, hugging the bottom the entire way. He surfaced on the far side and looked back toward Muldoon's camp. Except for a few patches of gray that floated above the water hole, the smoke stopped at the water's edge. He could see the body of the dingo that he had tripped over lying on the beach.

Fighting was still going on in the camp. He could hear shots and see muzzle flashes, but the shots were becoming less frequent. A slight breeze had come up and was starting to thin the smoke. Albert could see figures moving on the far side of the water hole and thought it prudent to move out of rifle shot before they could see him.

He climbed up on the bank and started jogging through the gum trees and into the hills on the far side of the water hole. Another cannon shell burst ahead of him and he could see smoke from the explosion. If he had any friends left, they probably had been the target, and he headed in that direction.

A hundred yards from the trees, he started coming across dead dingoes. They had been caught in the open, running toward the relative safety of the smoke-filled camp. They had been killed before they could strike a blow and, in dingo tradition, would remain unhonored where they lay. In time, the desert would reclaim the bodies.

Another shell flew overhead, and Albert saw where it landed. The shell hit in front of a large boulder, part of a rocky outcropping that had created another small hill on the desert floor. The minute the dirt from the explosion settled, TJ climbed onto the boulder and started waving his hat. The movement drew another shell, and TJ just managed to get off the boulder before it hit one of the other rocks. Stone fragments ricocheted off the face of the boulder. TJ climbed back up and started waving his hat again.

Albert heard the cannon go off, but there was no whistling and no shell fell. A minute later the cannon fired one more time and then there was silence.

TJ hesitated and then stopped waving his hat. He kept looking in the direction of the militia trenches. Finally he sat down on the boulder and put his hat back on. Jack limped out from behind the rock where TJ was sitting. He had Muldoon's peacoat thrown over his shoulder and was carrying TJ's Enfield in his good paw. He leaned the rifle against the rock, sat down, and put Muldoon's jacket across his lap.

Albert worked his way through the bush to the rocks as quickly as he could. He stopped next to Jack, who looked up at him and gave him a sad smile but said nothing.

TJ was still breathing hard from climbing up and down the boulder. He looked down at Albert. "I wasn't sure I'd see you again."

Albert looked around. "Where's Muldoon?"

TJ waved a paw toward the militia trenches. "He's up there somewhere."

Albert looked out toward the water hole and the ridge beyond. He could see movement in trees by the water hole, but the ridge was quiet.

"Did we win?" Albert asked.

TJ shrugged. "Wouldn't know. I've been stuck in this damn rock pile since the shooting started. It's been a hell of a fight, though."

Albert could feel the heat of the sun for the first time that day. He took his hat out of his vest and put it on. He heard a faint cry above him and looked into the sky. A crow flew over the rocks toward the far ridge. Albert watched the bird until it became too small to see anymore, then he looked over at TJ, who was struggling to get up.

"Give me a paw off this rock, would you, Albert?"

Albert saw a pile of stones behind the boulder, and he climbed up to TJ and helped him down. TJ leaned on him for a moment.

"I haven't seen a dingo since the shooting started at Muldoon's camp. When it sounded like you'd started a war down there, I couldn't hold them back. The cannon started up again, and that's when Muldoon took off. I tried to keep the gunners distracted, but I don't know if it helped much."

Albert looked over at Jack. The old wombat looked very tired, but managed another smile. "I told him I'd hold his coat, Albert. That's all anybody could ever do for Muldoon."

TJ took his paw from Albert's shoulder. "Who knows, we might have even won this damn thing." TJ held out his paw and helped Jack to his feet. "You head on out, Albert. Jack and I will be along directly."

"If it doesn't look good, you come back for us. A good run is always better than a bad fight and I want you to remember that," TJ cautioned.

Albert nodded and walked quickly down the hill toward Muldoon's camp. He looked back once to make sure that Jack and TJ were moving, then made his way into the bush.

Another crow flew over his head and landed in the top of a gum tree near the water hole. It began to call out and Albert followed the sound. He reached one end of the water hole and saw a few dingoes moving through the dead that littered the ground where Muldoon used to live. More crows were gathering in the treetops, and they watched with unblinking interest as below them the dingoes gathered up the guns of the fallen.

Albert hurried on past the camp. He had seen enough death that it held no fascination for him. He knew there were other bodies waiting for him on the ridge, and that was bad enough.

Small parties of dingoes searched for any of the militia that might have survived. They seemed indifferent to him and passed him by without any acknowledgment.

He reached the base of the ridge and walked up into the abandoned militia positions. There were a few dead kangaroos and wallabies lying in the first trench, but dead dingoes littered the slope all the way up to the gun on the top of the ridge. Muldoon's body was lying in front of the gun emplacement just beyond the last trench.

Albert walked slowly up the ridge, avoiding the dead as best he could. He stopped a few feet from Muldoon. The last shot from the cannon had carried away Muldoon's bad arm, but the explosion that close to the muzzle had killed the gun crew. Theodore's body lay in back of the gun, partially covered by bloody kangaroos.

A light wind blew gently across the ridge and ruffled the fur that poked through the torn fabric of Muldoon's purple tights. He lay on his back with his head turned to the side and Albert couldn't see the burns on his face. Except for the terrible wound that had taken away his arm and shoulder, he looked every bit the Muldoon he once had been.

The dingoes that had charged the hill at his side were all dead. There was no one left alive who saw Muldoon's last fight. If there had been any cheers, Albert hadn't heard them. Muldoon had fallen with the quiet companions he had had for the last eight years. In the end, he hadn't died alone.

Albert saw something shiny hanging around Muldoon's neck, but before he could bend down to look at it, he heard a hissing sound. Albert looked up into a set of goggles and the twin barrels of a shotgun.

Theodore was standing beside the cannon with his shotgun pointed at Albert. He started cackling, and foam began forming at the corners of his mouth.

"Zoo!" he whispered. Then he giggled and cocked the hammers of the gun.

"Zoo!" he screamed, as saliva dribbled down the front of his uniform. He giggled again.

Albert heard the report of the rifle before he heard the sound of the bullet hum past his head. The minié ball caught Theodore in the chest and knocked him back against the gun carriage. The giggling stopped, and Theodore slid into the dirt beside the gun.

TJ took the Enfield off his shoulder and let Jack help him up the ridge. It took a long time for them to navigate the trenches and the dead, but they finally made it to Albert and Muldoon.

They stood silently together. TJ took off his hat and bowed his head for a moment. Jack bent down and put the jacket he was carrying under Muldoon's head. TJ put his hat back on.

"Anybody have a pistol?" he asked.

Jack reached in his coat pocket and took out the pepperbox. TJ traded the rifle for the pistol, went over to Theodore, and carefully shot him five more times.

Albert bent over and looked again at the shining object that had caught his attention. A misshapen disk hung around Muldoon's neck on an old string. Albert bent down and looked closer. The melted metal disk said "Winner," but some of the letters were hard to read.

Dingoes had come out of the bush and were moving up the ridge scattering red earth on those who had died trying to silence the gun. Albert hoped that wherever Muldoon had gone, the red pigment might mean more to him than the medal around his neck.

30 ≋ A lesson in history

THE GATES OF HELL WAS DARK except for one dim light that flickered through a dirty window in the back of the building. Albert waited until TJ positioned himself near the back door, then he walked around the building to the front entrance.

He carried Theodore's shotgun under his arm. TJ had given it to him after the fight at the water hole. Albert had never been a good shot, and TJ thought he might have better luck with a firearm that was more forgiving than a pistol.

It had been three months since Muldoon had died, and TJ was impatient to finish what Bertram had started when he had invaded Hell. Except for a plumed hat lying in one of the trenches, there had been no sign of the wallaby after the battle.

That day, there had been no talk of looking for Bertram. A sadness had settled over the water hole and had replaced, in most, the relief of still being alive. Even the dingoes were quieter than normal and were quick to scatter back across the desert without feast or celebration. They just walked away and left the dead, both friend and foe, to be eaten by the crows that had continued to gather in the trees.

TJ had put all he had into directing the fight, and he was content to let Albert gather their gear and help him walk far enough into the desert to where the sounds and smells of the water hole were a memory and not a reality.

Jack had stayed with Muldoon's body while Albert gathered the packs from the rocks beyond the water hole. Then he, too, left the battlefield for the last time and limped after Albert and TJ into a late afternoon on the flats of Hell.

They traveled slowly, not really caring where they went or how long it might take them to get there. When it became too dark to continue, they made camp where they found themselves, one place seeming to be as good as any other.

Albert made a fire, pulled blankets out of the packs, and passed them around. At the bottom of his pack he found the whiskey bottle he had given to Muldoon. He passed the bottle to Jack without a comment. Jack took a drink and gave the bottle to TJ.

Albert sat down next to Jack and drank from his canteen. There seemed no need for conversation; they had acted out the parts given to them that day and their assignments for tomorrow could wait until the morning. One by one, they fell asleep.

At daybreak, they moved on in the same fashion as the day before, and so it went for two more days until they reached water. A small spring fed clear water into a small pool that overflowed into a stream lined with acacia and gum trees.

They stopped with an unspoken agreement that they had walked away from the recent past as far as they could, and it was time to live in the present and prepare for the future. The tasks they had done so many times before were done again with a certain relief in being able to escape into the familiar and the mundane.

Albert gathered firewood and hunted the water hole for crayfish. Jack searched the bushes for snakes, and when he was satisfied there were none he set up the tripod and made tea. TJ was still recovering from his wound, but he found the energy to wash his clothes and make sure that all the guns were loaded and in working order.

Over the weeks, a routine was established in the camp. Once the chores were done, they rested in the shade, swam in the water hole, and made conversation over tea and crayfish in the evenings. Several times, dingoes stopped by and would share their beetles and grubs in return for whatever TJ had roasted by the fire.

They never stayed long but would make signs to TJ, which he seemed to understand, then they'd leave as quietly as they had come. TJ said that the dingoes had saved the cannon for him, and as soon as their business with Bertram was sorted out, he was going to take the gun down to the coast. There was a chance the ship might show up again, and if it did, he was going to try and capture it and take up piracy. It was something he had never done before and he had an urge to give it a try.

Jack would smoke his pipe and tell stories about what happened to him or to Muldoon long ago in the small-minded towns that were scattered throughout Old Australia. He would often get confused and repeat the same story several times. TJ and Albert always pretended they were hearing it for the first time.

Muldoon was always there in Jack's stories, but it was the Muldoon from before the fight in Winslow. They were always young in the stories, with Muldoon's fame still ahead of them. In those days, each new town was just another adventure and not a tragedy waiting to happen.

Albert listened to TJ and Jack in the evenings, but he never told any stories of his own. His days in Adelaide were all he could have spoken about, but they were dark days, best left as fading memories. He hoped that someday he would be able to sit with new friends and relate to them the things that he had seen and done in Old Australia. But that hope lay in an uncertain future, and for now he was content to listen to familiar voices tell tales about places he'd never seen.

As TJ's wound healed, he became restless. At first he would take short walks up the stream, stopping to rest in the shade of the trees. The walks became longer and the rests less frequent. Soon, he began taking his rifle and disappearing into the desert for hours at a time. One day, after being gone from before sunrise until after dark, he came back into camp and told Albert and Jack that the time had come to return to the Gates of Hell.

The dingoes had reported that they had seen some lights coming from the building and there was a good chance that Bertram had returned. Even if Bertram wasn't there, they could destroy his printing press and burn the building.

It took them four days to reach the Gates of Hell. Jack was still dragging his left leg, and it slowed the march considerably. No matter how long it might take them to get to their destination, there had been no question about leaving Jack behind. He had been responsible for rescuing Albert in Barton Springs and had been under fire at the water hole. He had a right to be there when the Gates of Hell met its end.

Albert was pretty sure that Jack didn't hold Bertram responsible for Muldoon's death and in some ways might have been grateful to him for indirectly providing the relief that Muldoon had been looking for. But he knew if there was going to be a fire, Jack wouldn't want to miss it.

A large militia recruiting poster covered the sign by the door, but other than that the front of the Gates of Hell looked much as Albert remembered it. The wind had shredded the corners of the poster, and the glue holding it to the sign was beginning to give way.

Albert shifted the shotgun to his right paw and pushed the door partway open with his left. He listened for a moment and heard a faint scratching noise coming from inside the building. He slipped into the Gates of Hell through the half-opened door.

Bertram was sitting at the table in the center of the room. He was wearing a uniform jacket covered with gold braid and writing on a sheet of foolscap with a steel pen. A pile of papers sat on the table next to a candle and a full shot glass. There wasn't a tablecloth on the table, and the noise of pen on paper was clearly audible in the quiet of the room.

Bertram looked up briefly as Albert came in the door. "For a moment, I thought it might be Theodore."

"I wouldn't wait up for him, if I were you." Albert looked across the room and saw TJ standing in the darkness at the back of the room. The Enfield was cradled in his arms.

"I suspected as much. He was a brave and noble creature. I'll miss him." Bertram looked down at the paper and started to write again. "It's all in here. Theodore's valiant stand. His tragic end. How we saved Old Australia from the dingoes and their accomplices. In addition, I have included a section about how I rose from humble origins to the rank of General in the Armies of Old Australia. I'm hoping it will be an inspiration to others."

"I hope you're close to the end," TJ said very quietly.

Bertram looked over at TJ and shrugged. "I've already written the part where I am betrayed for the last time and murdered in cold blood by a foreigner and a platypus." He put down his pen and took a drink. "You will be long forgotten while my name will still be on every lip. A martyr to the preservation of the marsupial way of life. There will be a statue of me in every square."

TJ tipped his hat off the back of his head and let it hang from his neck by the chinstrap. He scratched an ear. "I never thought of that," he said.

Bertram smiled. "That's because you lack my imagination."

TJ kept scratching his ear. "Maybe we ought to let you go. What do you think, Albert?"

Albert was confused. He didn't want Bertram to escape, but he didn't like the idea of killing him in cold blood. "I don't know, TJ. He tried to kill us."

Bertram continued to smile. He took the sheet of paper he'd been writing on and placed it carefully on top of the manuscript. He folded the manuscript and put it in his jacket pocket.

"I know he did, Albert, but he wasn't very good at it," TJ said. "I look at it this way. As a constable, Bertram here got an entire town burned down. As a general, he got an army wiped out. If we let him go, he will get elected to public office, and inside of a week there won't be a live marsupial left in Old Australia." He started laughing.

For the first time Bertram became visibly angry. "Do

you think all that matters?" He stood up and reached back in his pocket and took out the manuscript. He shook it at TJ. "This is what matters. History is what matters."

TJ took the rifle out of the crook of his arm. "You talk too much, Bertram. Get out of here before I change my mind."

Bertram reached over and picked up the shot glass. He finished his drink and tossed the glass into the corner of the room. Then he started toward the front door, but he looked at Albert and hesitated. He spun on his heel and pushed past TJ.

"I still don't believe in demons," he muttered to himself, as he stepped out the back door and slammed it behind him.

TJ started poking around the piles of junk that cluttered the back of the room. "Might be something we can use in here. Help me look."

Albert slung the shotgun over his shoulder and went over to where TJ was. "Are you sure it was a good idea to let Bertram go?"

TJ smiled. "Don't worry, Albert. If he'd gone in your direction, I would have shot him before he got out the door. As it is, we've got friends out back."

Albert and TJ searched through the piles of furniture, stacks of barrels, and crates that surrounded the printing press standing along the back wall. They were still looking when Jack came in the back door. He waved to them and then he, too, began rummaging around at the back of the store.

Most of the barrels and boxes were empty, and the bolts of cloth moth-eaten. TJ found a couple of bars of lead and put them in a pocket. Albert was hoping to find his old rucksack that he had lost the first time he'd come to the Gates of Hell. He was sure the money that had been stolen was long gone, but he missed the rucksack.

Albert moved a dusty crate that had once contained parts for the printing press. Behind the crate something shiny reflected the light from the lone candle in the room. He bent down and took a closer look. The soft drink bottle he had brought from Adelaide was lying on the floor.

He picked up the bottle and wiped the dust off it with the sleeve of his coat. He had forgotten about the bottle. He didn't need it anymore, but it was all he had left from his days in Adelaide. As he put the bottle in the pocket of his coat, he smelled paraffin.

Jack was limping around the interior of the building carrying a large tin of lamp oil. He was pouring it on anything that looked flammable. When the tin was empty he threw it toward the front door and went looking for another one. TJ ran over and grabbed the candle off the table before the fumes could reach it and carried to the back door. Albert edged closer to the door and waited until Jack poured a second tin of paraffin all over the floor.

"I never had this much time before," Jack said. "It sort of takes the fun out of it."

TJ carefully opened the back door before he gave Jack the candle. "If you're not careful, there's liable to be more fun than you had in mind." He jumped out the back door with Albert close behind him. They were fifty feet from the building when they heard the paraffin ignite. They turned to see Jack silhouetted in the doorway and flames pouring from every window of the building. Jack took a long look into the fire before he limped back to where Albert and TJ were standing. He hauled himself a few feet farther and sat down on the desert floor, facing the fire. TJ and Albert sat in the dirt next to him.

The fire engulfed the Gates of Hell in a matter of minutes, and the shingles on the roof began to glow. Inside the building, the fire reached the store of signal rockets and they began going off. Some flew skyward through the burning shingles, others shot through windows and burning siding to skitter along the ground and explode somewhere in the darkness of Hell or to shoot into the boulder field and ricochet into the night of Old Australia. Flaming debris from the Gates of Hell blew into the sky, and the wind carried it across the desert as far as they could see.

Not far in the distance, Albert could hear the dingoes eating Bertram. The noise didn't bother him as much as it did when he had heard them eating O'Hanlin. But then, Albert had never cared much for Bertram.

31 ≋ The distant mountain

ALBERT WATCHED TJ AND THE two dingoes climb a low hill not far from where they had parted company. If it weren't for the blue bandana TJ had tied around his head, Albert would have had difficulty telling him apart from his companions.

They had left the last encampment at daybreak. Two young dingoes had come with them—not for any real purpose, just for something to do. The day was cool and the walking was easy. The mountain was still there on the horizon, seeming no closer than it had ever been. Before the sun was very high in the morning sky they came to the edge of Hell and the dingoes would go no farther. There were no markers on the desert floor to indicate that one patch of ground was different than another one a few feet away, but the dingoes knew that this was where their world ended.

The three old friends had stood on the edge of a new world and said good-bye to each other for the last time. In turn, TJ shook Jack and Albert's paws.

"You boys take care of yourselves and if you ever meet anybody else from California, you buy them a drink with the compliments of Terrence James Walcott."

"We'll do that," Jack replied.

TJ smiled.

"Well Albert, we can't say it hasn't been interesting, can we?"

"No we can't TJ, and that's for sure," Albert said. "Good luck in the piracy business."

"And good luck to you, my friend."

TJ turned and began jogging back the way they had come. The two young dingoes followed him and they soon disappeared into the bush, only to appear for a moment on the distant hill.

There had been some talk of staying together, but Albert knew that he wouldn't make a very good pirate, and there was not much chance that TJ would enjoy living anywhere shootings weren't a daily occurrence.

TJ had tried to talk Jack into going with him to capture the mystery ship. He told Jack that his limp might prove to be an advantage in the piracy business. TJ had heard that some of the best pirates had wooden legs, and a bad limp was just one step below having a peg.

Jack had thanked TJ for the offer but said that he was a little old for hopping around a deck trying to hit someone with a cutlass—and any day now he would go back to someplace beyond the lava field and take up prospecting again.

Albert knew he had no choice but to continue the journey he had started so long ago. He would walk toward the mountain that had been his guide ever since he had first left Ponsby Station. If Muldoon had been right and that everyone who walked far enough ended up in Old Australia, there was a chance that walking even farther might take him to the place he was really looking for. The dingoes had let TJ know that Hell stopped long before it reached the mountain. If so there might be another platypus out there somewhere the dingoes had never been.

Albert had asked Jack if he would like to come with him to the mountain. He knew that Jack's prospecting days were over and that leaving the old wombat alone with the dingoes wasn't a good idea. Jack's pride kept him from accepting Albert's offer for a few days, but he finally let himself be talked into going.

Jack and Albert made quite a show of deciding what to take with them and what not to take. In reality, all the things they owned amounted to very little, and they could have left an hour after deciding to go. But they needed to adjust to the idea of never seeing TJ again, and the time they spent packing helped make them feel a little bit better about leaving.

TJ stopped on the crest of the hill for a moment and looked back toward Albert. He raised his paw in the fashion of the dingoes. Albert did the same. TJ disappeared for the last time and Albert turned back toward the mountain.

Jack and Albert walked through midday, stopping often to let Jack rest. The land around them was changing slightly. The dirt was more rust colored, rocky outcroppings were becoming more frequent and acacia was giving way to stunted trees. Jack took no interest in his new surroundings, but now and then would look back in the direction of Muldoon's last fight.

A few hours before sunset, Jack told Albert he couldn't go any farther. Albert dropped his pack and helped Jack off with his. He put the packs on the ground and half carried Jack to the shelter of some rocks a few hundred yards ahead of them.

When Albert returned to the rocks with the packs, Jack was slumped against a large stone. He had tried to light his pipe but the effort had been too much for him. He sat there with his pipe in one paw and a box of matches in the other.

Albert took the pipe and matches and put them on the ground next to Jack. He took a blanket out of his pack and put it around Jack's shoulders. Jack thanked him and said he'd be ready to go in just a little bit. Then he closed his eyes and went to sleep.

Above Jack's head, Albert saw the picture of an animal carved in the stone. He looked at it closely, but windblown sand had eroded the picture and he couldn't tell what kind of animal it was. Albert looked around him and saw that the carvings were everywhere: stick figures of men, outlines of kangaroos, bandicoots, dingoes, wombats, and hundreds of other animals, some he knew and others he'd never seen before.

Albert walked around all the rocks and looked carefully, but he couldn't find a picture of a platypus. There was a chance that there had been a drawing of one and the wind had taken it away.

He sat down where he could keep an eye on Jack and see the mountain ahead of him. Even if no other platypuses had passed this way, the place he had dreamed of finding when he left the zoo was still ahead of him. He was sure that someday he would get there.

He had walked into Old Australia with an empty bottle, and he would walk out having learned about fame and friendship. He hadn't come from Adelaide to look for those things, but he had found them. He hadn't discovered why he had come to the place he was leaving, and he probably never would. The why of things had ceased to trouble him and he was content with what he'd been given. The soft drink bottle from the zoo was still in his pack, and he would carry it to the distant mountain along with all the things he had learned on the flats of Hell.

The late afternoon sun lit the desert in front of Albert in a way he had never seen before. Piles of rocks floated in a blood red sea of sand. Clumps of saltbush danced for him all the way to the mountain. Albert sat there in the beauty of that afternoon, glad to have Jack there with him, and grateful for days yet to come.

After the desert disappeared in the darkness, Albert walked over to adjust Jack's blanket against the chill of the night and found that Jack was dead. He adjusted the blanket anyway. Then he sat down next to the body and stayed there through the night, speaking to Jack about the life in Adelaide that had meant so little to him, as well as of all the things that he, Jack, and TJ had done together that had meant so much. By the time the sun came up there was nothing left to say.

Albert lay Jack on a blanket where he would be able to see the light of every morning and any star that fell in the night sky. He placed Jack's pack under his head and covered him with his old drover's coat. Then he put a can of sardines next to him, hoping he'd get a chance to share it with Muldoon somewhere down the line.

Albert packed his gear, put on his hat against the morning sun, and started walking into the desert toward the mountain on the horizon. Behind him, he could hear the stones begin to cry.

THE ART of Conversation

CATHERINE BLYTH

JOHN MURRAY

First published in Great Britain in 2008 by John Murray (Publishers)
An Hachette Livre UK company

1

A CIP catalogue record for this title is available from the British Library

Hardback ISBN 978-0-7195-2181-2
Export paperback ISBN 978-0-7195-2301-4

Typeset in Minion by Servis Filmsetting Ltd, Stockport, Cheshire

Printed and bound by Clays Ltd, St Ives plc

John Murray policy is to use papers that are natural, renewable and recyclable
products and made from wood grown in sustainable forests. The logging and
manufacturing processes are expected to conform to the environmental
regulations of the country of origin.

John Murray (Publishers)
338 Euston Road
London NW1 3BH

www.johnmurray.co.uk

For Vivian and Stephen

Contents

We Need to Talk

We need to talk.

When did this become a threat rather than a statement of fact? Is it a fact?

Walk into an Internet café and you might think speech obsolete. Visit a bar with widescreen sports, eat in a Planet Hollywood, see if you can sneak a word through the Dolby stereo barrier. On a bus, you might have no choice but to hear conversation, in Babel-like halves, but would you strike one up with a stranger? Go on, I dare you.

Some say this is the age of information, others, the communication age. There is no question that our ever growing means of keeping in touch have unleashed intelligence, creativity, passion and fun, offering countless new directions in which to stretch our hours. Yet these riches leave many of us feeling not so much lucky, as time-poor; as if life were

1

hurtling by in a fuzzy stream of images glimpsed from an accelerating car.

Fewer of us complain that conversation, especially face to face – for thousands of years the core of human interaction – is being pushed to the sidelines. But we should. We are losing out on one of life's greatest, certainly most useful pleasures. One that has the power to slow and enrich the passage of time, rooting us in a shared moment as no other pastime can. Potentially.

Yet have you never sat at a dinner, waited for someone to speak, watched a glittering frost of smiles seal the silence, and wondered how innocent cutlery can sound so very like the theme from *Psycho*? What about Christmas with the family? Lunch with the boss? The mute couples who garnish restaurants, pre-cocktails, on Valentine's Day?

Surely someone had something to say. Each had a life, and a pulse, presumably. It's tempting to assume that they couldn't be bothered. A more worrying possibility is they hadn't a clue where to begin.

If you haven't toiled in such deserts, lucky you. In my experience conversation breakdown is increasingly common, and other people are bewilderingly tolerant of it. I have seen otherwise savvy professionals struck dumb at supposed celebrations; been interviewed by Trappists posing as publishers; witnessed parties lurch from awkward chat to addled oblivion, while hosts revolve the room like circus plate spinners, frantic to keep it moving, their efforts drowned out by the crashing of bores.

Extreme measures are being taken. A friend's annual office jamboree, a fancy, candles-and-cleavage affair, was ruined by rude waiters. Until it was revealed that they were actors: the entertainment.

'But hey,' said my friend, 'at least it gave us something to talk about.'

Fear is understandable. If great conversation enhances any situation, when it flounders it can be hell. I love to hate my cock-ups because friends laugh at the retelling; however, alone, at night, ancient cringes still awaken spasms of shame.

So I feel for the man whom Samuel Johnson's friend, Mrs Thrale, mocked for having the ill-breeding to complain:

'I am invited to conversations, I go to conversations, but, alas! I have no conversation.'

(He had acquired a fortune in – whisper it – trade.)

In his era conversation was a status symbol. Thankfully we needn't take it so seriously; at least, not so formally. Still, even casual chat requires a confidence that seems to be waning, and I'm sure that in many blue-chip companies the con artist unmasked in G.K. Chesterton's *The Club of Queer Trades* could, with discreet marketing, coin it:

'A new trade,' repeated [the detective] Grant, with a strange exultation, 'a new profession! What a pity it is immoral.'

'But what the deuce is it?' cried Drummond and I in a breath of blasphemy.

'It is,' said Grant calmly, 'the great new trade of the Organizer of Repartee . . . a swindler of a perfectly delightful and novel kind. He hires himself out at dinner parties to lead up to other people's repartees. According to a preconcerted scheme (which you may find on that piece of paper), he says the stupid things he has

arranged for himself, and his client says the clever things arranged for him. In short, he allows himself to be scored off for a guinea a night.'

Winning witty points may be old hat, but conversation remains an art as well as a social duty. Somewhere along the way too many of us seem to have dropped the idea that it is something worth striving to be good at – as if we are either born great conversationalists or not. If only.

Conversation works in ways infinitely more various, and devious, than you might suspect. Take a closer look and you find an entertainingly candid portrait of the human animal, as well as a means to almost everything that you could wish for in life.

The Multi-Tasking Miracle

When it works, conversation can come close to heaven. Be it sharing a laugh with a stranger, transforming a contact into a friend; that joyful moment when you click, share a joke or spark a new idea; or just letting off steam with someone who knows how to listen, there are countless adventures between minds out there, waiting to happen, in each encounter, each day of our lives.

Networking is part of its value, although the word sounds chilly and strategic. Conversation is something bigger: it is the spontaneous business of making connections, whether for work, friendship or pure, fleeting pleasure.

Some writers have argued that it's where the raw stuff of life is spun into art. Speech – the gift of provoking thoughts in others' minds by rapidly modulated outtakes of breath – is

4

certainly a wonder, and conversation a miracle upon that miracle. Indeed, if evolutionary psychologists are right, it fathered language, out of grooming, the conversation of apes, when our ancestors sat about picking off fleas, flirting, working out who was boss.

But I find simpler reasons to treasure it. Get on with others, you will get on in life, and enjoy it more. Good talkers get dates, win contracts. They make job interviews fun, whichever side of the desk they are on. Furthermore, the qualities of a satisfying chat – vitality, clarity, wit, relish, tact, a light touch – are the same as we want of the people around us. Respect the rules of artful conversation and not only are you on your way to being a better person, but learn to steer discussion, to entertain, not dominate, and you're on the road to power.

Conversation is brilliant at both polishing thoughts and frothing up new ones, and although professionalism encourages us to wring the maximum from meetings in minimum time, serendipity produces many of the best ideas. Since information flows better through stories than year-end reports, censoring gossip – whether at the water-cooler or on e-mail – can dull a business's cutting edge.

Just as monarchs had their favourites and Arab rulers their salaried *nadim* ('cup companions') with whom to trade jokes and keep track of the court's mood, not to mention boost their own, so productivity and morale shot up when a Puerto Rican tobacco company started paying a cigar-roller the same hourly rate to down tools, sit in the middle of the work area, read papers aloud, natter and clown.

There are other benefits. Paul McCartney loves talking as well as crooning to audiences because, 'I remember stuff that

I'd forgotten for thirty years in explaining it.' Holocaust survivor Alice Herz-Sommer, a 103-year-old concert pianist, would agree. Asked about her fizzing social life, she confided she wasn't avid to hear about 'lives and problems' purely out of altruism or curiosity: 'This is good for the brain . . . better than a hundred pills.' How come she was so skilled at conversation? 'Chamber music is a discussion with your partner. You have to listen.'

More than words, conversation is music: its harmony, rhythm and flow transcend communication, flexing mind and heart, tuning us for companionship.

It doesn't have to be grave to supply life's turning points. When a young worker at Mother Teresa's Home for the Dying in Calcutta, novelist Jeffrey Eugenides was toying with taking up holy orders. But he couldn't work out why he lacked the spirit of his nice, somewhat oatmealy fellow volunteers. Until one day, strolling with a non-volunteer, he rediscovered something they had not: humour.

A beggar approached and Eugenides spurted a piety:

I said, 'Jesus said that whoever asks of you, you should give something.' And my friend said, 'Well, obviously Jesus has never been in Calcutta.'

Eugenides laughed, then quit.

At around six I had the most important conversation of my life, with a social worker who wanted to know how my sister and I would feel about another sibling. In the excitement beforehand, planning what to say, fantasizing about being a mini-mum – painting an alphabet frieze in this new child's bedroom, reading her stories, teaching her words – on some level, I realized that just talking could change a life, all our lives; or not, if this conversation didn't work out. But it did, and we adopted Heidi.

And random collisions mean the world. A drunken chat with a writer transformed my love of books, although this matters less to me than our friendship. A crack about the pre-digested look of the canteen slop for which we were queuing began another, a journey on a minibus, yet another – one that led, in time, to meeting my future husband.

Most thrillingly, conversation awakens us to each other, as in this rare happy tale from the wards of the Royal Hospital for Neuro-disability:

Young man with motorbike head injury in a coma. His mum, a keen evangelical, comes every day with friends to sing 'Onward, Christian Soldiers' by his bedside. She's hoping to stimulate his brain into action. It works: he comes round, but he can't speak. So they fit him up with one of those Stephen Hawking-type laptops, and the first words he speaks are: 'For God's sake, Mum, shut it!'

Two minds striking can kindle something magical. In his memoir, *The Diving Bell and the Butterfly*, Jean-Dominique Bauby, condemned to speak in eye-blinks after a paralysing stroke, snared it:

My communication system disqualifies repartee: the keenest rapier grows dull and falls flat when it takes several minutes to thrust it home. By the time you strike, even you no longer understand what had seemed so witty before you started to dictate it, letter by letter . . . I count this forced lack of humour one of the great drawbacks of my condition.

In short, conversation is second only to sex, a lot less faff, and it really matters.

Perhaps your meals are a respectful communion with a television set and perhaps you like that just fine. Still, in the frame of human evolution, you're a novelty, even a weirdo. Companionship ('the sharing of bread') has ever been, if not the bread of existence, then the spirit that refreshed it, and conversation, once a broad term for 'being together', used to be considered so delicious as to be a sin. Monasteries and convents forbade it and totalitarian states monitored it, because it is unruly, fun and seemed utterly instinctive.

Casanova, visiting Louis XV's palace, could hardly contain his laughter at the spectacle of the queen, dining alone at 'a table that could have seated twelve', while a dozen courtiers stood watch in a silence ruptured only by this solemn exchange, when she hailed a Monsieur de Lowendal.

'*Madame.*'
  '*I believe that chicken fricassee is the best of all stews.*'
  '*I am of the same opinion, madame.*'

But solitary dining, and living, no longer appear so unnatural.

Why Modern Life is Bad for Conversation

The irony of this communication age is that we communicate less meaningfully. Not despite but because of our dizzying means of being in touch. So many exchanges are conducted via electronic go-betweens that, what with the buzz, bleeps and blinking lights, it is easy to overlook the super-responsive information technology that is live-action, up-close-and-personal, snap, crackle and pop talk – one that has been in research and development for thousands of years.

Communication tools may bring us together, but, equally, they keep us apart, not least from the here and now. Laptops, BlackBerries and 3 billion mobile phones have perforated the division between public and private, and we're growing used to toting about portals of availability as if they were vital electronic organs. Men, women and children stride about, bellowing unselfconsciously into mouthpieces like deranged town criers, and entertainment permeates: children watch films in the backs of car seats; on buses, TV screens assail passengers with cod-celebrity news; motion picture ad boards entice the riders of London underground escalators.

Today's gizmogemony alters human experience in a way that trains, planes, automobiles, even the wheel, did not – nibbling at the conditions in which we operate, confusing the real with the virtual. Inevitably, this changes us.

Compared to face to face, Internet communication is two-dimensional. Yet the emphasis on appearances is growing, redefining how we relate, and with it, ideas of what constitutes a relationship. Many young people happily swallow the notion that textual exchange is interaction. Avid social networker Henry Elliss claims:

> *It's only fuddy-duddies who think it'll kill socializing. Did they say that about the telephone, or faxes? It's building relationships. I wake up in a cold sweat sometimes – if Facebook disappeared, those friends would be gone.*

If that's building, the foundations are weak. And where's the time or space to socialize, if, like him, you have 453 friends to hold vigil over? You hire a barn? Or are these perhaps imaginary friends, pulses of light on a screen?

As distractions multiply, fewer receive our full attention, and nuances are neglected. We don't look at the man selling us coffee, never mind shoot the breeze; we're too busy fiddling with our iPod. I've witnessed wedding guests with more qualifications than they have chromosomes text-messaging during the vows.

Developments, yes, but progress? Although these innovations crowd out conversation, it isn't redundant; rather, like an ancient, still mighty beast, it is endangered unless we appreciate, and carve out space for it. The nuances are no less valuable to us than they were to our forefathers, nor are the joys. Abandon them, and we miss out.

Admittedly, there are superficially sound commercial reasons why conversation should be whittled away. Business disdains it because, unless flogging goods by that unsteady zeitgeist vehicle, word of mouth, it is hard to monetarize (oh, woeful word). Worse, it guzzles airtime, face-time, eye-time; attention that could be consumed consuming or ogling ads. So fast-food joints have their fast-forward music, agitations of beats designed to drive you through your hapless meal and out of the door as quickly as possible. And J.D. Wetherspoon, owner of 691 British pubs, has announced that families will be served no more than two drinks.

Once they have finished the meal with the child, we would expect them to leave.

It is surprising formal restrictions should be necessary. Modern life may seem like a conspiracy against conversation, but we are complicit, and if we learned its skills by osmosis, this is less likely to be the case for our children. Psychologists fear that families are talking to each other less than ever, and there is plenty of evidence to support this.

Two trends pull us away from conversation: either it is underappreciated, or so highly rated that it seems daunting – as if, compared to e-mail, it were a luxury, couture form of communication, requiring special training, perhaps at charm school (yes, these are back in vogue).

Technology plays a large part. We want our toys, but short-term pleasures too seldom serve long-term interests. Nobel laureate economist Gary S. Becker observed: 'Individuals maximize welfare *as they conceive it*, whether they be selfish, altruistic, loyal, spiteful, or masochistic.'

Many twenty-first-century delights are individualistic, not to say onanistic; distractions that narrow horizons and, with them, social arteries. As Matthew Taylor of the Royal Society of Arts put it:

We have to ask ourselves why the Internet is so good for wankers, gamblers and shoppers, and not so good for citizens and communities.

If language was born of the evolutionary accident that our species thrived better in groups, then so, as we cease operating that way, conversation becomes less incidental. It cannot flourish in isolation. Nor can we.

A communication-fixated culture leads us to expect, by right, levels of understanding in our relationships that our grandparents would hoot at. Unfortunately, we're less practised than they were at the conversational give and take that might enable it, and feel – irrationally – crushed, even cheated, when our lofty aspirations aren't met. This is so prevalent as to seem almost banal, rather than what it is: sad.

Isolation magnifies disconnect and disenchantment. Many more of us live alone, bombarded by images of lifestyles to dream of, all of which feeds a sense of existence as a performance that we're failing at. Television scarcely features sociable conversation, because disagreement, like horrifying news stories, makes better drama. So pundits joust with pre-fab soundbites, and too many talk shows are either bland publicity exercises fluffed up by a comic, or non-celebrity punch-ups.

Understandably, we enjoy watching a good ruck of an evening when, by day, service industry culture demands niceness to order. Shouting at reality TV's latest Punch and Judy is sort of fun. But is it any wonder we fear confrontation, or prefer to hide behind our screens?

We may be in touch, potentially, with anybody, anywhere on the planet. Nevertheless, what kind of existence is lived 24/7, ever on call? Naturally, we offset our accessibility with portable solitudes and head-space expanders, first Walkmen, then iPods, to compensate for being packed cheek to bum in over-crowded trains. But while a soundtrack makes life seem more exciting, it also takes you out of it.

It's hardly surprising on-line activity should be addictive (and it is: in South Korea, the world's most plugged-in country, up to 30 per cent of under-eighteens are thought to be at serious risk, with government-sponsored boot camps to wean them off). Like the Latin *utopia*, the Internet is a 'nowhere', and, like all drugs, unsatisfying, whetting appetites that it cannot fulfil, stimulating the mind's eye as it starves our other senses. In so doing, it depletes users' sensibility and intuition, skills that may feel instinctive, but, like language, are acquired through being together. That is, in conversation.

Arguably, this saps social confidence. Certainly, unlike the pixellated peacocks that strut the cyber-playgrounds, out and about, face to face, even in innocuous situations, growing numbers of us seem so scared of saying the wrong thing that we say nothing. We think we're shy. We don't realize how arrogant, selfish and idle we seem.

It is glib to blame media scaremongers, drugs, images of violence for rising antisocial behaviour. Something deeper yet simpler is happening. Talk less, we understand each other less.

In 1958 philosopher Hannah Arendt pondered how bizarre it was that men could journey into space, yet few could discuss these Promethean powers sensibly, because science had leaped ahead of human intelligence, the spectrum of its possibilities beyond any single person's ken, let alone everyday conversation. For her, the fact that this development coincided with rising rudeness – complacent 'thoughtlessness' being 'among the outstanding characteristics of our time' – was no coincidence.

It could be that we, who are earth-bound creatures and have begun to act as though we were dwellers of the universe, will forever be unable to understand, that is, to think and speak about the things which nevertheless we are able to do. In this case, it would be as though our brain, which constitutes the physical, material condition of our thoughts, were unable to follow what we do, so that from now on we would indeed need artificial machines to do our thinking and speaking.

Unable to discuss the machinery that manufactures our human conditions, we're forced into blindness, an innocence that she feared would brutalize us.

If . . . knowledge (in the modern sense of know-how) and thought have parted company for good, then we would indeed become the helpless slaves, not so much of our machines as of our know-how, thoughtless creatures at the mercy of every gadget which is technically possible, no matter how murderous it is.

An atomized society, returning humanity to a mental Eden, but in a world of atomic bombs?

What worried Arendt was that we'd lose the ability to question: ethics, after all, derive from our feelings, and if we don't understand something, it is harder to sense whether it is right or wrong, let alone argue against it. How many of us can comprehend, never mind democratically vote on, nanotechnology, or genetically modified food, animals, embryos? Arendt may have been thinking nuclear. But how about brain-death by iPod?

Actually, you're more likely to be flattened if you cross the road talking on your mobile, according to studies of pedestrians at a busy Chicago junction. Why?

Conversation absorbs more of our senses than listening to music.

I don't hate technology: I used to thank Christmas I had television instead of a weekly gawp at stained-glass windows, or whatever passed for entertainment in Granny's day. (With TV, hell, who needed imaginary friends?) But I slightly fear it. Computers and their ancillaries are evolving exponentially faster than we human animals, supplanting our creature comforts, yet in no way altering our Stone Age emotional or social needs.

Are we serving tools made to free us, like the conscientious gym slaves who, rather than eat less, burn hours servicing the surplus calories of the low-input banquet that is the daily bread of the sedentary, developed world? Whatever else, like it, hate it, in and out of cyberspace, we're undergoing self-consciousness hyper-inflation.

Social psychologist Sonia Livingstone said of today's image-conscious teenagers: 'Celebrity is about people being interested in you when you fall over in the pub . . . There's an element of them being their own self-production.'

The change is as profound and spirit-pummelling as that brought by the mirror and the portrait, which in the seventeenth century heralded new levels of self-fashioning, guardedness and melancholy – to historian Lionel Trilling 'a mutation in human nature'. Just as the camera and the moving image, for all their inspiration, helped mass-produce self-awareness, alienation and longing, making (with the aid of mechanized murder) depression the black dog of the twentieth century.

But while we may feel splintered, juggling ten roles a day where our parents had two or three, we need our distractions too: that is what other people are for. As social networking sites and 3 billion mobile phones testify, we still crave to meet new people, hear what they have to say. And the joke is, despite the loquacious pyrotechnics that passed for the conversational genius of Oscar Wilde, conversation isn't a performance.

It takes two or more people and two things: attention and interest.

We can easily fold more of it into our life, and it's imperative that we try, not just for ourselves. The tide against conversation has a powerful undertow.

The Logic of Rudeness

Manners are shaped by their times. At medieval revels communal dishes gave an incentive to greedy guts with sharp knives and elbows. In ritzy Renaissance Italy, however, the new-minted fashion for genteel meals, with individual place settings and multiplying forks and spoons, reconfigured pecking orders and definitions of good behaviour. This created a niche, and conduct manuals, like Stefano Guazzo's 1574 bestseller, *Civile Conversation*, the earliest treatise on the subject, sprang up to fill it, with advice on how to plug gaps between courses with suitably pitched chitchat.

Today, industrialization is on the march, social fragmentation litters its progress, and as manners thin to accommodate overstretched lifestyles, a time-paring, talk-sparing attitude is spreading, and it stinks. If you're watching the clock, awaiting a text, how easy is it to sit back, relax and enjoy the present company? Think of the cannibalistic romantic scene parodied in *Sex and the City*, where dates are debated like commodity trades. Do you want to laugh or cry at the true story of Manhattan child Olivia Gopnik, whose imaginary friend, Charlie Ravioli, too busy 'grabbing lunch' to play, eventually hired an 'imaginary secretary' to keep Olivia at bay?

Yet some yearn for even fewer social niceties. Like Oscar-winner Halle Berry:

Being politically correct is bullshit. I want to know how someone really feels, what I'm dealing with. I want to know who you really are, and then maybe we can have a conversation.

Sadly, her dream of transparency belongs in la-la-land, and is far from universal.

Generally speaking, the more individualist a society, the more direct its manners. While many Americans prefer an upfront approach, collectivist societies tend to favour indirectness. Such as urban southern China, where *'laoshi'* ('simple and honest') is a cussword for country bumpkins, and the highest term of praise is *'congming'*, 'clever', in the Ancient Greeks' sense of *'mētis'* or 'cunning' (think Odysseus, not Achilles). Why?

To respect the maxim at polite behaviour's core: *do not embarrass the other person.* Analyst Robin Lakoff explained the logic behind the three styles of being polite:

Don't impose (distance) – formal
Give options (deference) – hesitant, euphemistic
Be friendly (camaraderie) – direct

Being deferentially friendly is the definitely maybe of getting along, and entails contradictions, since manners are asymmetrical and often what is polite for speakers to imply would be rude for listeners to say. ('Won't you have some juice?' versus 'I want some juice.') As a consequence, in super-polite company, the nuances can be a veritable merry-go-round of implication and suggestion, as my dad found, a relatively uncouth English child, visiting well-drilled cousins in 1950s South Africa. After a month he worked out the correct answer to 'Would you like some salt?' was not 'No, thank you' but 'May I pass it to you?'

In varying degrees, such push-me-pull-you diplomacy underpins all conversational exchanges; it is how we broker relationships. Therefore local differences, however filigree, are worth mastering. Alas, cultural variations are complicated by a further factor: scale. Where openness is sensible in small communities, in larger ones it becomes a liability. It cannot pay to be on nodding acquaintance with everyone in town – you'd dislocate your neck – or to ask the whole street in for tea: how could you trust them not to filch the kettle?

And if cunning is useful in towns, ignoring seems to make more sense in large multicultural cities, because stealth requires expertise; however, when norms are so diverse that a smile can be a come-on to one person, a taunt to the next, reactions are impossible to predict. So people shut down, conversation shrinks, resulting in a net loss in skills at reading others and self-expression. In such crowds, individuals become isolated and grab what intimacy they can get. The result?

$$\frac{\text{Rudeness}}{\text{(ignoring people)}} \times \frac{\text{Rudeness}}{\text{(being too direct)}} = \text{Rudeness}^2$$

Escalating rudeness is a logical outcome, but politeness is surely wiser, and safer.

Politicians extol tolerance, but what a chiselling aspiration this can be, so often freighted with hate. Rather than sympathize, it asks us to put up, shut up. This isn't sociable: it's antisocial. But if we don't socialize, don't master the reflexes of politic self-correction, we're stuck with clunking political correctness, which, as Halle Berry said, often seems not sensitive but imposed. And lip-service is as unlike to virtue as a fig-leaf is to innocence.

We need artful conversation. Co-operation is its operative principle, enthusiasm its divine breath, and its power to raise spirits supernatural. Not only can it make us less socially stupid, but also significantly brainier.

The Mind Mechanic

Some proclaim the Internet a great oom-pah-pah for literacy. Regardless of whether you see bloggers as scapegrace ego-casters or Samuel Pepys's worthy heirs, solo self-expression is feeble at training minds, the workhorses of communication. Linguist William Labov caused blushes when he analysed recordings from different classes and settings.

The highest percentage of ungrammatical sentences [appeared] in the proceedings of learned academic conferences.

It's no fluke that the monologue-asteries of lab and library nurture woolly jargon. Talking distils thoughts (we know they're unclear by the befuddled look on the other person's face) and book-learning is harder to absorb than education through conversation. What's less well-known is that studying the craft of conversation improves thinking all round.

In the late 1990s sample groups of eight- to eleven-year-old British schoolchildren took a course of Talk Lessons. Afterwards they accounted for thoughts as other classmates did not, more often using words like 'because', 'if' and 'why'. Tellingly, they outperformed in written intelligence tests too. Having learned to think aloud together, they were better equipped to reflect alone.

Conversation has been the engine of intelligence since *Homo* became *sapiens*. The species' evolution rewarded those with conversational skills – social and political skills – and these continue to select social leaders and spur cultural development. But as those schoolchildren and grammar-mangling academics prove, this tradition means diddlysquat unless each of us incorporates conversation into our personal evolution. After exhaustive exploration of the everyday conversations around and with babies in a cross-section of American homes, researchers Todd Risley and Betty Hart found that:

> *The large differences in the language experience that had accumulated before the children were three years old accounted for most of the equally large differences in vocabulary growth and verbal intellectual outcomes by age three – and many years later.*

How does conversation exercise the intellect? Knowledge is defined by neuroscientist Ira Black as a 'pattern of connectivity' between neurons and learning as modifications of this pattern. Similarly, communication follows social grammar, as we make connections by guile and guesswork, extracting signals from face, tone, gesture as much as words. As psychologist Nicholas Humphrey described, it's unbelievably artful; a dance, close to telepathy:

> *Like chess, a social interaction is typically a transaction between partners. One animal may, for instance, wish by his own behaviour to change the behaviour of another; but since the second animal is himself reactive and intelligent the interaction soon*

> *becomes a two-way argument where each 'player' must be ready*
> *to change his tactics – and maybe his goals – as the game proceeds.*

Conversation doesn't feel this hard, not if you practise it. But if you don't, as Stefano Guazzo wrote four and a half centuries ago:

> *He that useth not company hath no experience, he that hath no*
> *experience, hath no judgment, and hee that hath no judgment is*
> *no better than a beast . . . so the common saying is, that there is*
> *no other name meete for a solitarie person, but either of a beast,*
> *or a tyrant.*

The word Guazzo used was '*humanitas*' – 'communal conversation'. For anyone still unconvinced it can be learned or improved, I'm afraid it is how we all learn to learn. If we don't learn well, we limp through life.

'Goo-goo' is the most important word in the world, because when parents coo at babies, they're educating them in what behaviourists call 'musical companionship'. As babies goo-goo back, they absorb timing, taking turns, tone, co-ordination, gestures, facial expressions, story-telling – the orchestra of instruments by which emotions are transmitted and relationships formed.

No synthetic alternative will do, witnessed in a cruel experiment that showed an infant a video of its burbling mum (distressed, it withdrew). And babies who aren't talked to, or who are talked at abusively, grow into disruptive kids who can't express themselves. As do too many South Korean children, despite loving parents and the world's best education system. With little free time, some become socially malnourished,

seeking solitary solace on-line, trading interaction's challenges for virtual games – short-circuit gratifications that foster ingrown personalities and make their lives hell.

Dr Kim Hyun-soo, chair of the Association of Internet Addiction, explained: 'These people are very frustrated inside and full of anger.'

Any parent too busy to sit down for tea and ask about school should hear what teachers have to say about fading listening and learning abilities, or perhaps read the UNICEF report rating British kids' wellbeing the lowest in twenty developed countries, not least because Mum and Dad scarcely speak to them. Then have a weep, then think again.

Conversation can heal us. Children of talkative parents have higher IQs, know how to make connections, and friends. While we pay therapists to listen, in talking cultures depression remains a dictionary term. And the centenarian concert pianist's intuitions were confirmed by a study of geriatric nuns, which found that gunky brain cells don't equate with dementia, not if the nun keeps chatty, happy and takes the odd toddle.

As Nicholas Humphrey demonstrated, good conversationalists see others' perspectives, so have less destructive arguments. They don't, unlike the last, word-cudgelling President of the United States, inhabit an either/or universe. To assert 'you're with us or against us' is to quash debate, leading to bad decisions.

In 1940 Sir Kinahan Cornwallis, a British diplomat who helped forge the kingdom of Iraq, wrote:

The value of personal contacts and friendships has been proved over and over again in the Middle East, and the evil effects of aloofness and indifference are clear for all to see.

If only the lesson were learned. Not talking – failing to acknowledge the other point of view, never mind engage with it – polarizes, killing debate. In its absence, silence breeds suspicion, anger and violence, creating further distance – distance that comes to seem unbridgeable, faced with the unspeakable.

My hell is not, as it was for Sartre, other people. It is a twenty-first century with 6 billion-plus of us, on a shrinking planet, with dwindling resources, not talking. Lose the means to work out who we are, what we have in common, and we lose stories, the greatest consolation. Novelist John Steinbeck understood the creative balm of sympathy:

> *We are lonesome animals. We spend all of our life trying to be less lonesome. One of our ancient methods is to tell a story begging the listener to say – and to feel – 'Yes, that is the way it is, or at least that is the way I feel it.'*

Guazzo was right, conversation gives us humanity. Without it we're less than the sum of our parts, unable to improvise or be what roguish seventeenth-century philosopher Francis Bacon called 'a ready man'. And we need to be. Service industry is the future and if not the cheapest workers, we'd better be smarter to beat the competition. In a sense many of us are already courtiers. Yet the decline in everyday courtesy – failure to meet the eye, switch off that phone – attests to an urgent need to reawaken nerve endings.

Historically, the periods when conversation was most revered have been among the most fruitful for reason, invention and respect for the individual; times when people believed that their opinions could change the world. Think of the babbling coffee houses frequented by Samuel Johnson and enlightened chums; the great French salons, which brought together thinkers and artists and politicians, galvanizing mindshifts and freedoms from which the West continues to benefit. For Johnson and co, newspapers and print sped up talk. The Internet can do more for us, if we're sane about it. This is an exciting time for conversation. Potentially.

Stand on each others' shoulders and we can, like acrobats, build pyramids. Just as Jimmy Connors raised John McEnroe's game, so Coleridge spurred Wordsworth, so the Almohad court propagated scientific and cultural advance. What would Shakespeare, Jonson and chums have been had they not met in pullulating Elizabethan London and hung out at the Mermaid Tavern, where pub banter was

> *So nimble, and so full of subtle flame,*
> *As if that every one from whence they came*
> *Had meant to put his whole wit in a jest,*
> *And had resolved to live a fool the rest*
> *Of his dull life*

Einstein appreciated this: he trundled to his office in Princeton's Institute for Advanced Study solely for 'the privilege of walking home with Kurt Gödel'. Three freewheeling years of chatter led Francis Crick and James Watson to their epochal discovery of the structure of DNA. Do I hear you ask, 'But is it art?'

Were it not for mental and social workouts at a *tertulia*, a salon in Barcelona that he came to dominate like Barnum did his circus, seventeen-year-old Picasso might not have become a genius anecdote-teller, as well as a poet (little appreciated outside Spain), or won the renown and contacts that eased his scramble to the apex of the twentieth century's artistic pyramid. Walter Sickert, a lesser painter, famously donned his 'lying suit' to wow Mayfair dinner parties and butter the crumpets of rich admirers.

Conversation makes connections. For heaven's sake, it's a laugh.

There is No Right Way

On the other hand, if you want to kill a conversation, tell people you're writing a book on the subject. Either they feel like lab rats, or they turn nasty.

'Why you?' asked a doubting friend.

'Nice idea, but you can't make anyone better at it,' said a tactful teacher.

'So what's it all about then?' demanded a scary novelist.

'Oh, well,' I replied, 'you know, being interested in people.'

'Yeah?'

'But you don't want me to go on about that now, or I'll start reciting my manuscript,' I blustered, hoping to shuffle to another topic.

'Right.' But the look on the man's face said, 'Wrong.'

'Sorry, I'm tired. My defence is that you don't have to be a Grand Master to discuss chess, so I needn't be a brilliant conversationalist.'

'No,' he said. 'But you'd better be bloody good at it.'

Who am I to tell you what to do?

I've been obsessed with words and reading since I can remember, and, though shy, always loved talking, often dragged to the front of the class for it. But that's not exactly conversation skill.

My parents valued conversation, and sent me and my middle sister to practise on a long-suffering blind man, Colonel Colbeck (complete with curlicue moustache and much repeated tales of secreting whoopee cushions under bustles at Mama's Edwardian tea parties). Despite their efforts, I'm no Oscarina Wilde, and have often failed to keep the ball rolling. For work, I've navigated the challenges of interviewing celebrities, as well as publicized naked Russian poets and negotiated with wily agents – champion cud-chewers all. However, I also tend to interrupt, jump between thoughts, and on too many occasions, have had cause to wish my foot didn't fit so snugly in my mouth. And I have suffered bores.

I'm not an expert, but an enthusiast, an interested party, and this book isn't a script. There is no one great way to hold conversation. But certain approaches are more flexible, and there are plenty of avoidable errors as well as artful dodges. My ideal is to draw the best out of companions. Whatever yours is, appreciate conversation's finer points and your experience will be more rewarding.

Investigating this ancient art form, its great and its knee-grindingly dreadful exponents, has been like a mystery tour of what it means to be human; fascinating, and often hilarious. I'd never suspected that greetings were such important gate-keepers; that small talk is hugely significant, if you trim it to advantage; how creative listening is; how easily dynamics tilt for or against you. You will be amazed.

I have explored what topics are fit for purpose; why bores drain our wits, and how they can be stopped; the gymnastic arts of humour, flattery and seduction; the wisdom of lying;

tactics for shop talk, getting your own way, and, if truly necessary (but deeply satisfying), shutting people up.

Two conversations convinced me this book was necessary. The first took place on a train. I sat near a beautiful young man who was wearing a white cap. As the train rolled out of the station he took a small, leather book from his jacket. When he began chanting, I noticed he had no luggage except a couple of bags containing large, sloshing containers of fluid.

After the London bombings, I was paranoid, and ashamed: who was I to judge him? Ridiculous! Part of me wanted to change carriage. Instead, I asked if he was praying. We talked for half an hour about the Koran.

The second happened at a dinner. For two hours I sat by a self-styled publicity guru who regaled me with his postcode's wonders ('I love Notting Hill; all the same, I have the pleasure of being the most brilliant man in Battersea' – and this dinner was in Battersea), recommended his forthcoming book on self-promotion skills, but, apart from where I lived, asked me almost nothing.

If his is the direction of civilization, it is in reverse gear.

In 427 BC the orator Gorgias of Leontini conquered Athens with his defence of runaway bride Helen of Troy. It wasn't her fault, he said, but words, they 'stop fear, remove sorrow, create joy and increase pity' but they also 'poison and bewitch the mind'.

Two and a half millennia on nothing has changed. There is no greater power, no pleasure so serious.

Can conversation save lives? It certainly saves marriages and few would dispute it builds self-esteem. Shouldn't it be obvious it can also raise social esteem, generating the goodwill that funds the best in life and business? Neglecting it graffitis cultural DNA, muddles minds, and helps granulate us into extremists. But using it can rebuild our crumbling common ground. As researching this book has taught me, we are more complicated and magnificent than we realize: far from behind technology, we are beyond it.

Close your eyes a moment. Imagine saying 'Hi' to the strangers on your street. Imagine everyone saying it. Imagine it is the start of a conversation.

Is that so preposterous? It never used to be.

Let's wage war on shyness. With a friendlier environment, we have a better chance of making it into the next century. And enjoying it. As Alexander Pope nearly wrote:

> *True ease in talking comes from art, not chance,*
> *As those move easiest who have learned to dance.*

Understand the steps, you will hear the music.
We need to talk.

The Concise Manifesto

Attention + Interest = Conversation = Joy

What conversation isn't

    Performance art

    Competition

    Scripted

What it is

    Mutual appreciation

    Co-operation

    Spontaneous

Three Principles

    Generosity

    Openness

    Clarity

Five Maxims

    Think before you speak

    Listen more than speak

    Find the incentive for talking

    Never assume you know what they mean or that they
        understand you

    Take turns

Hello

On Conversation's Casting Couch

Don't talk to strangers? Don't speak until spoken to? Forget it. Inhibition is useless. How do you start a conversation? Simple: say 'Hi'.

It's easy to say. But as with flying, the critical phase of conversation is take-off, and greetings don't follow straight lines, but vary from place to place. Even chimpanzees have a host of hand clasps. Some grip, some press wrists, some grab and groom, and all respect one rule: the dominant chimp's hand goes on top.

By contrast, many humans bungle customary overtures. Some dive in; so keen to have an impact, they're blind to the impression they make. Other, shy coves stumble, mumble or say nothing. What does it matter?

The chimps get it: greetings announce who we are. They reveal plenty about a relationship:

'Hello, reptile,' she said. 'You're here, are you?'

'Here I am,' I responded, 'with my hair in a braid and ready to the last button. A very merry pip-pip to you, aged relative.'

'The same to you, fathead. I suppose you forgot to bring that necklace?'

(It is abundantly clear Aunt Dahlia adores her reptile nephew, Bertie Wooster.)

And they can shape relationships. When the Earl of Oxford was presented to Elizabeth I, he bowed, issued a loud burst of afflatus, and fled England in shame. After seven years' self-imposed exile, he returned to court. Her Majesty greeted him: 'My lord, I had forgott the fart.'

RULE ONE: *Greetings spark connections*

Initial impressions are indelible. Compare the shopkeeper who asks how you are with the one who snorts, her eyes glued on your down-at-heel shoes.

She may not mean to be rude, but she might as well turn her back. Yet in most towns, would this surprise you?

No word costs less or counts more in a conversation than 'hello'. Even in a megalopolis such as London there's something unsettling about a person who won't return it, like the man on my street whose liveliest response to 'Hi' is a grunt (usually he looks away). I'm not sure what I, or life, have done to him, but the sense of a person stranded in his own bleak world is strong. It crystallizes the importance of greetings for making contact and wiring conversation for sound.

How Greetings Connect

If conversation is music, then the start, the strike of a tuning fork, sets the tone and reveals others' key.

Greetings' exchange betokens a pact that people's attention is, for now, each other's. Not only does a casual 'Hi' or formally begged 'How do you do?' announce where you're coming from, but, like a diplomatic gift, the way you present it sends a message. However relaxed, it is a mark of respect, not an excuse to grab attention. (Which may shock U2's Bono. A friend's party was silenced when a bagpiper burst in, piped ten long minutes, then announced the rock singer couldn't make it, but had sent him to say 'Hi' instead.)

Not greeting emits a message too. Indeed, in Colette's novella, *Gigi*, the heroine, her mother and grandmother (the last two both retired courtesans) use it to dent the ego of an ageing roué and coax him into proposing marriage:

> *'Good afternoon, Mamita. Good afternoon, Gigi,' he said airily. 'Please don't move, I've come to retrieve my straw hat.'*
>
> *None of the three women replied, and his assurance left him. 'Well, you might at least say a word to me, even if it's only How-d'you-do?'*

RULE TWO: *Greetings are charms to open minds and doors*
Getting greetings right means hitting the same register as the other person – whether formal, friendly or intimate. Getting them wrong signals that you're uninterested, not on his wavelength, or an outsider; bad news in dangerous places. For instance, Tuareg nomads crossing paths in the Sahara desert

will reveal names only after trading set phrases like undercover spies. The lower status person (usually the younger) begins:

Younger: *Peace be on you*
Elder: *What do you look like?*
Younger: *Only peace.*
Elder: *What has gone wrong?*
Younger: *Nothing. Only peace.*
Elder: *What is new?*
Younger: *Nothing. Only peace.*
Elder: *Where are you going?*

Such rituals reflect the fact that manners are not universal but sprout up to serve regional circumstance. Nothing if not conventional, refined over millennia, they broker relationships, playing out social assumptions embedded in our cultural software, and so by their nature transcend finer feeling.

So Nigeria's Igbo, who believe the first person they greet dictates their day's fortune, happily ignore their own granny if there is a whiff of illness about her. So, to a Western Apache, introducing yourself is presumptuous (a keepsake of justified suspicion against men bearing gifts). Whereas in most urban societies not to do so – even if out of shyness – is rude, a bit like asking 'Don't you know who I am?' To which the reply must be, 'No, thank goodness.'

In complicated settings, negotiating the right to say 'Hi' can be a gorgeous dance. Intrepid Rory Stewart learned the worth of due respects hiking across Afghanistan, over mountains, in winter, shortly after tumultuous war. Initially he found the forms funny:

Finally a soldier marched in and, holding his right hand to his chest, said, 'Salaam aleikum. Chetor hastid? Jan-e-shoma jur ast? Khum hastid? Sahat-e-shoma khub ast? Be khair hastid? Jur hastid? Khane kheirat ast? Zinde bashi.'

Which in Dari, the Afghan dialect of Persian, means, 'Peace be with you. How are you? Is your soul healthy? Are you well? Are you well? Are you healthy? Are you fine? Is your household flourishing? Long life to you.' Or: 'Hello.'

But passing through shattered communities, Stewart soon mastered how to hail by lushly barnacled local custom, if need be invoking the forefathers of well-connected warlords who had guaranteed his passage. Time and again this, rather than gold, saved his life.

If seldom a question of life and death, like a letter of introduction clasped to the bosom of a Brontë heroine, greetings remain passports as well as the embodiment of the style by which you will be expected to behave. So if others bow, go ahead, and when in Rome, best do as they do, because respecting native customs is the first sign you can give someone that he should respect you.

The Origins of Confusion

I'm exaggerating? Of course, most of us pay greetings scant attention, precisely because they are conventional. But given the whirligig nature of globalized life, attending to their finer details is arguably more important than ever.

Thanks to globalization, a vast array of options beckons, with a profusion of gestures, from high-fives to continental high society's hovering *Handkuss* (uh-uh – no lips on Her Serenity's glove). Yet on closer inspection, amazingly few fit general use. Recall the nose-clash as you misjudge which cheek to kiss. The pause as you open a door, the other person hesitates, then you both walk into each other.

Confusion reigns because social codes are fading, and etiquette increasingly resembles a branch of astrology. Change is nothing new, but the information age has scrambled the software that programmes how we behave, multiplying distortions. We don't just copy our parents; we cut and paste from Web, film and TV. And although each walk of life looks increasingly the same, nuances proliferate and instincts are less instructive – fashion shifts too fast. (Try high-fiving a teenager and watch him sneer.)

Nevertheless, we form assumptions about personalities from the briefest encounter. I was utterly thrown when a business contact shook hands with her left paw (not coincidentally, she is a demon negotiator). Even with people we see all the time, jarring notes magnify into signs. Aren't you disconcerted by your Andalusian pal's ear-splitting air-smackeroos? The weirdo who winks when you buy milk at his shop? The aunt who still pinches cheeks? The tennis partner whose grip is like a drowning man's?

RULE THREE: *The first notes you strike should be on a general frequency*

Common sense ceases to exist when the pool of local certainties is awash with every other drop in the ocean. On the other hand, as your parents might have indicated, common sense has always been a thing of the past. One answer to the dilemma is to ditch greetings. Another is to get arty and improvise. Sure, you could twirl someone instead of shaking her hand (it happened to me). But why heap confusion upon confusion?

Trusty product of countless exchanges, the standard-issue gestures – the smile, the handshake – are already an amazing collective work of art, and evolved as they have for good reason. What is more, your opening – 'Hi' or 'Howdy?' – is already a bold tick in the social register, enough information for now, surely. This should be the easy bit.

RULE FOUR: *Smiling is a confidence trick*

It is apt that the first self-help guide, imaginatively titled *Self-Help*, should have been written by Samuel Smiles. Far from meek, anthropologists reckon baring teeth is as much designed to show yourself as an adversary with bite as to express warm feelings.

Our cousin the chimpanzee peels back his lips to warn of danger, suggesting that, as well as gently intimidating, the smile helpfully muzzles its wearer's fear; a confidence-boosting reflex, like giggling at splatter movies. Certainly, it is an assertion; bold, hardly modest, and some cultures prefer ladies to titter, a demure hand over lowered mouth. Admittedly, Tudor aristocrats had a brief grinning craze, when on-trend dames showed off blackened teeth to prove they were rich enough to rot them on costly sugar (and some resorted to fake blacking). But don't be put off. As Horace observed,

Smiling faces are turned on those who smile.

If you smile, the other person, unless very odd or hostile, will feel compelled to return it, for no other reason than that the mimicry instinct is so entrenched that smiles and laughter are contagious. (A 1962 hysteria epidemic in Tanganyika took two years' quarantine to stamp out.)

RULE FIVE: *Eyes make contacts*

Zulu has an elegant phrase for hello and goodbye: '*Sawu bona*' – 'I see you'. This encapsulates the power of greeting: it gives recognition. Not looking at the other person while doing it renders him invisible, implicitly declaring that either you're afraid to meet his eye, or he is beneath your contempt. Either way, it's bad manners, making you seem weak or pompous – a worse weakness still, for making conversation.

Faces reveal useful information, too. Your smile should reach your eyes because if the orbicularis oculi muscles don't contract, smocking your crow's feet, it will be read as false. Moreover, your eyes should reach into the other person's. True, not long ago debutantes embarking on the husband-fishing trip that was the Season were advised, 'Never look a man straight in the eye.' Such a gaze, counselled M. Dono Edmond, adviser to Queen Marie of Romania no less, informs its object that 'you are trying to probe his mind'. Heaven forfend.

But for artful conversation between equals, inattention tenders disaster. Take Ronald Reagan, never one to overlook niceties. At his adopted son's graduation, after he was famous but years before he was US President, he ambled around, extending his hand, saying, 'My name is Ronald Reagan. What's yours?'

Eventually he bumped into his son. Out went the mitt.

'*My name is Ronald Reagan. What's yours?*'

Isn't it tempting to read intimations of senility in his faux pas? Friendly as can be, yet so far, far away . . .

Missteps during greetings not only put people on guard instead of persuading them to lower it, but also prime them to expect that the blunderer isn't worth talking to. Charm can't work on autocue, and, as somebody should tell Bono, the truly charismatic don't show off; they're too busy, having eyes only for you.

Mapping Boundaries

The passive-aggressive grin makes a poetically fitting start to conversation, since it recalls that human relations have always been unequal parts antagonism and co-operation. Although smiling is an ancient primate inheritance, we hang on to it, because, at root, conversation is our species' miraculous innovation (catalytic converter?) for managing the tension between our desire to connect and our need for independence; a tension that has been nothing if not creative. As conversation developed, it allowed us to turn thoughts to words to collaborative deeds that led *Homo sapiens* out of the woods and on to run the planet – more or less.

Civility enabled this evolution. The word's meaning has been diluted, but to have a civil tongue in your head was once the prized asset of a privileged social group; like 'citizen', 'civility' spoke of a world that favoured discussion over violence or despotism (both derive from '*civitas*', 'self-governing community'). For Ancient Roman Cicero, the first thinker to explore the grammar of conversation, civility safeguarded 'community' by 'assigning to each individual his due' and making 'a habit of affability'. This remains true today.

RULE SIX: *Respect territorial claims*

We soon dread the kind woman we meet twice daily at the
school gate if each time she hugs us like a long-lost child,
because little civilities remain important protocols for cali-
brating intimacy. They pace out the distance between us at the
same time as drawing us together. And if conversation's
primary aim is to map common ground, greetings demarcate
personal space.

What contact is too intimate? The territory is fluid.
Although air kisses are bubbling up outside luvviedom, most
Britons still shake hands then draw back, and don't hug
strangers. However, five centuries ago Italian visitors to
England were aghast not at stiff upper lips, but at having to
smack them:

> *If a foreigner enters a house and does not first of all kiss the mis-
> tress on the mouth, they think him badly brought up.*

France currently favours two-way kiss trades, yet in 1831 Alexis
de Tocqueville, new to America, made a shattering discovery:
'Everyone shakes hands.' To a post-Revolutionary Frenchman,
such manifest egalitarianism was wildly touchy-feely.

Then again, unlike his predecessor Reagan, George W. Bush
considered handshakes high-risk. On first meeting fresh-
man senator Barack Obama, Bush offered a squirt of the
antiseptic with which he had been anointing the presidential
palm.

> *'Want some? Good stuff. Keeps you from getting colds.'*

In general an unlikely weapon for biological attack, a handshake remains the safest gesture for greeting someone new. In

fact, it came into use in more violent times, to show one did not wield a sword. Cicero would approve.

RULE SEVEN: *Pay attention and already you have a connection*

The bonus of conventionality is that while performing your handshake, saying 'Hi' or 'Howdy', your mind, if not quite on Reagan energy-saving mode, has space to take in the other person. So approach a new face like the start of a novel, magnetized for clues to an unfamiliar world.

Even handshakes reveal character, if only what a person wishes to project. Take note. Does she grip or squeeze? Lock eyes? Flick away? I tremble before knuckle-crunchers, and those pushy deal-closer types who place a second hand on top, trapping me, then pump away, as if to draw deep on the well of fast-drying friendship.

As for secret signallers, Freemasons et cetera, their clinches are no affair of mine.

Central Casting

Ignore a person at the fringe of a conversation and he'll soon go. Etiquette expert John Morgan explained:

> *In a curious way, until someone is introduced . . . socially they only half exist.*

He didn't mean this in a derogatory sense; rather, that recognition is all, and can create an advantage. In Ancient Rome senators hired *nomenclators*, who shadowed them around town, ready to whisper the correct form of address for approaching dignitaries, thereby enabling the senators to greet first, putting them in charge of the conversation. The same tactic is deployed by the infernal editor in *The Devil Wears Prada*.

Such power play illuminates the dark game of greetings and introductions. If the first business is trading names, a close second is establishing terms of engagement, offering enough information about each other for talk to crack on apace. But don't forget prestige is at stake: little status signals flash away, so the art of introducing someone else is to cast them in their preferred light, then bathe in the reflected glory.

In the past deference codes were overt. You could tell how to treat someone by how he dressed, and caps were doffed according to what, or not, sat on another's head (hatlessness being nigh to godlessness in times of epidemic headlice). In our socially mobile era, status is customized, making it harder to scan egos. At the corporate do, that unshaven, chainsmoking bum growling at all who graze his pungent biosphere will be the billionaire boss, his lack of grace, something for the 'little people', as effective a social barrier as a VIP's velvet rope.

But although manners alter, the human needs they exist to service – especially pride – remain. And of all social injuries, most avoidable is bungling a name.

The Name Game

Can't afford a *nomenclator*? Remembering is easier with the antique style of introduction: 'Zebedee, I'd like you to meet Aphra Jones. Aphra, allow me to introduce Zebedee Taylor.' But if this is *de trop*, why not repeat a name after you've been told it?

And be generous with your own. When introduced, if you detect the slightest hesitation, say it. Say it introducing yourself, even if you've met before, especially if the other person's name escapes you. In return, he should give you his. If not, prompt: remind him where you met. Equally, if it's your job to introduce other people, start with someone whose name you know, pause, then smile; hopefully, others will take the cue.

But if they're socially tone-deaf, own up. This can be positive: 'I couldn't forget you, but I'm afraid I'm hopeless at names.' Never, ever guess. (Sheila/Eileen, forgive me.)

Perhaps your memory is impeccable. Still, have a care how you show it. Some salesmen repeat clients' names to fast-track rapport, creating a faint yet oddly powerful sense of obligation to be nice back. Personally, I loathe it. And while it's good to drop a child's name into a bedtime story if you feel her attention wander, would you do the same when talking to an adult? Many do. But I know my name – why remind me?

Because someone else does not. To bring a fresh person into conversation without breaking momentum, try a slick lateral introduction: 'Zebedee Taylor, there you are. Aphra here was just going to tell us about her windmill.'

To 'Hi' or 'How Do You Do?'

So how to acknowledge status in introductions?

At a corporate event I once watched the chief executive of a multinational media conglomerate being introduced as the chief executive of a multinational media conglomerate to – *be still, your beating heart* – Don Johnson.

The CEO's TV-wide shades could not hide her perplexity.

She smiled, extended a lizard hand, rotating her head ninety degrees.

'And what,' she asked her host through unparted teeth, like a ventriloquist addressing a dummy, 'does Don do?'

The unfortunate host may have thought he was paying the CEO a great compliment in giving her such a fanfare to the *Miami Vice* veteran. He can't have been aware that, although greeting first means you lead an encounter, conversely, in introductions, the lower status person is traditionally introduced first – equivalent to the diplomatic gift, being offered the pasha. Not nice, but that's status games for you.

RULE EIGHT: *Introduce the higher status person (older, female) second*

Remember the playground chant? First the worst, second the best . . .

In a pub or bar, with close friends, who cares? But if in any doubt about the level of formality, pay attention; there are endless clues. (One grande dame used to pre-judge a function by the aerodynamics of the invitation: the stiffer the card, the further it flew when frisbeed across her dressing room, the smarter the togs she wore.)

RULE NINE: *Don't try to regrade the social register in greetings*

I've been in starchy situations where people act as if their personalities are in corsets, and most give the impression they'd rather not be (the alcohol intake usually confirms this). Even so, if you want to loosen up, it is the job of small talk, not introductions, to ascend the stair of friendship. Presuming intimacy from the off won't get you there. Old hands such as Princess Anne defy coercion. When she met the former premier's wife, Cherie Blair, the other said, 'Call me Cherie.'

'I'd rather not, Mrs Blair,' said the princess.

13 Unlucky Gambits for Opening Conversation with Strangers

1. A funny voice
2. Batting eyelids, twitching, itching, winking, etc.
3. The clothes inspection (radiates ill-will, regardless of whether you like the other person's look)
4. Touching, except the hand, cheek kiss, or clasping an elbow (for a power shake)
5. Refusing a hand
6. Holding on after its owner begins to withdraw
7. Wiping yours before or after shaking
8. Looking away during introductions
9. Laughing unprompted
10. That joke about the comedy surname
11. Rejecting a compliment
12. Saying, 'Oh yes, I've heard about you' without further elaboration
13. Silence

RULE TEN: *Introductions present the first thread for discussion*
Meeting a potential contact/employer/lover may feel to you like stepping under a Broadway hot-spot, but the other person may be equally intimidated, or thinking about what to buy for

dinner. At this point it's impossible to know. So if you feel self-conscious, invert it: be conscious of others, let your enthusiasm show, and focus on introductions, the primer for what you people might have to talk about.

An effective introduction is small-ad brief, splicing in only two ingredients per person:

A (who they are) + B (why they are relevant)

The salient information is not so much formal title (royals, snobs and servicemen excepted) as how you relate to one another or the event (housemate, client, mother-in-law, single male drafted in for ladies like you). Identify points of contact, charge people up, and you have a connection.

So put your best hand forward, smile, and remember the virtue of '*Sawu bona*': 'I see you'. It says the other person matters.

Now conversation can begin.

Typology of Bores, Chores and other Conversational Beasts

THE CROWD OF STRANGERS   *Tyrannoborus Rex*

You arrive late, as planned. The joint is jumping. There is your host, and there is everybody else you have never met.

Before a virgin expanse of unfamiliar faces, the prospect of mingling may feel little more alluring than staging a burglary. Simply saying hello can induce instant lockjaw. As can over-familiar faces, as at office parties, where, with shop-talk taboo, in non-work clothes and gauche mental mufti, colleagues may suddenly act like aliens without phrasebooks.

It's tempting to stay in the revolving door, as I once saw the actor Robert De Niro do, coming and going at a dog-eared film awards extravaganza. But for pity's sake, you've come this far. So think like a criminal: case the joint and find its weak points.

Best are fringe areas where groups break and re-form. Stand near food and drink and you've a ready-made topic, plus thing to do. If this is a house party, offer to help serve. (Hold the honeypot: bees will swarm.) And if you see a new group forming, stand by with an attentive expression; they may invite you in.

Someone nice is waiting to meet you, he just doesn't know it yet. He's the one not talking much who smiles, meets your eye. Or she's on her own, looking about hopefully like you, or he's studying the distant progress of a waitress, his glass as empty as yours. So join forces and catch her. Or hotwire talk with provocation. I once heard this shameless flattery: 'Magnificent skirt. Are you a ballerina?' (She pirouetted.) Once you've jimmied an opening, prepare to make small talk.

2

Small Talk, Big Deal?

On Striking Up a Tune

There was my target, deep in discussion with the museum curator. 'One Hundred Years of Cinema' was being opened by one bona fide British star. Just one hundred rooms to chase him through, as I sought my chance to strike.

At least, it felt like one hundred, and I felt like an assassin. In fact this was my first assignment for a gossip column. All afternoon I had read brown press cuttings on the antics and tepid shames of Jeremy Irons. Twenty questions? I had two hundred.

Until I started stalking and fear took over. Story – what story?

'*ACTOR VISITS MUSEUM SHOCK*'?

Finally, boredom slew fear: how bad could it be?

I went up, said my name and place of work. Irons smiled. I gulped. My throat and mind congealed. He smiled some more.

Then came the melt, starting in my nose, pores welling springs of treacherous sweat. At last he spoke.

'Good to meet you, Catherine Blyth of the *Evening Standard*. Have you met my wife?' He wafted a Hollywood-white hand. 'Sinead, Catherine Blyth, *Evening Standard*.'

'Hello,' I said, and fled.

Impeccable manners can nuke unwelcome intruders. Who was I, this sleek repetition of my credentials seemed to beg, to invade the Irons ether?

But the problem was mine: I had nothing to say. Without an ice-breaker, I froze, my body reacting as if his smile were sabre-fanged.

If you don't recognize the symptoms of social death, stop reading. You are a mathematician of genius, ruler of a minor principality, or possibly a sociopath. It may amaze you to learn that for many, even mild socializing is pathogenic. Such as the financial company directors, sent a questionnaire for a leadership course which asked: 'What in your work is most difficult?' As a chorus they replied: 'Small talk with clients.'

The Anatomy of Small Talk

Small talk has always had a bad name. The earliest reference in English, Lord Chesterfield's of 1751, is to

a sort of chit-chat, or small-talk . . . the general run of conversation in most mixed companies.

Stunted conversation, in other words. Like women, small talk has been derided as trivial, empty, even frigid (a 1905 tale refers to 'her colder, small-talk manner, which committed her to nothing'). As ever, prejudice masks insecurity and misunderstanding.

A character in Bernhard Schlink's novel *The Homecoming* observes:

> *I am no good at small talk: I can never quite find the right tone to make the weighty sound trivial and the trivial sound weighty.*

But small talk is neither a synonym for trite, nor about scaling topics to a set size. It can be many things: preamble to a meeting, networking, gossip, an exchange in the queue at the post office. At parties where guests are like bees bumbling flowers, it is a frivolous end in itself; for geishas, it is work. And wherever it occurs, however artless it seems, it is essential. As the wife reproves her husband in *The Painted Veil*:

> *If people only spoke when they had something to say, the human race would soon lose the power of speech.*

RULE ONE: *Small talk conjures intimacy*

Anthropologists liken small talk to grooming among primates, largely because it stimulates the snug sense of belonging that makes socializing a joy. Likewise, some academics stick it in a narrow box marked 'phatic' speech; those remarks meaningful less for what they say than what they signal. For instance, idle comments about weather are 'phatic' because their meaning isn't the information they contain – anyone can see it's a lovely day – so much as what they signal about the speakers' relationship: emphatically, you're on friendly terms.

This view minimizes small talk's multifangled role as conversation's warm-up act. Robert Louis Stevenson explained:

A good talk is not to be had for the asking. Humours must first be accorded in a kind of overture or prologue.

Not only does small talk enable the big by scouting topics, but it sets conversation's tone, pace and rhythm; scanning sensibilities, locking on to affinities, massaging minds and goodwill. All of which makes it a virtuoso instrument of social orchestration. What's not to like?

First, we do it most among strangers. Second, it can feel pointless. (The softer the topic, the harder the sell.) Third, it is bitty, quickfire, demanding disproportionate amounts of energy, rather like badminton, and pressure to perform may be cramping. (Who enjoys sparkling to order?) Fourth, as we send out grappling hooks, we expose ourselves, and if our offers are rejected we feel rejected. It's a striptease-cum-beauty contest.

This is why even Lady Florence Bell – a tireless Edwardian promoter of conversation, who launched Winter Gardens for the poor to congregate in on dark, lonely nights, away from the demon drink, and who was so far from shy that, by her daughter's account, she treated life as a play with 'herself . . . the leading personage in the drama' – even she so loathed small talk, so yearned for set phrases to stand in for it, like the pre-ordained pieties that nuns 'are obliged to say' if paths crossed at the convent, that she wrote a ridiculous book of them, *Conversational Openings and Endings.*

Wrong, wrong, wrong. The honour of small talk lies in paying others the compliment that they're worth talking to; the power in sparking the everyday magic of intimacy. Hell when it fails, it is eminently worth doing well, as the intimidated financial company directors understood.

The Rise of Small Talk

While most Anglo-Saxons joke about mothers-in-law, native Australians have 'mother-in-law' tongues, with dedicated vocabularies for use on taboo females. But such impressive verbal voodoo is fading along with other formal and deferential modes.

People are different, and it's daft to treat everyone the same, as did Sir Walter Raleigh's half-brother Dr Gilbert, 'a Man of excellent naturall Parts' who 'cared not what he said to man or woman of what quality soever', winning himself the accolade of sixteenth-century Britain's 'Greatest Buffoon in the Nation'. Yet growing numbers of us opt for the buffoon stance. Psychologist Steven Pinker observed:

> *Younger Americans try to maintain lower levels of social distance . . . I know many gifted prose stylists my age whose one-on-one speech is peppered with sort of and you know, their attempt to avoid affecting the stance of the expert.*

It's not just to be cool; in multicultural settings, hooked up through global commerce, or at international conferences such as the esteemed Pinker attends, user-friendly, low-key lingo translates more readily. But artful small talk is defter at making friends than what Chesterfield belittled as 'sort of chit-chat'. Or any other, kind of, like, you know, verbal padding.

RULE TWO: *Small talk is the social compass*
Rather than assume intimacy through blunt language small talk creates it, by pumping out friendly vibes and establishing connections between speakers who meet as equals. (Something of

a cultural novelty, born in the assembly rooms Chesterfield patronized, which may explain historic disdain for small talk as an upstart tradition that forced men to listen to – *ugh* – women.)

Its added bonus is the firing neurons and fizzing hormones that come of light stimulation – all of which enhance adaptability, indispensable to social survival in fast-moving, pseudo-egalitarian society, where talent for whisking up intimacy creates leaders among supposed equals. For instance, in ordering staff to 'call me Tony', ex-Prime Minister Blair astutely claimed friendship's privilege without conceding authority, making it harder to challenge him. Well, do you fight a mate?

The social instinct that made Blair an alpha operator is hardwired in us primates. Science writer Matt Ridley noted, before resigning as chairman of troubled building society Northern Rock:

> *The top male chimpanzee in a troop is not necessarily the strongest; instead, it is usually the one best at manipulating social coalitions to his advantage.*

We all must build coalitions, but as Ridley's fate testifies, this is an increasingly unwieldy task. Count the masks we wear, assigned by us, society, other people's perceptions . . . Shifting between roles, projecting different faces, is stressful (tellingly, the financial company directors hated *combining* small talk and business).

Humans are territorial animals. Exposure threatens us. Understandably, we feel the lack of a social compass. For sure, I dread what Philip Larkin called, explaining his refusal to be Poet Laureate, 'pretending to be me'. But to fear small talk is to miss its opportunity. It is the social compass, and with it we escape self-consciousness.

Disabling Shyness

Would you believe a professional performer finds small talk especially daunting? Ask Judy Finnigan, the chat-show presenter whose warmth makes her a friend to viewers:

> *The idea of conversation with strangers fills me with horror. When I'm with friends I'm totally relaxed, but with other people . . . I just don't like the whole small-talk thing. I even hate going to premieres now. I know that sounds ridiculously spoiled, but there it is.*

But her trepidation is reasonable. Famous people suffer the vast disadvantage that strangers imagine they know them intimately, which makes the task of building intimacy rather lopsided, and instant niceness the order of the day. Nonetheless, even for non-celebrities, who before entering a pub endure, like Kitty in *Anna Karenina*, 'a young man's feelings before a battle', and who bow down in thanks before the DJs waging war on conversation everywhere – including my hairdresser's, where it's being drummed out by the unstoppable march of techno – what makes small talk a tall order is performance pressure.

RULE THREE: *The more engaged we are, the less nervous we feel*

Research has found that with a serious topic and a good friend, we measure a conversation's success by how enthralled we were by what the other person said. Whereas the less familiar the other person, the more trivial the topic, the likelier we are to rate the experience by our own performance. An exception is between long-term romantic partners, when neither a topic's gravity nor either party's performance appears to effect post-conversational satisfaction – the negative interpretation being that they've stopped listening; the rose-tinted that they're so at one, the relationship is one unending symphony of sensitively cadenced talk. You decide.

Setting love-birds aside, it seems that if we're not invested in the subject of a discussion, or who it's with, we're self-conscious. Therefore the shortest path to bearable small talk must be to make it more involving – that is, to value it. Emotion inhibits this. However, harnessed by small talk, emotion is also the solution.

RULE FOUR: *Convert fear to imagination*

Philip Larkin's friend, novelist Kingsley Amis, suggested that human history is the tale of man, an animal, striving to forget he is an animal. Emotion exists to remind us of the truth. Embarrassment is the nephew of an ancient monster, fear. In bad cases we long for the earth to open and welcome us back, like the worms we were before life grew so complicated.

As anxiety prowls for evidence you'd be better off inside a large paper bag, nervousness ensures these fears come true, every time. Although such feelings are common with strangers, small talk is a correle, not – as many small-talk haters assume – the cause. The true horror arises from self-consciousness: the feeling you're on show, which paradoxically scuppers self-awareness, muffling your sense of the topic in hand, and, worse, sensitivity to interlocutors.

But fear is merely dyspeptic imagination. Set it to work on

thinking about the other person, remembering that he, if a stranger, is at an equal disadvantage, and embrace the opening courtesies (equivalent to those nosy things dogs do sniffing each other out) as an opportunity to express your feelings. Unless, that is, they resemble those of the man who crushed an old friend of mine. They were on a train, heading to an academic conference, sharing pleasantries and peanuts. Then, having inhaled the nuts, the other man picked up his book (almost certainly by Schopenhauer) and handed my friend the empty packet, saying, 'This is all our conversation is. Exchanging rubbish.'

The Principles

All relationships serve self-interest, including the laughs and tears we share with friends. Cynical? Hardly. This is what makes them meaningful. Similarly, conversation thrives if it is purposeful, so let artful small talk do the reconnaissance, delineating common territory and seeking a mutually agreeable direction in which to amble. Very often its point is no fancier than to find the point in talking to someone.

Not always easy. But as anyone fond of pubs or beauty parlours knows, chat need say little to be pleasant. Whatever the context, old friends or new, it is best if speakers respect five principles:

Put others at ease
Put yourself at ease
Weave in all parties
Establish shared interests
Actively pursue your own

These combine into the following strategy:

RULE FIVE: *Approach small talk like a treasure hunt*
Tools are:

> Elicitors: open questions, e.g. 'Have you come far?'
> (a House of Windsor special)
> Neutral topics
> Observations on your environment
> Ice-breakers: humorous questions and remarks
> Suggestions
> Enthusiasm

The most productive spirit is pioneering: sincere, curious, light, humorous. Radiate pleasure and non-Schopenhauer fans usually take it personally, opening like flowers in the sun. The only trouble with enthusiasm, as the wrung-out wife of an ebullient acquaintance confided, is you can drown in it. So if in doubt, leave it out.

RULE SIX: *Start in neutral*
Ladies and gentlemen once kept commonplace books, magpie hoards containing scraps of literature, historical facts, bons mots – any bauble that snagged the owner's fancy – that were consulted and memorized before engagements, lest opportunity arose to flourish them and impress the company.

Dare you disturb the universe with a tag from Ovid? Alas, today it's dangerous to presume shared knowledge or values, let alone puff your plumage. Better to think, as you approach that door, what is in the news, fashion, cultural affairs – whatever piques you. Try to combine elements in surprising ways.

('I was thinking of entering this outfit for the Eurovision Song Contest'; 'I see you're wearing Manchester United's colours.') Ideally, frame them to cascade clues about the other person. I wouldn't dream of suggesting you copy actress Imogen Stubbs and invent something:

> The Time I Died, *I think we called it – and tested it out at a pretentious party. The collective response? 'Oh, God, yes, so moving. I loved that book . . .'*

No, no, much nicer to mine uncontroversial territory. Keep it light: an observation, question, a thread to weave to something new. And revelations are out. I've never forgotten my first goring by an ex-boyfriend's horn-hided ex-belle: 'Did he tell you about the abortion?' Or my own clunker to an ex-colleague – standard issue, but still toe-crushing, and pointless – 'Any more children?'

If the answer's no, he doesn't want to say why.

Acts of Provocation

Some approaches ask for trouble – which might be just the thing to pep up talk. Compare 'I'm not sure about the coffee here,' with 'This latte's like breastmilk.' Between prejudice and opinion lie discussion and disagreement. But easy does it. Beware:

Generalizations: Can appear pompous, shutting off discussion.

Personal remarks: There's no accounting for neurosis. For example, 'I hate being told I look well,' confided a radiant beauty. 'It means I'm fat.'

Unsolicited advice: A charming fellow restaurant diner once told me, 'Order the fruit: it'll do your skin good.'

Health, wealth, creed: If you must know, there are other ways to find out.

Boasting: Let them see how marvellous you are.

Moaning: Need I explain?

Bitching: A hostage to fortune. Do you know them well enough to trust?

Teasing: Do they share your sense of humour?

Too much information: Enough said?

Unwarranted sympathy: Who wants to feel pitied?

Telling a woman where she got her dress: Obscurely insulting, and a form of boast.

'What do you do?' We've all asked, but who enjoys reheating their CV? If he loves his work, you'll hear soon enough. And you don't want to come over as a status sifter or salary sniffer.

If on the receiving end of this question and feeling puckish, why not take this ex-escort's advice: 'I say I'm a brain surgeon and see how they react.' Or copy ad director Vick Beasley and print bogus business cards (hers read 'BDI' for 'Beasley Detective Investigations': extra credit went to those who detected the pun).

Be prepared or toads shall hop forth from thy mouth. Like my unlucky friend who fell mute, to hide the effects of goldfish-bowl chargers of wine served by her boyfriend's intimidating older friends. But the soignée hostess wasn't having any of it and kept asking about her legal course. Somehow my friend spoke: 'Don't worry your pretty head about it.'

The shame outlived the hangover.

RULE SEVEN: *Find an incentive for talking*

What do you want to talk about?

To save time and tedium, seek what your fellow talkers would like. With antennae tuned, you can find common ground fast, then dig in. Trail topic bait, pouncing on subjects that light them up. Just one word – 'sport' – is a personality biopsy; gouts of useful information usually spurt forth. Or, if in season, mention Oscars: either they won't care, or they'll discuss films, gowns, or whoever's blubbing acceptance speech. *Voilà* your conversation's direction: another topic, culture, conspicuous consumption, or the grisly trade in emotica.

Watching faces also stems catastrophe. (I still picture my dumbstruck Anglo-Indian friend, Anil, at a barbecue, as evening darked to night, and I happened upon him cornered by a beery Blimp, who it transpired had been calling him 'O'Neill' and descanting on how Albion was awash with foreigners.)

Floundering? Then fabricate an incentive. Generous small talk automatically has a point, not least for you: Jonathan Haidt, author of *The Happiness Hypothesis*, found 'kindness and gratitude activities' the most enduring of mood improvers. I know a hotel publicist who finds the perpetual obligation to chat to strangers occasionally stifling. She wards off insincerity by finding ways to help: a restaurant tip, gallery to visit. This tactic works both ways, since being asked advice is flattering. Maybe they know a good butcher, book? A gift for a glum aunt? Specific enquiries reap detailed answers – richer small-talk material.

RULE EIGHT: *Tickle boundaries*

Discussion should enlarge by exploratory increments. Pace matters. Too neutral, too long and you'll both transmit beige personalities, but accelerate to war's evils right away and her son will be a brigadier. Instead, use discreet hints to flush the other person out.

If in doubt, the stair to intimacy has four steps:

Courtesies (Hello, how are you?)
Trade information (So what brought you here?)
Trade opinion (Isn't this music unusual?)
Trade feeling (Yup, I hate it.)

Pose questions that circle the personal, noting whether the other prefers a sharp or gentle approach, and adapting accordingly. And although small talk aims to please, don't make this too obvious. Unlike journalist Piers Morgan who, in uncharacteristically beseeching mood, asked Diana, Princess of Wales what it was like, 'being Diana':

'Oh God, let's face it, even I have had enough of Diana now – and I am Diana.'

Helpful of her to point that out.

It could have been worse: she could have said, 'So . . .' This tends to rear up then gently die after the preliminary flurry when basic parameters are established (who you are, why you're here). For such moments, we have ice-breakers. The best are funny. Such as the occasion Diana's alleged *bête noire* prince

Philip went to dine with the Governor of Agadir, and the British delegation was alarmed to see no cutlery. Not that this was unusual in Morocco, but nor was the Prince known for his sensitivity to foreign ways. Yet into the couscous plunged his fingers. 'Don't you find,' he said, 'eating with a knife and fork is like making love through an interpreter?'

RULE NINE: *Build talk up to scale*

Turn observations into discussion points by tagging on a question. For example, 'It's a beautiful evening, *isn't it?*'; or, 'I can hardly keep up, there are so many great American novelists/ new restaurants/ways to lose money these days, *aren't there?*' The implied compliment to listeners is that you value their opinion.

More provocative opinions can be smuggled in, potential offence cushioned by the note of query. But watch your tone: agreement-seeking can be discreet bullying. Or worse, in the case of the acrid yoga instructor who strode up to my friend, in the process of executing a perfectly humble down dog, and said: 'Have you ever been to a yoga class before, because this is an advanced class, isn't it?'

Just as hazarding a topic you've no passion for is unwise – without an opinion it's a dead-end – so you should aim to raise a subject with a follow-up comment or question in mind. Had I prepared one for Jeremy Irons, I could have averted full-body blush. Had I been less self-conscious, I might have seen what we already had in common: the place. If only I'd asked him about the exhibition. If, if, if . . .

The Algebra of a Follow-up: an Exercise

This is a topic-creation scheme. Instead of dollops of heavy material, information should be drip-fed. Try combining these ingredients:

A Situation – where you are; what people have been talking about
B The other person/people
C What you would like to know

Bald statements are hard to respond to (hence those fond of them seem pompous). Instead, fuse observations with questions that invite more than yes or no.

For example, at a welly-wanging contest held in Scotland by your pal Seamus:

$$A + B + C =$$ 'This is my first welly-wanging contest. You look pretty handy, Seamus. What is the best way to hurl a Wellington boot?'

$$A + (CB) =$$ 'These wellies are light but not very aerodynamic. How are yours?'

$$(AB) + (BC) =$$ 'Much as I love Seamus's welly-wanging contest, rowing across the loch gets harder every year. Have you come far, Jeremy?'

$$(ABC) =$$ 'What film other than *Welly-Wanging* should I bet on winning an Oscar?'

RULE TEN: *Be optimistic*

Worried something isn't worth saying? Heed the anonymous author of 1673's *Art of Complaisance*:

Small Talk, Big Deal?

The readiest way to become agreeable in any Conversation, is to banish all distrust, and to be confident that we are already so.

And what makes anything interesting? Well, how do you know a poem is a poem? Because it's marooned in white. Two things make its words art: the mind that selected them, and readers' faith that the choice was meaningful. And if you want to hold something up for consideration, it is already interesting: it interests you.

No idea why it attracts your attention? Mention it anyway; someone else might have a clue. With an open mind, you might learn something new about you. And try to extend the courtesy. If 'So. . .' is small talk's hardest word, nastiest is 'No'. As James Joyce found, meeting fellow belletrist Marcel Proust:

Our talk consisted solely of the word 'No' . . . Proust asked me if I knew the duc de so-and-so. I said, 'No'. Our hostess asked Proust if he had read such and such a piece of Ulysses. *Proust said, 'No'.*

Conversation hinges on reciprocity. You may sing like a nightingale on the dullest of subjects, but eloquence is no use, no matter that you're Joan of Arc or Joan Rivers, if nobody can answer you. If you speak, and I don't, a contract is broken. However, it isn't necessary to match word for word, revelation for revelation; the trade is emotional, not informational. What matters is to hear the invitation in what someone says: to speak, or to listen.

Typology of Bores, Chores and other Conversational Beasts

DEMOLITION BALL   *Pendulor blockheadibus*

Demolition Ball will let you get a word in edgeways. But don't mistake these interludes for him listening. In the lags between tirades, you can almost hear the groan of mental machinery as he swings back, preparing for the next attack.

Whatever you say, however you say it, DB will find something objectionable. Whether or not it is what you actually said. Why let facts stand in the way of a good argument?

His enthusiasms are little easier to take than his hates. Positive, negative, every opinion is delivered with such ferocity that people appear always to agree. It's easier.

The unfortunate by-product of rolling over to DB is that it appears to confirm he is right in all he says. This is particularly harmful since DB's operatic ego is in fact host to a tragic character, an aged toddler, still reeling at the discovery that he is not, as Ma and Pa suggested, the font of the world's hopes, dreams or wisdom. So the older he gets, the higher disappointment mounts, and DB punches out with ever greater force.

Tactics: Facing a monster it's tempting to play dead. But do as Perseus did to the gorgon Medusa: hold up a mirror to turn him to stone. It is because DB can't master his emotions that he messes with other people's. So step back, calmly identify contradictions in his arguments, and watch him writhe.

Can't be bothered? Then treat him like a tot: laugh or hug the helpless critter.

Pluses: In a Whatever world, DB's conviction that some things need saying, sense and sensitivity be damned, is rare. Consider him a whetstone to sharpen your wits.

3

Pay Heed

On the Acrobatics of Attention

When Marilyn Monroe married Arthur Miller, obtuse observers were confounded: what could an intellectual possibly have to say to a helium-headed bombshell?

But if Laurence Olivier is to be trusted, Monroe, not Miller, got the fuzzy end of the lollipop. He wrote to Noël Coward from the set of *The Prince and the Showgirl*:

> *The blond bottom looks and appears to be very good indeed . . .*
> *Arthur talks a great deal better than he listens, but I never found*
> *his talk very entertaining.*

Of all deterrents to conversation, most off-putting is the notion that great conversationalists are great talkers. Luckily, it's wrong. Conversation is two-way, three-way, as many ways as there are people. And however entertaining a night with Oscar Wilde might have been, compared to Arthur Miller, it would have been as spectacle, preferably at a distance, or you'd have risked supplying the warp for his wit.

Talk has hogged the limelight in part because listening lacks glamour. Politeness ordains it a duty, which has been mistaken for a measure of conversational power, with listeners the weaker vessel, to be filled by speakers' potent spirit. So thought society Rottweiler, la duchesse du Maine, daughter-in-law to Louis XIV:

> *I adore life in society: everyone listens to me, and I listen to no one.*

Unsurprisingly, her fashionable reign was brief.

RULE ONE: *Great conversationalists listen more than talk*

Surely the main reason listening is overlooked is that its masters deflect attention and cast it flatteringly elsewhere. Nonetheless, unlike madame la duchesse, the great French *salonnières* – who did so much, as historian Benedetta Craveri remarked, to make conversation 'a game for shared pleasure' – placed 'talent for listening' above speech, rating the brilliance of in-house wits according to the polish of their *politesse*.

Well, of course: if nothing else, drawing out other people is canny social politics. Stefano Guazzo, author of *Civile Conversation*, advised:

> *Keepe the mouth more shut, and the ears more open . . . In companie [ye] shall get the good will and favour of others, as well by giving eare courteously, as by speaking pleasantly. For wee think, they thinke wel of us, which are attentive to our talke.*

It can be the path to power. Witness the career of eighteenth-century courtesan Elizabeth Armitstead, who began in brothels yet bagged a top politician hubby, slinking into polite society by the grace less of her 'arts of display and seduction', than being a 'sympathetic listener', able to 'make every man believe himself the centre of the universe'.

And for any misguided person who imagines this is just for girls, another lady (opinion is divided as to whether she was Winston Churchill's mother or Queen Victoria's granddaughter) captured the difference between captivating talkers and heart-stealing listeners in two Prime Ministers:

When I left the dining room after sitting next to Mr Gladstone, I thought he was the cleverest man in England. But after sitting next to Mr Disraeli, I thought I was the cleverest woman in England.

Who would you prefer? In short, stuff duty. Far from talk's demure shadow, listening is its creative partner, able to shape conversation, forestall faux pas, forge connections, direct discussion, reap information and joy.

See how easily Dolly Parton bewitched this middle-aged magazine interviewer:

She totally focuses on me: how many female superstars could I say that about?

Or was it Parton's opening gambit that won her over?

I saw you in the corridor and I thought, 'Who is that attractive young woman?'

Actually, both.

Great listeners are irresistible because they sense what we want to hear. Soothing noises are part of their art. At its heart lie techniques to seduce purses, votes and minds.

The Rise and Fall of the Ear

Ears aren't just acoustic channels or pincushions for fashion statements. Their use and abuse as symbols throughout history tell a tale of social change. Where once power lay with gods, kings and armies, whom ordinary mortals had to placate, in our rackety world, with the assiduous propitiations of advertisers and other media, everyone seems to be grabbing of our attention, and we seem to listen less and less.

Ancient Egyptians exalted the aural organ to combat deities' and monarchs' indifference. Statues of pharaohs had jumbo flaps to display – and doubtless encourage – their willingness to heed the people. In hieroglyphics, the ear represented divine hearing, and worshippers left votive ear sculptures at temples to implore the gods to lend them theirs. Hear the wishful thinking in this 3,000-year-old hymn (etched with forty-four ears) to the god Ptah: 'lord of Truth, great of strength, the Hearer'.

Christ's final miracle before crucifixion was to replace the ear of the high priest's servant, Malchus, after the enraged disciple Peter struck it off: an act of forgiveness that serves as an emblem of Christ's openness to hear the prayers of all.

More sinister iconography adorns the Rainbow portrait of Elizabeth I, a branding exercise that depicts the childless monarch as divinely youthful (aged sixty-seven) and all-seeing, in a cloak spangled with ears and eyes; a baldly coded warning to any subject minded to foment dissent at a time when the succession remained uncertain. No wonder, condemned after a disastrous colonial exploit, Elizabeth's erstwhile pet Sir Walter Ralegh instructed his son:

Publicke affaires are rockes, private conversacions are whirlepooles and quickesandes. It is alike perilous to doe well and to doe ill.

(Likewise, the Queen's motto was the repressive '*Video et Taceo*' – 'I see all and say nothing.' Never mind that she rejoiced in conversation, in several languages at once when ambassadors came calling.)

Rather gorier propaganda took place in Japan in 1597, with the erection of the Mimizuka or 'Mound of Ears' outside Kyoto. This grim shrine contains ears and noses of up to 40,000 Korean victims of over-lord Toyotomi Hideyoshi's territory grabs into Korea and China (1592–8), an obfuscation that couldn't mask his ventures' ultimate failure.

Martial madness turned silly in 1739 when Spain and Britain began what the latter dubbed the War of Jenkins's Ear, named for a British captive who lost his to a Spanish privateer's blade in 1731. It was handed back with the words, allegedly, 'Take this to your king and tell him if he were here I would do the same to him.' Instead, seven years later, Jenkins flourished the wizened item before Parliament, demanding retribution, and the war raged for nine wretched years. But this noble revenge story masked the war's somewhat ignoble origin in a squabble over Florida colonies.

In the last century, the ear became a source of horror, figuring disconnection and alienation – whether in the lobe that crazed Vincent Van Gogh lopped off as a love-token, in the severed ear that besoils a white-picket-fence world in the film *Blue Velvet*, or the one sliced off a cop taken hostage in *Reservoir Dogs*.

The Dynamism of Listening

As art forms go, listening is a real Cinderella, little studied, scarcely taught. Yet there is no doubt it activates intelligence: infants snatch up words, with a vocabulary of up to 5,000 by their fourth year, largely spoken grammatically, whereas deaf children unschooled in sign language or lip-reading are severely mentally impaired. Are these dynamic skills, found in no other species, acquired simply by hanging around?

Not a chance. The opposite of passive, listening is an activity and it wires the minds of those of us who are lucky enough to be wired for sound.

RULE TWO: *Listening is the mother of relating*

Feedback is neither silent, nor invisible. It precedes talk and is first evoked by babytalk, what speech professionals call motherese. Although babytalk may sound like nonsense, it is instinctive and universal. Studies have found even premature infants automatically play goo-goo games with parents, and by four months they chime in to nursery rhymes, and, giggling, will mess with the beat – in effect, cracking musical jokes. Parents are no less programmed than their sprogs; as a child develops, babytalk unfolds in remarkably similar patterns across the globe, whatever the glottal idiosyncrasies of the parents' mother tongue.

In essence, it's a foundation course in the wind instrument, the voice, which is far and away the most complex sound system we can hear in nature. When the adult voice lifts and dips, roaming around inside and elongating vowels (consonants, the percussion section, are taught later), the exaggerations of pitch and tone sculpt points for the infant's untrained auditory cortex to seize hold of, educating it in how to differentiate sounds, and later words, from the voicestream.

The importance of babytalk to malleable young minds is evident in the case of so-called wild children, who, having grown up without human contact for the first several years of their lives, never learn to speak. But more than language, when the infant gurgles back to the parent, the two are duetting. Such musical companionship informs and enriches intellectually and emotionally, grounding babies in taking turns and timing: the key to social harmony.

By contrast, if babies are understimulated, they suffer. Depressed mothers' infants, who tend to experience lower pitched, less frequent vocalizations, are relatively flat, and clumsier at joining in, taking turns – negative feedback that gives their mothers less to grab on to, weakening the parental bond further. It would be wrong to accuse the poor mums of passing depression on. Rather, insufficiently turned on to the world, their babies struggle to gauge feelings or express their own.

Attention-deficit disorder, formerly known as annoying brat syndrome, is a clumsy term for a pervasive social blight: bad listening. I don't just mean those trying, shouty kids, who hear nothing at the word 'No' but an instruction to turn up the volume. However, they're a poignant illustration of what becomes of people who don't acquire, for whatever reason, the raft of facilities that we compact under the term 'listening', skills that children saw more of in less distracted times, but which are today increasingly scarce, whether in classrooms, pubs, clubs, or at dinner parties.

Can we improve?

You might think, Why try? Are we not doomed, set from the crib to our happy or unhappy parents' wavelength? Indeed, because we learn to listen before we speak, analysing it feels odd. But it isn't impossible, and it's worth it. Throughout life, listening makes us articulate, creating knowledge, attuning us to others' rhythm, helping us feel good. Like every aspect of conversation, it can be done better. Or worse.

In theory, it consists of two skills:

Projection – displaying listening
Detection – interpreting meaning and sentiment

In practice, detection breaks down to six tasks:

Hearing messages
Understanding
Remembering
Interpreting
Evaluating
Responding

But six is too modest a number. Words' melody maps the emotional curve of meaning, and as those who suffer from autism find, without sentimental equipment – what Jane Austen termed sensibility – following conversation is tough. So nimble listeners leaf through a *millefeuille* of different messages: not only assessing context and sense, but gleaning speakers' motivation, personality, agenda, mood, indigestion, sobriety . . .

That is, listening is harder than reading runes. Yet, by adulthood, most individuals' interpretative software is such that a study of people listening to football results found

as soon as the name of the second team is read out, you know straight away what the result is [win/lose/draw], even though you haven't heard the score yet.

In another, from recordings of 'forty seconds of surgeon–patient consultations' in which words had been wiped, leaving only tone, listeners could deduce which surgeons had been sued for malpractice. Surprise, surprise, they were the ones who sounded overbearing, not sympathetic. The moral of the story is that listening binds people to us.

RULE THREE: *Listening is the mother of invention: we make it up as we go along*

Although we might imagine we hang off a person's every word, this is a trick of our con-artist minds.

Three factors make listening creative, setting aside the not inconsiderable matter of weighing up the myriad meanings in every utterance. First, memory forms, as Plato observed, on a warm wax slab. Most messages self-destruct within half a minute, conversation following a thirty-second short-term memory track, which is built and dismantled as fast as its engine moves. So we lose thread, as actress Ronnie Ancona apologized for a tangent: 'My train of thought fell into my stream of consciousness.'

Second, listening is selective: we zone in on a voice, even if others in the vicinity are louder, in what linquists dub the 'cocktail-party effect'. Third, however much we might wish to, we can't hear everything. Expert Jean Aitchison explained:

> [*If we*] *assume an average of four sounds per English word, and a speed of five words a second, we are expecting the ear and brain to cope with around twenty sounds a second. But humans cannot process this number of signals in that time.*

Like inattentive yet imaginative secretaries taking dictation, our Houdini brains don't absorb every unit of each word but surf sound, improvising, glossing and predicting. Such feats show how listening elasticates our minds, springing us to conclusions with a gymnast's grace. Is it any wonder occasionally we slip, detecting words on the tip of another's tongue, and bite back before they have spoken?

RULE FOUR: *We're boundless adepts at piecing sense from nonsense*

Listening, like housework, is observed more in the neglect than the performance.

While no great treaty could have taken effect without arduous hours of ear industry, history's annals yield largely negative examples. If Henry II and legend are to be believed, four daft knights misconstrued a rhetorical question, 'Who will rid me of this troublesome priest?' for orders to dash off and dash off Thomas à Becket.

Critic Kenneth Tynan built a theory of Tom Stoppard's plays on one odd remark: 'I am a human nothing.' (Stoppard had said: 'I am assuming nothing.') John Mortimer found Kingsley Amis's revelation 'I hit my son with a hammer' almost as suggestive. Alas, no Oedipal tale, it was not novelist Martin, but Amis Senior's thumb that was black and blue.

These accidents happen because when we listen we iron out confusion with extraordinary, sometimes alarming efficiency, as was demonstrated in a 1967 'alternative psychotherapy' experiment. Subjects – college students – asked questions, receiving yes or no answers from a therapist in another room. Except there was no therapist: the experimenters had decided what responses would be given in advance, pre-preparing random sequences of yes and no. As a consequence, one guinea pig was advised first 'no' then 'yes' to stick with his girlfriend. However, although *he expressed surprise at the 'yes', responding that he had expected a 'no' [he] then looked for the pattern that made this [contradiction] intelligible. Students commented that the answers had a lot of meaning.*

Our ability to find patterns of meaning in the most arbitrary data is supreme, as was proved by similar tests, which created 'poems' from random lines in an anthology. Does such interpretive creativity destroy the notion of art? Not a bit. These experiments underscore that without interpreters, all meaning, all art, is air. In this sense every artwork is collaborative: a conversation between creator and viewer, writer and reader. (Suggesting that a monkey manacled to a typewriter for long enough could indeed type work attributable to Shakespeare – provided a human being in another room had even longer to explain why Shakespeare had written such tripe.)

And the improvised sense-jazz of conversation is surely the ultimate artistic collaboration. Excuse me if this sounds pseudy, but aren't you impressed how inventive we are?

RULE FIVE: *Signal attention to show you are happy to listen*

However, the rewards of listening aren't always obvious. Once I believed it a chore. Specifically, my first night at college, in the pub, sandwiched between two dry crystallographers for whom I served less as jam than bland conversational glue. I wondered whether, given limitless nods, smiles, and Really?s, I need ever speak again.

But I was being lazy, projecting satisfaction, instead of seeking an incentive to talk. And if attention is disengaged, what of communication? In a tart letter, Jane Austen mocked two women who 'spent their whole time in what they called *conversation*', yet

> *There was no interchange of opinion and not often any resemblance of subject, for Mrs Thorpe spoke continually of her children, and Mrs Allen of her gowns.*

Who enjoys the sensation that someone has lent you his ears, retaining his mind for his own, private use? However, very often this impression is unwarranted, because many who appear distracted are anything but.

How to Listen Actively: a Signaller's Guide

Strong listener reactions elicit livelier speech by projecting interest. Physical cues are: face the speaker, make eye contact, nod, smile, let emotions animate your face.

By way of experiment, fix an expectant gaze on a silent person in a group, as if they are about to say something fascinating. How long until they speak?

Take audible affirmative action too. Wow!, Really? and You didn't!, inane if insincere, are powerful used appropriately. 'Never interrupt', a cliché of conversational etiquette, should be ignored. Good interruptions aid the flow. Such as:

Supportive comments:	to encourage or evince sympathy, like ticks in the margin of your homework ('I so agree'; 'Exactly'; 'No!')
Overlaps:	when thoughts run gaily together
Summaries:	to clarify meaning, ensuring the right message is heard

Listening as Self-Expression and Repression

Signals are one thing. A responsive listener also shows, and knows when to veil his feelings. Or does he?

In the 1960s another experimenter, computer pioneer Joseph Weizenbaum, created Doctor, a software program that adapted a psychotherapy technique for bouncing back patients' statements as questions:

> User: *I have been rather depressed lately.*
> Computer: *Are you depressed often?*
> User: *Yes, almost all the time.*
> Computer: *Why do you say yes almost all the time?*
> User: *Right now I feel like I could cry.*
> Computer: *Is it because right now you feel like you could cry that you came to me?*

One morning he was appalled to discover his transfixed secretary at a computer, unspooling her sorrows into Doctor's clunky, copycat code.

I'm not shocked Weizenbaum was shocked (contrary as it seems, given this confirmed his program's success). Each of us swims in an amniotic consciousness, and we love, need, to feel understood, in order to dilute the solitude of our condition. So the thought that an echo is sufficient to convince us we're being listened to, that the bogus Doctor could seduce the secretary, carries the degrading suggestion that much of human complexity – those worries and wonders we store up and long to share – may also be illusory, empty, and that we are mere bundles of reactions, mysterious, and meaningful, only to us.

Such fears plague modern man, and to an extent explain the value vested in expert ear-givers – father-confessors, therapists – who restore faith in empathy as an art akin to shriving the soul. And whose friendship we needn't risk, troubles we needn't take on in return: a relationship dead-end, compared to fruitful exchanges with friends. Consolingly private, but pretty barren, this seems a perfect manifestation of the depressing direction conversation is taking.

RULE SIX: *Good listeners share a virtue: imaginative hospitality*
On the upside, Doctor's success indicates how accessible are the basic tools of empathy. Nonetheless, for meaningful understanding, imaginative engagement helps.

Its qualities have been quantified in an 'empathic communication coding system' designed to assess physicians' listening, which placed greater value on showing than telling. From best to worst:

Level	Type of listening
6	Shared feeling/experience
5	Confirmation of an emotion's legitimacy
4	Pursuit of the topic
3	Acknowledgement
2	Implicit recognition (but changing the topic)
1	Perfunctory recognition (autopilot)
0	Denial/contradiction

(I doubt this system advises British GPs to listen for a paltry average of three minutes before interrupting patients and telling them what is wrong.)

An open mind puts the censorious inner self on hold while

a speaker speaks. In theory. In practice, since listening is a process of selection and creation, with our inner voice providing a running commentary, mind clearance is difficult.

To improve, try to notice how you listen. Do you hear people out? Or are you, like me, so eager to show empathy that you're prone to talk over them?

And be aware of how you don't listen. Detecting the message in what someone says – the motive, goal – is guesswork of an eye-blink, which lends it the false, often deafening power of instinct or intuition. Ralph Waldo Emerson caught the difficulty:

> *What you are sounds so loudly in my ears that I can't hear what you say.*

In conversation, as music, it is easier to hear a false note than identify its source. Our minds are astonishingly able at judging, creating rules of thumb, prejudices. Holding back – not immediately attributing our irritation to the other person's character, but pausing to examine why we're annoyed – serves us better.

RULE SEVEN: *Trace the emotional line of expression*
Super-agent Mark McCormack urged aspiring tycoons:

> *Hear what people are really saying as opposed to what they are telling you.*

Likewise, actress Harriet Walter advised would-be Cleopatras wrestling with Shakespeare's verse to 'hear the need' in a character's speech – that is, find the emotional code to unlock its meaning.

Like arrows, words have impact through force and direction, but their point hits home only when listeners can account for where they are from and where they aim. And differences in conversational style add another 'direction' that can, if misunderstood, lead to personality clash. According to discourse analyst Deborah Tannen, a barrage of questions punctuated by finger-jabs is a friendly fumble to most New Yorkers; to a Californian, it is assault.

So reserve judgement, bearing in mind:

A speaker's native and personal style (his 'Omigod' may
   not be blasphemy to him)
How his words relate to the conversation so far
How his words relate to the agendas circling beneath
How emotions inflect what he says, and what you hear

And try to follow the emotional rollercoaster implied by tone and pitch, as well as posture, facial expression and gestures.

Sympathy Shutters: a Glossary

Thou shalt not give advice: the undeclared commandment of the Samaritans' helpline. Advice is a peerless strategy for not listening, and many words of seeming empathy are double-agents, closing down talk the speaker would rather not hear, or criticism cloaked in sympathy.

Here follow some false friends, which appear to hold out comfort but, like a cross brandished at a vampire, aim to drive others' woes away. In addition, some handy water-treaders that sound supportive without agreeing (ideal for tricky conversation).

The Art of Conversation

LINE	SUBTEXT
'Poor you!'	'Victim *again* – do we detect a pattern here?'
'You are in the wars!'	'Why do you keep picking fights?'
'Yes, when I did X. . .'	'Back to my favourite subject: me.'
'The same thing happened to Y. . .'	'You're not the only one with problems!'
'She didn't!'	'Stop exaggerating.'
'I can see why you felt that way.'	'Are you, perchance, being unreasonable?'
'If I were you, I would. . .'	'Thank heaven I'm not!'
'That's awful!'	'Enough already.'
'I understand.'	'And have for twenty minutes. Where's your fast-forward?'
'Why do you think he said that?'	'Look in the mirror, honey.'
'That must have been hard.'	'But note my use of the past tense: move on.'
'Next time. . .'	'New topic, please.'
'Can't be easy.'	'Hey, could be worse.'
'That's hilarious!'	'I don't get it.'

RULE EIGHT: *Hear the unstated*

Comic Joan Rivers says no to shrinks ('There goes my act').
Poet Rainer Maria Rilke was little more enamoured:

> *Something like a disinfected soul results from [psychoanalysis], a non-thing, a freakish form of life corrected in red ink like a page in a schoolboy's notebook.*

He was too suspicious. Responsible therapists tease out discontinuities and slip-ups in what patients tell them, not to smooth away quirks of personality, but to unearth tensions and conflicts, and break down hidden causes of pain – painful as this enzyme may be.

In any situation understanding is deepened if we listen out for insights lodged inside inconsistencies and non-sequiturs; telling details that can identify the knotty kernel of a misunderstanding from which problems have grown, or reveal interesting kinks in a mind's architecture.

For example, Elizabeth I shot down rumours of a dalliance, vehemently denying 'anything dishonourable', then spoilt it by adding, so what if she led a 'dishonourable life'? As queen she 'did not know anybody who could forbid her'. These statements coalesce the conflict she faced between being a woman, servant of chastity, and a monarch above men's laws – a conflict that, in a cooler temper, she strove to put on ice by assuming the sterile role of Virgin Queen.

On a practical level, when you hear a contradiction – say, the airline claims your flight's cancellation is not the same as bumping you off, therefore compensation isn't due – unpack it. Not only can this be therapeutic and forestall misconceptions, but you may cajole someone into revising his tune (for extra intimidation, write the explanation down, calmly checking spellings and punctuation – see 'How to Complain', p. 258).

Attend to speech patterns, too, as these are living autobiographies. If the new boyfriend gabs in unalloyed jargon, clichés or swear words, what does this say? If the prospective client talks down to you, how will he do business?

And heed omissions. What does the estate agent pass over in silence? If the car dealer keeps returning to the design, ask again how the machine moves.

Let Her Eat Cake

Philosopher J.L. Austin suggested statements have three dimensions: words' sense; the meaning implied by that sense; and the speaker's underlying aim. This idea suggests a recipe for X-ray listening.

Take a statement: 'Marie-Antoinette has eaten all the cakes.'

Now picture it as the message iced on a three-tiered cake: the top layer consists of the message's meaning (what the speaker is saying); the middle, an implied opinion tucked inside; and at bottom, the speaker's sly conversational purpose.

Icing: 'Marie-Antoinette has eaten all the cakes.'

Top: Greedy Marie-Antoinette looks fat.

Middle: Fat is not a good look.

Bottom: She makes me sick; I wish she made you sick too.

This prompts a final question, the plate: Why is this speaker making this statement?

The answer depends on your view of the context. In this case, I imagine my bony speaker addressing a boyfriend, who, his eyes lost in Marie-Antoinette's creamy cleavage, replies, 'Let her eat cake,' wishing she'd let him scoop up the crumbs.

RULE NINE: *Listen to construct the meaning you want to hear*
When the reluctant suitor Ziggy told fellow *Big Brother* contestant Chanelle that he wanted 'to finish this', she shot back, 'This conversation?'

It took him another week to dump her.

Her rat-trap response demonstrates how effectively replies can nail the meaning of a preceding sentence, whether or not this happens to be what a speaker intended. Similarly, paraphrases elucidate speakers' views, and may sneakily alter them, tossing them back, refashioned in so pleasing a style that others happily mistake them for their own – spinning conversation wherever you would go . . .

For this reason, La Fontaine compared a skilled conversationalist to 'the bee who gathers honey alike from every different flower'. He might have been describing Lord Rendel, politician friend to egotist Gladstone, who could

start a new trend of thought with the most innocent suggestion; some challenging remark, casually interposed . . . With the gentlest pressure on the rudder, he could give a turn to a conversation, confirm or moderate a trend of policy.

Effective listeners reach inside minds to place a hand on conversation's controls, an ability that helps avert the danger to every bearer of bad tidings: getting shot. Like business consultant Rick Huttner, who inoculates clients to unpalatable truths by building rapport, using listening and questions to train them to his way of thinking.

I respect all the input they give me. I listen for what they really want from their lives . . . [the job] is really listening, listening, listening and at the appropriate time adding something to the conversation, and then change happens.

Thus advice emerges as the product of a joint-thinking venture. Which, of course, it is.

So before saying something challenging, see if skilled mid-wifery can't persuade it out of the other person's mouth:

Listen
Wait to be sure a speaker is finished
Question
Summarize
Empathize
If you must, offer a different view

But you may get further saying nothing at all. Pop artist Andy Warhol might have been a big noise. Still, he understood listening's craftiness, according to singer Deborah Harry:

'He was a terrific listener, that was his genius really. He just sucked it all in, and made a point of never saying too much. That's a skill,' she says, and to prove the point, stops and smiles.

Not least of listening's virtues is that it reminds us to cherish silence.

Typology of Bores, Chores and other Conversational Beasts

THE APOLOGIST

Perfica Nervosa

She's so, so sorry. She's three minutes late. Her fault: the trains weren't working. She's always expecting them to be – silly her – that's probably why the drivers strike! Has she ruined the meal and everything? And dear me, she's only brought wine, chocs, flowers, no cheese. Sorry, they were clean out of Lafite '78, she had to settle for '75 – isn't it awful how old bottles' labels peel off, all that nasty dust. And it's such a pity the roses look as if their petals will drop off next week. If only she'd brought a nice bush . . .

While having her round for coffee is trying, steel yourself before tea at the Apologist's glossy-mag-proof home. As she wheels out the feast (only truffled unicorn; the phoenix got burned), pointing out asymmetrical holes in her home-fribbled fig foccacia, if you don't hug her, you'll club her.

Although bent on increasing others' happiness, the Apologist has much in common with her introvert sister, the Paranoid. That is to say, she is a mite selfish. In her relentless quest for perfection, she neither hears the pain her sonorous angst inflicts, nor senses that self-flagellation is inverted boasting, compelling others to give reassurances that, as a result, are never entirely sincere.

Tactics: If you care about the Apologist, don't be drawn into her sado-masochistic reward system: shut down the apology airspace to set her free. If she starts, laugh and change topic. Or say if you didn't know better you'd think she was fishing for compliments.

If you don't love her, the same tactics apply. Otherwise she'll drive you nuts.

Pluses: Maddening, yes, but the Apologist proves how hard it is to be nasty to someone who beats you to it (a useful ploy to remember when you're in trouble).

NOTE BENE

Sorry, but, the celebrity apologist: The public display of supplication has become an inevitable chapter in the narrative of any self-disrespecting twenty-first-century celebrity. A jolt of scandal, plus foaming boot-lick to the people that a waning star has let down (all potential exercise DVD/redemption-memoir purchasers) may offer a brief sequel in the public eye. But never confuse a good-hearted Apologist with this suppurating imposter, Sorry, But.

4

The Rest is Silence

On Not Speaking

Silence's advocates tend to be discreet. But unusually self-effacing journalist James Hughes-Onslow spoke out after someone complained that, for all his juicy insider knowledge, having him to dinner was like 'feeding a corpse'. He argued this was polite:

> *Any intervention of a merely factual nature would probably bring the conversation to a complete halt.*

Do you hold back? Despair of those who do? However lively your patter, however focused your charm, occasional air pockets in conversation are unavoidable. Whether they're golden, or deadly, is debatable. But then, the same is true of talk.

When Egypt's pharaoh sent Solon, founder of Athens' democracy, an animal to sacrifice, he took the chance to test the

Greek's famed wits. Would Solon kindly select which part of the beast he judged best, which worst, and send both back? By return, came a single item: the tongue.

If words may be misread, the trouble with silence is it's nothing if not ambivalent. Since it requires discipline, it has long reflected power, and been affiliated with both good and evil. While the Roman goddess Isis vanquished 'the lamentable silences of hell', to Quakers and Buddhists freedom from the word brings higher consciousness. However, these days the negative view is in the ascendant.

The noisier life becomes, the more technology and social isolation gnaw at face-to-face talk, the less conversational silence seems to be valued. Residents of febrile urban environments dread it far more than those reared in gentler, rural settings – as if the absence of speech were as threatening as a Pinter pause.

To me, rising hostility is slightly paradoxical: if we don't converse so much, you might think we'd feel easier with silence. But it also seems logical, as an extension of our declining prowess at reading conversational subtleties. Certainly, the bias is so entrenched that research finds hesitant speakers are routinely taken for doubtful characters: either mad, sad, shifty or – a telling contradiction, this – powerful. Meanwhile powerless pre-school tots are being diagnosed with 'selective mutism' (fear of speaking in social situations), a condition formerly known as shyness, that is dosed with Prozac.

There's bleak humour in busy parents contracting out responsibility for their offspring's social graces, like this father, flourishing a cheque at an analyst:

'Ask any price you want. My son doesn't talk. So do whatever you want as long as you make him talk, and then let's not talk about it any more.'

But when did speech cease to be a freedom and become compulsory? Is silence an illness? And what parent licenses strangers to 'do whatever you want'?

Whatever is going on, it is sick (if happy news to Pharm-Corps).

It is time to speak up for silence.

RULE ONE: *Confidence not talking increases confidence talking*

That those who fear silence also grasp its strength is clear from the popular belief that quiet people are arrogant, with some justice in the case of US President 'Silent' Cal Coolidge, whose disdain spayed many a conversation.

'How could they tell?' asked Dorothy Parker, on hearing he was dead, and it's thought that it was she who enlivened a dinner by saying she'd bet on getting more than two words out of him. His reply? 'You lose.'

But the prejudice is more often a projection of self-doubt, as when American *Vogue*'s Anna Wintour became a target to murderous ex-reporter Peter Braunstein:

There were many high-profile editors and God knows they had big egos . . . But Wintour? She just never talked to peons like us. It was beneath her.

Braunstein's inadequacies reflect a widespread (fortunately rarely homicidal) malaise. In individualist society, if self-promotion seems nigh on compulsory, those who don't play the game may seem above it all, and above us.

Hence a newspaper interviewer felt moved to note that Churchill's biographer, Martin Gilbert, was unafraid 'to leave long pauses as he mulls over a thought or searches for a precise word' – correctly implying that self-restraint and pedantry, handy traits in a historian, are eccentric nonetheless; signs of social deviance and awesome self-assurance.

Are silent people a danger to polite society? The uncon-fident ones are, according to research which finds that lonely people fear silence most, with anxiety about how to fill it, or seeming needy, compounding the problem by cramping their conversational style: too scared to ask questions, offer opin-ions, their introverted habits of speech pretty much guarantee more silence.

Perhaps the chief conversational threat of a quiet person, however, is that his sphinx-like bearing acts as a verbal laxative on those less able to keep their own counsel. Believe me, I know. A former boss was a clam. During one of his rare after-work outings, desperate to fill a void, I began riffing (I knew not why) on the unlikely, not to say barking, possibility that a business rival's bizarre taste in white, pointy loafers had con-tributed to his recent coronary.

Then I glanced down. What did I see on my boss's feet?

Yes, it's worth getting to grips with silence.

RULE TWO: *Silence is meaningful*

You may imagine that silence says nothing. In fact, in any spoken communication it plays a repertoire of roles. Just as, mathematically speaking, earth should be called sea, since most of the planet is covered in it, so conversation might be renamed silence, as it comprises 40 to 50 per cent of an average utterance, excluding pauses for others to talk and the enveloping silence of those paying attention (or not as the case may be).

Outside speech, silence serves as background, frame or cue to talk. (Like the white page around the words of a script, plus added capacity to give emphasis or tug the playwright's sleeve and beg further and better particulars, if anything's unclear.) And within speech, it can be a unit of communication or punctuation to pace, pattern and shade meaning.

Conversation gourmet La Rochefoucauld distinguished between the 'eloquent', the 'mocking' and the 'respectful' silence, as if there were clear-cut types. However, no silence is inherently good or bad. Yes, sometimes it expresses empathy and promotes good talk; others, confusion and distance. Then there are silences of power: as a shield, weapon, or to encourage others to speak. But silence never comes with a label attached, and ambiguity multiplies, since each instance is custom-made, we each have a personal dictionary for interpreting the unsaid, and while your pause may be devoid of intent – say, you're thinking or breathing – it always conveys a message if a listener interprets it as meaningful. All of which increases silence's potential to wound and confuse.

I remember the call from a friend.

'I'm pregnant,' she said.

The moment stretched.

'Silence,' she said, by way of prompt.

Rude as it seemed, my silence wasn't empty, but clamorous with questions. So I quickly said, 'Wow. Are you happy?' Then immediately wished I hadn't.

Rather than let silence get the better of you, appreciate the virtue in its flexibility: a communication tool that's as versatile as the queen in chess. Heed Benjamin Franklin:

> *As we must account for every idle word, so we must account for every idle silence.*

Which sounds onerous, but, on the contrary, you've everything to gain. Discreet conversational omissions can fuel thought, exercise tact, prompt laughter, drama, flush people out, and push prices up, or down, swifter than any fast-talk. Or as Aelfric Bata, tenth-century monk, teacher and midget (proudly signing work '*brevissimus monachus*') scolded novices:

> *It is stupidity to be so talkative and full of words. Chattering garrulity and garrulous chattering are hateful to God.*

RULE THREE: *Be a connoisseur of pauses*

Listen carefully and dumb silence tells you plenty – after all, the pause is for thought.

Two kinds occur in speech: for breath or hesitation. Only around one in twenty are the former, because respiration automatically slows when we talk. (Maybe the abbreviated monk Bata was right, chatterboxes really are dumber, their poor grey cells starved of oxygen.) Often these fall at grammatical breaks, where, in writing, would be punctuation.

Far more suggestive are hesitation pauses, which comprise between a third and half of ordinary speech, and can pop up anywhere in a sentence, grammar be damned. And, despite our popular mistrust of halting talkers, linguists judge hesitations as marks of 'superior' spontaneous speech; like fins breaking

the water's surface, they indicate thoughts snapping and circling as speakers plan ahead.

Whereas, for at least one disgruntled academic, smooth talk
betrays a phoney:

> *Either [speech] has been rehearsed beforehand, or the speaker is*
> *merely stringing together a number of standard phrases she*
> *habitually repeats, as when the mother of the 7-year-old who*
> *threw a stone through my window rattled off at top speed, 'I do*
> *apologize, he's never done anything like that before, I can't think*
> *what came over him, he's such a good quiet little boy usually, I'm*
> *quite flabbergasted.'*

So don't be down on gappy talkers. Rather than hedging, their
broken sentences may stake out high-grade truths.

Alternatively, they could be super-manipulators. Masters of
silence may be taken for master talkers – not always a mistake.
Infinitely foxy French statesman Talleyrand sat up at night,
polishing his epigrams. Then he

> *would often sit through a party without saying a word, but then*
> *suddenly come out with a sentence which people said was the sort*
> *they never forgot.*

Well-honed shafts of wit strike harder, resonate further, than
buckshot bons mots because listeners must give greater weight
to each word (as a cracking twig can convince the lone traveller
that a host of dangers lurk in the shadows).

Notice how speakers use controlled pauses, like stage managers, to prompt others to talk, to clarify meaning, to increase
drama or suspense. A pause may say, 'Wasn't that something!'
or 'Listen up!' Or draw attention to what a speaker isn't saying,

inviting listeners to fill in, as wicked Iago does throughout *Othello*, misleading the imaginative Moor. Or mark a channel hop, as a speaker brakes before – ahem – changing subject.

Frequently pauses are tacit invitations to others to speak. If unsure whether you're being asked to leap in, note turn-taking's three laws:

> If a speaker invites another to speak, he must stop and let the other start
>
> If nobody has been invited, anyone can speak next
>
> If nobody volunteers or has been selected, the speaker may go on (but is not obliged to)

RULE FOUR: *Use pauses creatively*

Investigation into music's physiological effects has found that listeners' pleasure and relaxation peaked, if that isn't a contradiction, not during slow movements but at junctures of silence in a melody, when tension breaks. This shows how subliminally manipulative silence may be, suggesting why the great waves of a rousing harangue of a speech, such as Hitler went in for, are so effective. How easily may entranced listeners mistake the rapture they experience in the interludes for a mark of the righteousness of the words?

But pauses are just as easily a force for good. Listen to how newsreaders' seesaw cadences help words slip down – even though in some respects their delivery is utterly unnatural. And while it's well known that listening to music impedes students' concentration, fewer of us are aware that silence enhances intelligence. A 1970s 'wait-time' study in American schools found that if teachers gave students just a few extra seconds to answer questions, their responses and engagement greatly improved, as did their year-end examination results. Equally, evaluation of psychotherapy has found that sessions in which least is said are most effective.

In part this is because the longer a pause lasts, the more meanings germinate in speculative minds; like the lull before a joke's punchline, it deepens reflection. Indeed, silence's spirit of incantation may be very sexy, cloaking the reticent speaker in mystery. Scantly interviewed icons, such as Greta Garbo or Kate Moss metabolize this to mystique, and women who gripe about male emotional inarticulacy persist in swooning over word-shy hunks, like *Pride and Prejudice*'s Mr Darcy, who seem impregnable to pressure to talk. Why say she looks good enough to eat with a spoon if you can say it in an indolent glance and let her imagination roam? Practise the seductive art of tailing off . . .

And see if you can't splice a few more breaks into your speech to underscore what you've just said, to build anticipation, swell significance, slow pace (useful in arguments) or grab attention – if only to free a moment to break off and meet listeners' eyes. Your words will weigh heavier, you'll seem more self-possessed, and others will listen closer.

RULE FIVE: *Silence pressurizes others to speak*
Alexander Pope dubbed silence the 'varnisher of fools, and cheat of all the wise!' Occasionally, it creates too positive an impression, as film executive Kate Philpot discovered when overstretch led to breakdown:

> *Too tired to speak in meetings, I would just smile and nod, hoping nobody would notice. Ironically, given the chance to talk*

uninterrupted, clients sang my praises and recommended me to others.

Her tragicomic predicament illustrates how effortlessly silence compels others to talk – a chance to gain information and insights, as well as speak volumes about your confidence. In power games, be aware of three tactical properties: as silencer, shield and negotiator.

For Sigmund Freud, rebuffing a bumptious writer, it was a blunt but effective instrument.

[Freud] made no answer and was not troubled by the silence this caused. It was a hard silence, a sort of weapon in his hand.

Use silence to kill. Asked a nasty question, pretend you didn't hear. Don't want to say why you're late? Don't, then. Not reacting also guards against unhelpful revelations, whereas hasty complaints provide recipes for how to wound further. And it overrides embarrassment, as a Frenchman found, watching eighteenth-century Londoners relieve themselves into chamber pots in, *horreur!*, the dining room, 'undisguisedly', and at 'no interruption of the conversation'. So if you balls up, shut up: talk will perforce move on.

Silence can sidestep commitment, signalling acceptance without an irretrievable yes, since tacit consent is always deniable. Instead of disagreeing, saying nothing keeps channels open, defusing potential confrontation. It also turns tables, forcing others to plead their case. (How weak Richard II seems in Shakespeare's play, for all his eloquence, before the quiet avenger and future king, Henry Bolingbroke.)

Maintain it as a smokescreen, forcing opponents to speculate on what you're thinking, hiding, planning . . . This may inflate their perception of your position. What is more, if they're ferreting around, wasting time, worrying, you've weakened them – so the illusion is eminently material. And always wait to respond to an offer: if they come back again, you know they're desperate. Even on the phone or face to face, hold back. The pressure to fill silence is so alluring that they might just improve it.

Remember what CJ, the merrily tyrannical boss in *The Fall and Rise of Reginald Perrin*, would say, as he kept underlings waiting outside his office?

One, two, three, four,
Make 'em sweat outside the door,
Five, six, seven, eight,
Always pays to make 'em wait,
Nine, ten, eleven, twelve,
COME!

RULE SIX: *Silence is a window of opportunity*

Of all silence's powers, perhaps greatest is the chance it gives you to mend a hole in conversation, winning everyone's gratitude. Or, if you prefer, to kick talk into touch and skedaddle. Either way, politeness requires that you revive talk first.

First diagnose the silence: is conversation dead, or has it skipped a beat? If so, why? Miscommunication? Too much information? An agenda better saved for another day? A faux pas?

Think hard. In my experience, offence can bud out of anything from scorning lemon-yellow cars, or calling a child 'little devil' (admittedly, it was a christening), to querying the name Kenton (her husband's).

Once you have identified the cause, smile, invoke a new topic or prepare to say goodbye.

And if ever in future silence troubles you, try to count the ways in which it is full. Welsh poet Dannie Abse recalled life with his late wife:

There are so many different qualities of silence: the breathless silence that follows a war explosion; the stony silence of a religious sanctuary. There is also the agreeable, comfortable silence of two people who love each other and who have lived together for years. I knew that silence.

Maybe, for a moment, words are unnecessary. Maybe something better has passed: something understood.

Typology of Bores, Chores and other Conversational Beasts

LIMPET   *Nugo*

Pendens

Limpet tries to blend in. He shows no sign of life. It isn't clear who invited him, or why. But as he clings to conversation, rock-like in silence, he stands out ever more.

Alternatively, garrulous Limpet sizzles with news you've already heard, stories that end well before their telling is told; impervious, indestructible, like a fossilized creature mysteriously reanimated. Oh yes, she says (and this explains everything), she's known the host an age. But thank heaven for Facebook. Otherwise, they'd have, like, totally lost touch!

To either species, grim or garrulous, time is an abstract notion. Limpet adheres like a useless limb, unbudgeable by hint or yawn, and drags at conversation until all others' spirits are limping.

Tactics: Show Limpet the kind of interest he must experience rarely – how else has he developed such a concrete coat of a personality? Perhaps a story lies behind the creation of the carapace. Ask questions, explore passions: you might prise off the shell to find a remarkable person.

Pluses: Limpet reminds us that anyone is boring if he outstays his welcome, and that diverting others is a duty – its neglect punishable by withdrawal of social security.

5

Fit Subjects

On Topics in Search of Good Homes

What do you want to talk about?

This can be a question of social life or death. One Hollywood producer feared for Victoria Beckham and her husband, the ageing footballer David, on moving to LA:

> *They're good-looking and rich, but I don't know where they're going to fit in . . . They don't really have anything anyone wants here. I mean, they're not going to be in movies. You're certainly not going to see them at Warren and Annette's for dinner, talking about politics. They're going to have to find an 'issue' if they want to be taken seriously: maybe something like breast cancer or the environment.*

A pet subject is the only passport to some circles. In less elevated settings, to be without a cause may not make you a rebel, but you had better have something to say.

You need a topic.

Timeless Measures for Tailoring Topics?

We think of topics as abstract nouns with capital letters – Love, War, God – but the terrain shifts with time and tide. A minefield once yawned between men and women, so much so that evil Queen Victoria strove to deter suitors for her youngest daughter (whom she wished to retain as a companion in old age) by expedient dullness. One man recalled:

> *Sitting next to a beautiful princess is a reward for bravery in fairy stories, but if the gallant man were popped down every night next to Princess Beatrice, he would soon cease to be brave. Not that she has nothing to say, for when the subject moves her, she has a torrent, but what with subjects tabooed, the subjects she knows nothing about, and the subjects she turns to the Queen upon, there is nothing left but the weather and silence.*

Still, rationing spurred ingenuity. A debutante snaffled Britain's richest duke with graceful disquisitions on 'ghosts and the royal family', honouring the double-edged ethos that gals should lead conversation, but never, ever come over as clever. My granny held that wherever she was, however grim the circs – and as a nurse in the Second World War, grim they often were – babies and the price of fish perked things up. But her modest topic store would not stretch far today.

Now information is wireless and free-range, no princess may be sequestered from it, however high her tower. And if Granny's generation could confidently assert do not discuss War, Politics, Money, Sex, God or Death, such iron certainties toppled before the Iron Curtain, attitudes drifting from nothing to anything goes. It might even be argued that conversation skills have slackened because we're spoilt for topical choice. Imagine the stamina necessary to eke out ghosts and the royal family over the duration of a dinner date, before tabloids made them such toothsome subjects.

Yes, we have it easy. But as anyone who has put his foot in it will testify, there remains such a thing as the wrong topic of conversation. How do you tell?

By the silence.

RULE ONE: *Good topics create talk*

Far from fixed Abstract Nouns with Capital Letters, the elusive What we are talking about keeps moving, slipping down side alleys, emerging as something else entirely, due to conversation's spirit-charging ability to summon up ideas.

It's the law of the conversation jungle: either fresh talking points sprout from the old, new ones are grafted on, or the whole fragile ecosystem conks out.

RULE TWO: *Topics are unstable mixtures of attitude and subject*

Aristotle had a neat concept for explaining what enables topics' polymorphous perversity: the active intellect. In brief, inside *Homo sapiens*' lively mind lie imaginary versions of the world, and in the collective craft of conversation we trade perceptions and ideas: a wondrous capacity that has enabled us to transform each others' views, and with them, the world.

On the small scale, simply exchanging words is alchemy, altering topics each time they pass from person to person. Just as syntax, the arrangement of words, shapes meaning and clarity, so conversation has its own dynamic syntax, as thoughts conjoin and separate with the ripping speed of Velcro. The better they do, the better we get along.

🗨 **RULE THREE:** *A topic's fitness endures with the thrill of the chase*

In an ideal world, as the libertine author of 1673's *Means to Oblige in Conversation* wrote, a subject, 'the quarry of two heated minds, springs up like a deer out of the wood'. However,

> *There is nothing in a subject, so called, that we should regard it as an idol, or follow it beyond the promptings of desire.*

As for where to hunt, his advice was simple: 'Speak . . . to the purpose'. Which seems sensible: the original Greek word, '*topos*', means 'place', so a topic can hardly be out of it. (The word is Aristotle's, from his *Ta Topika – On Commonplaces*.)

🗨 **RULE FOUR:** *Topics must be relevant and accessible*

That is to say, a good topic is whatever you want to discuss, and most fertile are those on which anyone can comment – the richest, like evergreen pop icon Madonna, morphing before they date.

But hang on, aren't some topics bad?

Yes: generally the ones we gossip about, then regret at our leisure. Like this seventeenth-century English lady, Lucy Hutchinson, repining her racy youth, before Civil War divided cavalier from puritan, and Charles I from his head.

> *I was not at that time convinced of the vanity of conversation which was not scandalously wicked . . . I became the confidante in all the loves that were managed among my mother's young*

> *women; and there was none of them but had many lovers, and*
> *some particular friends beloved above the rest.*

Can't you sense her yearning to say more about these 'particular friends'? And doesn't the fact that virtue starches her lips increase your desire to hear, three-plus centuries on?

RULE FIVE: *Questionable subjects whet appetites*

Scandal and conflict have ever been the spice to conversation. In the Bible's first chat, Eve and Eden's serpent discuss pilfering the tree of knowledge, and the earliest recorded literary dialogue, in the Mesopotamian epic *Gilgamesh*, is between a father and his hunter son, fretting about the hairy eco-warrior sabotaging their traps. The association remains fitting because although, as Aristotle suggested, accessible topics hail from the common ground, hot topics map faultlines and points of difference.

Paradoxical? Hardly. Without such border skirmishes, where would we be?

In a dull, silent world, free of opinion and all the troubles and triumphs it brings.

What we really want to talk about are pleasures, frivolous matters of taste (market researchers confirm this: launching a pop group or a chocolate bar, they court neighbourhood cool-makers, but not for conversationally unfriendly products such as life insurance); and perils, as well as those piquant phenomena that don't quite square with our notions of how life should be. In other words, when it comes to good and bad topics, puritan and cavalier attitudes continue their squabble, speaking in us with forked tongue, as we shiver at a murder, deplore a filmstar's cellulite, and get our juices flowing.

Hot topics' appeal isn't entirely prurient. We huddle around them like a fire, trading titbits of information, taking intoxicating nips of *Schadenfreude*, to render the monsters out there a little less scary and reassure ourselves that we aren't alone in our fears, or that worse could happen, indeed has: to somebody else. The best topics – even the bad – make us feel better, one way or another.

The Choice

So which subjects should be hoarded for sustaining conversation, and which froth up a light chat? In his *Art of Pleasing in Conversation* Cardinal Richelieu (the real one, not the *Three Musketeers*' villain, although they've plenty in common) counselled:

> *Obscure Sciences and great Affairs must have a less share in their discourses than agreeableness and diversion.*

But jolly humanist Erasmus ridiculed sententious attitudes in the tale of a banquet.

A guest sat by the fire. Another said, 'I want to tell you something.'

'Is it serious?'

The man frowned. 'Not merry.'

'Then save it,' said the guest. 'Serious things after the feast.'

He was not happy when he saw his burned cloak.

There is no formula. Instead, read the mood, and bear in mind that edgy subjects, though risky, tend to trail conga-lines of meaty potential topics. And whatever you pick, it will say something about you . . .

The Menu

Births, marriages, affairs, divorces, deaths?

A category better known as local news. Learning what has befallen family, friend and foe is great. Provided it is your family, friend or foe. Like many wines, local news may bring transports of delight in its native land, but it doesn't necessarily travel.

Still, gossip is conversation's bread and butter (two-thirds concerns our local world). The word originates from Old English 'godsybb' – 'spiritual kin', such as godparents – and it still serves as social glue, reinforcing ties of kith and kinship. Just as apes groom to bond as much as to clean, even salacious talk is a form of solace and back-scratching. Its devilish reputation is deserved insofar as it features material we may not mention to the parties concerned. But talking behind backs forestalls exchanges like this:

> (Friend who shall be nameless): *'Hello, Mrs X. Where's your husband?'*
>
> Pause. Mrs X turns green, gulps: *'He died two weeks ago.'*

To me gossip is a growth industry, ever more essential in atomized urban society, as family ties weaken and networks grow wider, looser and diffuser, and most bonds are inked in friendship. While monitoring a virtual crowd of Internet pals can accentuate loneliness if you're not truly in touch, gossip remains friendship's primary medium, as well as good for business. If I could, I'd buy shares in it.

Risk: Misjudging your audience; too much information; too little

Opportunity: Information; titillation; sense of superiority
Scenario: Reunions; christenings; bar mitzvahs; and (at low volume) funerals

Sex?

Once upon a time my friends and I shared further and better particulars, for research you understand, but detailed accounts have been off-limits since the last door slammed on my teens.

Does sex talk turn you on? Does your listener want or need to know? Certainly the Mitford sister, Diana Mosley, found it dry fare at a lunch with the ageing widow Wallis Simpson, Duchess of Windsor, who was evidently keen to remind guests that a king had once preferred her charms to ruling his country.

> *Pathos personified, about nine people including a nurse (in a green silk dress) & she (Duchess) tried to get the ball rolling by saying how nowadays people are only interested in SEX, well as we were all well on the way to the grave the ball refused to roll.*

Risk: What you think flattering may not be if your listener's mind's eye isn't soft-focus
Opportunity: If it turns you on
Scenario: Locker room; doctor's surgery; bedroom; bathroom; kitchen . . .

Current affairs?

A fair bet once. But as a surfeit of topics rushes in via radio, TV or Internet, like Cleopatra, 24/7 news 'makes hungry where most [it] satisfies'. Hourly are we buffeted by vistas of calamity, but our relation to it is image-deep – dulling shockability, jading interest. So where our grandparents avoided talk of war out of consideration for those who wished to forget, we are likelier to shun it out of boredom or that guilt-salving euphemism, compassion fatigue. Not that we think of it like that. In fact, we'd rather not think about it, since it makes us feel futile.

Nonetheless, discussing big stuff with baby boomers remains more mind-expanding than numbing, thanks to their halcyon memories of 1960s protests. And many – their mortgages paid off, their offspring schooled and resolutely deferring the production of time-consuming grandchildren – are also doing something concrete to set the world to rights. Let them fire you up and you might find yourself getting out there too.

Risk: Depression; tedium; argument; revelation of dubious beliefs

Opportunity: Catch the latest; quell a bore; raise consciousness

Scenario: Student union; pub (for sport haters); dinner party; Saga holiday; sixtieth birthday

Heavy weather?

The British classic: where others have climates, UK skies are ruled by the capricious goddess, Weather. Except, with climate change, weather has gone global – no longer a demure neutral topic of discussion, but a titan, hauling an unruly retinue of visions of imminent, overheated apocalypse, as we dodge hail in July, sunbathe in October. Want to talk about it? Do canapés go with melting polar ice caps? Up to you.

I say, reclaim weather; acquaint yourself with its fluffier side and go cloudspotting.

Risk: Cliché; inconvenient truths; environmental depression

Opportunity: Remember umbrella/sunblock; better than old ladies' bunions

Scenario: Start of conversation; passing time of day with strangers on street, anywhere. Go on. If only for one day a year, imagine how nice it would be

In God/State/King we trust?

The forces that shape us are sometimes fascinating, sometimes dull, and always divisive. Formerly, such topics were forbidden from mixed company, but this stricture is at an end. However, if you want to curdle a conversation, toss in a remark about your Undear Leader. You'll soon learn who is a political animal, and who doesn't give a monkey's.

As with current affairs, discussing creeds, whether social, political or theological, can coagulate conversation, since it reminds unbelievers how little dust our little lives, for all their busyness, actually raise. Worse, many of those who get on hind legs to such topics are ranters and ravers, who talk as if atop invisible podiums.

Take this scene in Katherine Mansfield's story 'Germans at Meat'. The other hotel guests are agog that the narrator might not want a baby (in fact she is ill):

> *'Germany,' boomed the Traveller, biting round a potato which he had speared with his knife, 'is the home of the Family.'*
> *Followed an appreciative silence.*

Minds worn shiny by prejudice offer few conversational footholds for those who don't mirror their opinions. So before you enquire, ask yourself: do you care about the answer? Equally, do you mind too little? If, like pioneering psychologist William

James, you regard religious belief as a vehicle to convey us through choppy existence, to prick another person's convictions is to tinker with the engine of meaning in his life. Equally, to press your own on him is in effect to demand that he show you his, since conversation is a trading game. Who would do either?

Someone itching for an argument, is who. Thin-skinned nineteenth-century painter Benjamin Robert Haydon, a committed Christian, griped about a dinner party:

> *Shelley [the Romantic poet] opened the conversation by saying in a most feminine and gentle voice, 'As to that detestable religion, the Christian . . .' I looked astounded, but casting a glance round the table easily saw by [Leigh] Hunt's expression of ecstasy and the women's simper, I was to be set . . .* vi et armis.

Admit it: baiting is fun.

Risk: Depression; tedium; argument etc.

Opportunity: Tranquillize bores; wind someone up; get down with a teenager

Scenario: Drinking holes; rallies; temples; high tables; golf course; after Christmas lunch

Money?

If two-thirds of the average conversation consists of window-shopping one another's lives, naturally, the price tag arises. Nonetheless, traditionally money talk is taboo. Food writer and successful businesswoman Prue Leith recalled:

> *In my family, you never discussed food, money and sex. Only complete vulgarians discussed them. I think that's absolute nonsense. Food, money and sex are all great pleasures in life.*

Of course money is fun. If you have it. If not, it may be a talking point – but a pleasure? And advertising wealth exposes insecurity. Take note, self-declared tycoon Peter Jones:

> *If there has been resentment about my success it's gone unnoticed, because I simply wouldn't care. I am positive there are people out there who are jealous.*

Er. He is positive. Therefore, he cares.

If money talks to you, make no mistake, others' envy funds the pleasure. Be subtle, as a 1587 conduct book advised nouveaux riches brides:

> *Guide your guests around the house and in particular show them some of your possessions, either new or beautiful, but in such a way that it will be received as a sign of your politeness and domesticity . . . as if showing them your heart.*

But after your latest acquisition's price has been tagged, really, what more is there to say? Despite strong recent growth, this conversational weed shouldn't be mistaken for a fecund topic.

Risk: Unpopularity; crassness; mistaking price for worth; silence; 'So what?'

Opportunity: Funny, perhaps, as ABBA suggested, in a rich man's world

Scenario: Office; accountant; estate agent; bank; marital bed; divorce lawyer

Here comes trouble?

'How are you?' To which the reply is: 'Fine. You?'

Any alternative should be broached with caution. Unless,

that is, you wish to bring conversation to an end; in which case, trouble talk is a swift means to do so.

In general, enquiries after health and happiness are not diagnostic. Their aim is the friendly gesture, doing the metaphorical job of a wave as we pass someone's home: if not on intimate terms, rarely do we expect to be invited in and told how unhappy is its resident. (Similarly, Anglo-Saxons routinely close conversations with symbolic invitations to 'see you soon', as a foxed Russian acquaintance found, turning up on London doorsteps as she thought had been arranged.)

While you may consider painful topics, like scabs, best picked in private, in Turkey, however, complaining is art, with seven different verbs to capture its nuances. Of Istanbul students surveyed, 30.4 per cent identified 'personal problems' as their top topic, 37 per cent of women selecting the slightly grander 'problems for students/the young'. Some argue this predilection expresses a national romantic, melancholy streak, others blame fear of the evil eye (unguarded talk of fortune is asking for trouble). But I see the pleasure of whingeing, with the right person, as philosopher Francis Bacon wrote:

Communicating of a man's self to his friend works two contrary effects, for it redoubleth joys and cutteth griefs in half.

Complaining can be modest, extremely funny, and gory details are bliss. A cynic might add that tales of misfortune – told sparingly, with wit – stoke popularity. A Machiavellian might go further, and tell you that the novel *Vanity Fair*, Thackeray's masterly mockery of social aspiration, features a gentleman who did ' little wrongs' to neighbours 'on purpose, and in order to apologise for them in an open and manly way afterwards' – and for this troubles was 'liked everywhere', earning a lucrative name for honesty.

Risk: Lost prestige; attract by losers; self-pity; yawns

Opportunity: Feel better; make others feel better; analyse problems; laughs

Scenario: Best friends; mothers (in limited doses); lovers (ditto); frenemies (when moaning is coded showing off – as in, 'I'm so busy with my projects/babies/holidays/work-life-holiness balance to juggle')

True confessions, secrets and lies?

Blame Freud, blame TV, blame the Pill: the twentieth century saw a mass deregulation of taboos. But while our hot-lipped media imply that anything is up for discussion, unsolicited revelation from non-friends remains a burden. Spare a thought for hairdressers and bartenders.

Although morsels of mischief pep up talk, overdone they leave a sour taste. For conversation to feel truly intimate, traction between minds and an easy flow are what count.

Risk: Bad name; aftertaste; know who you're talking to?

Opportunity: Thrills; spills; risk; they might show you theirs

Scenario: Father-confessor; doctor; therapist; best friend; officer of the law

Dearly beloved?

Romance, pets and children fall under what I term the Baby Problem.

Why are babies boring? They're not. As P.G. Wodehouse observed, many resemble homicidal fried eggs, and of course, in little blossom's greedy gaze we see the wonder of the world reborn. The problem is their makers.

Hormone-foamy, knackered or plain self-centred, parents, like lovers, fondly imagine that what makes them happy is equal cause of celebration to the rest of us.

Well, I'm happy you're happy. And as it happens, I like hearing about affairs of the heart and children; I love talking to said miniatures, and I enjoy patting dogs. Do I want details? A recital of little Timmy's latest trumpet-tooting triumph? Oh, a *story*? A real live anecdote? You're on.

But my, how fast stories about children grow; must be pesky time that goes slow.

However loved-up you are, it's no excuse to ditch conversational technique. Litanies and lists do not a tale make: keep a long story short to make the pleasure mutual.

Risk: Tedium; envy; the opposite of envy

Opportunity: Laughs (now or later)

Scenario: With other interested parties; at school gates; featured in deprecating jokes, etc.

Hobbies, sport, arts, books, films, music, gadgets, widgets and other esoterica?

With fellow enthusiasts, go for it. Even with the uninitiated, a light top-note of titbits and trivia make conversation sing. Aside from radars for identifying common ground, discussing extra-curricular interests has the advantage that enthusiasm spawns enthusiasm.

Poet Leigh Hunt, who cheered on Shelley's teasing of Benjamin Robert Haydon, seemed to have forgotten his meaner streak when he advised 'topics fittest for table' are

cheerful, to help digestion; and cordial, to keep people in heart . . .
reminiscences, literary chat, questions as easy to crack as the nuts,
quotations flowing as the wine, thoughts of eyes and cheeks
blooming as the fruit.

The Romantic era may be over but even acid-tongued
comic Ricky Gervais admits: 'Nothing makes a connection
with me like a piece of art, a song or a painting . . . I'd rather
gush about something that changed the world than be embarrassed.'

Try to imbibe a bit of culture; if only to distract yourself from
routine matters. Should you be too busy for first-hand research
into the latest must-read/-see/-listen, take heart from Pierre
Bayard's *How to Talk About Books You Haven't Read*:

Among specialists [literary critics] mendacity is the rule, and we
tend to lie in proportion to the significance of the book under con-
sideration . . . the books we talk about are only glancingly related
to real books.

The oddest interest can ignite a conversation. Whatever
grabs you. In moderation.
Risk: Riding hobby horse into ground
Opportunity: Information; warmth; passion
Scenario: Anywhere. Up to a point

Immediate surroundings?
What is going on? What prompted the smile that just scudded
across your companion's face? Why did that woman wear that
dress? All such minor mysteries may be enlisted for your battle
against silence.

The joy of topics triggered by your environment is that because they occupy common ground, they limbo dance under the usual etiquettes and you may raise them, interrupting a given line of discussion, without offence. So if bored, keep eyes and ears skinned and you can bounce talk elsewhere. Be imaginative ('Nice flowers' is not juicy). And cautious. Jibe at the man in the mauve catsuit and he will be her dad.

Risk: Worth talking about? Can you make it worth it? Is it safe?
Opportunity: Distraction; filling gaps
Scenario: Any time, any place, anywhere

Them?

Smooth-talking Disraeli remarked,

> *'Talk to a man about himself and he will listen for hours.'*

But don't enter your interlocutor's private space without invitation. Wait to ask what he does, if he's married, has kids, until he's flagged these topics as safe. Take the side route, and stalk subjects that excite him.

Risk: Is it interesting? Is it safe?
Opportunity: Big return for small investment of enthusiasm
Scenario: Need you ask?

What next?

And finally, the topic so overused that we're hardly aware it is one: arrangements.

Many conversations round off in an exchange about the next occasion to meet/talk/do business. So if you want to say goodbye, but not for ever, ask, 'When can we do this again?'

This sends a polite but unambiguous message that this conversation is already in the past.

Risk: Making false commitments
Opportunity: Getting on with your day
Scenario: When the end is nigh

Here ends my menu. Perhaps yours is longer. Whatever subject you choose, let it matter. G.K. Chesterton was right:

> *There is no such thing as an uninteresting subject; there are only uninterested people.*

Neither an encyclopaedic imagination nor a spontaneously combustible topic makes conversation whoopee if speakers don't engage. It became clear to me that a job interview masquerading as lunch had turned belly-up when, without warning, my would-be employer began rabbiting about her cat (she hoped, by obscure methods, to 'raise Sheba's consciousness').

What went wrong? Hard as we'd tried, I didn't care about her interests, and the indifference was mutual. We had failed to tie our topics together.

Typology of Bores, Chores and other Conversational Beasts

SHOWGIRL   ***Ostentatrix Ludi***

You smile. She laughs. You say she looks well. She says you look incredible. You have a new job. She just bought her company. Going on holiday? Guess who is heading into tax exile . . .

Showgirl understands that life is competition. Anything you can do, she does it better, with knobs on, and glitter, and if you're lucky, lucky, lucky, she will tell you how.

Men, call them Preens, employ similar methods. But Showgirl respects a distinctly feminine tradition. If she had an emblem it would be a titchy silver spade, disguised as an accessory. Although insecure to the bottom of her high-kicking heels, she never undermines directly. Rather she takes every opportunity to smuggle information into conversation to big herself up, most perfidious, as a worry preying on her mind. Will her cloth-of-gold gown shed dodo feathers at the Academy Awards? Will she be shuttlesick on her voyage to Venus? Will that rock star stop trying to convince her he isn't gay?

Invariably thrilled to hear your plans, Showgirl does all she can to advance your cause. But isn't it odd how often she converts your news into ways she can help? You'll never leave her company walking taller: that little spade builds her foundations by nicking earth from yours.

Tactics: Isn't it gratifying she wants to impress you? Her machinations are also painfully informative, given she targets your weaknesses: listen for what riles you and you'll hear your insecurities talking. With this guide, set about shoring up your perimeter walls.

Pluses: There is something breathtakingly brazen in how Show-girl boosts her interests. Such focus, drive, chutzpah: useful armour, and worth assuming from time to time.

6

Into the Groove

On Steering Controls

If having nothing to say is bad, too much is possibly worse. Millionaire American politico and doer-of-good Arianna Huffington 'bubbles over with questions':

> *'Do you like to dance?' 'Can we talk about perfumes?' 'Do you think the breast stroke is more feminine than the crawl?' 'Do you like Leonard Cohen?' 'What do you think of my lipstick?'*
>
> *She says this is all part of her innate 'capacity for intimacy'.*

But gush and it may wash over them.

'Only connect,' wrote E.M. Forster in *Howards End*: a motto for life, but it does as well for conversation. At its best, in animating our views, conversation reveals who we are and, when sympathies chime, we relate to one another. Slipping between topics makes connecting possible.

Even military men should cut a tippy-toed dash. Captain Orlando Sabertash's 1842 gent's conduct book advocates a

graceful and pleasing manner . . . from 'grave to gay, from serious to serene'.

Sound silly? Think of a person you met recently. Do you remember what was said or how you felt talking to him? Emotion dwells in the memory longer than the neatest verbal twist, and whatever topic you discuss, conversation's visceral pleasure emanates less from the beauty of words than the harmony of its pace, rhythm and flow.

RULE ONE: *Flowing topics smooth social dynamics*

Jumpy talkers unsettle us by darting from topic to topic, like squirrels in a forest fire. Wordsworth's friend, the opium eater Thomas de Quincey, suggested all would run smoother if we appointed a 'symposiarch'. A similar approach is used to broker talk in fashionable 'dialogue' workshops, at which mediators instruct speakers to pass batons, even bananas, to divvy up airtime (only the banana-clutcher may speak). But isn't that bananas? Think what is lost if you can't share the insight a remark has sparked, or overlap sentences, in terms of spontaneity, ideas, momentum, connection . . .

Like the industrious fairy-tale gnome, Rumpelstiltskin, who spun straw into gold, dexterous talkers transmute dross subjects to dazzle by spinning threads that draw people together and lead to new treasures. But magical as it may sometimes seem, conversation's flow proceeds by cues and signals little more complex than traffic lights. However, because we follow them, like rules of grammar, largely unconsciously, and often converse with our mind elsewhere, or running ahead to what we want to say next, signals can be missed or skipped. Indeed, many encounters go wrong purely because topic signalling is on the blink. We just don't notice. Instead we blame the situation or the other person: so gauche, rude, dull! Or become defensive, inhibited, and stop doing our bit to tease out common ground – short-sightedness that cheats us of fun and friendship.

E.M. Forster was on the money. 'Only connect.' Topical connections are the joinery of relating.

RULE TWO: *Bid for a topic tactically*

Throughout conversation we broker topics. Negotiations can be comically protracted.

> *'Does this red top go okay with my colouring?'*
>
> *'Yes, dear.'*
>
> *'You don't think it's too loud?'*
>
> *'No, dear.'*
>
> *'It doesn't clash?'*
>
> *'No.'*
>
> *'It's just the way my hair's been acting lately . . .'*
>
> *'You look fine.'* [Sound of TV channel being switched.]
>
> *'I DYED IT GINGER LAST NIGHT. HAVEN'T YOU NOTICED?'*
>
> *'No, dear.'*

But bidding is simple. I offer a subject: 'Hear about Fred and the banana split?' And you either agree: 'No, what?' or bid for another: 'Yeah. But did you hear about Mary and the hell's angel?' or, if a real schmo, offer nothing more: 'Yeah.'

Nonetheless, how we bid alters conversation dynamics. The options are:

Direct bids

Statements: 'I have to tell you about Fred, the biker and the vanishing banana.'

Questions: 'Heard about Fred's hell's angel?'

Previews: 'Guess what Fred's done now?'

Indirect bids

Oblique comments, statements or observations: 'Fred is in the custard.'

Your style of bid indicates whether you wish to lead discussion. Open bids – 'They say Fred is brilliant,' or 'Heard about Fred?' – let the other person either react passively or take charge of developing the topic. Closed bids – 'Tell me about Fred'; 'Guess what Fred did' – leave no room for manoeuvre. So be wary of bidding as an expert: 'Let me tell you about my ormolu clocks.'

In sensitive situations, indirect bids tactfully point out the door without forcing the other in. Say someone else mentioned John's striptease at the harvest supper, you might ask the guilty man: 'You partied out?' And if you can't ask where Jean's been, fish: 'I would've invited you but there was no answer when I called.'

RULE THREE: *Exercise editorial rights in your reactions*

Just the tone of an answer is illuminating, able to signal desire to spin in a given direction (green); support without furthering a topic (amber); or hint enough, already (red):

Green: Add new material to be developed ('Fred, eh? Fearless for his height.')

Amber: Neutral, no extra topical reference, adding nothing ('Poor Fred.')

Red: Yawn ('Uh-huh.')

Be aware of how our responses actively select topics by shining a light on what interests us. Think how to train them. For instance, I met a man, call him Jake, who boasted: 'I have a weakness for fast Italian cars.' I said nothing. He elaborated.

> *'Laid my hands on a beaut of a Testarossa. Bright green. Can do up to 220mph on a fast road. Dealer couldn't sell them for horse meat at first. Ferrari discontinued the run, but now there's hardly any, they're worth a mint.'*

Each extra tot of information was the seed of a new topic. Had I smiled and said, 'Ferrari?' at 'Testarossa', this would have focused his mind on that marque as a subject to expand on. If I'd said, 'Gosh, where can you drive that fast?' after 'fast road', that might have steered us away. Stupidly, I smiled, wasting a month's ration of Really?s.

How you structure statements may engender or neuter talking points. Consider these reactions to 'Silent movies are so evocative.'

> *'I don't remember any. Maybe because I'm obsessed with words.'*
>
> *'You're right, they're hypnotic. Maybe that's why I find it easier to remember scenes from talkies. Or that could be because I'm obsessed with words.'*

Same information, different message. The first says: 'I have completely different opinions. Want to hear about me?' The second shows respect and supplies at least three fresh topics (hypnotism; favourite scenes; words).

Conversely, play a defensive game with amber signals, use clichés to suggest a topic is not for debate, or flattery and polite comments to baffle difficult topics, e.g. 'That is an interesting question' (see chapter 13). The subtlest curb of all is not matching enthusiasm: 'Oh yeah?', softly spoken, announces that this news is already stale.

The Reason I Called

You feel it circling. A shadow passes overhead. For some reason it doesn't swoop. Instead, the person at the other end of the phone chatters on. But you aren't fooled. You know this conversation is heading towards something – something you probably won't want to hear.

Who likes being ambushed? But, charming as wittering may be, it may be kinder – not least to your schedule – to open conversational airspace and guide the agenda in to land.

First, step back, highlight the oddity of the call: 'It's been a while since we spoke.'

No response? Hint you know something's up: 'Everything all right?'

Does she say 'Fine'? From a friend, this answer should make you nervous.

Take courage: ask. 'So what can I do for you?'

'Oh. I— No, nothing.'

Now you have a choice: press on – 'You sure?' – or take this at face value and let yourself off the hook: 'Right. Only, I was in the middle of something . . .'

If she doesn't spit it out now, don't worry. She'll be back.

Staging Topical Takeovers

Fed up with Ferraris? Time to change the subject. But take your listeners with you. There are six methods to shift between topics without audibly scraping gears. Pick yours according to whether the subject you wish to introduce is a

Shift: New
Contrast: Variant on a line of discussion
Familiar: Extension of the given topic

The fresher a topic, the greater the work required to weave it in. This is marked in how we speak, whatever our language. Evaluations of French and German speakers have found that pitch and volume rise according to how new a topic is. So use your voice to grab attention. (Monotone speech is uninvolving because so much of words' meaning – their emotional force – is lost.)

Now, choose your topical knitware. Consider these links marketing tools and pitch a topic by connecting it to the other person's needs, wants, hopes and fears. Better still, be gossipy, introducing a tinct of secrets hidden, details forbidden. 'I'd better not say,' makes anything twice as interesting. Want to wind somebody up? Root the topic in her insecurities. ('Talking of Christmas, Aphra, how's the diet?')

1. Topic-tying: Good old grammar. To keep clear, ensure listeners grasp which 'he' or 'it' is in play, even as you introduce new 'he's and 'it's as you go along.

2. Step-wise progression: Good for complicated subjects. So, to explain your job at the café is hell, you might say, 'First the bananas arrive, then the hell's angels, then Fred throws a wobbly with the custard,' progressing to the conclusion: 'It's hell!' Bridging components – 'first', 'then', 'after that' – create coherence by presenting elements as part of a story. Not only do they help reach topical destinations, but they are invaluable for escaping one you don't fancy. For example, ending a relationship you might begin: 'It's not you . . .' At first, this is clichéd. But go step by step, itemizing issues you wouldn't wish to foist on the other person, and the topic ceases to be 'You're dumped' to become 'Tomorrow begins my quest for Shangri-la'.

3. Touching off: Trade off previous talk, introducing a topic by latching on to something mentioned earlier. Say, 'As you rightly said, bunions and wellies don't mix . . .'

This is endearing, in a subliminal way, as it demonstrates how engaged you are. We're all suckers for apt quotations. Think of the cheap laughs TV quiz show panellists bag by referencing previous jokes: it isn't so much that what they say is funny, as it shows off their quick wits, and we feel included; somehow, recognizing the allusion makes us feel wittier by association. Similarly, in conversation, a touch-off, witty or otherwise, enjoys the privileged status of an in-joke.

4. Thematic touch-offs: Topics may springboard to others by touching on shared themes. Such leaps of thought ask us to attend to buried meanings – the implied, the unspeakable – giving a certain frisson. Indeed, half the pleasure of conversation with old friends is how much of it may be woven from thematic touch-offs. It feels like glorious mind-reading, because it is.

Hence thematic touch-offs are among the fastest ways to feel more connected to strangers, as well as escape a dull topic. Be warned: they can seem random. If in doubt, make the link explicit: 'Kangaroo keeper? Wouldn't a pouch be cool! I hate handbags.'

5. Triggered topics: Triggered topics also play off previous talk but are even more unruly; conversation's equivalent to tickles. A keyword – say, mention of a friend's labour – might cue a fresh topic ('Speaking of monstrous births, seen Hilda's kids?'). Or the trigger might be a pun. If you're walking in the park, you say, 'Ice cream?' and he says, 'I can make you,' this platonic friendship may be up for review. An added bonus, as with topics triggered from observations of your surroundings, is these bypass the etiquette of bidding for a topic.

6. Listed topics: Or agendas, as at business meetings. These require no topical interweaving, and make duff social conversation, e.g. catalogues of activities in reply to 'What did you do on holiday?' However, invoking the idea of listed topics can be handy. For example, to cut off her inventory of buffet dishes served at the Hotel Paradiso, say, 'Now, the other thing I wanted to mention is that'. At a stroke, you've introduced the impression of an agenda, implicitly declared the previous subject closed and conveyed that your time is limited, even if hers is not.

Topic Plasters and Signals:
A Glossary for Glueing Talk

Out of inspiration? These nifty words and phrases cobble together the unlikeliest topics.

If truly in the doldrums, try the ones with stars: all by themselves, they should provoke fellow talkers to return to the floor with a fresh topic.

Casual

'Hey'
'Listen'
'Guess what'
'You have got to hear this'
'Let's see'
'Now then'
'Here's the thing'
* *'Erm'*
* *'Right'*
* *'So'*

Retrospective

* *'Well'*
* *'Anyway'*
* *'Still'*
* *'Did I interrupt you?'*
* *'As I was/you were saying'*
'I meant to say'

Formal

'The reason I called'
'This might interest you'

Ominous

'Incidentally'
'By the way'
'I was wondering'

RULE FOUR: *Dare to be conventional*

You needn't be a smoothie to win points for keeping talk going. As a teenager I was prissily averse to platitudes, clichés, and never knowingly remarked on the weather. More fool me. Stating the obvious is perfectly acceptable. And a little local knowledge can pay dividends.

An agonizingly gauche banquet very nearly wrecked President Nixon's historic visit to China, by showing how little each side had to talk about, despite their nations' supposed new understanding and the effort American delegates had made beforehand to learn the use use of chopsticks (famed TV reporter Walker Cronkite sent olives flying), not to mention a White House memo containing useful conversation tips such as 'The Chinese take great pride in their food and to compliment the various courses and dishes is also recommended.' While Nixon traded insipid remarks with the Chinese Prime Minister, his Secretary of State, William Rogers,

> *told long stories about his hero, the great golfer Sam Snead, to the Chinese Foreign Minister, a tough old revolutionary who had no idea what golf was.*

If only Madame Mao had been there. Then Mrs Nixon could have salvaged the moment with this age-old Chinese conversation opener:

> *'How is Your Excellency's favoured wife?'*

To which Mrs Mao would have replied, equally conventionally:

> *'Thank you, the foolish one of the family is well.'*

Typology of Bores, Chores and other Conversational Beasts

THE GRAND INQUISITOR   *Sciscitator Nasutus*

You may imagine you have embarked on a light chat. To the Grand Inquisitor, this is contact sport. Neither has she a private thought, nor encountered a private grief. No topic is too sensitive to be aired, shared and shredded. In her favour, her candour matches her nosiness.

A fine specimen at a dinner was a radio presenter who eagerly asked each guest's age, leaned in for a closer look, cocked her head and said, 'Are you sure?'

Later in the meal she cried out: 'Ladies, who do we fancy, handsome Henry or sexy Simon?'

Then smiled at the man beside her, neither Henry nor Simon, saying in a voice of unutterable pity, 'No, not you.'

Her husband, also neither Henry nor Simon, grimaced. 'Her family call her the social hand grenade.'

Tactics: Don't be offended, be awed she's made it so far, missing so many filters. People like her build business empires. Watch carefully. If only to replenish the stock of your Shut-up Shop (see chapter 14).

Pluses: A great how-not-to, valiantly she proves why social protocols exist. Watch her at work, carefully noting the boundaries as she crashes through.

7

Do Go On

On Wrangling Boredom

'As I was saying—'

Yes, he has been at the smoked salmon blinis. You turn your head. He mistakes your ear for an invitation and leans a little closer, his canapé breath hot on your cheek.

'What I was saying was—'

He stops. Out shoots his glass. A passing waitress tops it up: his fourth refill. How long have you been trapped?

The bore totters, regains his balance and looks you up and down, confused.

'What's your name again?'

Your eyes coast over to your friend, chatting merrily. She sees you, smiles, carries on. Damn her.

He notices. 'I'm sorry, am I boring you?'

'No,' you lie. 'Not at all. Please, do go on.'

He beams, then frowns.

'Now, what was I saying?'

Boredom provokes desperation. It was either that or disco rage that propelled my father from a Christmas party to walk seven icy miles home. A friend of mine consoles herself in similar circumstances by writing – on her ankle, with the toe of her shoe, under the table where no one else can see – 'BORED', 'I'M DYING', 'HELP', 'THE END IS NIGH'.

History does not relate if anyone has in fact been bored to death, although the entertainment provision in many care homes for the elderly suggests this is not for want of trying. When you're cornered by a bore the sensation of life ebbing away – and going on elsewhere, where the people laugh and the sun still shines – is palpable, and painful.

To be boring is beyond bad manners. It is theft. Take that lady who wouldn't dream of picking your pocket, yet thinks nothing of squandering your time, detailing the plot of a book you already said you've read. What is she thinking?

The short answer is: she isn't. While boredom is easy to recognize when you're inside it, it is more difficult to tell if you are its cause. But it is your duty, and in your interests, to try.

Are you an unwitting time-thief? How to judge? How to stop? And can anything be done about those dullards guaranteed to bore all of the people, all of the time?

Absolutely. Although our social lives might improve if we could sort bores from non-bores, the word's a label, a perception, not an essence of soul. That dolt may think the same of you, or pep up, given encouragement. Bores are made, not born.

Good news! Redemption is possible. Instead of hunting tame bore, then, the task is to truffle out instances of the verb 'to bore', explore its causes, then trample it.

What is Boredom?

Historians argue that boredom isn't a timeless human dilemma, but rather an evolving concept, wafted across the English Channel, ghost of the dandified ennui that held court among moping French aristocrats before the guillotine intervened. They have a point.

Though a sin, medieval 'sloth' shares little of modern boredom's character. If you spent your peasant days hacking a living from unyielding fields, rustling up tithes for fat abbots, you would not be bored, but fervently desire, as old graves do, 'Rest In Peace'. Peace and quiet were valued commodities then, not boredom's yawning ladies-in-waiting.

The antisocial sense of the verb 'to bore' sauntered into the language around 1750, on the arm of the expression 'French bore', 'boredom' making its belated literary debut the following century, with languid Lady Dedlock in Dickens's *Bleak House*. Lexicographers can't decide how it came to mean what it does, or displaced its ancestors, apathetic 'accidie' (affliction of famished monks, tormented by pre-lunch sugar lows in the form of 'noonday devils'); peevish 'spleen'; or mundane 'dullness' (as defined by Samuel Johnson: 'to make dictionaries is *dull* work'). My theory is bores got their name because they bore a hole in conversation out of which enthusiasm rapidly drains.

If the notion was born of the age of industrialization, on a practical level, tedium today is mass-produced by leisure, be there nothing to do, or so much choice none seems worthwhile. The latter is commonly diagnosed as an illness, 'options paralysis', and privileged Westerners seem to be suffering an ennui epidemic (in 2007, 36 per cent of Britons, beneficiaries of the world's fourth largest economy, rated themselves 'very happy', compared to 52 per cent in poor, grey 1957). Feelgood businesses are booming and we have a brand-new science, positive psychology.

The idea of a Wellbeing Institute at Cambridge University (est. 2006) may strike you as certifiable, but boredom is no laughing matter. It drives change; indeed, anthropologist Ralph Linton argued:

> *capacity for being bored, rather than man's social or natural needs, lies at the root of cultural advance.*

And it raised conversation to art. France's first salon began in tedium, after a twelve-year-old Italian newlywed, the marquise de Rambouillet, arrived in Paris in 1600, found nobody to talk to, and imported *conversazione*. Salons became sanctuaries from the dull court, *salonnières* became unbeatable talkers (excluding unmentionable courtesans: see chapter 10), and grave topics flourished, inadvertently helping to finish off their stifling world. Shortly before the Revolution, the prince de Ligne observed: 'In salons these days one speaks of politics and finance where once one spoke of nothing but love.'

What Makes a Bore?

Boredom has two causes: too much of something (overload renders all information equally meaningless) or too little.

Similarly, there are two extremes of bore. At one end stand those besotted with their own voice; at the other cringe feeble, silent types.

Most conspicuous are the former, who draw all life and light to themselves and, like black holes, give none back. Disgraced media baron Conrad Black was a world-class attention thief. Blessed with an excellent memory, his social climbing consisted of courting famous people with lectures on history and current affairs (at dinner).

The latter sort, stealth borer, is subtler but no less selfish, so conversationally risk-averse that when persuaded to speak, he says effectively nothing: either clichés and platitudes – silence thinly disguised – or remarks that lead nowhere.

For instance, stealth borer says, 'Yes, I went to Japan once.'

You say (excited: first hard fact), 'Did you! Where/ when/why?'

'Um. I forget/Ages ago/Holiday.'

On a good day he'll add, 'It was nice.'

The anti-hero of Herman Melville's story 'Bartleby' is typical. 'Pallidly neat, pitiably respectable, uncurably forlorn', he replies to all requests 'in a singularly mild, firm voice, "I would prefer not to." '

Don't pity Bartleby. His bogus shyness is contempt, buried in a coy shrug. Stealth borers may find the rest of us boring. Talking to one of them is like putting coins in a slot machine that doesn't even cough up the flashing lights.

It's tempting to ignore bores, but switch off and the conversational circuitry soon breaks down. Hence creative solutions are preferable. I don't say it's easy. Bores aren't good company because it doesn't occur to them that they're anything less.

Maligns sense no obligation to engage others' interests; benigns fail to perceive that their interests aren't universal. All inhabit a pre-Copernican universe, in which they are the axis about which the world spins.

In essence, they lack nerve-endings, like Christopher Monkton, Third Viscount of Brenchley, a conundrum of a man, who lost a million pounds on his (he thought) 'insoluble' Eternity puzzle, yet seems immune to embarrassment:

> [*He*] *talks with irrepressible good humour and impervious authority on this and any other subject I raise, from the Forestry Commission (spectacularly incompetent) to the* Guardian *(ditto). He laughs without restraint at his own anecdotes. He is not a man, you might say, who seems plagued by self-doubt.*

Funny as bores may be in retrospect, talking to them presents conversation's highest challenge: to make the bore interesting.

First, diagnose the boredom, including your role in it.

At root, the bore is someone you don't want to listen to. Although there are therefore as many varieties as people to be bored by, the structure of every boring conversation is basically the same: a conflict of interest played out as hostage situation.

Boredom fills the deficit between the attention a speaker demands and the interest he commands. The more intrusive the bore, the less entranced you are, the more confinement chafes – pain magnified a thousand-fold if you're stuck.

Contextual variables – loud music, hunger, tiredness, bad temper, urgent desire for a pee – play their part. And of course, although someone may look bored, eyelids droop for many reasons. Telepathy has a way to go, but when conversation stagnates, we may interpret the signs and make a judicious guess as to whether we're with an unresponsive Bartleby, or ourselves acting the part of an impervious Black.

RULE ONE: *Read the listener*

Be reasonably confident your listeners' interest is lost if:

They reply with monosyllables, random comments, new subjects, silence

Their eyes wander or assume a fish-on-slab glaze

They glower, never nod, keep twitching their watch cuffs

You find yourself repeating yourself

Chains of 'really's are not dialogue. And don't be encouraged if their tone lends 'Hmm' a sleepy question mark (translation: 'Like I care?').

Barring sleep, physical clues to listener fatigue are ambiguous. Some people pitch forwards when they're interested, but settling back also equals settling in for a meaty chat. Whatever body language experts claim, crossed arms signal concentration or fed-up-ness as much as defensiveness, and one girl's eager grin is another's clenched, mute, 'God, you're weird'. There is no universal grammar.

Reading ennui is not an exact science, more a descriptive art. As, logically, it can only be, given that boredom – an instinct for social survival, evolved over countless generations – makes itself known first in feeling. Nonetheless it is amenable to analysis, which offers clues on how to fight it. By way of experiment, if you're really bored, divide the minutes (T) a person takes up by your level of interest (I) in what they have to say (from a low of

1 to a high of 10). This is their tedium index ($\frac{T}{i}$). The higher the number, the greater the bore.

There is a further nuance, in that most people's interest rate, however high it soars initially, will deflate with time.

RULE TWO: *Keep it brief*

Sadly, listening talent is on the wane, with patience in dwindling supply. So if your listener looks tired, or your Guinness is still brimming, its foam flat, and everyone else's glass half empty, shut up. Every subject has its use-by date.

Shut-up test: Imagine you're soft-boiling a modest egg. Have you talked over three minutes? This better be a great dinosaur egg of a fascinating topic. Stick to the point. If they want more, they'll ask.

This advice may puzzle raconteurs who believe themselves marvellous conversationalists – writers and actors in particular. The likes of Gore Vidal are lionized for their ability to sustain lengthy anecdotes. Personally, I'd rather eat glass than sit next to him. Virginia Woolf, too, was a conversational dominatrix. Her biographer writes, apparently approvingly, of Woolf's amazing

> *flights of fancy, her wonderful performances in conversation, spinning off into fantastic fabrications while everyone sat around and, as it were, applauded.*

Leave it out. They want theatre? Let them buy a ticket.

Good conversation is a team sport; pace and energy keep it alive. The poet Shelley captured the giddy joy of high-tempo rallies with Byron:

> *the swift thought,*
> *Winging itself with laughter, lingered not,*
> *But flew from brain to brain.*

And if you want each word to sink in, take a leaf from poetry. Researchers Marc Wittman and Ernst Pöppel have found that our brains prefer data sorted into three-second bundles – be it in music, speech or poetry. This bias transcends cultural differences:

> *Experiments were conducted using poems in different languages*
> *that were spoken aloud. Independently of the language, it took the*
> *speakers circa three seconds to recite the individual lines.*

We're all suckers for this rhythm. How else to explain the mysterious power of three? 'Education, education, education,' cried the politician. 'Love, love, love,' chorused the Beatles.

Better then to ditch three-minute declamation for three-second soundbites.

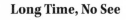

Long Time, No See

The old friend is an old friend for a reason. You know, she knows, but it's impossible to ignore her without offence. For a nippy, packaged small-talk getaway, turn to Aristotle, who argued that stories have a beginning, middle and end. Equally, a catch-up conversation will gallop by if structured to deal first with the past, the present, then future plans, a strategy that also creates a natural exit.

For example:

Past   'Hello. How long has it been?'
'. . .!'

	'Wow. Wasn't that at X's? How is she?'
	'. . .?'
Transition	'No, I haven't seen her for a while.'
	'. . . .'
	[Awkward pause.]
Present	'You living around here?'
	'. . .!'
Transition	'That sounds great. We're hoping to do that one day. Any tips?'
	'. . . .'
Future	'Excellent. I'll remember that. Oh, look, I'd better catch up with Y before he leaves. It was great to see you. Let's do it again some time.'

RULE THREE: *Take turns*

Your listener remains unresponsive? Dispirited as you may feel, don't give up.

Note the Latin '*conversare*' means 'to turn around often'. Sharing is the core social principle, and most people like talking about themselves, so unpack your conversational toolkit to help them join in. Frame questions to offer scope to roam on to other subjects (not 'Do you like chocolate?' but 'Can you believe cocoa is a health food?'). Equally, when – if – you're asked a question, supply an answer they can mine, don't bat it straight back. That's not playing the game.

I know a diplomat's son whose childhood was awash with insipid drinks parties. He and his siblings survived the small talk by setting challenges (odd words to weave into conversation, e.g. lecithin, penguins, telescope, fanny). Today he's ace at converting questions into questions, flicking on the conversational ball.

Finding out what he thinks, on the other hand, is like catching eels with chopsticks. Sometimes it's tiring. But still, at least he acts interested in me. There are superbores, invariably male, capable of consuming five courses without asking any questions of their companions, usually long-suffering females. (Travelling alone, especially by air, pack earplugs.)

RULE FOUR: *Act interested to be interested*

How we behave contains numerous instructions as to how others should treat us, so one of the most effective tactics against boredom is refusing to acknowledge it.

This applies both when bored and when you suspect you're at fault. At a friend's birthday I met a man who, when I excused myself (nature called) said mournfully, 'I'm very boring.' At once I believed him, even as I loudly disagreed, then had to wait five minutes before dashing to the loo. Worse, till that self-pitying moment, I'd liked him.

If ever tempted to say 'I'm boring you', take this as a warning from your subconscious and say goodbye instead. And remember, to be bored or boring isn't affable. Often it is the bored person's fault: a failure to engage with the other person's point of view. In that frowning toad may crouch a prince so give him the benefit of the doubt and smile encouragingly.

Perhaps the most important revelation of the Tedium Index (above) is that the intensity of a listener's engagement materially alters the value of what is said. The more interest you bring to conversation, the more interesting it will be. Even if you fake it. Why bother? Enthusiasm – originally Greek for 'possessed by god' – kindles energy and warmth through the friction of thoughts darting back and forth. Just like magic.

So detonate your bore with this tactic, from a journalism course's seminar on pepping up dull interviewees: whip the droning along with monosyllables – 'Yup . . . yup . . . yeah . . . right . . . wow!' – all the while smiling, nodding, doing lively things with your eyebrows.

When speaking, act animated and you'll not only carve up the sense of your words more clearly, but seem more engaging too, as politicians appreciate. They karate-chop the air to lend gravity to the hot stuff steaming from their mouths, a venerable tactic. In Attic Greece, Cratylus disguised his flummery by

> *hissing aggressively and shaking his hands; for these things are persuasive* [*to people*], *because the things they know become tokens for what they do not know.*

He played angry, they believed he was justified. Alas, it worked for Hitler too.

RULE FIVE: *Scavenge for material*

Nothing to inspire you? Excuses, excuses. Imagine doing zip-all, beautifully, full-time, and having to entertain bored masters, potentially on pain of death? Courtiers, muzzled by etiquettes and sheer monotony, somehow unravelled viable material from their cocooned existence. Their techniques repay study.

Sei Shōnagan, a tenth-century Japanese lady and the empress's chief wit, was more constrained than most. Sitting behind a screen (one could not be seen) duelling poetic ripostes with a man was life at its most thrilling, and writing verse, off the cuff, in public, a frequent, terrifying ordeal. Relief came in light conversation. What, in such a shuttered existence, did she talk about? Her technique was to watch everything closely, sucking joy from minutiae: the hush of blossom falling, ice shavings sweetened with syrup, snow on a sunny day.

Look around and you'll find endless material. Like bitching, only nicer (if you avoid needless risk: remember the mauve catsuit), observations bond people by ranging them metaphorically side by side – facing outwards instead of at each other, wondering what to say.

Admire the whiskies behind the bar, wonder how so many Scottish islands can support distilleries. Does that arch frame a bucolic bosky view? Did you love climbing those kinds of trees when you were a child? Is that man over there wooing that woman? You like that necklace? Then admire it. Observe the effort the boring host has made, aloud. He may light up. You might jump-start something new.

RULE SIX: *Watch the waffle*

Equally sharp was Shōnagan's eye for bores. High on her list of 'disagreeable things' comes the 'insignificant person who talks a lot and laughs loudly' and 'uses too many words', unaware that he is ridiculous, too self-involved to recognize that his listeners are better informed. Overlook Shōnagan's snobbery and here is the bore's fatal flaw: significance.

It's generous to offer listeners more than one topic; blether on and you'll seem self-obsessed, and rightly so because, if only out of naivety, this shows no awareness of the imperative to focus discussion and invite others to sign on to a topic.

If listeners can't relate, every word is a waste of energy, like throwing a ball without taking aim, which is why all tangents and remarks that loop nowhere are freighted with boredom – whatever their inherent interest. And verbiage is certain to wax listeners' ears. I heard a woman put down a slavish man (he was in love; she feigned not to notice): 'Gee, you're spewing inanities this morning.' But he wasn't. He was trying to impress her, in self-consciously florid terms. So if on the receiving end, listen harder: within the pomposity may be a pearl worth knowing.

Or not. For a time I worked at an arts institution. To stay awake during epic meetings, I translated, silently, into English, the jargon-laden prattle (most of which turned out to be about money). But the director had a useful catchphrase for silencing quarrels: 'I take a Brechtian stance on that.' Nobody could answer back because they couldn't understand.

I left.

RULE SEVEN: *Divert, don't dictate*

Ideally, conversation takes us out of ourselves. This is totally at odds with the bore's social strategy. Some bludgeon with fixed opinions, others rule with silence; all dictate to conversation by being its dead centre. What to do? Soldier-philosopher Sun Tzu observed: 'The highest warfare attacks strategy itself.' To beat bores, challenge their monopoly and their tactics: divert them.

Sociologist Max Weber compared ideas to railroad switchmen, able to redirect a culture's evolution. I'd add they fuel the engine. Why not attack a monologist's monoculture with a virus: a fresh idea? Just don't thump invisible lecterns or neglect to observe your listener: ask yourself, is this news to him?

Teasing may also throw bores off their well-worn tracks. I watched a self-important politician melt when a flirt tweaked his ruddy nose. Still, gently does it. If cheeky courtiers quickened the pulse of their jaded patrons, some went too far. The Earl of Rochester, Charles II's on-off favourite, got the boot for this squib:

> *God bless our good and gracious King*
> *Whose promise none relyes on*
> *Who never said A foolish thing*
> *Nor ever did A wise one.*

But the king soon fetched him back. Life grew too dull. (How could he do without the man who began a poem 'Her father gave her Dildoes six'?)

RULE EIGHT: *Use the difficulty*

Don't forget, a little learning can be a fun thing, sprinkled on the right company. As the anthropologist said, boredom spurs invention. Follow the example of novelist Sir Walter Scott, and milk for information:

> *There are few persons from whom you cannot learn something,*
> *and . . . everything is worth knowing.*

The exception, in my experience, being an aficionado of Swiss fridge magnets (the cow, when you wagged its tail – guess what? It went moo).

Still, as your bore talks you through his client list for the umpteenth time, try to capitalize on this opportunity to polish conversation skills. If he's exceptionally nasty, you could play outbore the bore, doing unto him what is done to you. But I doubt he'd notice, and you'd soon bore yourself.

Is boredom ever a virtue? Psychotherapist Adam Phillips

reckons it's a 'developmental achievement' and that adults are 'oppressive' to demand that children 'should be interested . . . Boredom is integral to the process of taking one's time.'

Perhaps he's right, we're too quick to cry 'bore'. We entertainment-rich consumerists are all a bit like Charles II: we demand to be amused.

Recently I took a train from London to Bath, in the designated family carriage. Most passengers read or snoozed. But one boy whined and moaned, all the way to Bath. The same boy whose top-drawer laptop computer delighted everyone else with top-volume war-game noise, all the way to Bath.

Every so often his parents told him to shut up and play his game, then went back to their books.

The elderly lady opposite me muttered, 'He needs a good talking to.'

We exchanged a grimace, went back to our books.

In retrospect, I feel sorry for that boy; unable to amuse himself, his parents acting as if this was solely his problem. Couldn't they have talked and played together?

Adam Phillips might argue that he needed to be ignored.

Believe me, I tried. I should have talked to the old lady instead.

RULE NINE: *Closed minds are bored minds*

The rough manners today bewilder older generations. Grannies lament the toys kids are given; when we were young, they say, we made our own fun. Old bores?

They know far better than TV-drenched we how to tell stories, take turns, listen.

Then again, in her old age Rebecca West had unforgiving memories of meeting Nobel laureate W.B. Yeats, who 'boomed at you like a foghorn'. The younger writer had far preferred frisking with other young writers present, and decades later remained astonished that 'Yeats wouldn't join in, until we fussed round and were nice to him . . . What he liked was solemnity.' Yes, even in her dotage, it didn't occur to West that the grand old man of letters might justifiably expect these literary whippersnappers to be interested in what he had to say.

That whiskery chap with the slow way of speaking has a trove of experience. So be patient, let him share it. You'll be the richer.

RULE TEN: *Be kind to the bore*
One day, he could be you.

Typology of Bores, Chores and other Conversational Beasts

DEAF IN BOTH EARS   *Ambiaures Inauditae Egotissimus*

Least forgivable are those ostensibly interesting bores, bereft of curiosity, complacently accustomed to consider being in their presence a privilege. Anyone who has been pursued by famous, rich or older men will recognize the problem. You say gold-digger; I say danger money.

With a shrug DIBE kills the question he dislikes. With a swivel of the eye he heckles any other who durst hold the floor.

'The point is,' he says, a prehensile fist smashing the table, if you venture a comment that strays from his preferred narrative line.

But while his self-importance often reaps fat rat-race rewards, DIBE usually has a dead-eyed spouse in tow, as well as an entourage of failed relationships – consoling testimony to the social limits of tunnel vision.

Tactics: Remind DIBE you exist. Make comparisons, seek advice, offer counter-examples to curtail the monologue: 'Reminds me of when I did X.' If DIBE is toxic, attack the core: smugness. Sympathize at each boast: 'How awful looking after so many houses!'; 'Don't businesses like that go under?'

Pluses: Since the demise of *Dynasty*, how many opportunities exist to pity the spoilt rich? Those sad, lonely billionaires . . .

8

Wit to Woo

On Humour as Social Engineering

Is your catchphrase 'Just joking'? Perhaps it's time to revise your repartee. How about this:

Two cannibals, eating a clown. One says to the other, 'Does this taste funny to you?'

It worked for Tommy Cooper, the madcap magician-comic, who knew well that humour, like clown-meat, is a matter of taste. But now, if I told it, quietly, in a quick, breathless burst, I guarantee the gag would pass you by.

I never crack jokes. Not that I don't try to be funny; I just prefer a side approach, smuggling humour into comments so that, if nobody notices, the custard pie is not on me – or so I like to think. Why bother at all? Robert Louis Stevenson nailed it:

Talk has none of the freezing immunities of the pulpit . . . A jest intervenes, the solemn humbug is dissolved in laughter.

If nothing else, Harvard University investigators have found that those who stride on life's sunny side outlive misery-guts, which may well be because they are not lonely, since humour is the electricity of intimacy. It helps us forget ourselves, braces emotional suspension, exercises minds, garnering friends and power, from bedroom to boardroom.

Cicero recalled Julius Caesar as a young lawyer,

so superior to one and all in wit and repartee that, even in foren-sic speeches, he prevailed over the arguments of other advocates with his conversational style.

Anyone can profit from humour. Yet I'm not alone in my fear of skidding on the banana skin of a slack wisecrack, nor my tendency to chuckle at the merest sniff of wit from someone else. Such cowardly tendencies are prudent social politics. And for all the mystique misting ideas about what makes something funny, laughter turns out to be an ultra-practical conversational fix-it. Eight times out of ten, wit has nothing to do with it.

What can this mean? For a start, anyone can be funnier – without being funny – if they appreciate how laughter works.

The Social Conjuror

Imagine there was a magic word that could, like a snap of the fingers, wind someone up, calm him down, make him listen, draw him near, send him packing, change the subject, or let you say what you want and get away with it?

There is. It's 'Ha-ha-ha'. And that's not all it can do.

Neuroscientist Robert Provine had a hunch that laughter was more significant to communication than some fellow academics credited. With difficulty, he raised funds to investigate 1,200 'laugh episodes' (moments of dialogue followed by laughter, in typical social situations). To his amazement, 'only about 10 per cent to 20 per cent of prelaugh comments were estimated by my assistants to be even remotely humorous.' Typical laugh-getters included 'I know!', 'Look, it's Andre!', 'Nice meeting you too', 'What can I say?' and 'How are you?'

If rarely a response to humour, what is laughter for? Provine speculated it expresses 'grunts and cackles from our animal unconscious', hand-me-downs from ancestor apes. Perhaps. We can't ask them. More useful is the notion that, like so much else in talk, laughter is a grooming device for smoothing and restyling interaction.

RULE ONE: *Laughter is a social organizer*

When we 'get it', 'it' is not only the joke, but the effervescent intimacy with everyone else laughing. And in those eight out of ten cases, where no joke is in sight, laughter serves as social punctuation: like an exclamation mark, it says, '*Really* good to meet you!' or '*Andre?* So it is!' On an emotional level, this shows approval: 'I'm talking to *you* and I *like* it!' On the practical, it denotes a change of topic.

So to laugh after 'What can I say?' is a way of saying, 'Not a lot on that topic! Any other offers?' And at Andre's arrival, its punctuation opens a gap in conversation, to let Andre in, or let out the person who spies him (noticing being a classic conversation getaway).

Laughter also opens trapdoors in serious moods and we use it tactically, as a matter of Machiavellian instinct. For instance, most of us laugh after raising troubling topics, a reflex that gives listeners two options: to laugh too, or to react seriously and talk. Hence we're wise to quip at our blunders. If others laugh, the moment is burst, conversation levitated out of awkwardness, and speakers are returned to an equal footing. No matter if their first impulse was to laugh at you, now it is with you: your quip gives permission.

This illustrates how laughter not only gives conversation rhythm, but also regulates intimacy, releasing tension, communicating emotion, performing a similar job to those dials you twiddle on stereos, equalizers. Without its pulse talk feels dead and social syntax buckles, because, in very precise ways, laughter synchronizes conversation's dance. Muff the joke, miss the beat, giggle too late, and you'll soon feel out of the loop – making humour a status game.

RULE TWO: *Laughter is a status moderator that can lift you up or down*

Casanova trod the knife-edge in 1750 Paris. New in town, seeking friends, he was chatting to a plump man at the opera when he spied a lady, 'covered in jewels but enormous in size':

> 'And who,' I asked my fat neighbour, 'is that fat pig?'
>> 'The wife of this fat pig.'
>> 'Oh! I beg a thousand pardons.'

Luckily the man, 'choking with laughter', promptly asked him to dinner, a coup later crowned when an aristocrat sneered that an actress admired by the Italian lothario had 'terrible legs'. Casanova replied:

> '*I cannot see them, monsieur; and anyway, in judging female beauty, the first thing I set apart are the legs.*'

The fortuitous pun won him 'immediate standing'.

But the easiest way to make people laugh is be their boss. I remember, a lowly assistant and new to a company, making a barbed remark in a meeting. Silence. Then the man next to me repeated it, and everybody needed straitjackets. Maybe they didn't hear me, maybe they disliked me, maybe my timing was way off. I prefer to think the problem was social position. Until this point I'd communicated in shades of blush, whereas he was resident funny man – far better qualified than me to be funny.

RULE THREE: *Humour melts barriers*

If I'd been more laid-back, however, banter might have brought me real influence. On-target laughter is a powerful weapon. Fourteenth-century artist Giotto vaporized social boundaries with backchat, winning the friendship of the King of Naples.

One scalding summer's day the king said, 'I'd stop painting if I were you.'

'I would too,' said Giotto, 'if I were you.'

This seems ample proof of George Bernard Shaw's claim:

> *To tell people the truth, you'd better make them laugh or they'll kill you.*

You can get away with murder if you make people laugh because a minor mental explosion disables thought and body.

Sportsmen exploit ridicule to scuttle opponents' concentration. In particular, Australian cricketers are maestros of 'sledging', aka ball-breaking. My favourite was yelled as England's Phil Tufnell moseyed over to the wicket:

'Oy, Phil, lend us your brain? We're trying to build us an idiot.'

Similarly, bons mots are slicker than pig grease for squeezing out of tight spots. Ninon de Lenclos, *salonnière* and calumniated pioneer of rights for women, such as changing lover every three months, sharpened her wit repulsing amorous suitors. Just as well. One day the queen, pressed by scandalmongers who accused Ninon of poisoning the flower of French youth, sent an order to quit town for 'a convent [*couvent*] of her choice'.

'I pray you,' Ninon told the messenger, 'say I choose the Grands Cordeliers.'

Punning on '*couvent*' (also 'monastery' in French), she had selected one whose monks' debauches were legendary. The stunned messenger returned to the palace and repeated her word for word.

'Fie, the villain,' said the queen with a laugh. 'Let her go where she wants.'

Comic Steve Allen explained the paralysis caused by laughter as a 'short-circuit' because humour plays games with our mental processing. The brain begins 'filing away the material according to what appears to be its face-value meaning, when suddenly . . . our consciousness perceives that there is more than one interpretation of the material. The brain is therefore momentarily startled, and its normal function interrupted. We suddenly face the fact we have been tricked.'

The tingly adrenaline rush that follows makes it harder still to be angry at the laughter's cause. Happily, this mind–body trade flows both ways, and physical ruses can tickle an unsuspecting mind into feeling funny.

Laughter Without Wit: Some Tips

Philosopher Henri Bergson observed that 'all laughter is inherently social', and psychologists confirm that nothing eats away a sense of humour like isolation and its concomitant, self-consciousness. Conversely, there's nothing like other people to make us laugh.

Experimenters asked some seven-year-olds to listen to comedy tapes on headphones. Alone they laughed little, but with another child their giggle rate shot up. What is more, the closer they sat the more both laughed. Even if only one could hear the tape.

Not only is laughter a reflex, but it is contagious. Hence broadcasters go in for 'laughspeak', a giggly style of talk, to tame interviewees; hence laugh-tracks are dubbed over sitcoms; hence, while traditionally it is wrong to laugh at your own jokes, laughter analyst Robert Provine found that speakers laughed on average 46 per cent more than listeners. And just as it has been observed that we laugh harder at people we find sexy, so the reverse is true: the more you make others laugh, the more they'll be attracted to you.

All of which suggests some wit-free techniques for magnifying mirth:

Relax: be informal, focus on them (inhibition squishes laughter)
Stand close: the nearer, the more they'll laugh
Touch them lightly, occasionally
Use eye contact

Show your amusement

Don't fake smiles or laughs: always obvious (real smiles reach
   the eyes)

Be near laughing people, the more, the merrier

Bring others in (*note*: laughter's SOS will attract others, helping
   dilute bores)

Expect to be amused: optimism optimizes humour

Laugh at your own jokes, except in larger groups (with an
   audience, joking becomes performance, and the same
   criteria apply as for stand-ups)

Drink alcohol

What is Funny?

If humour is organic to certain situations, can it be cultivated?
What is funny anyway?

Defining humour seems almost the definition of foolish,
like trying to sculpt sunbeams or bottle rainbows. Indeed,
fitting farce ensued after Clarence Richardson, fifty-five,
of Wessington, South Dakota, died in 1946, bequeathing a
princely $30,000 to whoever sent his postmaster the best
definition of 'joke'. Seven thousand entries in, the postmaster
went to court, and the will was quashed on the grounds the
deceased had been of unsound mind.

I suspect Richardson had an entirely healthy sense of
humour. However, stern philosopher-wit Voltaire, a friend
of Ninon de Lenclos, cautioned:

*A joke explained ceases to be a joke. Any commentator of bons
mots is a fool.*

Then again, Voltaire might have been protecting trade secrets. Although comedians harp on about how analysis destroys comedy, this is a bit like surgeons saying the leg is a marvel of nature and shouldn't be chopped up: so it is, but they still understand the mechanics, can dissect and repair it. What comedians really mean is that talking about what makes something funny isn't a barrel of laughs. But none can deny they work at it, and, as Ninon demonstrated, a spot of apprentice work comes in handy.

RULE FOUR: *We laugh hardest at the stuff that is hardest to talk about*

Comedy jigs on the borders of our discomfort zones. Ricky Gervais, star-creator of *The Office*, claimed humour has no taboos. But tampering with taboos, snapping at sensibilities, is comedy's *raison d'être*. Each joke has a victim: there must be an 'it' to 'get'; even if 'it' is a belief, it is attached to someone, and a reductive view would be that the butt's invariably the listener, laughing at himself for being fooled.

However, lines of attack tend to be indirect. Anthropologists found that jokes in North American tribes skirt seven topics:

Sex and gender
Shortcomings or social deviance
Sickness, suffering, death
Religion
Wealth
Power and authority
Social stereotypes and relationships

These targets, sources of desire and weakness, strike nerves everywhere because comedy is a fairground mirror, monstering what disturbs us, making 'it' – our fear, our folly – ridiculous. It defangs threats, deflates authority, transmuting the funny-peculiar into the funny-ha-ha, reminding us that nothing matters, but plenty's worth knocking.

And we shouldn't overlook the enduringly popular, ever economical joke resource: its machinery. Wordplay, such as the pilloried pun, is humour's junk food, embezzling laughs from bamboozled listeners' brains. Unburdened of anything so portentous as a comical idea, the average pun has little to say for itself beyond 'Duh, gotcha, filing error!' Which may explain why people are so down on them. Still, seven- to twelve-year-olds of all ages remain in thrall, including me.

RULE FIVE: *The right target is what others are prepared to laugh at*

Jokes, like taboos, shift with society, and Russell Brand disproved Ricky Gervais on 12 September 2001, getting fired from MTV for presenting a show dressed as Osama Bin Laden. Brand had forgotten humorist James Thurber's dictum:

$$\text{Tragedy} + \text{Time} = \text{Comedy}$$

Although jokes thumb a nose at fears, they work best as 'an epitaph on an emotion', not when feelings are live and kicking, and cracks at others' expense may cheapen you. So aim at listeners' assumptions. Even better, joke against yourself.

In unfamiliar terrain, only a bold, brilliant or socially suicidal wit should tackle:

What others in the room look, smell, sound, feel, or taste
   like
Wives, husbands, kids, siblings, parents
Pets (wake me when it's over)
The poor and needy
Genitalia, odoriferous effluvia, biological hazards
Obscure hobbies, chess, philately, maths, physics,
   esoterica
How wonderful life is, how brilliant you are
Plague, famine, war, pestilence
The horrid food/drink/guests (to the host)
The horrid host (unless it's you)

RULE SIX: *For wit to woo, better to amuse and be amused than ape a stand-up*

Despite Britain's pride in our nation's sense of humour, a 2007 survey found the average citizen remembered only two jokes. Surprised? Don't be.

Social humour is generally triggered by situation, not ready-canned, and the monopoly conditions in which professional comics operate have none of conversation's companionable to and fro. Indeed, so antisocial is the audience-performer dynamic that jokes can de-emulsify conversations into gag contests – not always desirable. Be that as it may, professionals' comic wisdom can be culled to boost everyday wit.

Attitude: 'Never, never try to be funny!' commanded *Producers* genius Mel Brooks. Following this advice doesn't mean never laughing; rather, relaxing to lower the stakes. Try quips, not shaggy dog stories, and smile: the more confident you seem, the less exposed you feel, the clearer your voice will be, and the funnier you'll appear.

Pitch woo: If misjudging the audience is the commonest cause of humour failure, second is knowing the audience too well, and letting on, by jabbing at their insecurities. Don't tout your sharps, oversell or announce 'Here's a funny one' before testing the water. Instead, do as comics do: build rapport, lob the odd compliment.

Recognition: Read a group, ensuring it can read you. Humour has a regional accent, dramatized by actor Simon Pegg in this exchange between friends (B is British, A, American):

> B: *I had to go to my grandad's funeral last week.*
> A: *Sorry to hear that.*
> B: *Don't be. It was the first time he ever paid for the drinks.*
> A: *I see.*

Observe what makes listeners tick, ideally taking the truth and twisting it. Or as another comic advised, don't give a funny opinion: give an opinion in a funny way. Forget rococo riffs on harpsichords: people will more readily endorse the comic value you assign to, say, the horror of opening beer since the ring-pull's demise, or winkling a favour out of a miserly neighbour, or ploughing through Ikea on an August bank holiday.

Style: Humour speaks with forked tongue – in double-meanings, incongruity, image, metaphor and so on – but over-complicate it and no one will get it. A cleverly bowled joke deceives just enough to be caught; listeners' pleasure being in their mind turning somersaults, then making a clean landing. For instance, a phrase like 'bungalow mind' places an extra processing load on the brain, which effort makes it stick.

So be economical, gulling listeners' imaginations into being your collaborators. Use as few words as possible, employ vivid, visual language, and act out stories with body and face. (Like actress Lucille Ball, who was so adept her scripts featured 'light bulb' or 'puddle up' as facial stage directions.) Dazzle their mind's eye and they won't see a punchline hurtling at them.

Pace: Stand-ups say: 'Never step on your punchline.' Meaning: savour the pause before a gag, defined by Ajaye Franklin as 'the lighting of the fuse'. Telling a funny tale, build suspense, letting misunderstanding and expectation coalesce in listeners' minds, adhering to the principle: don't say it until you have to.

Surprise: No doubt Julius Caesar's witty conquests in court taught him: 'The most powerful weapon of war is the unexpected.' Mix maladapted elements to wreak comedy havoc: praise the bad, exaggerate, understate, fake anger, feign delight. Use inversion: rather than 'What a big pancake roll!' say, as a lawyer did to me, 'This pancake roll wants to devour me.'

Humour works by guile, not advertisement, but play with comic expectations and punchlines may be discarded. A Bill Cosby routine began: 'One time I had a sore throat, bad sore throat.' He paused, preparing his audience for a joke, then resumed in a cross child's voice, 'I have a sore throat.' They cracked up; as much because the pause primed them for a gag.

Follow the way of woe: In funny-land nothing gets better: the trajectory is always bad gets worse gets more and more absurd. Such as the time I was whining about my expanding bottom. My husband – sighing, eyes shut, in bed – said, 'Not at all.' So in I hopped, to a loud crack. My side of the bed had gone through the floor. My husband groaned, got up, and we lifted it out. Another crack. The leg on his side had snapped. Finally, so did he.

The Anatomy of a Joke

Jokes embody in miniature the short, dapper definition of comedy given by the short, great Charlie Chaplin: 'Two opposite ideas that collide.'

The simplest come in two parts: the set-up (building comic expectation) and the punchline (exploding expectation to reveal the skulduggery). Like mathematical equations organized on absurdist principles, a good joke's incongruous ideas are so deviously intertwined that the deception dissolves only at the end.

Think of it as a tale of two stories. If the set-up implies one storyline (the one listeners believe in), the punch reveals a second has been tucked inside all along. But the equation never quite adds up: it defies logic, like a magic trick. The mind boggles, and so we laugh.

$$\text{SET-UP} + \text{PUNCHLINE} = \text{LAUGHTER}$$

Or alternatively,

$$\text{INCONGRUITY} \times \text{CREDULITY} = \textit{SURPRISE!}$$

To be effective, the first story, the set-up, targets a specific audience assumption. Only if the aim is accurate will the trap spring, two ideas crash-bang-wallop, and then bumble about, rubbing their heads, quaking with mirth. This chicanery relies on intellectual prestidigitation;

somewhere buried in the set-up is a slippery item about which the joke turns, which stand-up Greg Dean calls the 'connector'.

Here's a Dean special:

For Father's Day, I took my father out – it only took seven shots. I could always drink him under the table.

This double-yolker has two connectors: 'shots' and 'took out' (both our flexible friends, puns). But the method only works if your aim is true, landing bang on listeners' target assumptions. Which is why the best jokes are:

Concise (only telling details, no superfluous or repeated words)
Easy to follow (expressive delivery and weighted
    pauses, focusing attention on the connector and the reveal)
Timed to maximize misunderstanding and surprise

Save the punch till the last word.

But play it how you want it. Roseanne Barr's feisty Lady Caliban comic persona grabbed audiences by the throat, but liked to leave them hanging. She began with a premise, took a little journey ('the hook') drawing out the first storyline, sinking it in listeners' imaginations, and then . . .

Premise:	He comes in and he says, *Roseanne, why don't you try to be more aggressive in bed?*
Hook:	So, I thought about it and the other night, we're lying there and he reaches for me . . . and I said,
Pause:	
Punchline:	[screaming] *NOOOOOOO!*

And the target assumption? Barr's character: that she would want to please her man.

Please.

RULE SEVEN: *Let humour shift the temperature*

But the best humour is organic not premeditated, and medicinal, according to American Norman Cousins, who beat 500–1 odds of recovery from an agonizing condition with an inspired hypothesis: If illness is psychosomatic, why not wellness? Treatment began with episodes of *Candid Camera*.

Cousins's smart inversion has suggested a sneaky humour tactic. Why sweat up a quip if you can snatch laughter from the jaws of the social need it serves, by taking the mood and shaking it?

To neutralize a problem, isolate, then ironize it. Use repetition. Say she says, 'Don't get me started . . .' You say (warmly, not snootily), 'Don't get her started.' He spills wine? Say, 'My shirt. My shirt!'

Dropped a clanger? Make light: 'Is it time to talk about the weather yet?' or 'This reminds me of a joke. Shame I can't remember it.'

Nervy? 'Don't worry about my wobbly voice, I'm just terrified.'

He said something funny but the feeling isn't mutual? Don't let silence gouge an embarrassing hole. A light eyebrow-raiser – 'You!', 'Honestly!' – is enough to let conversation continue smoothly.

We tease those we care about, because this flattering liberty assumes the other person will get the joke. Use the power. And if pressed by a pachyderm pest, try this boaster blunderbuss, overheard by cocktail-talk collector, Andrew Barrow:

Congratulations. Are you frightfully pompous now?

Typology of Bores, Chores and other Conversational Beasts

CAN YOU BELIEVE IT?   *Mendax Mirabundus*

Thank heaven for eyebrows. How else to sustain that look of amazement as Can You Believe It launches into another vertically challenged tale?

Few companions are as wearing. Coercive little phrases – 'Wasn't that incredible?' – reach out from her flat-as-yesterday's-lemonade recitals, pulling her audience by the ear, demanding that they a) show amazement b) wake up.

To an extent, such cues are welcome clues: how else to know which parts are meant to be fascinating? However, emotional stage directions pre-empt spontaneous wonder, and subject to such bullying, the rebel in us recoils while the nice conformist affixes a smile, wondering why we're annoyed as well as bored. (A fastidious friend took agin an old roommate at a reunion, not so much due to the exhaustive sermon on her visit to a cathedral, but because it ended in the command 'Just think!')

What is worse, CYBI is so busy imposing reactions, she never learns what truly rocks our world.

Tactics: CYBI means well, and we've all been in situations where our excitement gets lost in translation. If it so happens that not only would you believe it, but you've a better story, take the floor (and give everybody some respite): say, 'Yes, reminds me of when . . .'

Pluses: If you start issuing Wow!-prompts, this is your subconscious hinting that an encounter is on the slide. Seek more creative means of support, or get out of there.

9

How to Tell a Lie

On the Detection of Untruths

It suits us to believe that liars are punished and their schemes backfire, but this is self-deception. There is a reason witnesses in courts of law tell the truth, the whole truth and nothing but the truth, 'so help me, God'. If we went about our business voicing our every suspicion, lust and grievance, we too would need a divine bodyguard. Imagine:

'You as daft as you look?'

'My elbow has more personality.'

'Your brat stinks.'

RULE ONE: *Trimming the truth is a social skill*

Our species' success comes of sociability, serving four social goals – collaborative, convivial, competitive and conflictive – none of which correlates with truth unmodified.

While getting along means being trustworthy, could we gain each other's trust if we were totally honest?

Take the dilemma of vet Yoav Alony-Gilboa, eating rabbit at a 'posh restaurant'.

> *Halfway through I hit a bone and thought to myself, 'This is not right.' I checked another bone that, for a rabbit, shouldn't be there, and it was. I realized we were eating a cat, beautifully seasoned, tender and moist . . . I didn't complain, however, as it would have been too embarrassing for my hosts.*

Sociability requires self-sacrifice, and kindness, self-censorship. Skipping awkward bits, sparing feelings, saving face: these are the lies that bind, invisible stitches of untruth, as we tailor conversation to our audience, but so intrinsic to the process that we scarcely notice we are doing it. Ideally.

But although lying is innate, found in gorillas and human toddlers, and deception well documented in grizzling infants who find instant succour in their parents' arms, tact is something only socializing can teach.

Worryingly, saving lies are falling from fashion. Confession is a flimsy alternative to a fully paid-up conscience, yet the often invasive mantra of 'sharing' is little challenged. The soap operatics of self-revelation are free to all in the access-all-areas info swamp that is the Internet, with scanty particulars on full display. And the 'home truth', seldom less than self-serving – a warrant to bully or pass problems on, breaches of social trust in the name of honesty – passes for virtue.

An unsuspecting friend received a call from a recovering addict, an acquaintance long out of her life, who outlined the vintage sexual fantasies in which she had starred, back at school – a violation prescribed by his therapist! The road to responsibility?

RULE TWO: *Directness is a privilege of intimacy*

A representative defence of directness comes from singer Mutya Buena:

> 'People say, "You're so pretty but you're so rude; you shouldn't be talking the way you're talking." Excuse me? [*Imagine extravagant hand gestures here.*] I can't help the way I am. I've grown up with four older brothers so I've learned not to take any nonsense . . . People seem to be intimidated by me, even small children.' She laughs. 'I think that people took my bitchiness for being horrible, rather than just being me.'

Being herself means being bitchy but not being horrible? Such contorted thinking from such a bright woman shows how easily we think well of ourselves, and how much is lost if we forget directness is a right we earn. Only a friend can say you look vile as a favour.

Honest Delusions

Is directness honest? Depends what you call truth. Watching a philosopher grapple with it can feel like watching a fly fling itself at a window, unaware that the glass it bashes (its perceptions) is both what inspires its attempt to get outside, and the barrier to success.

We're all stuck inside ourselves; what we see is partial and only fickle language is available to comprehend it. Worse, our truths reside in memories, which aren't static entities but unreliable, imaginative acts, each recollection a minor physio-logical miracle, as electricity and chemicals surge, switching on allied brain cells – physical alliances that themselves ebb and shift with fresh experience and time's sifting sands. In a sense, we are but figments of our imagination.

So why don't we go mad?

RULE THREE: *We're biased to believe and tell convenient truths*

In *Consciousness Explained* Daniel Dennett reflected:

> *Our fundamental tactic of self-protection, self-control, and self-definition is not spinning webs, but telling stories, and more particularly concocting and controlling the story we tell others – and ourselves – about who we are.*

Stories save us, thanks to our amazing capacity to fit evidence to expectations and believe the best of ourselves. Paradoxically, the self-serving editing by which we confect our identities shows how important integrity is to us, how much we long to be right – whether screwing a good deal, saying an affair hurts no one, or claiming bitchiness isn't rude.

By contrast, politic social awareness asks us to sense that truth is a contest between facts, their relevance and their meaning, which, like memories, alter with time and new information; to acknowledge that others see things otherwise, and our truth isn't The Truth. Thus conversational caution keeps us honest, by reminding us to take turns, hear other points of view and frame our words accordingly. Thank goodness.

Imagine, if truth were all that mattered, and a one-size-fits-all fundamental law identified it? We could forget ethics, humility. We certainly needn't worry about getting on, having a conversation. No, we could disappear up our fundamentals, stamp on all who disagreed, assured of our own supreme righteousness. Even former US Defense Secretary Donald Rumsfeld, unbending in war, appreciated relativism:

Needless to say, the President is correct. Whatever it was he said.

The Good Lie: A User's Guide

So what is a lie? Concealment? Fabrication? Deception? Omission?

A useful recipe for an active lie comes from William Hirstein:

I lie to you when (and only when)
1. I claim *p* to you.
2. *p* is false.
3. I believe that *p* is false.
4. I intend to cause you to believe *p* is true by claiming that *p* is true.

RULE FOUR: *A bad lie is antisocial*

If we accept the premise of doctors' Hippocratic oath (do no harm), we can define a bad lie by the test set in 1999 by the British judge who backed the Reynolds defence (named after the former Irish prime minister, who felt he had been libelled, but lost the case).

Is the untruth stated knowingly, maliciously, recklessly?
Which implies that:

RULE FIVE: *A good lie may mean sincerely well*

This fits with thinker Bernard Williams's evocation of truth's dual personality, as consisting of sincerity and accuracy. The laws of good manners – don't impose, don't embarrass – resolve the problem of when sincerity and accuracy don't get along (you sincerely want to thank your hosts; mentioning the cat is superfluous).

And after all, competing truths redefine facts. Is the attentive, deferential doctor a docile wife or a walkover mother? Should she be? Different rules govern each role we play, and not framing our words to a particular situation or relationship courts hazard. (So if your sister had taken you to the restaurant, the cat might not be off-limits after all.)

Do as Emily Dickinson ordained:

> *Tell all the Truth but tell it slant.*

Tell a Lie?

If we depend on convenient untruths, surely we need also to detect them. But while evolutionary psychologists view lying as an adaptation to aid social survival, one that hastened the growth of man's twisty-turny brain, evolution is rather lagging on our capacity to ferret out lies.

Investigations have found that the average person has a 40–60 per cent chance of rumbling one, and professional lie-hunters fare no better. And for each cliché about how liars act – they scratch their nose, fidget, their eyes roam, they look up and to the right – there is zero evidence.

Might as well flip a coin? Not quite.

Although each liar lies in his own way, all suffer three pressures:

Emotional (nerves, excitement)
Cerebral (they have to keep track)
Behavioural (they try not to fidget, stutter, etc.)

These pressures produce clues that, if many appear together, may well tell a lie.

Non-verbal clues:
Eyes don't complete the smile.

Decreased movement, gestures, blinking (the extra load on a liar's mind stills his body).

Seems unco-operative or uninvolved.

Vocal clues:
Voice sounds tense, negative, its pitch is slightly higher than normal.

Verbal clues:
Stories sound implausible, rehearsed.

Statements are short on details, especially visual, sensual, spatial or temporal (the liar is unlikely to observe a place was cold, smelly, dark, etc.).

Language is less immediate, more uncertain and negative, with passive clauses and indirect statements (e.g. 'The man told me he felt ill', rather than, 'The man said, "I'm going to vomit" ').

Most reliable are verbal and vocal clues. Of course, abnormal behaviour will be apparent only if you know what normal is (another reason to prioritize face-to-face talk).

And be warned: adroit, practised liars doctor the facts to feel like truths they can believe in. All tests agree that the best liars are sales professionals. But for them, selling the hell out of a product they don't rate isn't insincere but a sign of devotion – so by Bernard Williams's measure, aren't they good, honest workers?

Whereas second-rate liars overcomplicate things, going out of their way to avoid fabrication, preferring ambiguity to committing to a yes or no. They omit information, claim a faulty memory, don't answer questions, meet allegations with generalizations or subjective truths, heap up irrelevant details, as if to hide untruth in a thicket of unrelated truth, and garnish statements with groves of excess verbiage. They answer, as did one-time US Secretary of State Alexander Haig,

That's not a lie, it's a terminological inexactitude.

Guidelines for Snaring Liars
(Or, Alternatively, Not Getting Caught)

We're prejudiced in favour of words that confirm our expectations.
(Say what they want to hear; they will deceive themselves.)

We're biased to believe those we find attractive, friendly and confident.
(We believe what we like to see: smile, meet their eyes, dress well.)

The higher the stakes, the likelier a liar will seem stressed or rehearsed.

(Psych yourself down by shrinking the significance of the lie, and keep it simple, precise and no quibbling.)

Falsification is harder than omission, so make the suspected liar account for himself.

(The best liars believe what they say. Stick to the truth, edited.)

Look for a liar and you'll be misled by expectations. Instead, sieve behaviour for indications he may be lying. Does he look tense? Is he thinking hard? Playing for time?

(Don't over-control behaviour: fidgeting and gestures are normal.)

Don't rush to conclusions about whether odd behaviour means he's lying: instead, seek explanations for any mismatch between what he says and how he acts.

(Imply alternative reasons why you might seem under pressure.)

Act suspicious and you put the liar on guard.

(Assume everyone is suspicious; act as if they've every faith in you.)

Increase the cognitive load: ask him to repeat things, darting back and forth in sequence.

(Get the other person talking. Can you tell your story in any order?)

As he retells his story, does his tone or style alter, the level of detail drop off?
(Lie as if reliving it, keeping immediacy and amount of details consistent.)

Is he going out of his way to tell you something you didn't ask?
(Never lie unless you have to.)

And remember the clichés. To be believed, carry a hanky; never scratch your nose.

How to Spot – or Mask – a Bad Idea

Verbal sharp practice may hone the appearance of reason. Equally, many a bad case has stifled a good idea. Don't be misled by rhetorical feints, or, alternatively, miss an opportunity to beef up your argument. Here is a catalogue of alluring nonsense, baseless assertions and fallacious conclusions that arise in conversation at work, rest and play.

The assertion-request
A blackmail technique for leveraging demands with an emotional but evidentially challenged premise. As in, 'Everyone has one, Mum. Why can't I?'

Character assassination
Ad hominem/feminam arguments discredit ideas by attacking the advocate. Or conversely, they collapse distinctions between actor and act. They call the child naughty because it has done a naughty deed. Or call the man evil because they call the word evil because, once upon a time, an evil use has been made of it, e.g. the plot-spur to Philip Roth's novel *The Human Stain*, a misunderstanding over the word 'spook'.

If X, then Y
'If they hoiked up your salary, then they should mine.' Says who? Note that 'then' is not the same as 'therefore'.

'We have no reason to doubt'
But no reason to believe either. (Popular with politicians.)

Wrong case, right answer?
So they use a rubbish argument for why the sky is blue (Jupiter spilt his ink). Does that invalidate the proposition?

Begging question
These clever smears can smuggle assertions into questions. Such as: 'When did you stop beating your wife?' Or 'Ideal for curing orange peel.' Since when is cellulite a disease?

We are the great and the good; our quango is great and good
Logicians call this the 'composition fallacy' – assuming that a group has the qualities of its members.

Britain is rich; every Briton is rich
Oh, sure. The reverse of the composition fallacy, this is the divisive fallacy, which assumes all members share the qualities of the group. As in, each Beatle is a towering musical genius.

If X, then Y. Not X, therefore not Y?
Not true! Just because the business made lots of money last year and we got bonuses, now the profits are down our bonuses shouldn't automatically flop.

Either X or Y. X, therefore not Y
Again, says who? Why not both? Who says they're contingent anyway? For instance: 'This pie tastes awful. Either the blueberries were off, or I

forgot to add sugar. The blueberries taste funny. So I must have added sugar.'

Bogus analogy

Misleading comparisons, comforting though they may be, lead to loony conclusions: 'Shakespeare was a genius and he never learned how to use the Internet. Therefore I can still be a genius but foxed by Google.' 'Saddam is like al-Qaeda. Therefore, blast Saddo, bye-bye al-Q.'

What a dilemma!

Another either/or fallacy, whereby false equivalences are linked to form the basis of a decision. As in: 'Either I lose weight or I'll never be happy.'

Unhappy averages

The golden mean fallacy is what democracy rests on: the notion that the best solution is a blend of all the different views out there. But think about it: if applied in the realm of interior decoration, the average wouldn't be golden, but a world in sludge-grey.

Nice argument, shame about the premise

You can build logic on a wild idea, but it won't make the argument right. As in: 'In a world made of strawberries, sugar and cream would be fatal, due to maceration . . .'

Upgrading evidence

You may have data; this cannot determine ultimate values. 'No skin cream smooths more soothingly, say our tests on twenty-three women basted in it for a week. Ergo, this is the elixir of youth.'

After X, therefore because of X

So she left after you burned the toast: that doesn't make Breville the reason why.

Do I smell fish?

Don't let a niffy red herring throw you off the scent: presented with data, question whether it's relevant enough to be called information.

Price = Value

Our management consultant cost a lot therefore his advice is good? Well, if it makes you feel better . . .

Value by association

The language of hope gums together spurious marketing claims.

Regard with caution: 'help', 'like', 'virtually', 'acts', 'works to', 'can', 'up to', 'as much as', 'looks like', 'fortified', 'enriched', 'strengthened', 'fights', 'combats'. (All code for: 'But not quite what you'd like it to do'.)

You too!

Projecting the weakness of your case on to someone else. For example, the man accused of racism accuses his accuser of discrimination.

Minimization

So it was your first time. So you only broke one teacup. So? You broke it. (My catchphrase as a toddler: 'Didn't mean to, doesn't matter.')

Straw doll

Redescribing someone's position to make it seem weaker:

'You want to spend all day getting dusty and thirsty and burned?'

'No, I want to go to the beach.'

'Oh.'

Typology of Bores, Chores and other Conversational Beasts

THE INSINUATOR

Iago Scabpickus

Are you haunted by the third person? During arguments, does the same name keep popping up? '*She* said you like mountaineering'; '*He* told me vintage jewellery is for cheapskates'; '*She* said you said that I said I didn't like her.'

This person is the Insinuator, often a nimble youngest child, schooled in sowing discord, using elder siblings as Trojan horses for advancing his own agendas.

Fishing techniques differ: some Insinuators favour hooks, some flies, some scratch their catch's belly. But all want something, if only a reaction. To that end, annoyingly – this being the point – they'll assume private knowledge of your desires and dreams, then poke holes in them. Common baits are under-the-rib comments: 'Bet you didn't like that' or 'You scrub up well'

.

The Insinuator believes himself a politician. In fact, he missed his vocation on the stage. This is never more evident than when delivering what he considers bad news. It isn't his voice, good though this usually is, soft as a velvet paw, the merest gleam of a claw in its anticipation of your reaction to what, sadly, he must impart . . . No, it's how he engineers the blanks between words. The Insinuator is a Pinteresque purveyor of pauses – extended to span canyons, which panicked listeners populate with Bosch-like visions of horror.

The good news is the script usually falls short of its . . . dramatic . . . punctuation. No news can be that bad . . . Can it?

Tactics: The lever of his power is irritation, so meet taunt with tease; he'll rise like a neurotic trout.

Pluses: If the Insinuator is hard to spot initially, once a victim, you won't forget.

10

Pillow Talk

On the Languages of Love

Once, conversation was a dirty word, embracing every form of congress of the flesh. The association remains fitting. The way to a heart may lie through the stomach, but more potent are those aphrodisiacs fed via the eyes and ears.

Among the craftiest seducers were courtesans, rated since the *heterae* of Ancient Greece for their limber minds as much as their pliant morals. Many were poets, but their finest art was sales. Elizabethan traveller Thomas Coryat warned of the Venetian hired siren's

> *Hart-tempting harmony of voice . . . A good Rhetorician, and a most elegant discourser . . . shee will assay thy constancy with her Rhetoricall tongue.*

Nineteenth-century *grande horizontale* Esther Guimond remarked it was strange 'that we courtesans alone be worthy and able to converse with philosophers'. But nothing pricks desire sharper than our erotic dream machine, the imagination, and ingenuity at caressing it upped a lady's price. And if agile tongues open purses, they engorged minds in the salon of her rival, La Païva, according to poet Théophile Gautier: 'Conversation was always sparkling, original, rich in unheard-of ideas and expressions.'

In our noisy world, words still arouse: sex phone-lines prove it. Yet when we like someone we're often tongue-tied by nerves and adrenaline, elemental to sexual chemistry, and worry about finding the right words. This can be enough to silence us.

Is that such a bad thing? Across the world and time, people have lured lovers in a glance, *à la* Romeo and Juliet, in throbbing nightclubs, or, like traditional Apache teenagers, whose courtship may entail sitting together for up to an hour in silence.

'It's better,' said one seventeen-year-old. 'You don't know how to talk yet.'

Many techno-literati favour indirect approaches, like dater Andrew MacGowan:

I knew what I wanted and the Internet cut out the middleman. You can meet people in bars and clubs, but then the first element is attraction. I wanted to use a medium where you talked to someone on the phone before meeting and saw whether you formed a bond.

Yes. Then again, you lose the precious early bonding moments and the memories that form close up, as well as risk inspiring fantasies that bring needless disappointment when you meet.

And can you know what you want before seeing it? Sex rewards serendipity.

Communication doesn't just create or conserve relationships; it is their essence, and face to face matters since so much lies beyond speech. I could tell I liked someone by the butterflies that jived in my belly when we met, and the daydreams after – second-guessing the meaning of a hesitation, a lowered voice, the shade of a smile; promises that neither e-mail nor telephone deliver.

In eighteenth-century Madrid under the Inquisition, prohibition heightened desire and eloquence at expressing it: 'On their walks, in the churches, at the theatre, [ladies] speak with their eyes to whomever they wish, and have a perfect command of this seductive language.' But the most spellbinding gaze speaks louder with words. Chat-up lines abound, and some work; however, subtler methods exist to ramp up tension, signal bad intentions and ensure your pillow talk doesn't send lovers to sleep – not even in a relationship's mellow autumn.

Sweet Talk, Hard Sell: The Rising Price of Negotiating for Love

Romance makes chess of the most humdrum conversation because in love and lust, all are strategists. We can't help it; millions of years' evolution and millennia of cultural change have conditioned us to massage our words to attract value-added partners. But recent decades have shaken up the curriculum of our sentimental educations, and romantic values have metastasized, with the length and style of courtship as unpredictable as ladies' hemlines. Conversation – seeing others' point of view, speaking to their desires – has never been so necessary.

For centuries men traded women in deals weighed by dowries, like so many gold balls and chains, and for all the mist swaddling romance, the marketplace persists and is increasingly volatile. In 1993 economists Theodore Bergstrom and Mark Bagnoli dubbed courtship 'the waiting game', because in traditional societies the richer the groom, the older he tended to be, and the younger his pretty bride. They predicted that as female autonomy grew, women would marry later, to men closer in age. Almost right; however, divorce and singledom are soaring.

They had overlooked the strains of negotiating for love in a free-market sexual economy. In *The Challenge of Affluence* Avner Offer demonstrated that as wealth rises, marital satisfaction falls. Why? Just as money doesn't end problems but precipitates new ones, so it is with choices. (Call it the quantity theory of insecurity.) Desires alter when we needn't wed to be kept, fed or watered.

Ask model-actress-poet Jerry Hall, who in 1985, still embroiled with Mick Jagger, memorably drawled:

My mother said it was simple to keep a man, you must be a maid in the living room, a cook in the kitchen and a whore in the bedroom. I said I'd hire the other two and take care of the bedroom bit.

By 2007, the focus was less on what she could provide than get:

You know the kind of guy I'm looking for? A guy on my own wavelength. A guy I can have a conversation with. I've tried toyboys,

I've done lots of sexy guys, and some have been very smart and nice, but you can't talk to them about anything. Maybe I'm not going to enough cocktail parties.

Hall could always take care of herself, of course. Nonetheless, this trend affects everyone in upwardly mobile economies. If we can meet our needs, we base decisions on wants and we want it all: to be caressed, supported, entertained, preferably by a partner of similar status, personality, IQ and background (the well-educated, far from less superficial, fret most about partners' 'collective desirability').

But social change has outpaced biology and cultural ideals. Pregnancy remains a bigger deal than ejaculation, and cookie-cutter ideals of macho and girly, formed when sex roles embodied the division in male and female spheres, remain deeply embedded, and continue to shape desires and tactics for meeting them; breast implants, for instance. Women still wish to be treated like ladies, men still wish to be 'real' men; all want independence, but none, if they can help it, to pay the escalating bill.

RULE ONE: *Romance is a dance and an audit*

So romantic conversation today has to play some very old games, hurdle towering contradictions, scale sky-scraping aspirations, as well as glean mate-rating data.

Luckily it is brilliant at the latter. Even a speed-date, the same duration as the three-minute pop songs and foxtrots our parents and grandparents had to tickle each other's fancy, is enough to assess if you two might have more to discuss. A survey has found that even though snap judgements rest on surface details, our instinct draws us to physical traits – age, weight, height – that, unlike eye or hair colour, give ultra-reliable clues to the socio-economic factors we care about. And not forgetting our voice, which, from vocab to grammar to accent, is a treacherous informant on everything from geographical and social origins, to aspirations to temperament to health.

At the start of a relationship, then, the chief difficulty for would-be pillow talkers isn't so much working out if you share common ground as shimmying alluringly over it. Flirting is at a premium in contemporary metropolitan society, sexy because those who can get along have more options. And while nineteenth-century Japanese marriage codes allowed 'she talks too much' as one of seven grounds for divorce, and while chaps once joked that they proposed marriage to fill an awkward silence (after the frantic blab of courtship dried up), nowadays, settling down doesn't mean an end of conversation.

We should be so lucky. Today, quality communication is an almost oppressive ideal, expected day in, day out, in the talka-thon of a long-haul relationship. *Über* eligible, *über* talent scout Simon Cowell rationalized his reluctance to get hitched:

> *The superstitious side of me goes, 'I couldn't follow that'. [My parents] were as happy as I've ever seen two people, mainly because they never stopped talking. From the second they woke up to the second they went to bed, yak yak yak, all day long – I used to call them the chipmunks.*

Except, when is there time for meetings of minds? Infatua-tion must be hot-housed (like all dopamine-releasers, it is an addiction). But we have so much else to do, plus endless sexual window-shopportunities – from porn, to on-line dating services, to the ethereal, not to say fictional companionship available in virtual worlds. Anyone may have a harem on his/her hard-drive, and some may think that if it steams their wetware, hardens their software, it's good enough.

Other snipers are at work. Now sex roles are unmoored, modern couples' lives must be custom-built and it's all up for debate: who cooks, works, holds baby. As if the basic challenge – recalibrating two people's wants and needs over the vagaries of time – weren't enough. Never have men and women had so much to discuss. And still we dream of The One. Then again, with artful conversation, we might find him, or her.

Courtship, Love Bombs and Other Verbal Attacks

Courtship does more than kindle intimacy, make loved ones feel loved. Castiglione observed in his 1528 conduct-book, *The Courtier*:

> *If the means by which the courtier is to win her favour are to be nobility, distinction in arms, letters and music, and gentleness and grace in speech and conversation, then the object of his love is bound to be of the same quality as the means through which it is attained.*

RULE TWO: *The style of approach advertises, or masks, the game being played*

Different means signal different ends, and ignorance is no defence if hints are misinterpreted. Flirty G.B. Shaw reported how E. Nesbit, the nice lady who wrote *The Railway Children*, chastised him (after 'I refused to let her commit adultery with me'): 'You had no right to write the Preface if you were not going to write the book.'

So pick tactics, including pace, advisedly. Play slow, for risk assessment and research, if intentions are serious, but if intentions are light, so should talk be. Discreet messages are deeply influential since they establish terms of engagement. For instance, scotching the competition is an important element of the game and, argued psychologist David M. Buss, a heterosexual woman looking for a quickie should tell the object of her desires that a rival is 'a tease' (by implication, she isn't). However, for slow-burn amour, better call her a slut.

First, get his or her attention. There are two options: overt and covert. One sends up flares, the other issues ambiguous smoke signals. Different means, very different ends . . .

Love bombs

We've a rich tradition to draw on: half literature's pearls co-alesced around the gritty challenge of breaking a chaste resolve. 'Had we but World enough, and Time', Andrew Marvell's narrator chides his 'coy mistress',

> *An hundred years should go to praise*
> *Thine Eyes . . . But at my back I always hear*
> *Time's wingèd Charriot hurrying near*

'Get a move on' never sounded so gorgeous. But how many more masterpieces will be written, in the West anyway, to beg a woman to strip? The obstacle race from lust to bed seems so short, with both sexes free to play for whomsoever they like.

Still, transmitting the spark of interest, in spark-sparking style, hard enough when a boy had to traverse a ballroom to ask a girl the pleasure – and trek back to his laughing mates if she turned him down – seems little easier in the mosh pit. The Arctic Monkeys devote a song to the anguish of uttering a first word to a 'future bride' on the dance floor (as if she could hear it).

For such dilemmas are chat-up lines, fishing hooks to snag attention and, in theory, lead to where up-chatters wish to go. Although the strategy – disarm by surprise – is sound, gambits tend to the crude, and always have.

In 1661 John Gough celebrated the end of the puritans and licentiousness's return with Charles II's ball and sceptre by publishing *The Academy of Complements*, a treasury of thesaurus-varnished lust for youths who'd witnessed little public flirting. In it, breasts are 'twins where Lillies grow', 'Ivory balls of listing pleasure' or 'soft Pillows of love'. (Do you like that positive visualization, steering her mind to bed?)

RULE THREE: *Use outrageous chat-ups for fast-food love*

The logic of a ready-baked chat-up is it takes pressure off the chatter-upper, putting it on the chatter-uppee to joke back. Alas, this is slightly flawed. Asked to perform, the logical response must be, why should I? How many strangers are game for instant verbal ping-pong?

Writer Toby Young went to mortifying lengths to find out, donning a surf-dude wig and brandishing ten lines from *How to Pick Up Girls* in ten Manhattan hot-spots. Finally, in desperation, he whipped out the humdinger:

'Are those space pants you're wearing?' I enquired. 'Because your arse is out of this world.'

She gave me a look of total amazement: Did you really just say what I think you said? Then, miraculously, she started smiling.

'That's the worst line I've ever heard,' she laughed. 'I can't believe you've ever picked up a girl using that line.'

'You're right,' I responded. 'I haven't.' Then, just as I was about to walk away, my new, be-wigged personality took over. I fixed her with an unflinching stare: 'Until now, baby.'

A triumph, thanks to his quick quip. So much for the easy option.

A knock-back is odds-on unless the line's purveyor is Adonis or Aphrodite. Yet this is the cheap merit of cheesy chatups. They won't brain someone into fancying you; rather, they're tests to find out if they do. Admittedly, clowns can appeal. Comic-lothario Russell Brand profited from childhood pester power:

Having to lobby so relentlessly to secure a pet [gerbil] set me in good stead in later life when seducing pious women. 'Please take your bra off! Please?' 'Can I see your bottom? Oh go on?'

All the same, his Byron-nicked-my-eyeliner good looks must have helped.

A love-bomber who doesn't want to rule out long-term romance should keep it simple, using an ice-breaker, ridiculous flattery, or an off-centre remark, avoiding the quickfire banter conundrum by coming armed with a follow-up: ask for a dance or buy a drink, and immediately you can ease into a gentler pace of talk.

Try to surprise. A creep I knew enjoyed fiendish success congratulating women's dainty teeth and ears, and publisher George Weidenfeld, whose conquests some considered disproportionate to his appeal (and allegedly furry derrière), used tactical psychology, praising intelligent ladies' beauty, and vice versa. Psychologists concur that gorgeous women seem to lack faith in their other strengths. Apparently this is not a problem for beauteous males; make of that what you will.

Smoke signals

I offer no chat-up lines from women because I found so few.

Possibly because until recent decades women were under parental lock and key, possibly they were too shrewd to be overheard, but more likely because chat-up lines are the bastard progeny of courtly romance, of lovelorn swains hurling gravel at flint-hearted Madonnas atop unassailable pedestals, whereas women have their own tradition of strategizing with friends that starts in school. Although clucks of hen-nighters aren't averse to heckling a hotty, and mores are changing, when looking for long-term action females remain pickier mate-hunters than men, and by adulthood many hours have been invested in decoding and programming would-be loved ones. After this relationship homework, a bias against chat-up lines is understandable.

RULE FOUR: *You're never sure an artful flirt is flirting, but you should want to be*

A chat-up line is as rude as a pinch on the bum, pushing for intimacy, yet leaving choice to the other person. So the chatter-upper isn't only vulnerable, but he ditches seduction's mightiest weapon: doubt. Whereas flirting evokes a fugitive sense that intimacy *might* be possible.

It is an illusion any can nurture. The top-flight courtesan's true genius was surely her reverse-sell, persuading clients she must be persuaded to tumble – and it was true; the best had their pick of suitors. And super-cocky male Jack Nicholson favours anti-chat-up lines, decanting the confidence of Hollywood sylphs with corkers like, 'When did you get pregnant?'

RULE FIVE: *Activate their interest: look ready to be interested*
To begin a flirtation, attract attention without showing your hand. The best signal of availability to talk was 'Do you have a light?' Then, as eyes locked over the flame . . .

Smoking, rest in peace. Fitness lovers should buy a dog. Strangers happily coddle and compliment by proxy, so make yours a pattable pet avatar.

Lesser substitutes include handing round refreshments at a party. Elsewhere, ask the time or where you can leave a coat. Or place yourself in the room's liminal zones, near food and booze. Don't look lonely: talk to someone who makes you laugh.

Try an 'accidental' eye-clinch. Move into the target's sightline, then do what anthropologists lyrically term allogrooming, i.e. twiddle your hair, lengthening the torso and narrowing the waist. (Men not blessed with Samsonesque lovelocks may fiddle with their collar.) Now catch the target's gaze, hold it a moment. Later, do it again and smile.

Just agitating your body can be enough. I watched actress Kristin Scott-Thomas unman the Wolseley Restaurant with

a feline stretch, and a minx do something horribly effective involving flashing marble-smooth, indubitably fragrant
armpits. At. My. Man.

Invisible Flirting

Can words convert attention to attraction?

As Yves Montand and Mae West proved, in the ravishment
of hearts you can talk, croon or coo your way past an imper-
fect face. There is nothing like friendliness to hatch a romantic
mood. Even in a laboratory, men given the mildest attention
were found by behaviourists to believe that they shared interests with a woman despite reading unambiguous written
evidence to the contrary.

Practice makes the flirt, so develop a habit of turning incidental transactions into satisfying interactions. This isn't about
being cheesy, turning it on solely for those you find attractive,
or faking it: become a compulsive bestower of artificial sunshine and you'll drain your reserves. (A friend in PR attributed
her divorce to being girdled in niceness all day – for which she
compensated with a grand unloosening of barbs at the end of
it.) Simply trade pleasantries in a queue, greet the waiter, the
bus driver, chat while your purchases are scanned at the
check out. Immediately your days, and you, will seem brighter
– a low-watt equivalent of the glow that people in love emit.

RULE SIX: *Synchronize your speech*
If you like what you're hearing, intensify engagement with a
little romantic legerdemain, a tactic which should continue to
work, however long you have been a couple.

Talk's rhythm, bounce and flow conjure the delicious sense of having clicked, a process you can help along by becoming conscious of the other's pace, volume and tone. Don't slavishly copy. An experiment on students concluded that only perceived similarity in speech rate increased social influence; extra slow or fast speakers were irked by over-accurate imitations, unaware of their own oddity, just as most of us fondly believe our voice to be deeper and richer than it sounds to any other (our skulls are hospitable to bass notes that scram when our voices project through air).

Also attend to your target's vocabulary. Words imply sensual preferences, according to neuro-linguistic theory, so adjust your vocabulary to appeal to the other's dominant sense. Listen. Is he visual? Or does he talk of feelings, textures, smells, sounds? Now echo this language in your speech.

You could try grafting yourself direct on to their romantic mainframe. Hypnotist Paul McKenna claims a friend (*friend?* pah!) uses speed seduction: 'He asks [women] if they've ever been in love, and what they felt like, and then attaches himself to that feeling.'

RULE SEVEN: *Exploit rules of engagement*
Charm's good luck turns on a simple equation:

Be interested = Interest them in you

This can be a low-input endeavour. Women fought duels over the 'polite and quietly humorous' eighteenth-century duc de Richelieu (model for Valmont, the rake in *Dangerous Liaisons*) because he listened. Smitten intellectual Emilie du Châtelet raved: I can't believe someone as sought-after as you, wants to look beneath my flaws, to find out what I really feel.'

Listening has the further advantage of unselfconsciousness, and, relaxed, your confidence will unburden confidences. Director Ang Lee hypnotized actress Tang Wei into sharing

secrets I've never told anyone. Right away I can feel that he really wants to know me. Other directors look at you as a piece of flesh and refuse to meet your eyes. But Ang looked into my eyes. It was like he wanted to know my heart.

As with humour, those who are direct and clear (but not overbearing) slip under our radars because their bearing implies that we're already intimate. Physical cues are:

Close distances
Eye contact
Touch

Move the other person to feel closer to you: lower your voice, and your interlocutor will lean in and feel like an ally. What is more, primates are profoundly susceptible to mimicry, unconsciously mirroring each other. Watching somebody hold their breath, it's peculiarly difficult not to hold your own; and in police interviews, interrogator and suspect's body languages converge after three minutes (hence body language and its experts are always suspect).

So step nearer. Don't invade the other's comfort zone: the gentlest touch is effective. In a test, waitresses who grazed a customer's arm or shoulder when leaving the bill received 25 per cent higher tips, yet customers were unaware of having been touched, let alone extra generous.

And verbalize the positive. Linguists term some impassioned talkers 'high-involvement speakers'. They favour:

Direct, strong language, full of positives and intensifiers ('must' not 'could')

Few weedy diminutives (no 'slightly', 'possibly', 'might have been')

Personal and relational pronouns ('I', 'me', 'we', 'ours')

Just the word 'we' can be enough to create a feedback effect.

Such is the power of social influence that high-involvers inspire hesitant speakers to talk more passionately, which may explain why opposites attract. By contrast, the gappiest conversation occurs when low-involvers meet. Instead of joking, expanding on themes or offering fresh material, their comments peg limply off the surface text of what others say – unwilling to raise new topics, scared to pass comment – sapping vital forward momentum: a drag for everyone.

Trepidatious conversationalists with distant verbal ticks are as difficult to converse with as pompous boors who cling to 'I' instead of venture 'you'; both make feeble talk-makers, entrenching their isolation by not building topical, or by extension emotional, connections. The diabolical cost of in-grown communication habits, in worst cases, such as the angry young Internet addicts of South Korea, is that they incarcerate people within in-grown personalities. But for anyone, desire increases the social risks necessary to transmute an encounter into a relationship that might satisfy it. (Did your knees not knock in the vicinity of your first crush?)

So minimize the risk, look after what musicians who play

wind instruments call their 'embouchure' and keep up your pecker with friendly chirps at people behind counters, on phonelines. Equally, if a shy mouse catches your eye, you can – must! – coax it out of the hole.

Wage war on shyness.

Raising the Game

To ascend to romance proper requires that elusive devil, emotion, which scientists find consolidates and activates memory (as author Siri Hustvedt observes, 'What we don't feel, we forget'). It makes sense to communicate memorably, stoking those stomach-plummeting sensations that ruthless salesmen exploit: doubt, fear of loss.

RULE EIGHT: *Imagination feeds romance, feeds attraction, feeds love*

There's nothing like uncertainty to make you think, giving romance its tragicomic tinge, as is most perfectly realized in the novels of Jane Austen. She knew whereof she wrote: her own, ultimately unfulfilled, *tendresse* with Irishman Tom Lefroy, had been nourished by ambiguity

> *in a series of meetings, some of them accidental and some con-trived, at which feelings were only partially revealed, desires only half expressed.*

Be unpredictable, deploy silence; add layers of mystery, walk away. And don't look too eager. Regency strumpet Harriette Wilson inflated her market value with spirited perversity. Her memoir records first meeting the Duke of Wellington (it was she whom he told, upon threat of blackmail, to 'Publish and be damned!'). Having paid a procuress 100 guineas for his introduction, the old warhorse took Harriette's hand. At once she withdrew it.

'Really,' said the modest maiden, 'for such a renowned hero you have very little to say for yourself.'

On and On and So On?

The language of love changes as relationships shift from lust to attraction to attachment. These are specialized activities: different hormones, different behaviours, even different parts of the brain light up with each phase. What we want of a mate – kindness, warmth, openness – doesn't entirely square with the aggravating erotic incertitude of infatuation. Yet most of us yearn for one person who can press all three buttons, and don't expect love to leave lust behind.

Some doomy scientists argue that sexual destiny is inscribed before birth, with men likelier to be gadabout short-term maters the more testosterone swam inside the womb. (An indicator of *in utero* hormones is the length of index and ring fingers: if the latter is longer, apparently he may not be the marrying kind.) Yet myriad benefits come with pair bonds, and according to behaviourists, people disinclined to intimacy face 'heightened stress and lower life satisfaction'.

Luckily, mind can rule matter. Artful communication lets lovers fulfil the three-in-one ideal, hopping between channels to meld the practicalities of co-habitation and cupboard love with affection, enthralment and animal desire. If communication falters, however, the firmest partnership may fall into the fourth, dead zone that psychologists dislike talking about: indifference.

So what is lovers' conversation like?

At first, urgent, hoovering up details in an attachment process similar to that by which babies imprint on parents, as we do what John Donne describes in his poem 'The Sun Rising' and contract the world to our little room, frequently confecting our own babytalk too. To others nauseating, this private language can be enduringly powerful; even in the dog days of marriage, my husband can access it to shut me up ('Choglet' remains particularly effective, when he wants the last in the box).

As a relationship is established, conversation becomes less intense, but no less important. The joy of rubbing along, side by side, facing a shared future instead of drowning in the beloved's lash-wide stare, is a bond with exceptional practical benefits. However, as the thrill of performance, being witty, droops – with a sigh of relief, if the relationship is to be a refuge from the importunate world – the worth of keeping communication fresh remains correspondingly high. Get too cosy, stop entertaining each other, and undifferentiated coupledom can tip into complacency, boredom sneaking in with his pipe and slippers.

A fifty-six-year-old, otherwise happily married mother, still capable of orgasm, bemoaned the lack of ladies' Viagra:

> *I'm rarely in the mood . . . I want something that will affect my state of mind before sex. I can still remember the level of interest I used to have. That's what I want to recapture.*

How depressing. There is an unimprovable mood enhancer. Not in the medicine cabinet: between her and her spouse's ears.

RULE NINE: *Communicate to stimulate imagination*

Proximity doesn't equate with intimacy if you lose awareness and the relationship becomes wallpaper whose pattern you don't notice.

Some couples go to extremes to perpetuate exciting distance, like Gallic thinker Bernard-Henri Lévy, who addresses his glamour-puss wife by the formal '*Vous*'. Others take a pragmatic line. Lévy's countrywoman, Colette, earwigged on the conversations between 'snobs of vice' in neighbouring villas on the Côte d'Azur.

'Lend me your wife,' asked a husband.

The other nodded. 'If you lend me your eldest son.'

Partners who care not to share recharge all three levels of intimacy: they listen, say nice things, but also tantalize, tease, balancing the comforts of routine with surprise, never so stuck in their tracks that they forget to admire the passing scene.

To cultivate conversation, don't make it (and make it a chore). Enable it. Introduce spaces in the day where talk might flow, not cut off by other noise. Just being in the same room doing chores ensures companionship remains a relationship's hub and heart, unlike the hedge-fund couple outed as communicating by e-mail – at home.

Turn the radio down, the TV off, face each other when you're eating, give the dishwasher a sabbatical, wash and dry up together. Then go for a walk. Give a dog a home. And hold a glance, remembering how it was when you couldn't be sure what that mind was thinking. Sure you can now? How presumptuous. Find out.

How to Row

Ever felt trapped in a soap opera: same storyline, faintly different script? You are. Most couples row about the same set of issues, and how tends to matter more than why. Psychologist John Gottman, at the helm of US's 'largest love and marriage lab', found

some argue a lot but find that the thrill of making up more than compensates for the cost of the conflict; some argue very little, preferring to skim over disagreements and concentrate on the positive side of their relationship, and some spend so much time compromising that disagreements rarely occur.

These approaches work because resolution is not essential for conflict to be good, since airing problems releases tension. But two poison heart and health: carping, the steady drip-drip of contempt; or ignoring, denying a partner's point of view by withdrawal into silence. Although superficially different, both attitudes deny intimacy by attacking the central idea of a relationship: the shared bond. And by extension, immune systems, according to Gottman, with the attrition of stress leaving the henpecked and the cold-shouldered more vulnerable to disease.

Watch your argument tactics. There are six:

Pass: the complained-at ignores the complaint
Refocus: the complainer or complained-at shifts the subject of complaint
Mitigate: the complainer downgrades their complaint
Respond: the complained-at acknowledges the complaint's merit

Not respond: the complained-at denies the complaint's merit

Escalate: the topic of complaint expands, hostility rises

Hell-bent on break-up? Adopt either of the last two.

Otherwise, dilute gripes with positives – ideally, reckoned Gottman, a cocktail of five nice comments per negative. To me this sounds as random as governmental exhortations to eat five fruit and veg a day, but can't be any more harmful. And stand back and pick a technique for difficult conversation (see chapter 13).

RULE TEN: *Know when not to speak*

Happy couples may duet, like Simon Cowell's mum and dad, from dawn to dusk, but the least happy I know also keep babbling, like two-headed monsters; deaf, dumb, sadly not mute.

The difference is in imaginative sympathy, as defined by counselling service Relate: 'Good communication, empathy, caring and emotional intelligence.' Which is why the faith that fostered a million therapy sessions – that if we have a problem, we must discuss it – should, in my opinion, come with a health warning.

Take the biggest interactive challenge a couple can face: when two become three. A study found that new parents routinely kept quiet on issues causing them grief, discussing only those on which they agreed. Initially researchers were shocked, but why deplete yourself quarrelling over minutiae when huge change is already upon you?

Partnership is a three-legged race that should make clearing obstacles easier – but will not if you keep stopping to debate whose leg goes where and why. Relationships stumble if we forget that how we relate, converse, keep in touch, are their very substance. If there's a secret, it's the same as for any conversation: you get what you give. Negative, positive, at least 50 per cent is up to you.

Spies set honeytraps because love loosens lips. So relax, and if your pillow talk keeps you awake, I hope it's for reasons other than nightmares.

Typology of Bores, Chores and other Conversational Beasts

BITCH   *Canicula*

Bitch is a spin doctor by another name. Her smiles are sabres, her words knives, and her sallies detonate, like good jokes, moments after delivery. Consider this, from hardy music perennial Keisha Buchanan of Sugarbabes, a charm fiesta in person, but who has the publicity nous to rib her popstrel rivals in print:

Being famous, there's pressure to stay thin, but thankfully I'm in a group where we sell records based on our music, not what we look like. It's much harder for Girls Aloud.

How brilliant to suggest their asset, pulchitrude, is mere camouflage for other failings.

Bitching isn't exclusively female. Rap music proves men love doing it, if only beefin bout their bitches, and entrepreneurs and Ozzie cricketers excel. These gabsmiths display the panoply of skills bitchcraft involves.

There are two branches: direct (vituperation, laceration), and indirect (rearview stilettos). The latter is great for bonding, bringing us together by focusing on a usually absent third party – what in drama is called an opposition figure, such as the snotty vixen, generally brunette, who makes you root for your Bridget Jones/Cinderella.

Indirect bitchery is therefore socially acceptable, provided you mask it; preferably, as bitching about an alleged Bitch. Direct bitchery is riskier (notice nifty Keisha Buchanan kept hers oblique: you laugh at her cheek, so are less inclined to condemn her). But always a guilty pleasure to watch.

Tactics: Don't mess with her: bitch about her and win new friends.

Plus: It's no fun being her scratching post, but eminently inform-ative. She has a surgeon's eye for victims' vanities. Might she have a point?

11

The Fine Art of Flattery

On Love in Measured Doses

Confucius said:

> *Soft words and ingratiating expressions are rarely paired together with humanity.*

But what did he know? Demi-deities have little call for compliments, being in the business of persuading us that their wisdom is superior. In mortal endeavours, to neglect them is less than human, and not a little daft.

Flattery fine-tunes conversational overtures and is an unparalleled instrument for making us feel good. Yet few aspects of interaction are so maligned. Why? There are suspicions of insincerity, manipulation, yes, but the underlying problem is difficulty.

Compliments require diplomacy as delicate as for buying

presents. Every gift, by word or deed, reveals its giver's opinion, or misunderstanding, of the receiver. Indeed, compliments stake a claim for a relationship, by boldly assuming reciprocity. Better to give than receive; all the same, who doesn't expect something back?

RULE ONE: *Artful compliments are never too great to be returned*

Flattery shouldn't be confused with boot-licking. Minimal effort and imagination can throw out delicious back-scratching hooks to bind people closer to us. To show you're listening approvingly, emulate octogenarian charmer Deborah, Dowager Duchess of Devonshire, who talked with

> *great economy and clarity, albeit punctuated with sudden bursts of flattery – 'You are so right!' 'Absolutely spot-on!'*

Incompetents think that more is more and overdo it, causing embarrassment, killing talk (if the flatteree doesn't know you, or is speechless, she will struggle to say anything back). It is worth remembering that flattery, far from self-abasing, is, as novelist Benjamin Markovits remarked, 'sometimes the sincerest form of arrogance' and highly assertive. After all, to offer a compliment is to presume you are qualified to give it. Novelist James Salter mischievously downplayed his inclusion in critic Harold Bloom's hit-list, *The Western Canon*:

> *The question is: does [Bloom] know anything? . . . In the end, flattery is wonderful so long as you don't inhale.*

By contrast, Chaucer, father of English letters, well understood that writing his own *Troilus and Cressida*, a tale told and retold by the great classical authors, was a status-grabbing act, claiming a literary title for himself as much as his vulgar native tongue. But lest readers miss the point, towards the close he commanded his 'litel bok' to go 'kis the steps' where Virgil, Ovid, Homer, Lucan and Statius had walked – an act of obeisance that, by implication, anointed himself their worthy successor.

RULE TWO: *If flattery is self-serving, it should hide it*

The underlying concept of flattery as indirect power play is best expressed in the musty phrase, 'to curry favour'. To grasp fully its metaphorical sense, picture not a vat of simmering 'favour' stew; instead imagine Favour, a handsome steed being groomed with a curry comb. Never a straight bow of humility, paying homage is courtship, designed to massage the homagee's feelings and steer his responses in your favour. Ride him too hard, you'll both be saddle sore.

Heed the example of those repositories of royal caprice, court favourites, who only survived if they trained a discriminating eye on their job's two-way political function: as lightning conductor (on hand to be blamed by lesser courtiers for a monarch's whims, as a bad influence), and as persuader-in-chief (to intercede for lesser courtiers). For them, as for parents who heap exorbitant praise on children's rare good behaviour, flattery was often spiked with inverted criticism or advice. As one of Elizabeth I's lapdogs was told:

> *Never seem deeply to condemn her frailties, but rather joyfully to commend such things as should be in her, as though they were in her indeed.*

Their egos may be more prominent, but otherwise absolute monarchs are like you and me. We'll yield to stroking, so long as the flatterer's will to power is veiled; and even perhaps to advice, so long as the person issuing it puts the accent on his own faults.

How to Flatter

Be appropriate: Obsequiousness is grotesque because it is out of proportion, exuding surplus oil, making wheels too slippery to turn. Good flattery is weighted to the moment. Medieval historian Geoffrey of Monmouth recorded approvingly how Julius Caesar placated the rebellious Gauls:

> *He who had once raged like a lion, as he took from them their all, now went about bleating like a gentle lambe, as with muted voice he spoke of the pleasure it caused him to give every-thing back to them again. This soft caressing behaviour contin-ued until all were won over again and he had recovered his lost power.*

Be unpredictable: The unexpected is both memorable and, because original, seems more authentic. So it is flattering to subvert hierarchical relations – gently – deferring to assistants, cajoling bosses ('managing up'), or smarming to vassals (see Caesar, above).

Glorify in hope, not expectation: Abbasid poet Ibn al-Rumi recognized that flattery is lyrical, not literal – an expression of power, a wish, rather than truth:

God has reproached poets for saying what they do not do, but they are not guilty of this alone, for they say what princes do not do.

Similarly, artful compliments take their recipients on a holiday from drear reality. Why say, 'Your eyebrows are dark', if you can liken them to dancing calligraphy? Provided you're sincere, the other person will know you mean it. Remember, this grooming exercise attends to the demands of the idealist super-ego. Indeed, giving a compliment, it is effectively rude not to exaggerate, since you are expressing a feeling, a desire, not a mathematical exactitude.

The one you love is always the most beautiful in the world, because you're asserting the primacy of your world, not Brad and Angelina's. We expect to hear this, even as we understand it isn't factually true. Trust Shakespeare (Sonnet 138).

> *When my love swears that she is made of truth*
> *I do believe her, though I know she lies,*
> *That she might think me some untutor'd youth,*
> *Unlearnèd in the world's false subtleties . . .*
> *On both sides thus is simple truth suppress'd.*

Forget sunshine: bring some flattering candlelight into someone's life.

Be indirect: Choosing what to compliment, for subtlety, aim at something allied to a person's prestige or a quality from which you could benefit, as supplicants to irate sultans are wise to trumpet their mercy.

Unpopular trainee geisha Sayo Masuda bought her way out of a reputation for stupidity by cynically playing on it, setting herself up as a compliments broker:

When I could see that a customer was important to a particular geisha, I'd watch for a moment when no one else was near and then say something like: 'Elder Sister's always talking about you, you know. She must really like you. I like you, too! And Sister likes you even more than I do. I guess that's what it feels like to be in love?' Then I'd flash him a big, innocent smile. Since they all were convinced that I was a bit weak in the head, they'd take me seriously and be really pleased. The customer would tell my Elder Sister. Elder Sister would feel flattered and start taking me with her to parties. And before long, all this effort began to bear fruit. I became popular.

In the same way, playwright Aphra Behn flattered her king, Charles II, in her dedication to *The Feigned Courtesans*, by bigging up his mistress, ex-orange seller Nell Gwyn:

Who can doubt the power of that illustrious beauty, the charms of that tongue, and the greatness of that mind, who has subdued the most powerful and glorious monarch in the world?

The better you know someone, the greater the praise: A compliment swells according to intimacy. Equally, not to offer one to a friend you haven't seen lately might be construed a tacit suggestion that she's changed, but not for the better. I enjoyed an encounter with my husband's employer, who gallantly roared that I looked no different from a decade ago. Then spoilt it: 'Which plastic surgeon?'

How to be Flattered

Compliments present an etiquette puzzle.

Until we hit puberty it's good manners to say 'Thank you' to a compliment. But after that, at least in Britain, the protocols of politeness demand we say something more elaborate: simply accepting seems somehow smug. This makes flattery peculiarly helpful to conversation, especially early on, because the requirement not to count our laurels compels us to use ingenuity and find something else to talk about.

We obey what I call the Law of Compliments Disavowal:

Acknowledge the compliment; never simply accept it.

Ideally, this means turning the compliment into an opportunity to be modest and then give a compliment back. To 'That is a lovely dress', you might say, 'Oh, I got it in the sales. But yours is *gorgeous*.' A competitive element can creep into self-deprecation ('Think this dress is supposed to resemble an over-stuffed sausage?' 'No, it's lovely. But I look like the Bride of Wildenstein's offcuts'). Nevertheless, at bottom it's all about showing solidarity and building a comfort zone. Even if you and your friend end up squabbling about who has the gravel-liest skin.

Envy is flattery's handmaiden, so the more truthful a compliment, the wiser you are to acknowledge but not assume it. Gracious composer Franz Schubert thanked Graz Music Society for making him an honorary member, saying he hoped 'one day [to be] really worthy of this distinction'. And US chat-show host Tyra Banks was artfuller still to dismiss 'quickly but with a smile' a journalist's suggestion she was 'the new Oprah Winfrey, her heroine'. Such a response seems only to confirm the merit of her ambition.

Just as no sensible celebrity complains of his isolation, no sage beauty says, 'You're right, I am.' Professional good-looker Liz Hurley dutifully flicked off an interviewer's suggestion of her gorgeousness by drawing attention to her 'ugly' hands. Celluloid-melter Michelle Pfeiffer claimed to another that she looked like a duck. Pure genius, that. Immediately you super-impose a wee duckling over that lovely face, and at once think, Gosh, far from unattainable ice maiden, Michelle is cute.

With Reservations...

Then again, were Tyra to congratulate Michelle on her un-withered charms, the only polite answer would be 'Thank you'; anything else and Tyra might think she was fishing, or weird. In part, because Tyra herself is an infernal radiance and honesty between equals is more permissible, with no power imbalance to offset. But there is also a cultural difference. Pride in merits remains a keynote in America's meritocratic dream; apart from at high school, there's little terror of tall poppies or being one, and no class-war-stained angst about looking down, or up. So stateside, don't match compliment for compliment unless you mean it. As for knocking one back – forsooth, for shame, fuhgeddaboutit.

And tread carefully in Germany, where some take no-nonsense compliments a step further, delivering backhanders with a spin worthy of Boris Becker. A Berlin theatre designer found the concept of writing a diary column for a newspaper hard to grasp. Finally we translated.

'*Klatsch*?' – 'Gossip?' (rhymes with '*Quatsch*', German for 'trash').

She stared, as if to verify this being before her was human.

'But you are a serious person!'

Typology of Bores, Chores and other Conversational Beasts

CREEP   *Ickydemus*

Creep arouses similar feelings to a slug: either you want to stamp on him, or run. But it doesn't end there. These uncharitable sentiments create a negative feedback loop: you feel bad for feeling revolted, then angry at Creep for making you feel bad, and so on, *ad infinitum*. What fuels his repulsive force?

Speech-act theory explains that statements don't simply communicate ideas, but are themselves actions with social goals. The trouble with Creep is that his noisy aims drown out his words – primarily, with the slurp of sucking up – often lending his speech an undead quality, as if scripted in advance. And since he equates boosting your esteem of him with boosting your self-esteem, he goes in for vertiginous, stack-heeled compliments that only make you shudder, wondering, What is he after now?

As Amy Sedaris said, in conversation there's no greater compliment than talking to someone who is really 'in the moment' – that is, into you, here, now. Regrettably, Creep never imagines you might like him for himself; fatally, he is too condescending to see his objectives ooze transparently from each over-egged word. Many politicians exude the same miasma: we know their smile really says, 'I want your vote.' Hence we feel like prey. Liked not for ourselves, but as means to their ends.

Tactics: Creep is a vampire, so unless you invite him in, he has no power. Don't feel obliged to be nice. Say stop if he is embarrassing you.

Pluses: Creep reminds us of the importance of sincerity, style and engaging with others, not trying to get in with them.

12

Shop-Talk

On Conversation as Work

It was a Sunday in April, but the sun was strong and the sky pressed down like a clammy hand. Nobody in the garden felt like networking, and all seemed in need of refreshment – all except the rosy Irishman, draining the last cool glass of champagne.

'Communication is simple,' he said, tapping his head. 'All you have to do is get something out of here, and into here,' he added, tapping mine.

He knew what he was talking about; he was an ambassador. But rarely does it seem so simple at work. As for the compulsory socializing: business lunches, Christmas dos . . . And however pleasant our boss, how many of us haven't felt, as Voltaire did of his some-time patron Frederick the Great, that when he calls you ' "friend" he means "my slave" '?

The social knit of office life is riven with power imbalances and knotty with contradictory demands: to get along and get ahead; to compete and co-operate. At worst, fear and loathing make it purgatory, as in Joseph Heller's novel, *Something Happened*:

> *In my department, there are six people who are afraid of me and one small secretary who is afraid of all of us. I have one other person working for me who is not afraid of anyone, not even me, and I would fire him quickly, but I'm afraid of him.*

At best, it encourages rapport, passion and imagination – the lifeblood of zestful talk. Nothing can beat conversation for managing the conflict-riveted camaraderie of the workplace. Even when it must be, of necessity, antisocial.

The Challenge of Shop-Talk

All communication is hampered by a problem that might be summarized as (*pace* Donald Rumsfeld): 'I don't know what you don't know that I don't know you don't know.' Never is this truer than at work, and it is more problematic than in normal conversation, thanks to the social influence we must quietly exert while playing the good professional.

RULE ONE: *Never assume that people understand you*
Imbalances of power create imbalances of knowledge, and in professional encounters too often we fail to account for the ignorance or otherwise of the person we're talking to. Have you ever staggered away from an accountant, lawyer or surgeon *not* confused? Had a free and easy exchange with an IT helpline?

Conversely, the less powerful wonder what the powerful are hiding, and tend to second-guess. This compromises the flow of information, sometimes feeding dangerous Groupthink, in which a meeting's cyclonic dynamics ensure that leaders hear only what they want to. Think Iraq, or the calamitous Bay of Pigs invasion, which almost tipped cold into nuclear war.

It may be deliberate: Tony Blair unblushingly expected Secretaries of State to clear submissions in private before discussing them in Cabinet. Or teams' expertise may be so specialized that managers neither comprehend nor respect it – a risk, foretold by Hannah Arendt, blamed for woeful communications at NASA that led to the homicidal Challenger shuttle disaster.

In business, these issues are further complicated by a basic tension. Each worker, from CEO to envelope-stuffer, faces a dual requirement: to be himself, and to play his part to get the job done. If the personal and the professional conflict, there can be drama.

RULE TWO: *Artful shop-talk mediates emotion, information and power*

One solution might be to copy what a bestselling author told me she did to survive speaking engagements: 'I put on a rubber head.' But nine to five, a smiling mask chafes, and phoneyness is repellent. Which isn't to say you shouldn't put up a front. Substituting 'if' for an optimistic 'when' levers deals. Certainly, without the chutzpah – i.e. fibs – of Tim Smit, co-founder of the Eden Project, regarding other backers' 'firm commitments', Cornwall's wildly popular botanical showcase would have remained a fantasy.

Every worker should strive for something beyond balancing

personal and professional. To excel means harnessing emotion, severing personal from professional concerns yet building relationships; heating discussion without searing pride or hazing priorities; and communicating clearly, without talking down, or over heads.

Oh, and ideally, all contacts should be personal, as Dee Dee Myers, ex-Press Secretary to Bill Clinton, advised *West Wing* actress Allison Janney:

> *Your relationships aren't determined by the boundaries of your job. It's by who likes you.*

Face to face cements connections that 10,000 e-mails cannot. Sadly for party-phobes, research has found that newcomers who attend just one corporate social in their first eight months feel greater attachment to a company than those who don't. Not that they identify paint-balling or pub quizzes as the cause: the binding is subliminal.

In the end, said agent Mark McCormack, people buy from a friend. To succeed, treating colleagues and clients like one is the place to start.

What about creative tension? I've worked in companies that set employees at each other in survival contests that rewarded the fittest at politicking (not necessarily those fittest at their tasks). Sure it was chatty; but cost-effective? Backbiting ate time and morale.

This may seem to support the line used by vending-machine salesmen in the 1960s to convince factory owners that canteens carried a hidden cost: camaraderie – staff talking, griping, forming loyal bands able to mobilize and strike. But it can be costlier if employees don't talk.

A business is, in effect, its workers' acts, and the knowledge driving them is a capital asset – and a liability if underdeveloped, or it leaks. Photocopy company Xerox found this out in the 1970s when engineers and scientists, who saw each other as arrogant dweebs and 'toner heads', stopped talking, and upper echelons failed to appreciate the scientists' ideas. But corporate outsider Steve Jobs spoke the scientists' language, saw a chance, and licensed their innovations. Apple Computer ripened them to bear glorious fruit.

Miscommunication lost Xerox the PC. But just nattering is hugely valuable. So much of twenty-first-century activity is obscure or shrouded in jargon (specialization being one of conversation's arch foes) that sharing with others who get what we're on about is a huge boon. The hardest-hearted manager should appreciate, as Socrates did, that dialogue percolates knowledge, and the stories shared in breaks, handily sorted by cause and effect, dole out user-friendly training on a coffee spoon.

Since Steve Jobs's giant leap, globalization has accelerated competition and adaptive 'learning organizations' like Toyota thrive. Smart businesses see employees as their nerves, and seek to unlock the cutting-edge know-how in their fingers and put it to work. But wherever we toil, however unenlightened its communications may be, artful conversation can awaken our own and others' tacit knowledge, make it articulate, wire us into work's quasi-social matrix, and maximize our assets.

Mechanics and Fluid Dynamics

Productive work conversation means not more meetings, those drains of enthusiasm, but rather making words work harder, co-ordinating brain and spirit, and saving time.

The instruments are no different from normal conversation, just worth using more stringently than down the pub. And while dialogues – interviews, sales pitches – have different dynamics from group meetings, the same basic principles apply in each. Primarily, that communication is a two-way transaction. Sender and receiver should feel equally responsible for ensuring that messages ring out loud and clear.

RULE THREE: *Make allowances for the blinkers of your position*

The imbalances of power or information in most business exchanges skew perceptions further. For instance, sociologists find that those in charge are biased to perceive unequal outcomes as fair, and less powerful parties strategize far more for encounters, so will be, understandably, correspondingly less satisfied. As if we needed sociologists to tell us that.

Effective communicators compensate for these biases, as golfers account for the slope and swell of the green when they putt. The best go one better and find an advantage. Use these dynamics deftly and you may ensure that others emerge happy from an exchange regardless of whether it is the outcome they wanted.

Tony Blair once had a wizard-like ability, an awed civil servant observed, 'to make people walk away feeling taller – having opposed them'. Mateyness is less effective, however, if a listening ear doesn't appear to hear. Andy Duncan, formerly of Unilever, then Channel 4, impressed his previous chairman as 'open and informal', a great team leader. Yet cynical underlings saw Duncan's 'toe-curlingly' pally style as a rubber head, claiming he exploited it to bounce off dissent,

> *maintaining there will always be those who disagree . . . His supposed inclusivity was equally disarming: people were invited to talk to him, about anything, to voice their opposition to something, then he did what he set out to do.*

So an enlightened boss should go out of his way to engage staff loyalty, presenting tasks as exclusive to them, i.e. strategize as hard for encounters as underlings. Meanwhile, enlightened employees should appreciate their boss likes feeling good, and deploy positive presentation to make rewarding them easy. Good news gilds the bearer . . .

RULE FOUR: *Every communication is a chance to make business easier*

Managing up, down or sideways, the communication goal is identical: keep channels open, relationships flexible, feelings positive.

Before anything else, we must manage ourselves, using analysis and planning to compensate for our self-serving inclinations to blame others instead of examining causes, and, likewise, to personalize success when surfing a lucky break (like stockbrokers with Master of the Universe complexes, deluded that their success is down to unique investment acuity, rather than prevailing fortunes brought by fair economic winds).

Complaining a boss is woolly is self-defeating; better to enhance communication, clarify what is asked of you, and be a joy to employ. The pious view is to see it as entrepreneurial conversation, able to catalyse difficulty into a learning opportunity.

The basic recipe for successful shop-talk, like successful relationships, is finding common ground, then stretching it. Its basic ingredients are tact, salesmanship and a firm grasp of the mechanics of communicating and receiving a message.

Dear Prudence

By Machiavelli's measure, prudence is analytical and stoical,

> *Able to assess the nature of a particular threat and [accept] the lesser evil.*

Deciding whether to communicate, let cost-benefit analysis be your guide. That is, ask, So what?

Say Hayley in sales is taking credit for a deal your contacts secured. Before speaking up, ask, Is it worth it? Nobody likes a sneak. So what is there to gain? Is your motive power play, to let off steam, or for mutual benefit? Will speaking out serve either your or the business's long-term interests? So what if you don't?

If it's really the shortest route to meet them, plan it.

Salesmanship

We all sell when we communicate, be it an idea, opinion or joke, just as all workers must flog their skills. Many seem unaware of this, in part because the idea of selling intimidates. Fools imagine it is all deals, but serious salesmanship forges relationships, using passion and personality as tinder to clients' enthusiasm. Without it there would be no business. Anyone who imagines selling to be beneath them should know it comes garlanded with philosophical plaudits. Aristotle anatomized it in his *Art of Rhetoric* (persuasive speech), identifying three aspects, in ascending importance:

Logos – The virtue and style of the argument
Pathos – The emotions of the audience
Ethos – The credibility of the speaker

As Aristotle discerned, an insight borne out by twenty-first-century research using brainscanners, the best idea matters not a jot if it leaves audiences cold. Even if your words move them to tears, to get a message inside heads, first they must believe in you – and want to. Smart work communication doesn't focus narrowly on hearing, or saying, yes, but building faith, credit and the long-term conversation that is a relationship. It:

Shares spoils
Gives credit where due
Expresses admiration and gratitude
Is amusing and amused
Speaks up for the weak
Apologizes frankly and first

A suck-up's charter? It's only human to use rapport to shore up your position. That's how primates do business, with similar networking ploys seen in monkeys. Call it generosity, aloud.

But however casual a work conversation, beware of presuming intimacy. Or humour, that insuperable friendship coagulant – a qualification only time brings. In a 1950s London department store, anthropologists found, incoming workers had to wait three dull weeks to be included in banter, three more before cracking their own jokes.

Mechanics

Each work conversation is a three-part task, entailing regulating, sending and receiving.

Regulating: For an organized communication, think in advance: when; where; how long; what issues to cover; in what order; what note to strike; what interests and goals are at stake; how to meet or improve them.

At the encounter, greet, introduce (if unfamiliar), and trade pleasantries. This both respects rapport and neatly places it out of harm's way, because the transition into business signals that what follows isn't personal, and it ensures everyone knows who is here and why. (Had he done so, my husband might have avoided the university interview throughout which a don shuffled papers, addressing him as 'Joanna'.)

Preamble small talk also tests and sets the tone, so may shift the frame of subsequent discussion. Hint you've brought an alternative proposition, for instance, and the other side's conversation strategy is in tatters. Or, off home turf, lead greetings and you may lead the next moves too.

When discussion begins, state purpose and agenda, then explore propositions and decisions, step by step, repeating agreements at the end. Whatever transpires, a friendly farewell helps to restore lost face. And in the absence of minutes, circulate action points afterwards to avoid confusion.

Sending: To resonate, present your message as Castiglione's ideal courtier, never lacking 'for eloquence adapted to those with whom he is talking'. And be, as director Gurinder Chadha advised wannabe filmmakers,

absolutely clear about what you want to say . . . What's your vision?

Don't leave your personality at the door. Karl Marx knew how to package his punches, blending 'philosophical seriousness with the most biting wit'. Trim vocabulary, pace and tone to the occasion, aiming at simplicity and concision, using keywords, humour, surprise and arresting images.

Consider how near listeners to sit; when to look at them to sink a punch, grab their attention; when gestures can add oomph. Draw them onside with open questions (not answerable by yes or no). And use your voice: volume, pace and emphasis.

In his 1854 *Rhetoric of Conversation*, George Hervey advised:

Do not seek a reputation for humility by always daintily avoiding the pronoun I.

But at work 'I think' admits this is your impression, tacitly inviting others to correct it.

Receiving: Judicious listeners adhere, at least on the surface, to the premise innocent until proven guilty, seeking and sifting clues as to where someone is coming from, before deciding where they're going, never mind offering an opinion about whether or not it is a good idea. A methodical approach explores data, then opinions, then propositions, then solutions and decisions. To focus talk, pose questions, repeat, paraphrase. Acknowledge sentiments even if you don't agree to the interpretation ascribed, and if conversation bogs down, step outside it: observe it has become sticky, inviting others to explore why.

There is no better means than listening to avoid destructive power games, which fritter a business relationship's huge asset: the sense of obligation. Indeed, obligation can create a relationship. Benjamin Franklin tamed an ardent political enemy by asking to borrow a book: a small debt that brought a new topic of conversation, then a bond.

Two-Way Dances and Hydra-Headed Monsters

Nice and easy? So it is not always simple. (See chapters 6 and 13 for nipping and tucking awkward moments.) On the other hand, in most business conversation, whether a dialogue or a many-mouthed meeting, you will have but one motive:

RULE FIVE: *Find the best solution – usually yours*

For this, the message to get across is: You want to work with me. A service ethos can carry you anywhere. Noam Gottesman, mega-bucked founder of GLG hedge fund, attributed his success to

> *Paranoia. The secret is about what the clients want. We work in a 'what have you done for me lately?' business.*

Don't we all?

Showing what you've done lately, like showing what you can do next, means convincing the other side that your solution fits their needs – and, very often, convincing them precisely what it is they want. Here is a checklist of tactics for doing so:

Research: Where do interests and advantages meet and diverge?

Align: Map your offer on to their requirements.

Anticipate: Likely questions and objections. Can you build positive answers to potential concerns into a pitch? (A five-year degree? All that charity work . . .)

Timing: Think when is most expedient to raise issues or throw in something unexpected.

Lead/follow: In pitch situations, the seller leads – preferable to interviews where you dance to another's tune, offering a mini product trial. (My nadir? An hour waiting for Liza Minnelli's ex, David Gest; twenty minutes more as he ordered snacks and chatted to someone else. Finally he removed his shades: 'Soooo. Talk.' I corpsed.)

Soften the dynamics, but don't ignore them. Interviews are voyages of discovery, each side tacking in a different direction: the interviewer pushes for information while the interviewee pulls the interviewer into an avuncular, advisory mode. If either overdoes it, conversation will feel a jumpy failure. So read the signals, match the other's pace.

Wait: If silence is the enemy, rush to fill it and you become your own. Pity Topman clothing brand director David Shepherd, on being asked his target market:

> *Hooligans or whatever. Very few of our customers have to wear suits for work. They'll be for his first interview or first court case.*

Fear not: Lower emotional stakes to increase confidence. Consider interviews as ways to meet interesting people, and bring your own comfort zone: memorize five points to convey and you'll feel less like prey (avoiding palpitatory fight-or-flight feelings).

Be easy to look at and hear: Locking eyes announces this is a meeting of equals. When her daughter Floella said she had a job interview, Veronica Benjamin sat her down, beaded her hair, and said, 'Do not take your eyes off the interviewer.' Floella was soon capering in dungarees on children's show *Play School*.

Milk the target: Use questions to show off research, expose preferences (what happened to the last employee?) and points from which to link your wares to their needs. Explore objections: do they stem from misunderstandings, excuses or material problems?

Mind the gap: Flummoxed? The question is your life raft. Repeat, clarify; show how you think on your feet. (See chapter 13.)

React: There is a tale of an Oxford University interviewer who removed his shoes and socks to clip his toenails. Demonic strategy? Madness? Who knows. If someone is determined to unsettle you, view it as a test. Joke (my husband could have said, 'Only friends call me Joanna'). Reframe a negative positively. Admire the damned clippers.

Bend Your Wiggle Room: a Negotiator's Guide

Negotiating may feel like poker. Trace your negotiating space beforehand to improve the odds. Its co-ordinates are: what you want, points you can and can't concede, what you'd settle for; and these same parameters for the other side (guess). Where these overlap lies territory for settlement.

Outline concessions, planning points to trade, then step back. Is there wiggle room? Review each side's interests and aspirations. Might something else, not on the table, satisfy both? If so, this is your ace in the hole. Now imagine the consequences if agreement isn't met. Any alternatives? Aim to walk in knowing you can walk away.

At the meeting, explore motives and assumptions behind the other's stance. Clarify and you might shift a position. Don't be shy of stating your criteria or aims either: however shrewd, the other side may not have thought these through, but should.

If both sides want to do business again, you've won, preserving the long-term deal: your relationship. So never confuse what is fair with what is right; history is strewn with noses cut off to spite owners' faces, as we don't act in our best interests, preferring nothing to a mean deal – just as chimpanzees in tests refuse to perform a task if their reward is a piece of cucumber, but their partner's a succulent grape, even if ordinarily they like cucumber. Why? Fairness isn't logical but psychological: about saving face. Good negotiators keep deals sweet by keeping them short. Talk too long, positions petrify, and each side thinks the time invested means they deserve more (forgetting that the other side has spent just as much, but the pie/grape/cucumber is no larger).

Follow My Leader: Mental Care for Meetings

'The multitude is wiser and more constant than a prince', averred Machiavelli, after the Medici put him out of a job.

That greatest wisdom dwells not in the greatest minds, but the aggregated views of the crowd, is an insight as old as democracy. All the same, a group thinking aloud isn't necessarily the slickest means of aggregating them.

Analysts find the most successful management teams argue

hard, but hold it together because the tone isn't personal: the focus is on gains. Without good governance, however, meetings degenerate into either a brawl or a pack, because dialogue spurs people into increasingly extreme positions. Furthermore, Parkinson's Law of Triviality asserts that the less important an agenda item, the more time is spent on it. Can you doubt it? We speak most freely on matters that won't burn us, or for which any number of solutions is possible and equally desirable.

The net consequence is that all meetings have a natural lifespan beyond which dementia sets in. A brief biography:

An issue is born.

Slowly, voices are raised, frail heads of opinion sprout. Some find the light, are watered, grow, others shrivel in the shade, until one vast opinion takes over, draining resources, until an axe falls . . .

The job of attendees is to represent their positions as best they can, with a keen sense of when and how to back down. The chair is axeman. But his duties also encompass those of circus ringmaster.

There's nothing like repetition to persuade people an idea is right (see politicians, advertising, organized religion, etc.). So it's vital to challenge monopolists, reach nuanced decisions not herd opinions, and nip madness in the bud. Stick to the drill:

Agenda: agreed and circulated in advance
Fixed time frame: never too long, never after lunch
Venue: quiet, conducive
The right people: no time-wasters

RULE SIX: *Keep discussion light and well-ventilated to weigh matters fully*

The ideal chair doesn't lay down the law but the shape of discussion, creating rounded decisions by speaking last, listening hard for what is not said, ruling against:

> *Rambling, tangents, grand-standers, monopolists, personal attacks, leading questions, debating stunts, dodging, negativity, shillyshallying*

And for:

> *Mutual interests, uncovering assumptions, testing propositions, exploring alternatives, the devil's advocate.*

Wise business leaders would do well to recollect the example commended in Sir Thomas Elyot's 1531 treatise, *The Book Named the Governor*. Belinger Baldasine, 'a man of great wit, singular learning, and excellent wisdom', counsellor to the King of Aragon, who liked taking 'doubtful or weighty' matters home. After dinner he would summon his servants and set a riddle

> *wherein was craftily hid the matter which remained doubtful, would merrily demand of every man his particular opinion, and giving good ear to their judgements, he would confer together every man's sentence.*

In the meantime, savvy communicators will accept social influence for what it is: the engine of communication. They'll do their utmost to wire into the network, to please the powerful, cultivate the weak, and prosecute their cause as persuasively as possible.

Neurological Fireworks

Otherwise known as brainstorming. It's an unbecoming image: a cerebella blizzard, or hobnail-booted soldiers stampeding an unyielding cortex. My preferred definition is organized mindfunk: a conversation designed to open minds, bestir synapses and blizzards of fresh ideas – not to reach judgements. Although it should liberate participants to say whatever pops into their heads, without structure it will puddle into buffoonery.

Tackling a product or concept, corporate communications expert Linda Conway Correll suggests listing:

1. Facts about it
2. Sensory observations (possible even if the 'product' is as abstract as mathematics: think graph paper, protractors, curvy zeroes, fork-like fours, headaches . . .)
3. Experiences of it
4. Uses for it

Then do a spot of associative outreach, taking words from these lists to come up with fresh lists: things that share the product's quality; things it isn't like; combinations of elements to describe a new use for that product (for instance, a dog could, conceivably, be renamed a love-alert). Find points of similarity between dissimilar elements, mine these lists for weird new definitions of your product, and soon it'll look very different.

But keep it snappy. Think pinball, not chess.

Typology of Bores, Chores and other
Conversational Beasts

Networking isn't popular. Some sneer it smacks of corruption. But business turns on trust and personal relationships, and few hermits lead corporate takeovers.

Sally Morgan, one-time government fixer turned business adviser, denied exploiting contacts yet conceded, 'It's easy for me to pick up the phone.' And what is a contact but someone you can touch?

Networking is a posh word for knowing who to talk to and how to make them listen. It's nothing new. Visiting, familiar to costume drama fans, could be a grave social duty. In 1801, decades before becoming Byron's crabby Venetian landlady, Lucia Mocenigo trudged around Vienna on an exhausting mission of social work to restore family fortunes. She

diligently wrote down [names], together with their addresses, in a brown leather notebook that was to become her personal social registry. She used those initial introductions to gain access to other illustrious houses, and planned her courtesy visits dividing the city up by areas and neighbourhoods. She called on an average of two to three houses a day, and always wrote down the address and the date. She drew a map and kept a precise tally.

Facebook seems almost tempting. But ideally, networking brings as much pleasure as profit. I know a delightful couple, great party-givers. Numerous threads connect their guests, many of whom might be deemed more powerful than the hosts; but

237

because they meet *en masse* at the hosts' house, the hosts become the gravitational centre, generous spiders in a web of influence. It's a parable of social influence: be good to get good. No wonder Zeus was often worshipped in the form of the God of Guest-friendship.

Still, networking sometimes feels like dentistry, yourself patient and probe. Sounding out strangers is mined with hazards; touchy subjects like money and professional status. And while being nice, or naughty, or both, to get in with someone, lies behind most conversation, nonetheless we are hypocrites and the tang of an agenda makes us suspicious. Keep yours discreet.

In the presence of the king, those who do not speak of what they need will obtain more than those who do.

(As Casanova misquoted Horace, in the presence of a king, when funds were short.)

A good networker regards everyone as king, himself too. Unlike this nerveball:

His voice was quick, anxious, slightly high-pitched, as though he were worried I would leave before he had finished his sentence.

Enter a room believing the bargain is unequal and awkwardness is guaranteed. What is more, it's unnecessary, because if someone interests you, it's likely you will him. He isn't doing you a favour: you both are, by talking. See this as small talk plus.

Successful networkers charm widely, aware that the more sparks they kindle, the more they sparkle. To indefatigable *salonnière* Carole Stone, maladroits are unmistakable:

They glide into the room, head straight for the most influential person and hog their attention, before breezing out without a glance at other lesser mortals.

Think what you might discuss, with whom, but don't button-hole, and focus away from workaday matters even if these are what attracts you (that jolly doctor really doesn't want to discuss your sore toe). Showing off homework won't always win gold stars: I was nonplussed when a stranger elaborated my Google CV, a compliment I couldn't return, knowing nothing about him. But I love talking to people who make me see things differently, offer fresh ideas. Trivia, humour, mild provocation . . .

Approaching your agenda, sidelong questions are advisable. But unless the other volunteers the topic (and you may plant the seed) what need you now but contact details? Win him over, follow up promises. If he's happy to take your call you have connected.

13

Choppy Waters
On Navigating Difficult Conversation

So ravishing was the tongue of Madame de Staël that contemporaries rated her one of Europe's three powers (alongside Britain and Russia). Literary titan, political dynamo and seductress, if not beauty, she encrusted her salon with the great and the good, and helped to gather the forces that toppled Napoleon.

If anyone could twist a conversation to her ends, you might think it she. But no.

Once she had chased the Emperor. She wrote, expressing regret that a 'genius' should be saddled with a nonentity 'Creole' wife. No reply (he laughed and avoided her). Finally she tracked him down to Talleyrand's and handed him a laurel branch, demanding:

> '*Who is the woman you most respect?*'
> *Napoleon replied, 'The one who runs her house best.'*

'Yes, I see your point. But who, for you, would be the greatest of women?'

'The one who had the most children, Madame.'

No wonder she had it in for him. The moral of her story is, if you have a proposition, tender it sensitively. The moral of his? If you must repel someone, do it nicely. Their ticklish encounter illustrates that every conversation is a negotiation, and bungling one can balls up a relationship. However, the reverse is also true.

RULE ONE: *Difficult conversation transforms relationships, for better or worse*

Conversation's challenges are as varied as we, but fall into distinct categories. Active: to ingratiate, confront, appease, mediate, seduce, persuade, oppose, rebuke. And defensive: parrying unwelcome approaches, fielding criticism, diverting attack.

Hardest are conversations with the wounded, whether or not the injury is ours to heal or repeal. What do you say to a person sliding down the razor-blade of life? Nothing can feel easier than the wrong thing. You might tell yourself, or him, or her, to let sleeping dogs lie; no use crying over spilt milk. Countless platitudes are on hand to block a messy turn in conversation; arguably, clichés were invented for that very purpose ('shut up' disguised as cockle-warming folk wisdom). All are alibis for engaged sympathy.

What is wrong with skirting sore points? Often it is a shrewd kindness: the shoulder to cry on can get soggy, undesirable by association with past woes, and agony aunts can turn nag, unable to hear when advice is no longer sought. But say nothing and, if a problem is grave, contrary to King Lear's admonition to reticent Cordelia, something will come of nothing, and it won't be nice.

RULE TWO: *Assuming conversation is difficult makes it so*
Although challenges exist, expecting the worst is what tangles us in knots. Many men are silenced by shame at sharing fear, and neither ovaries nor oestrogen make women any less gauche. Mortally ill Sarah Hitchin wrote heartbreakingly of being penalized by friends, unable to believe she still liked 'a giggle'; as if she, accessorized by cancer, was no longer she:

> *Now, if they do ring, they whisper, 'How are you feeling in your-self?' One has lost contact after 24 years of friendship.*

In the name of openness, unpleasant talk is increasingly outsourced to paid ears, with the unintended consequence of impoverishing the communication skills and thinning the relationships of the rest of us – as was satirized by mordant teen novelist Nick McDonell in this sterile exchange between a mother and daughter:

> *'Is something wrong? Is something upsetting you?'*
> *'No.'*
> *'Because I was thinking if something was, upsetting you that is, then you might want to go and see this doctor I know.'*
> *'A shrink?* [. . .] *I don't know what I would talk about.'*
> *'Oh, you'd find things to talk about.'*

Then the girl warms to the idea, recalling the bodacious lies her mates tell their shrinks.

Choppy Waters

RULE THREE: *Avoiding difficult conversation weakens relationships*

Today indirect communication is on the up, with so many alternative methods to defer confrontation, fob people off: by e-mail, letter, text . . . We might imagine it easier to read bad news, to avoid misunderstanding. As if.

A friend's parents-in-law are great letter-writers, issuing regular bulletins on how he should coddle his kids, cosset their daughter. No doubt they would be shocked to learn these land like a punch in his gut, read not, as written, in calm rumination, but amid the tug-of-war of toddler breakfast. They can't suspect that using a one-way medium inherently renders their message a judgement; that not speaking, abdicating power over their voice's inflection, ensures that it strikes their harassed son-in-law as hectoring, strident, a wee bit mad.

All communication is dialogue, its meaning not its speakers' intentions, but its effect on sender and receiver. Want miscommunication?

How simpler than to bisect the dialogue?

If we ditch the myriad non-verbal cues that help meaning ring out loud and clear, if we lack messages from the other's face, we can't tell how news sinks in, adapt our words to their reception, incorporate new information, correct misperception, or stop before we say too much. And the person at the receiving end can't hear our words' emotional force, tone, let alone counter false impressions or exercise his right of reply.

To say writing obviates difficulty is like saying conversation is clearer wearing blindfold and ear plugs, in separate rooms.

RULE FOUR: *Tough topics demand flexible conversation*

Social scientist Michael Moore has found that face-to-face negotiation conjures a rapport e-mail cannot, a disadvantage that may hamper outcomes. To resolve a problem and preserve relationships, mutual understanding is imperative, and I'd argue no technology supersedes the high-definition, multi-channel parallel processing system of two beings' brains, faces and bodies, talking and listening together.

You can't kiss and make up by phone or fax (although you can dump someone that way, as a famous actor allegedly jilted his pregnant lover). Whereas the authentic look of remorse is a priceless addition to the word 'sorry'.

RULE FIVE: *Great conversation is difficult conversation that worked out*

Of all the idiocies of dodging tough talk, perhaps worst is the missed joy. What may be lost if we choose, wrongly, silence over risk; laugh instead of listen; say yes, but don't mean it; say nothing for fear of hearing someone doesn't feel the same way?

And how can you tell in advance whether a conversation will be difficult? Act by Crow's Law, invented by Second World War intelligence whizz R.V. Jones:

> *Do not believe what you want to believe, until you know what you need to know.*

As the cliché goes, grasp the nettle. First pick a strategy: evasion, mediation or persuasion? Then, tactics.

Evasion

Good for defensive situations and sloughing off tricky topics.

Absorb: Don't rise to the bait and you don't give others power. A writer was mesmerized by 'unexpectedly likeable' hypnotist Paul McKenna, whom she found 'intensely straightforward'. Why? He proved 'impossible to embarrass', taking 'pretty much everything I say as a compliment.'
Opportunity: Teflon is proof to minor conflict.
Risk: Becoming impervious to genuine problems, smug, and therefore vulnerable.

Quip: At the start of his reign Tony Blair was a gifted hook-wriggler, high on the vapours of Cool Britannia. In July 1997 he hosted a reception for its leading lights and met Oasis rocker Noel Gallagher, a rumoured champ of South American energy aids:

> I told [Blair] that we stayed up till seven o'clock in the morning to watch him arrive at [Labour Party] headquarters and asked him, 'How did you stay up all night?' He leant over and said, 'Probably not by the same means as you did.'

(How different from the man who, years later, told novelist Ian McEwan he admired his paintings. I'm a writer, McEwan corrected. No, Blair insisted; he really liked his art.)
Opportunity: Deflect or deflate without addressing the central issue.
Risk: Being insufficiently funny or quick.

Flirt: Spectacular at disabling reluctant flirtees. Prince, the artist formerly known as squiggle, deployed ruthless coquetry to stall rock critic Mick Brown: batting eyelashes, 'touching my knee', sulking, gazing into the distance if he disliked a question, seizing on words as objects of wonder – anything, indeed, but answer.

> *'Hedonist?' He arched an eyebrow and smiled. 'For years I didn't even know what the word meant . . .'*

Brown likened the encounter to 'fencing with a wraith'.
Opportunity: Amusing.
Risk: Annoying the wrong person.

Meet question with question: Why not?

My sister-in-law flips questions like pancakes. A stranger demanded: Why did she elope to Finland? Amanda smiled. 'Lovely country. You been?'
Opportunity: Fun with the distractible and the persistent.
Risk: You might not like the answer.

Reframe questions: Questions are like predictions, framed to shape answers. So use your answer to shift focus and wendy-i-wander from traps.

The wiles of David Linley, Princess Margaret's son, did not escape this scalpel-sharp interviewer, but might pass un-noticed with the unsuspecting.

> *Isn't it a bit scary becoming chairman of Christie's? 'Yes, but I've done scary for so long.' But then he smoothly revises his answer: 'To me, it's less scary, more honour . . .'*

Other jiggery-pokers include repeating a question, with modifications to encompass whatever you would rather discuss. Or bamboozling: say 'I'm glad you asked that,' or 'Yes, that is important, which is why . . .' or 'That's an interesting question'. This may be followed by a statement that doesn't answer it, without seeming rude, because lip-service has been paid to dialogue's to-and-fro.

Sadly, many listeners are so inattentive, they'll accept decoys as explanations if presented as such. I suspect this is why, according to a book called *Yes!*, 'because' is often enough to make someone do your bidding: as in, 'Please may I jump this queue because I need to buy something' – or, as Mum said, 'Because I say so'.

Opportunity: Limitless.

Risk: Have your wits about you – and hope your interrogator doesn't.

Diffuse: Interpretation is up to you. So address an enquiry's theme instead of particulars, as actors do when journalists seek to vivisect their private lives. Cate Blanchett routinely steers 'conversation away from the personal to the abstract'.

Another interviewer met pitiless resistance from Joseph Fiennes:

> *I say, let's try again: do you fall in love easily? 'I love travelling. I love cultures.' I ask, do you travel to other people's souls easily? [Fiennes] says, not laughing: 'You'll have to ask them. I love life. I'm fascinated by human behaviour because that feeds back into my work . . .'*

Opportunity: Co-operate while turning tables.

Risk: Seeming untrustworthy or maddening.

Persist: They won't listen? Plough on. Fashion designer Dame Vivienne Westwood

has advanced skills in avoiding interruption. When she senses that you are about to jump in, she furrows her brow, breaks eye contact and, without disturbing the deceptively soft rhythm of her voice, hauls on through.

As Prince showed, looking away makes it harder for someone to pitch in, and helps you concentrate. Or say 'Hang on', and counter-interrupt: 'Yes, but what I was trying to say . . .'; 'Maybe I haven't put this well . . .' Naturally, you want to hear what the other person has to say – in a minute or ten, once your point has been made . . .

If a point is extra sticky, talk long enough, you may substitute another. Memory is so brief, questioners may not recall what was asked, or fear another monologue too much to try again.

Opportunity: Attack disguised as defence, this tactic shows full attention has been given.

Risk: Arrogance. Westwood's frustrated interviewer observed: 'Those she works with seem to regard her with more respect than warmth.'

Blank: Try forgetful (he claimed) author Douglas Adams's invincible riposte:

I refuse to answer that question on the grounds that I don't know the answer.

Without details, lines of enquiry fizzle. Filmmaker David Cronenberg nuked questions about his childhood with 'Quite ordinary, really.'

Opportunity: Skip flimflam.

Risk: Credibility. Does the enquirer know more than you suspect?

Mediation

For when engagement is unavoidable, indeed desirable. Good in business, negotiation, conflict. As a rule, try to separate issues from personalities to dampen negative emotion.

Go slow: Singer Diana Krall cannot trill publicists' tune. One writer labelled her 'a cow' because her 'reserve' and 'desire to think about a question before giving a response' led to 'disconcertingly long pauses'.

Hers may seem a poor example of the virtues of taking time. But in arguments (as opposed to faux-cosy interviews) going slow is a bonus, counteracting the kinetic back and forth that may, if heated, accelerate dialogue to insult rally, crisis to drama. Curb that energy: ruminate, cleave to the point. You won't be sidetracked, and will compel the other side to slow down, think and listen too.

Opportunity: Stabilizes volatility, helping information to sound out clearer.

Risk: Rather than reining yourself in to think constructively, you simply act hoity-toity.

Break down: Active listening – repetition, agreeing a précis of a position before moving on – replaces the emotional propulsion of argument with the cooling balm of analysis.

Show respect by inviting the other party to 'help me understand'; seek information; check and repeat ('If I'm right, what you're telling me is . . .'). Gently, without blame, remind others you aren't privy to their thoughts – which may seem obvious, yet is necessary. Think how maddened you are when people don't see how they are impinging on you. But do you tell them?

Opportunity: Dissect difficulty into segmented topics, create an agenda, identify goals, and conversation becomes a process, not combat.

Risk: Apparent condescension.

Ten Commandments for Emotional Ventilation

Most conversational difficulty consists of emotion, but explaining that someone should feel differently is the rudest non-advice (trust the old English adage, 'Proffered service stinks'). Instead, carefully air injuries and you may simultaneously acknowledge their validity while diminishing their emotional power.

1. Explore – don't ignore – feeling ('I see you're upset')
2. Acknowledge the other person must address a problem (even if you don't think it one)
3. Don't react emotionally or judgementally
4. Let the other person talk, don't finish sentences
5. Only offer opinion or advice if sought
6. Don't agree or disagree until you must
7. Limit interruptions to supportive statements
8. Repeat key words, to show your grasp of issues and re-route rambling

9. Display listening: face the other person square, keep eye contact, an open posture
10. Question, summarize, and seek opinions on how to proceed

Persuasion

You know it is a good idea. Help them to see why.

Prepare the ground: Breaking hard news, open with a statement that announces, like a sinister puff of dust on the horizon, the character of the words to come: 'I'm sorry', 'I have to tell you . . .' Then pause. Often, the other person will complete the sentence.

How you broach a topic can affect reactions, so give it a spin. Say, 'You know what I'm going to say, don't you?' Even if your news is unexpected, having agreed, your listener will probably persist in the flattering belief that he knew all along.
Opportunity: Diminish impact.
Risk: Overstretch the preamble and you'll wind the other person up.

Make it look easy: My boyfriend went to lunch with his boss, a journalist who affected the bearing of a parchment-stiff brigadier. Over coffee, lighting a cigar, the boss asked if there was anything else he wished to discuss. Not really, said my boyfriend, then mentioned our relationship (we worked together). 'Oh!' the man cried, spluttering Havana flakes. 'Well, you've done nothing wrong, but she'll have to go.'

According to a well-placed source, he held officers oughtn't to consort with foot soldiers. Nevertheless, my boyfriend's error was to present the situation as a problem: far better to offer a solution. Castiglione's *Courtier* advises a sage favour-seeker:

> *Skillfully make easy the difficult points so that his lord will always grant it.*

As for my boyfriend, he has had time to rue his mistake. Reader, I married him.

Opportunity: People are lazy.

Risk: Suspending disbelief a bridge too far . . .

Play dumb: Teenager Jellyellie exhorted parents who want to talk about birds, bees, or bongs:

> *Start off chatty and informal – never sit your teenager down for a discussion and call them into the room, as they immediately think they've done something wrong and will be nervous for the rest of the conversation.*

Similarly, Brendan Duddy, for decades the undercover link between the British government and the IRA, claimed that many breakthroughs took place not seated at tables, but in breaks, 'over a cup of tea', when guards were down and people relaxed.

So why let on this is a talk with a capital T? Take an oblique approach: ask for thoughts on a tangential issue. They may lead you to the point.

Overplay the cod-casual card and nobody buys it. (My father quails at 'By the way'; my mother quakes at 'Incidentally'.) Yet the opportune moment may be decisive, and is often unanticipated, when mind or body is otherwise occupied. Aristotle believed lessons were better learned while out walking (his pupil, Alexander the Great, was a fine advertise-ment). Endorphins boost mood, and in difficult situations, if you are not confined, not confronting the other person's face, you remove dimensions crucial to the drama of antagonism (dimensions that in happier situations deepen engagement).

Why not enlist the optimism inherent in making a journey to suggest changes are not only necessary but easy, desirable? ***Opportunity:*** Act normal and conversation may well be. Serious isn't a synonym for difficult.

Risk: Be unsubtle and the other person may use irritation at your ruse to shunt you off piste – attacking your tactics instead of engaging with the issue.

Play games: Broadcaster Evan Davis puzzled over how to come out to his family. Then he turned it into a game, starting with his brother:

'I have something to tell you, can you guess what it is?'

His brother guessed right, then suggested Davis tell their parents in the same way. After Christmas lunch he popped the question. His parents drew a blank, so his brother pretended to guess. Then another brother cracked a joke. No drama, no tears. ***Opportunity:*** Make light of a revelation to dispel an atmos-phere of conflict.

Risk: Appropriate?

Dim the opportunity: Why attack a proposition if discreet sabotage can downplay its appeal? Use belittling language, diminutive descriptors (sort of, kind of, stuff); sow each sentence with a negative. Recast the scenario ('You're absolutely sure you want to spend eight hours a day doing nothing on dirt?' – my take on beach holidays). Infuse fantasy with dreary practical considerations. ('If we did this, and A, B and C, then X happened, then Y, then Zzzzzz . . .') For more tips, remember how your parents spoke to you in adolescence.

Or emulate Mark Antony in *Julius Caesar* and use the other side's weapons against them. Caesar's assassins tell the mob they are 'honest', then Mark Antony appropriates the word, repeating it in ever less apposite contexts, making the claim seem progressively ironic, and the assassins, by extension, utterly false.

So take the keyword or the emotional tug of a bad argument ('I gambled away our life's savings for you'), hold it up to an unflattering light, and strip it of value and force.

Opportunity: Depersonalize objections.

Risk: The other person is so attached to his crap idea, he takes the attack personally. Perish the thought . . .

Courtesy corral: How do you tell a girl her ivory gown makes her look like cling-wrapped cottage cheese?

Don't. Say the plunging damask shows off her antelope neck instead.

Anna Valentine, the couturier who attired Camilla Parker Bowles for her wedding to Prince Charles, cajoles brides-to-be by swathing them in attention, ushering them towards comely frocks by focusing on their most flatterable bits. Such schmoozing works on babies, business leaders and the most tyrannosaurus divas. Swarm over every detail, keep each hint soft-focus, gag potential protest, inducing a diabetic coma from all your sweetness. Few illusions are more intoxicating than that we are captivating. Indeed I watched an otherwise talentless woman propel a meteoric career almost entirely by facelift-obviating smiles, emphatic nods and resourcefulness at telling people they were fabulous.

Opportunity: Get what you want in the guise of providing a service.

Risk: Exhaustion. Sustaining disbelief.

Peel an onion: Things aren't going your way? Use emotional levers to jack up your position. Quit the crying and moaning – too near blackmail, as well as liable to make victims fractious. Instead, make feelings instrumental by attaching them to positive arguments for your cause: 'I'm so passionate because . . .'

Opportunity: Move them to sympathy.

Risk: Seeming out of ideas/unreasonable/potty.

Mind Your Language

In the seventeenth century Thomas Sprat described how Britain's first scientific institution, the Royal Society, enacted a purge to win kudos with rich, influential merchants (hitherto science had been the preserve of highfalutin polymaths like Sir Francis Bacon). Members asset-stripped their vocab in favour of a

> *close, naked, natural way of speaking; positive expressions; clear senses; a native easiness; bringing all things as near the Mathematical plainness as they can.*

The learned members had a thoroughly modern appreciation of how words open the minds that open doors. In persuasion, the task isn't to offer a balanced view, but win people over. To do this, what matters is how you jigsaw the facts to the picture you wish to present, and frame it to fit listeners' views. But it is a process, and each step should be contrived to bring them with you.

Engage trust and this is tantamount to loyalty, according to hostage negotiation expert Mitchell Hammer:

> *Various studies have shown that when we say we trust someone, we are less critical, we require less information, we share more aspects of ourselves, and we give people the benefit of the doubt.*

Language can be an incantation to trust, inducing a co-operative frame of mind without advertising to listeners how the mood has been achieved. Social workers talk to clients of 'our' strategy to reduce debts. Similarly, police negotiators increase feelings of immediacy by using present over past tense, and language to imply that a co-operative relationship already exists:

'This'	not	'That'
'These'	not	'Those'
'Our'	not	'My'
'Here'	not	'There'
'We'	not	'I'

The underlying message – 'We're in this together' – resonates subliminally, summoning the sense, delightful in any conversation, of a moment shared.

And the more positive, the better. Mine your situation for opportunities to say yes. Don't browbeat like chef Gordon Ramsay, for whom 'Yes?' seems to be a full-stop. (Actually, the question mark is debatable: he yaps it like an order.) Rather, find things the other person can nod to and you begin to establish a pattern of agreement.

Start from their needs, and repeat what they say: 'So you want a new car?' gets your first yes. Impregnate possibility in every sentence. Say 'Let's'; 'We could'; 'Would it work if . . .?' Conversely, to evade responsibility or downplay a situation, use distancing language. 'Due to funding problems'; 'Collateral damage was sustained'; 'An accident has occurred'; 'It has come to my attention that your daughter has crashed our car.'

To conserve your power of influence, exert it sparingly. The wizard Merlin bewitched the king with his prophecies. But when the king begged Merlin to peer into the future for fun, according to chronicler Geoffrey of Monmouth, he refused:

> *'Mysteries of that sort cannot be revealed . . . except where there is most urgent need for them. If I were to utter them as an entertainment . . . then the spirit which controls me would forsake me in the moment of need.'*

Merlin, or rather Geoffrey of Monmouth, was clairvoyant enough to see that if you scatter wisdom like poppyseed, the oracle becomes a clown.

The 'spirit' that made Merlin's prophecies credible was the king's urgent need to credit them when in dire straits. So, whatever the situation, how your listeners feel about you matters more than what you say, because conversation, like poetry, works not by convincing but stirring. Emotion nixes reason every time. Experiments by psychologist Drew Westen discovered that, presented with a bad argument by a politician whom they like, partisans' brains go out of their way to 'turn off the spigot of unpleasant emotion':

> *The neural circuits charged with regulation of emotional states*
> *seemed to recruit beliefs that eliminated the distress and conflict*
> *... And this all seemed to happen with little involvement of the*
> *neural circuits normally involved in reasoning.*

Irrational? Perhaps. On the other hand, without passion, can we be ethical? Feeling is the ultimate judge of our deeds' merit, not the chopping blade of logic. And since we all feel before we think, inevitably feelings have the power to drive our thoughts where our beliefs would send them. This is why the most persuasive argument in the world is what we want to hear, from someone we enjoy listening to. Lawyer Clarence Darrow averred: 'The main work of a trial attorney is to make the jury like his client.'

So don't try to change someone's mind; use what is there. Learn what he likes. Focus on his face; read his feelings; hear messages in his voice. Smile, even when talking on the phone (the muscles alter the tone of voice). Put yourself in his shoes, speak to his interests, and he will find it easier to range himself alongside you.

Conversare: to turn around often.

Who needs argument, if you can convert him?

How To Complain

Complaining troubles those for whom it is a confession of weakness (self-censorship at which adherents of the stiff upper-lip tradition excel). The consumerist ethos is emboldening many. Still, in private life, asking for more, or less, or better, or faster, can be daunting.

Thank Dr Thomas Gordon for his handy three-part complaint formula:

When you do X I feel Y because Z

This neat assertion of cause and effect imputes no blame; indeed, it presumes the culprit is unaware of what he is doing. And it is literally undeniable, because only you know how you feel. Whether he feels you should feel that way is another matter.

So if you've bought a pair of dirty shoes, bitten through an elastic band in your salad, or been bumped off your flight and are stranded in Rotterdam at three in the morning, consider how unwelcome orotund rages will be to the person on the other side of the counter – the only person who can help. No need to wheedle; simply assume he wishes to resolve the situation as much as you, and take it by degrees.

Level one: Present your dilemma, but let the other person define it – thereby taking ownership of the problem. As in, 'I took them home, got them out of the box, and then I noticed'; 'Look what I found in my lollo rosso'; 'We're stuck.'

Level two: Has he upbraided you for sharp teeth? Is he thick? Workshy? Still assume co-operation, using questions to outline, without dictating, what you think he should do to help. 'Can I have the refund direct to my account, or do you have another pair?' 'Shame, I was really enjoying the salad. Perhaps you can throw in pudding.' 'Which hotel do you usually put people up in?'

Level three: No advance? Try a forceful yet positive statement: 'In the past this was okay. It would be a huge help if . . .' 'Please remind me of the procedure for claims . . .' As you raise the stick, keep the carrot dangling: 'It is really kind of you to take the time/lend me your pen . . .' He may be doing his job to the barest minimum; nevertheless, help him feel good about helping you, and act as if it's a great personal favour. He may succumb to the undertow of obligation you've implied.

Level four: He is blaming you, implying you wore the shoes, arrived too late for your flight, etc. Try mild self-assertion, focused on how he gains from solving your problem, and seek advice: 'I'm sorry to inconvenience you. We realize you don't set the policy. How can we get out of your hair?'

Level five: An absurd excuse deserves commemoration. Write it down, asking him to repeat it, 'to help me understand' his position. Check spellings and punctuation, ask for the complaints form, his assistance filling it in. The goal is to make it less trouble to satisfy than refuse you, with passive-aggressive attrition. Don't be fobbed off: grin till your teeth hurt.

Level six: Outright accusation, such as you went breakdancing in those sneakers, or ordered that £500 bottle of St Emilion knowingly (so what if you drank it). This is a gift, breaching the service industry code: The customer is always right. Show how hurt you are. 'Are you calling your customer a liar?' Write his answer down, acting the detective, of the genial, Miss Marple variety.

Level seven: Cry.

Typology of Bores, Chores and other
Conversational Beasts

THE UNIVERSAL EXPERT   *Omniscientus Caudex*

No sooner has the Universal Expert asked what you do than he is explaining how to do it better. Fussily furbished minds can lack sensitivity. At a hotel the *sotto voce* dining room was nightly kebabbed by an amateur food critic's commentary: 'This is good', 'This is not good' or 'Almost good – but not quite', severally repeated, between each bite.

I met a quintessential UE at a dinner. He claimed deep knowledge of each passing shade of a topic, and didn't hesitate to illuminate each dim corner. Towards the evening's premature end (no second helpings) he announced proudly, 'The most fascinating conversations I've had lately were with complete strangers. Funny, isn't it?'

The host, a relative, smiled wanly. I pictured the man's friends: all strangers, innocent all.

There seem to be growing numbers of UEs; barricaded in industry jargon, gazing down from high pulpits of data, the frail body of their opinion studded with spurious fact. They may not mean to condescend, they may even be clever, but they're too daft to get along. Theirs is an infallible system for avoiding threatening meetings of equals, but as conversation, a cheat. Or worse. After the funeral of a doctor, fellow medics approached the bereaved family, and, fishing for something to say, enquired about the sudden illness, then outlined in clinical detail exactly how she would have died.

Tactics: UEs are easily flattered, and easily led by questions. If he means well, you might joshingly suggest your interest in Albanian abattoirs is limited. If not, don't josh.

Pluses: A learning opportunity. Maybe.

14

Shut-Up Shop

On How to Wage a Word War

Remember those hopeless insults? Custard pies that boomeranged back, splat, on you?

When sorely tried, letting rip may feel deeply satisfying but ultimately, like swearing or smacking a child, it's a loser's game. Far smarter is playwright Alan Bennett's policy:

> *I'm all in favour of free expression provided it's kept rigidly under control.*

There is an art to verbal sallies. While the right put-down is glorious, the wrong one is shaming. An ex-colleague once made the office cringe by boasting of her triumph over a youth who had been slow to admit selling her a grubby pair of shoes.

'This is why you are a shop assistant,' she told him, 'and I am a manager.'

(She worked in publicity.)

If cruelty will show you up, showing you can't take it is little less damaging to prestige. The best policy is to rise above it, like Ivan Vasiliev, a dainty Belarussan ballet dancer known as 'the boy who can fly', who confessed to measuring his stature daily,

> *because I have the complex of a small man! In the Bolshoi they have many tall men, so they're always telling me I'm small.*

Did he punch them?

> *No. I just do something that they could never do.*

If flight is beyond you, try a sharp retort – not so much cutting as polished. When words are weapons, counter-intelligence spares pain, and it saved lives in ancient Arabia. Before storming into battle, scimitars a-bristle, opposing tribes would send forth their best satirist for a poetic slanging match. This not only dictated morale, but often, if the loser suffered a rout, his tribe would slope off without further ado.

Similarly, the ideal rejoinder muzzles the opposition. I know: I suffered the stiletto of Yorkshire wit William Hague. I was at Associated Newspapers, waiting for the lift, when I glanced down into the atrium and spotted the young politician's gleaming pate. It was 1997, Labour had just swept to power, Hague aspired to be Tory Party leader and to that end, I assumed, he had come to woo the influential editor of the *Daily Mail.*

There was something mournful in how Hague sat, alone on the bench, no retinue in tow; like an old codger watching pigeons in the park, or a miscreant schoolboy awaiting a caning. Naturally, I pointed this out to passers-by.

'Look, there's William Hague. Isn't he *sad*?'

Finally the lift came, stuffed with journalists. My friend Vince walked out.

'Hey,' I said. 'You see Hague sitting down there, all by himself? Tragic!'

Vince widened his eyes then scarpered. Puzzled, I entered the lift.

A familiar voice spoke. 'He's not alone any more.'

I, alone, laughed.

I cannot guarantee your sallies will attain Hague's élan, but a little effort can kick-start invective kung-fu, and help avert that baleful *esprit d'escalier*, that sense of opportunity lost, which Mark Twain captured in his definition of repartee: 'Something we think of twenty-four hours too late.'

Shut-Up Shop

This is war, and begins with a protocol.

RULE ONE: *Ensure defence is necessary and justified*

As the Spanish proverb has it, 'Insults should be well avenged or well endured.' Or you will end the fool.

If there is no outright aggression, first ignore it. If the offence persists, check the offender intends to be as rude as he seems. Ask if he meant to say that. You could say he is making you feel uncomfortable. He may shut up.

But with a persistent bigmouth or bully, prepare to fight. Your aim is two-fold: to silence him and retain moral high ground

Now consider tactics. Meet slur with slander, take the fight to the lowest verbal skill level, and not only may you cede the high ground, but you may also make it far too easy for your opponent to reply in kind.

RULE TWO: *A smart riposte raises verbal and intellectual stakes*

For minimal effort, maximum effect, don't vituperate: cogitate, baffle and confuse, taking the battleground out of an opponent's comfort zone and attacking his mode of attack.

If you can be politer, wittier or shift the focus from his target – preferably on to him – you will put him off balance. And if he looks foolish, his thrust only injures himself.

Here, in ascending difficulty, follow twenty tactics.

1. Do nothing

As the fourth of China's hallowed *Thirty-Six Stratagems* has it: 'Relax while the enemy exhausts himself.' An approach for the supremely confident and powerful (think stoic mum versus apoplectic toddler). Fold your arms and smile like you're being paid to.

2. Laugh

3. Challenge

Flip back a challenge, forcing the attacker to defend her attack. Repetition will do:

'Idiot!'

'Idiot?'

Elizabeth II walked to a photoshoot at Buckingham Palace

with Annie Leibovitz of *Vanity Fair*, sizzling with irritation at having to don her fiddliest ceremonial fig (cumbersome Order of the Garter robes plus tiara).

'I'm not changing anything. I've done enough dressing like this, thank you very much,' said the octogenarian to a flunky hefting her train.

Unfortunate then, that at the shoot Leibovitz asked Her Maj to remove the tiara to look 'less dressy'.

'Less dressy?' demanded the Queen. 'What do you think this is?'

She did not need to add that Leibovitz had failed to grasp the import of her robes of state, hardly a casual ensemble one may dress down for a stroll with the corgis . . .

4. Embrace

Why expend energy on repulsing a strike when you can welcome it: 'The pleasure is all mine,' or 'You're too kind.' Can't swallow all their bile? Then share the wealth: 'I know, we have much in common.'

5. Quibble

Tackle the terms of your attacker's criticism, rather than the central charge: 'Sure you wouldn't rather I parboiled my head?'

Another English queen, Elizabeth I, excelled at such parries. Late into decrepitude, as death drew nigh, she took to lolling in her chamber on heaps of cushions, gawping at nothing like a baked fish. Anxious courtier Sir Robert Cecil ventured to say: 'Your Majesty, to content the people, you must go to bed.'

'Little man, little man,' she tutted. 'The word *must* is not used to princes.'

6. Reject

Put the onus on them: 'Prove it.'

7. Deflect

Feign confusion. Refocus the problem: 'Somebody upset you? Let me at them'; 'Don't put yourself down'; 'That's no way to talk about your wife.' Or be slightly patronizing: 'Watch out, someone might take that personally'; 'Poor you!'

8. Reverse

This might be called 'hold up a mirror'. I dedicate it to Griff Rhys Jones.

Life is tough for this millionaire comedian, TV presenter and producer. He is always being recognized. As somebody else. Culture vulture Melvyn Bragg once introduced him to his daughter (his 'biggest fan') as actor 'John Sessions'. More often he is mistaken for Hugh Laurie or Hugh Grant. And when he met the real Grant, the *Notting Hill* star asked him what he was up to 'these days'. Hours later Rhys Jones thought of a comeback: 'Well, a hell of a lot more than you!'

But I'm glad he didn't use this peevish one-upper. Far mightier, if a mite arch, would have been a straight reversal: 'The question, Hugh, is what are *you* up to?'

This tactic is very effective for blunting sly digs. ('Well, fancy meeting you here!' 'No, fancy meeting *you* here!') My favourite anti-compliment came from a woman who told me, 'You look great! Isn't this bar's lighting wonderful. Soooo flattering.'

'Yes, it is,' I said (in my head, twenty-four hours later). 'You look great!'

9. Killing kindness

Spleen feeds on outrage, so starve it: stifle the abuser with niceness.

Recently I was at a house party, my first all-nighter in years. In the queue for the loo, a mad-eyed man glowered at me. So, in what I thought a candyfloss, thoroughly amenable manner, I said something along the lines of: 'Gosh, it's ages since I was at a house party like this, into the small hours. I feel like a teenager!'

'What do you mean?' he demanded.

'Well, what I said,' I said. 'Makes me feel young. Wonderful, isn't it?'

'That is an incredibly arrogant stance,' he roared, and strode off.

Later I found myself next to him on the dance floor. He was chewing off a woman's ear. I heard the words 'superficial' and 'desperate'.

'What's up?' I asked sweetly.

'This, all this,' he cried. 'It's so fake!'

'Oh, that's terrible. Why suffer? Don't do it to yourself. Go home. Now.'

'You're absolutely right,' he beamed, then asked me to join him.

10. Invert

Can you invert the jibe and find advantage in alleged weakness? An ageing politician was attacked by a younger for his ripe years and sparse hairs. In reply, he promised not to exploit the advantage experience and wisdom gave him over the callow youth.

11. Prick the pompous

At the sharp end of a lecture? Dull it with a tease: 'I'm afraid you can't reform me.' A seventeenth-century lady of leisure ended a suitor's diatribe on the conduct of Philip II by asking, 'Why, sir, will you be wise from morning to night?'

12. Ironic praise

So there he is, face like a psychotic tomato, spitting ire. Take a deep breath and try this trick used by advocates in Ancient Greece: eulogize a minor and unrelated aspect of the assailant, which should highlight the gravity of his crime, or at least disconcert him. Say: 'That colour suits you'; 'You have wonderful teeth'; 'You haven't aged a bit'; 'Incredible tan. Gran Canaria?'; 'Who told you you're sexy when you're livid?'

If they fulminate long and hard, emulate the Fat Man, Mr Gutman in *The Maltese Falcon*, who swats off Sam Spade/Humphrey Bogart's cracks as if they were confetti. Say you admire a man who knows his own mind, how elegantly he slings his mud . . . Or thank him: 'It was considerate to let me know you had a problem, and in such detail.'

13. Escape the moment

Try an ominous question. Say: 'I wonder how you'll remember this conversation'; 'Feel good now? Remember, feelings change.' This one, overheard by party-talk collector Andrew Barrow, should pull a ranter up short: 'Know what I'm thinking? Good job you don't, because it's very rude.'

14. Mock the mocker

Conservative politician Ken Clarke once vaporized an opponent's tirade by scoffing, 'The Right Honourable Gentleman sounds like a shopping list.' (In their laughter, most MPs forgot the charge-sheet.)

If someone is crude, you might venture: 'I bet you can't say that backwards'; 'Now spell it'; 'And words of more than one syllable?'; 'I'd hate to meet you on a bad day'; 'This isn't your first language?' Or offer, 'Another drink?'

15. Instruction
You might suggest, as Mr Bennet does his unmusical daughter Mary at the piano in *Pride and Prejudice*, that your assailant has delighted you long enough. So will he, kindly, shut it.

16. Take him on a journey (a strategem for the strong)
Play consequences, showing what his attitude will cost: flash a Clint Eastwood smile.

David Geffen, then a Warner Brothers exec, went up to Eastwood after the studio screening of his new film *The Outlaw Josey Wales*. 'I only want to suggest one thing. I think it would be better if it was twenty minutes shorter.'

Eastwood thanked him. 'I'm glad you took the time to see the picture, and I appreciate your comments. But why don't you study the picture some more and see if you have any more thoughts. When you do, give me a call over at Paramount.'

'Why over at Paramount?' asked Geffen.

'Because that's where I'll be making my next movie.'

'The picture is perfect,' said Geffen. 'I wouldn't change one frame. Thank you very much.'

Clint said, 'Thank *you*.'

17. Distract

Create a sideshow. Mount a demi-attack (implied rather than outright lampoon). Ask: 'You always wear your hair like that?'; 'Did you plan that outfit?'; 'Your dentist still in practice?' Or say: 'Don't let me keep you, your next drink's waiting'; or 'Perhaps you'd like to share these thoughts with your mistress. There she is.'

18. Back to school

Be childish. Puerile comments are utterly disarming, because they lift calumny to a comic plane – with the happy possibility of fettering an assailant in giggles. And if he reacts badly, he appears worse than childish, humourless. So say: 'Unnnh! I'm going to tell on you.' Or try for an absurd aspersion.

For instance, the body slam. This stupefyingly infantile compound item pairs an aspect of the aggressor's physiognomy or personality with an unthreatening adjective to form an absurd epithet (alliterative or rhyming for extra impact). Such as: yoghurt-pants, caterpillar features, cheese-brain, mirkin-mouth, Brillo-brow, dolcelatte-legs, sensitive rhino, subtle clod, pocket primadonna, shapely dolt, spam-head, parsnip nose, spud-u-like, iguana-face, Picasso-girl, leech-lips, george bush.

Puzzling similes and metaphors are fairly dumbfounding: 'When you're emotional you look just like a boiled boot/ electrocuted jelly/wronged flamingo/rhubarb fool.' Or label your opponent as something small, dainty or innately cuddly: 'Okay, squirrel/koala/chicken wing/petal/mouse/wee thumb/ diddle-diddle-dumpling/champ.'

Or personify your assailant's mood: say, 'Sorry, Mrs

Depressing/Mr Moan/Professor Crosspatch, what seems to be the problem?'; 'Show mercy, Dr Angry/Mistress Irate.' Ask a daft question: 'Have you curvature of the brain?' If fired up, issue a mock-heroic curse: 'May your granny toss salad in Hades'; 'May you give birth to humungous hedgehogs.' Or a foolish invitation: 'Go wild! Smash a grape!'; 'Hence, distended dong of a disenfranchised donkey.'

For slurs with staying power, paint a picture. Sixteenth-century literary nitpicker Gabriel Harvey slandered rival Thomas Nashe as 'the toadstool of the realm'. Alan Bennett neutered a monstrous uncle with a diminutive 'Australian hamster'. Popular British buffoon-politician Boris Johnson dismissed rumours of adultery with the haunting 'inverted pyramid of piffle'. A pity the piffle proved true.

19. Bash the basher (not for use on the violent)

Take it up a notch with a hecklerism. There are answers for these (in brackets), so handle with care.

'Why don't you take a long walk on a short pier?'	('Age before beauty.')
'Here's the reason for birth control.'	('Daddy/Mummy!')
'Millions of sperm and they had to pick you!'	('I'm a good egg.')
'I can recommend a psychiatrist.'	(*'Quelle surprise'*; 'Keep him busy?')
'Is your personality terminal?'	('Yours is critical.')
'I bet you're a genius from the knees down.'	('And I have ankles'; 'We can't all be heels.')

'I'm sure you're nicer than you look.' ('I'm sure you look nice in the dark.')

'Want to give me a piece of your mind? Can you spare it?' ('I like giving to the less fortunate.')

20. The most deserved assault in the world

According to Kingsley Amis, Princess Margaret had a 'habit of reminding people of her status when they venture to disagree with her in conversation'. How sad.

There is no greater conversation-shirking cowardice than pulling rank. If asked 'Do you know who I am?' use a boast gag:

'Elvis?'

'Memory trouble?'

'I'd rather not.'

'No, who do you think you are?'

'Yes, but I'm prepared to overlook it.'

Rude Art

Excoriation has a riotous history. Here is an inspirational selection:

Putdowns

Beethoven to another composer:

I liked your opera. I think I will set it to music.

Ninon de Lenclos, liberated lover, on toffy-nosed marquis de Sévigné:

He has the heart of a cucumber fried in snow.

Sydney Smith to garrulous historian Thomas Babington Macaulay:

You know, when I am gone, you will be sorry you never heard me speak.

Shut-Up Shop

Woodrow Wilson on Warren Harding:

He has a bungalow mind.

Poet Robert Burns, dissing an anonymous critic:

Thou eunuch of language . . . thou pimp of gender . . . murderous accoucheur of infant learning . . . thou pickle-herring in the puppet show of nonsense [etc.]

Model Jean Shrimpton, on being asked about her relationship with snapper David Bailey:

Sex has never been high on my list of priorities.

Old Lancashire favourite (not for hotpots):

A waste of skin.

Disraeli, converting dour political rival William Gladstone's virtue into a vice:

He has not a single redeeming defect.

Retorts

Lewis Morris, poet: *It is a conspiracy of silence against me, a conspiracy of silence. What should I do?*
Oscar Wilde: *Join it.*

Oscar Wilde to painter James Whistler: *I wish I had said that.*
Whistler: *You will, Oscar, you will.*

Lord Sandwich to libertarian John Wilkes: *Sir, you will die either of the pox or on the gallows.*
Wilkes: *Depending on whether I embrace your mistress or your principles.*

The Art of Conversation

Waiter in Annabel's nightclub to an elderly patron, upon being asked to help find false teeth, which had fallen on to the dance floor: *Certainly, sir. What colour are they?*

Winston Churchill's contretemps with fellow politico Nancy Astor are notorious, but worth repeating.

Astor: *Winston, you are drunk, horribly drunk.*

Churchill: *And madam, you are ugly, terribly ugly, but in the morning I shall be sober.*

Astor: *If I were your wife I'd put poison in your coffee.*

Churchill: *If I were your husband I'd drink it.*

Clare Boothe Luce, letting Dorothy Parker enter a door first: *Age before beauty.*
Parker: *And pearls before swine.*

William Wordsworth to Charles Lamb: *I believe that I could write like Shakespeare, if I had a mind to try it.*
Lamb: *Yes. Nothing wanting but the mind.*

Elizabeth I, greeting jester, Pace, on his return to court after brief banishment for being rude: *Come now, Pace, let us hear more of our faults.*
Pace: *No, Madam, I never talk of what is discoursed by all the world.*

But perhaps the boldest retort, certainly the most learned, came from ninth-century Scottish scholar John Scotus, dining opposite the Emperor Charlemagne.

'What is there,' asked the emperor, 'between *Sottum* and *Scottum*?' (Meaning, 'between a fool and a Scot'.)

In a flash, the scholar replied, 'The width of this table, Sire.'

Typology of Bores, Chores and other Conversational Beasts

SAYING SORRY   *Coprophagy*

Jaded representatives of the world's press gathered in Vancouver for an up-close and personal at the dress rehearsal for the first show on the Spice Girls' comeback tour. Only, no girls. Then:

Suddenly, the five appeared in a flurry, like a flock of goldfinches alighting. They had come to offer their apologies for the delay, explain the frazzled condition of their nerves, promise that none of their costumes would fall apart, and hope we enjoyed ourselves. In a long lifetime of attending large concerts, I have never witnessed anything remotely as charming. Some might say this was the work of conniving minxes, but then they weren't there.

Stunt or not, this keep 'em waiting, treat 'em nice manoeuvre is highly effective, building expectation, then earning honesty credits from an inconvenience of your own making. Not that I'm suggesting you contrive any such thing. My point is, what is lovelier than humility?

When you cause offence, how you acknowledge it, or don't, can deepen the injury. 'Never apologize, never explain what you think happened', said to be Elizabeth II's motto, might work for monarchs, but reticence is a cat's scratch from rudeness. So say 'sorry' instead.

Or should we? The word is under attack. Novelist Sandra Howard argued it has become so devalued as to be meaningless. Certainly, often it prefaces self-justification or refusals to compromise: 'Sorry, you had it coming'; 'Sorry, but it was your idea';

'Sorry you feel that way, but we will go ahead.' However, as these examples show, the word isn't at fault; the problem is tagging others on to it, demoting 'sorry' to the prelude to a squabble over responsibility.

Apologizing is a finely balanced art, of judgement more than self-expression. Far from a negotiating point, 'sorry' should be a final concession, and every self-exculpatory word you add puts more blame on you. If the story is complicated, explain what you think happened, showing your regret without accepting full responsibility. If the fault is yours, say so.

Yielding should steer a dispute to an end. And bear in mind that rolling over too soon may be damaging. Charles I advised Lord Wentworth,

Never make a defence or an apology before you be accused.

But then, as history relates, had Charles bowed to his people, he might have kept his head.

15

Are You Receiving Me?

On Stitching Conversation into Your Life

Why did ex-supermodel Christy Turlington cast her BlackBerry in bronze?

To save her marriage.

Adultery with an elfin communication console has yet to enter the statutes, but how many of us have not felt, like this lady, harassed by

> the sudden violent irruptions of unnecessary possibilities into our daily lives, the incessant wrenching of the mind away from one subject and bringing it to bear upon another, the constant need of making decisions, albeit of the most trivial and unimportant kind. How is it possible under these conditions to think to any purpose? How can our rolling minds gather any moss?

Lady Florence Bell, to give her full title – she of the absurd small-talk book – was bemoaning the invention of her namesake, Alexander Graham Bell, the telephone. She was writing in 1907. One century on, her objections have a sinisterly modern ring.

But unless you're a multimillionaire yogini or aristocratic aesthete, junking technology and retreating to the tranquillity of an eco-friendly yurt, while assistants take care of business, probably isn't an option. And would you wish it?

Modern conveniences free time to talk. Julie Burchill defended superstores for

the buzz of getting things done quickly *so one can then move on and do something one loves, be it sex, conversation or lazing away the day on the sofa or the beach.*

All the same, what if home is a towerblock, or you don't own a car, or you live alone?

Conversation need not have a purpose to have a point. Unfortunately, the price of many of our conveniences is the loose change of socializing, with inconvenient long-term costs that sociologists, teachers and psychologists are only beginning to count. Points of contact that once sewed the day together are being unpicked: the rise of electronic banking, the demise of post offices and corner shops, condemn many, especially the old and poor, to stay at home.

I don't deny technology makes life more kaleidoscopic. On the upside, with communication technology, fresh opportunities to make connections abound. I love that I can witter to a guy in Albuquerque about gorgonzola cheese. On the downside, it rarely encourages us to prize unalloyed moments together, and I would point out to Professor Martin Jones, author of *Feast: Why Humans Share Food*, that TV dinners

bring families no nearer the conviviality of our grizzled ancestors, gawking at crackling fires, than the Victorian dining room
did – at least, not in promoting talk; not unless there is only
one TV set and no phone, stereo, Xbox or computer to
compete with. However, in 2007, 40 per cent of British under-
fours had a TV in their bedroom . . .

Our gizmos make great diagnostic tools for measuring
other people's crapness – as they exacerbate or even invent it.
'Why doesn't he pick up the phone?' we ask, without asking,
'Why should he?' Who hasn't complained of the unanswered
e-mail, or wasted time waiting, checking, interpreting, specu-
lating? How much likelier are we to screw up or offend if we've
so many messages to process that they receive only cursory
attention? How much worse if we lose traction with our most
sophisticated communication medium, conversation?

Something must be done. Luckily, it need not be much.
With a little effort, you can tame the attention-eaters and draw
conversation into the centre of your life.

RULE ONE: *Say hello*
And goodbye, to everyone you have dealings with. In shops,
queues, on buses, customer helplines . . .

RULE TWO: *Ration your attention*
I applaud the sign at my off-licence:

> *Customers talking into mobile phones will not be served: it is
> rude!*

Ignore the phone, better still turn it off. The answer service is
there to be used.

Train people not to expect instant feedback. Only deal with e-mails and so on at a set time, and don't answer colleagues outside paid hours except in emergencies; even if they work abroad, they should respect your time zone. Otherwise your day will become 24/7, and you'll be so fried soon everything is an emergency – giving employers a more worth less.

RULE THREE: *Think before text*

According to a survey in 2008, seven out of ten Britons text or e-mail when a face-to-face conversation is possible, believing this saves time. But does it? The average employee spends one and a half to two hours a day panhandling streams of verbiage, and a friend in industry is tormented by confusions that stem from trigger-fingered co-workers' hare-brained e-mails. Even e-mail etiquette gurus Will Schwalbe and David Shipley are susceptible:

> *By the time we had sorted out our timetable, three weeks had passed, lots of e-mails had been exchanged, and a question that should have taken one minute to answer had eaten up hours. We had come face to face with one of e-mail's stealthiest characteristics: its ability to simulate forward motion. As Bob Geldof, the humanitarian rock musician said, e-mail is dangerous because it gives us 'a feeling of action' – even when nothing is happening.*

Before tapping the keys, ask: is this the best way? Why agonize over an annoying e-mail if you can see your colleague?

Just for a week, use e-mail and text solely to send documents or schedule phone or face-to-face chat. How much time do you free up?

RULE FOUR: *Appreciate the voice*

Computers screen a great deal, as a Ready4Life etiquette course teacher told students:

> *You're losing so many of your social tools on e-mail. We can't see the other person. Are they smiling? Are they angry? We just can't see it.*

Text is weak at expressing tone, the emotional dimension that gives words much of their meaning. For this reason, the expressive typography popular in the last communication revolution, the eighteenth century – a Ballyhoo of Capital Letters, Zany – Punctuation, and *emphatic italics* – is reborn in dastardly emoticons. :-(

But as Pebbles, seventeen, a Ready4Life student pointed out: 'Everyone perceives them differently – like that sarcastic eye-rolling one'. Similarly, columnist Sophia Money-Coutts endured paroxysms over text message politesse:

> *She asked me whether I signed off with a big kiss (X) or a little one (x). 'Is there a distinction?' I asked, aghast that I might have committed romantic hari-kiri by sending big ones. 'I'm not sure,' she replied, 'but isn't it all just so unclear?'*

Indeed. There is the phone, in your hand. So, as David Gest would say, talk.

RULE FIVE: *Question your definition of problems*

Things once central and convenient – family dinners were cheaper, playing with kids kept them quiet – have come to be seen as optional, or obnoxious. Far from pleasure, play is a problem to Scott Huskinson, vendor of Tadpole (rubber cases that turn iPods into toys):

I thought how parents all over the world use in-car DVD players,
but there's no solution for entertaining kids once you leave the car.

The concept of quality time (invented in 1970s corporate America, gaining general currency in the cash-and-grab culture of the 1980s) implies that we sense much of time is impoverished. But such language is also a licence to dole it out grudgingly, as if to convince us it is proper most hours should be distracted, second best or negligible; a warrant to neglect that we like to imagine is benign. Why else are there TVs in toddlers' bedrooms, DVD screens in backs of car seats and teddies with computer games in their bellies? Today's kids not only play with toys but expect them to interact. Does this help them interact with one another? I lost a year to a Donkey Kong game, in the playground, with a similarly fixated Mario Bros. fan. Her name? No idea. But I remember the girls at dance club.

Does your attention-seeking teenager have a point? Is that chore a joy in disguise – something satisfying to do while catching up with someone you like? I was never convinced by invitations to: 'Come paint my flat – we'll have beers, it'll be fun!' or 'Build dry-stone walls in beautiful Cumbria – only £699!' But I'm prepared to rethink.

RULE SIX: *Spring-clean routines*

Anyone can clear space in routines for conversation. Mealtimes, bathtimes, relaxation, hobbies – all potential shared times. Co-ordinate timetables, be in the same room. Turn off the central heating. If you can, leave the car, walk and, yes, shop together. Want to spare the other person the trouble? If you're trogging around Tesco's while they watches telly, you're depriving her of quality interaction: the best way to unwind and create distance from stresses and strains is to talk and put them into perspective.

And be hospitable. Invite someone to tea, elevenses. These rituals once paced out the day, but have been downgraded to snacks grazed on the hoof, depleting their soul food: talk. As writer Bee Wilson points out, they're kinder to host and guest:

> 'We must have you round to dinner' seems to slip inevitably out of one's mouth as soon as a friendship reaches a certain stage. But how much more fun life would be, for lots of reasons, if we had people round for afternoon tea instead. The bliss of tea is that it brings no expectations.

A slice of toast will do. Less fuss, less outlay, more fun for you.

RULE SEVEN: *Make plans*

Why fix to meet if we can improvise on the hoof?

Because you might not get around to it. Flexibility makes us flaky, and many city friends see each other less than out-of-towners because they feel less urgency about keeping in contact. Don't settle for catch-ups by phone or e-mail, which can deceive us we're in touch at the same time as displace direct encounters. Be a stickler, buy a diary, fill it with indelible arrangements.

RULE EIGHT: *Make it matter*

Once you're with them, leave the phone alone.

RULE NINE: *Relish silence*

Inevitably time feels impoverished, experience intangible, if we don't notice spending it. Fast for a day: no TV, computer, music, Playstation, film. Unplug the toys, plug in, be a tourist in your world, and you'll find there is no silence: too much is going on.

What will you see? Who will you meet? Perhaps you'll have a conversation.

RULE TEN: *You tell me (www.catherineblyth.com)*

Conversation Survival Kit

Nervous? Prepare and travel light. Remember five points:

1. Attention
It's not about you: prepare to listen. Watch others' faces, the clock by which to measure turns on the floor.

2. Imagination
Every utterance contains the seeds for further discussion (except, possibly, 'Fine').

3. Enthusiasm
The fount of inspiration.

4. Focus pull
Direct conversation to the other person's interests: you'll soon find what interests you about them.

5. Ingredients
Review topics as you might before a news quiz. One headline issue; one trivial; one gossipy.

There is no shortage of communication, but is it not telling that globalization has created Globish, a nuance-stunted anglo-lingo spreading like ivy across the globe, which contains only 1,500 words? Its codifier Jean-Paul Nerriere, once of IBM, hymns its limits:

> *It is designed for trivial efficiency, always, everywhere, with everyone . . . One thing you never do in Globish is tell a joke.*

Guidelines include: repeat yourself; avoid metaphors and colourful expressions, and keep sentences short. However, with so few words to play with, this isn't always possible (rather than 'siblings' you must say 'the other children of my mother and father'). Conversation friendly it is not.

So much of communication transcends language, conversation's telepathy – seeing behind screens, hearing what is told, not what is said – is invaluable. Friendships flower from such tiny prompts: the twitch of a mouth, a shared glance, all the unsaid, perhaps unsayable things. Henry James wrote:

> *Small children have many more perceptions than they have terms to translate them; their vision is at any moment much richer, their apprehension even constantly stronger, than their prompt, their at all producible, vocabulary.*

It's true of us all. But even remote encounters make life better.

One day I called my bank to check a credit. A sing-song voice said it had arrived, then perhaps she asked what the money was for; anyway, somehow we began talking about books and exchanged recommendations. I asked where she was based and she said Wales.

'Out of the window I can only see green. Nothing else. We're surrounded by trees,' she said. 'Where are you?'

I described my London street, said how lucky she was.

'Yes, it's beautiful.' She sighed. 'But it's blooming boring. That's why I read.'

And we laughed.

In 1956, Dorothy Parker said: 'Civilization is coming to an end, you understand.' But ever since it was thought of, civilization has been failing: that is why we work at it.

Conversation's finer points may be lost without our world tottering. Still, as communication, it is unimprovable. Of all arts, the oldest and most captivating, it is also the easiest, free to all. As prices soar, and time shrinks, and space compacts, it is one luxury that costs nothing. Protect it, prioritize it and reap the wealth of a companionable, convivial life.

Let conversation bring you the world.

PS

Are you fond of farewells? Is the person with you rather less so?

Shoving to the exit, or dawdling, a hint of other business hanging like a bad smell, is awkward. But there are gentle ways to usher conversation to its close.

First, choose a line or topic that will suggest this is the end, my friend:

Arrangements: Talk of the Next rings the knell for Now.

Any statement starting 'Finally', 'Lastly': Suggests an agenda is nigh complete.

Troubles: Having plumbed the depths, re-ascending to froth is somehow psychologically impossible.

Satisfied customer: A labelling comment to convey a job has been ticked off the list: 'Well, I just wanted to check everything was okay.'

Farewell by implication: Pre-goodbye goodbyes: passing regards to the wife, etc. (Further reason to remember the personal details of time-guzzling clients and employees.)

Past tense: To kill the Now without committing to future encounters, say, 'It was great seeing you again', 'This was fun.'

Or ask, 'Was there anything else?'; or 'Now what did I mean to tell you? No, no, it's gone.'

Time's wingèd chariot hurrying near: That oh-so-pressing world you must be getting on with, or the missus will kill you, or the shops will have run out of Christmas trees, or the kids will be starving . . .

Rescue remedy: Is a loved one being mumbled in the maw of a bore? Are you tired? Be direct without offending the third party by implying that your loved one is reluctant to go, but inadvertently imposing on you.

'Dear one, we must leave now'; 'I'm sorry, but I'm going to have to drag you off, early start'; 'The babysitter?'; or this treat, overheard: 'David, you're liable to capsize any moment!'

Mustn't keep you: To say that you're halting their day is polite, but be warned, use repeatedly and it gains a tinct of condescension (so you're busy: so say so).

Now an exchange of verbal bows to ensure both parties agree our work is done.

Me: 'Well?'
You: 'Well.'
Me: 'So!'
You: 'So.'
Me: 'Okay then!'
You: 'Okay.'
Me: 'Bye.'
You: 'By the way . . .'

Can you hear the questioning uplift in the first speaker, the downbeat of the second? In effect, you are engineers, running through final items before clearing the plane for take-off ('Check?' asks Engineer One; 'Check,' confirms Engineer Two).

Similar exchanges occur to tread water when a conversation stalls. They're all opportunities: to raise another subject or prise open an exit. Just wait for a 'So. . .', introduce a turning-point word – 'well', 'listen' or 'now' – then say it's been great talking, but, sadly, you must go . . .

If ever you wonder, Why are we still talking? it is time to say how much you have enjoyed it, then goodbye. A little thing, like hello, it joins the dots of our increasingly dotty lives.

Knowing when to leave, wrote salon moralist La Bruyère, is 'An art that vain men rarely acquire.'

Like the art of conversation, you cannot attain it in vain.

Goodbye.

Acknowledgements

This book has enjoyed indecent amounts of luck. Here are some of the reasons why.

First thanks must go to my magnificent agent, Eugenie Furniss, out of whose conversation the idea sprang, and to my inspiring editors, Eleanor Birne, Erin Moore, and Helen Hawksfield. I'm grateful to all at John Murray, especially Nikki Barrow, Morag Lyall, Sara Marafini, Roland Philipps, Janette Revill, James Spackman and Leigh Wells, and the other unseen hands who helped usher this book to the shelves; to Bill Shinker and the Gotham team; to William Morris, in particular Alice Ellerby, Rowan Lawton, Shana Kelly and Jay Mandel; and to Henryk Hetflaisz and Remy Blumenfeld, who live in the realm of the possible and make it contagious.

Many individuals provided help and guidance, including: Emily Anderson, Jessica Axe, the late Shereen Baig, Nicola Barr, Andrew Barrow, Vick Beasley, Chris Blackhurst, Heidi Blyth, Jenny Blyth, Stephen Blyth, Vivian Blyth, Caroline Bondy, the staff of the British Library, Helen Burdock, Jackie Burdock, Emily Charkin, Kay Chung, Pete Clark, Vin De Silva, Andrea di Robilant, John Elliott, Theo Fairley, Max Gadney, my grandmother, the late Frances Gillam, Jane Gillam, the late Michael Gillam, Vince Graff, Clare Grafik, Louise Haines, Louise Harding, Carolyn Hart, Robin Harvie, Emily Hayward, Alice Horton, James Hughes-Onslow, Virginia Ironside, Gillian

Acknowledgements

Johnson, Alex Key, Irma Kurtz, Leonard Lewis, James Lewisohn, Michael Mack, Oliver Mack, Helen Marshall, Francesca Maurice-Williams, Harriet Maurice-Williams (a fine classicist whose help I corrupted), Walter Meierjohan, the staff of the North Kensington Library, Emma Parry, David Patterson, Chrystalla Peleties, Harry Phibbs, Gerrie Pitt, Dominic Prince, Rose Prince, Robert Procopé, James Ribbans, Andrea Rossini, Laetitia Rutherford, Professor Sophie Scott, Amanda Shakespeare, Christopher Shakespeare, Francesca Shakespeare, John Shakespeare, Lalage Shakespeare, Nicholas Shakespeare, Matthew Sturgis, Ben Summerskill, Petra Tauscher, Anne Turner, Dominic Turner, Susan Urquhart, Edward Venning, Sarah Venning, Marilyn Warnick, Hywel Williams, John Williams, Andrew Wilson, Bee Wilson, Katie Wood, Beverly Yong, Toby Young.

Not forgetting what is owed to some wonderful teachers: Brenda Atkinson, Dick Clarke, Gary French, John Glover, Dr Paul Hartle, Hazel Hill, Dr and Dr Holding, Neil Jarvis, Tom Morris, Dr Jonathan Smith and, most of all, Professor Germaine Greer.

Studying conversation can feel like chasing butterflies, but some ace netters eased my task: thanks to the interviewers, reporters and analysts who catch idiosyncrasies on the wing.

And lastly, to my husband, Sebastian Shakespeare, who has had enough conversations about conversation to be forgiven for wishing no more, but is still talking to me.

Select Bibliography

Aitchison, Jean, *The Articulate Mammal*, London, Routledge, 1998

Andreae, Simon, *Anatomy of Desire*, London, Little, Brown, 1998

Arendt, Hannah, *The Human Condition*, Chicago, University of Chicago Press, 1998.

Aristotle, *The Art of Rhetoric*, London, Penguin, 1991

Bacon, Francis, *The Essays*, London, Penguin, 1985

Belot, Michèle, and Francesconi, Marco, *Can Anyone Be 'The One'?*, London, Centre for Economic Policy Research, 2006

Brown, John Seely and Paul Duguid, *The Social Life of Information*, Boston, Harvard University Press, 2000

Brownell, Judi, *Building Active Listening Skills*, New Jersey, Prentice-Hall, 1986

Buss, David M., *The Evolution of Desire*, New York, Basic Books, 2003

C., S., *The Art of Complaisance*, London, John Starkey, 1673

Casanova, Giacomo, *The Story of My Life*, London, Penguin, 2001

Casey, Neil, *Social Organisation of Topic in Natural Conversation*, Plymouth, Plymouth Polytechnic, 1981

Castiglione, Baldesar, *The Book of the Courtier*, London, Penguin, 2003

Cicero, Marcus Tullius, *On Obligations*, Oxford, Oxford University Press, 2000

Collier, Jane, *An Essay on the Art of Ingeniously Tormenting*, Oxford, Oxford World's Classics, 2006

Correll, Linda Conway, *Brainstorming Reinvented*, London, Response Books, 2004

Craveri, Benedetta, *The Age of Conversation*, New York, New York Review of Books, 2005

Dean, Greg, *Step by Step to Stand-up Comedy*, Portsmouth, Heinemann, 2000

Elyot, Sir Thomas, *The Book of the Governor*, London, J.M. Dent, 1962

Select Bibliography

Fisher, Roger, Ury, William and Patton, Bruce, *Getting to Yes*, London, Arrow Books, 1987

Goldstein, Noah J., Martin, Steve J. and Cialdini, Robert B., *Yes!*, London, Profile Books, 2007

Gourevitch, Philip, ed., *The Paris Review Interviews, I*, Edinburgh, Canongate, 2006

Gristwood, Sarah, *Elizabeth and Leicester*, London, Bantam Press, 2007

Guazzo, Stefano, *Civile Conversation*, London, Constable, 1925

Hickman, Katie, *Courtesans*, London, Harper Perennial, 2004

Hirstein, William, *Brain Fiction*, Cambridge, MIT Press, 2005

Humphrey, Nicholas, *Seeing Red*, Cambridge, Harvard University Press, 2006

Hunt, Leigh, *Table-Talk*, London, Smith, Elder, 1902

Irwin, Robert, ed., *The Penguin Anthology of Classical Arabic Literature*, London, Penguin Classics, 2006

Karpf, Anne, *The Human Voice*, London, Bloomsbury, 2006

Leech, Geoffrey N., *Principles of Pragmatics*, London, Longman, 1983

Levinson, Stephen C., *Pragmatics*, Cambridge, Cambridge University Press, 1983

Levinson, Stephen C., and Owen, M.L., 'Topic Organisation in Conversation', 6810/2, London, Social Science Research Council, 1981

Macdonald, Scot, *Propaganda and Information Warfare in the Twenty-First Century*, London, Routledge, 2007

Malloch, Stephen N., 'Mothers and infants and communicative musicality', *Musicae Scientiae*, Liège, ESCOM, 2000

Masuda, Sayo, *Autobiography of a Geisha*, London, Vintage, 2004

Mercer, Neil, *Words and Minds*, London, Routledge, 2000

Miller, Stephen, *Conversation*, New Haven, Yale University Press, 2006

Monaghan, Leila and Goodman, Jane E., eds, *A Cultural Approach to Interpersonal Communication*, Oxford, Blackwell Publishing, 2007

Monmouth, Geoffrey of, *The History of the Kings of Britain*, London, Penguin, 1966

Morgan, John, *Debrett's New Guide to Etiquette and Modern Manners*, London, Headline, 1999

Nilsen, Don L.F., *Humor Scholarship*, London, Greenwood Press, 1993

O'Connell, Sanjida, *Mindreading*, London, Heinemann, 1997

Pinker, Steven, *The Language Instinct*, London, Penguin, 1995

Poole, Steven, *Unspeak*, London, Abacus, 2007

Provine, Robert R., *Laughter*, London, Faber and Faber, 2000

Ridley, Matt, *The Origins of Virtue*, London, Penguin, 1996

Romaine, Suzanne, *Language in Society*, Oxford, Oxford University Press, 1994

Rovine, Harvey, *Silence in Shakespeare*, Michigan, UMI Research Press, 1987

Runciman, W.G., *The Social Animal*, London, HarperCollins, 1998

Schwabe, Kerstin, and Winkler, Susanne, eds, *On Information Structure, Meaning and Form*, Amsterdam, John Benjamins, 2007

Shapiro, James, *1599*, London, Faber and Faber, 2005

Shepherd, Margaret, *The Art of Civilized Conversation*, New York, Broadway Books, 2006

Shōnagon, Sei, *The Pillow Book*, London, Penguin, 2006

Stevenson, Robert Louis, *Memories and Portraits*, London, Chatto and Windus, 1900

Stewart, Rory, *The Places in Between*, London, Picador, 2005

Tannen, Deborah, *Conversational Style*, Oxford, Oxford University Press, 2005

Tannen, Deborah and Saville-Troike, Muriel, eds, *Perspectives on Silence*, New Jersey, Ablex Publishing, 1985

Van der Molen, Henk T. and Gramsbergen-Hoogland, Yvonne H., *Communication in Organizations*, Hove, Psychology Press, 2005

Vasari, Giorgio, *The Lives of the Artists*, Oxford, Oxford World's Classics, 1998

Westen, Drew, *The Political Brain*, New York, PublicAffairs, 2007

Williams, Justin H.G., 'Copying strategies by people with autistic spectrum disorder', in *Imitation and Social Learning in Robots, Humans and Animals*, Cambridge, Cambridge University Press, 2007